SAILING AGAINST THE WIND

WRITINGS FROM AN UNBOUND EUROPE

Sailing Against the Wind

A Novel

JAAN KROSS

Translated from the Estonian
by Eric Dickens

NORTHWESTERN UNIVERSITY PRESS
EVANSTON, ILLINOIS

Northwestern University Press
www.nupress.northwestern.edu

Printed in the United States of America

10 9 8 7 6 5 4 3 2 1

Library of Congress Cataloging-in-Publication Data

Kross, Jaan.
[Vastutuulelaev. English]
Sailing against the wind : a novel / Jaan Kross ; translated from the Estonian by Eric Dickens.
p. cm. — (Writings from an unbound Europe)
"First published in Estonian under the title Vastutuulelaev: Bernhard Schmidti romaan in 1987 by Eesti Raamat in Tallinn, Estonia. Copyright © The Estate of Jaan Kross. Published by arrangement with Werner Soderstrom Ltd. (WSOY), Finland."
ISBN 978-0-8101-2652-7 (pbk. : alk. paper)
1. Schmidt, Bernhard, 1879–1935—Fiction. I. Dickens, Eric. II. Title. III. Series: Writings from an unbound Europe.
PH666.21.R6V3713 2012
894'.54532—dc23

2011031105

∞ The paper used in this publication meets the minimum requirements of the American National Standard for Information Sciences—Permanence of Paper for Printed Library Materials, ANSI Z39.48-1992.

CONTENTS

TRANSLATOR'S INTRODUCTION

Jaan Kross (1920–2007) is regarded as the most important Estonian prose author of the latter half of the twentieth century. His major works consist of two types of prose: historical novels set in Estonia, and semiautobiographical novels and short stories. The author focuses on the psychological makeup of the protagonist within the context of a search for national as well as personal identity and fulfillment. His heroes are always of Estonian or Baltic German ethnicity; the former are usually from a humble background, the latter from the upper social stratum of Estonian society. German was spoken as a minority language in Estonia for several hundred years. Like neighboring Latvia and Lithuania, Kross's native land has suffered occupation and the subjugation of its national identity for centuries, and has only been a sovereign nation twice, from 1918 to 1940, and since 1991. Estonia has at various times in history been part of the Russian, Swedish, Polish, and Danish empires.

Jaan Kross was born in the Estonian capital of Tallinn, where his father was a skilled metalworker. In the late 1930s, Kross began studying law at Tartu University. But then Estonia was occupied, three times in succession. First came the Soviets, from the summer of 1940 to the summer of 1941; during that time the whole Estonian government and many members of parliament were deported by the Soviet occupier to Siberia. Then came the Nazis in 1941; they arrested and exterminated the Jews. Finally the Soviets returned and occupied Estonia until 1991. These occupations put to rest any dreams of a legal career Kross might have entertained. Both the Germans and the Russians were suspicious of the young law student. During the Nazi occupation, Kross, suspected of Estonian nationalist activities, spent a few months in prison. He was ultimately let out and managed to dodge the draft into the Waffen-SS, only to fall afoul, a few years later, of the new occupying power, the Soviet Union. He was once again accused of Estonian nationalism, but this time was not so lucky; he spent the years 1946 to 1954 in the Gulag and internal exile in the region of Vorkuta in Russia, until the post-Stalinist thaw led to amnesty.

When Jaan Kross returned home to Estonia, he started out as a poet writing witty commentary on current affairs veiled in historical guise, safely within the strictures of the Soviet censorship apparatus. Soon, however, he moved on to prose. And his greatest achievement is the fifteen or so novels and several short stories that he produced from the 1970s onward.

Kross always did his homework regarding background detail. Many of his works describe the lives of real historical figures in fictional form: a medieval chronicler, a Baltic German dissident, an Estonian soldier serving the czar, a legal expert collating czarist treaties, a painter, and a freedom fighter and diplomat in the turbulent years around 1920 as Estonia gained its independence (in the novels *Between Three Plagues, The Madman of the Czar, Michelson's Matriculation, Professor Martens' Departure, Three Crests of Hills, Untouchability*). The periods covered range from the sixteenth century to the 1930s. For these novels Kross did meticulous research in libraries and archives, in the days before the Internet and search engines made such things easier. And he always had to face the challenge of cudgeling out historical documents through the inscrutably convoluted Soviet library system, pitting his wits against the censors.

In his semiautobiographical brand of novel, Jaan Kross described people he met personally at school or university, in prison, or in the Russian labor camps (e.g., *The Wikman Boys, The Ring of Mesmer, Excavations, Treading Air*). Here it was more a question of personal encounters than archival research, and here memories became interwoven with fiction.

In more than a thousand pages of published memoirs titled *Dear Travel Companions,* the author reviews his life from childhood until around his eightieth year. In this two-volume work, readers of Kross's fiction come across episodes described in the novels and short stories, episodes that had sometimes seemed farfetched, yet turn out to be based on real life. One such episode during the Nazi occupation relates how Kross cheated the army doctors by taking medicine that affected his pulse so that he would be declared unfit for military service. Otherwise he could have ended up fighting for the Nazis. After his return from the Soviet labor camp in the mid-1950s, Kross's life remained relatively peaceful, and he gradually became a respected writer and even enjoyed some fame in Russia.

Apart from his involuntary sojourn in Siberia, Kross traveled later in life to places as varied as Finland, Sweden, Hungary, Morocco, Canada, and California. Kross and his family lived in the center of the Estonian capital of Tallinn, but spent the summers at their summer house on the small island of Kassari, just off the larger island of Hiiumaa to the west of the Estonian mainland. Here Kross found the necessary peace to write. The two ferries needed to reach Kassari prevented a surfeit of visitors.

Most of Jaan Kross's major novels have been translated into Finnish, Swedish, and German; some have been translated into Russian, French, Spanish, and other languages. This novel is the fourth to become available in English; the other three are *The Madman of the Czar* and *Professor Martens' Departure,* translated by Anselm Hollo, and *Treading Air,* translated by me. A collection of stories in my translation *The Conspiracy and Other Stories* is also available in English.

As explained in the author's preface, *Sailing Against the Wind* tells the story of a real-life figure in fictional form. Bernhard Schmidt (1879–1935) was an Estonian-born instrument maker in stellar optics and a designer of astronomical telescopes. He was born in Estonia, but lived in Germany soon after the rise of the Nazis, and died there. During his working life he first polished lenses used for large astronomical telescopes. Later on he also designed various such telescopes, some of which are still to be found in Germany, Spain, Mallorca, and one, the "Big Schmidt," at Mount Palomar in California.

The bulk of this novel nonetheless describes, in semifictional form, the struggles of the man Bernhard Schmidt with himself. Although a product of his age, Schmidt was by no means the average Estonian working abroad. He was an islander, from the northern Estonian island of Naissaar (Swedish: Nargö; German: Nargen), in other words an outsider even when visiting Tallinn. The German and Swedish languages are socially relevant to the novel. Until World War II, there was still a minority of Swedish speakers living on Naissaar and other Estonian islands. These Estonian Swedes fled to Sweden in 1944 along with many other Estonians. And Baltic Germans still dominated the upper echelons of Estonian society during Schmidt's lifetime. Despite his German-sounding name, Schmidt was neither an Estonian Swede nor a Baltic German. But German was the language of education in school at the time, which helped him when he moved to Germany.

Estonian nationality plays a key role in Schmidt's life. Estonians were often regarded as bumpkins by Germans and Russians until they succeeded at something. Then Estonian achievements tended to be appropriated by Germany or Russia. Throughout this novel we find instances of Schmidt making protests, however minor or futile, against the fact that he is not recognized in Germany for what he is: an Estonian inventor. As the Nazis become more powerful in Germany, Schmidt, a foreigner by birth, feels more and more alienated—ultimately leading to tragedy.

Another key factor that shaped Schmidt's life was the loss of his right hand as a teenager in a fireworks accident. He fought doggedly against this handicap, and instead of working mainly with abstract ideas or becoming bookish he started manually polishing lenses and mirrors with his remaining hand, to a perfection that remains a mystery to this day. The fact that Schmidt was largely self-taught also plays a key role in his life, as he never felt fully accepted by the academic and scientific fraternities, either in Estonia or in Germany. He was never schooled and socialized to become a member of scientific circles, where the normal progression was from a university degree to a higher degree and then on to a career as a professor. In both the small German town of Mittweida, where he was loosely associated with the technical college, and the astronomical observatory at Bergedorf near Hamburg (both of which still exist), he was always regarded as something of a reticent, foreign oddball. And yet this autodidact ultimately invented astronomical telescopes that are only now, in the early twenty-first century, beginning to become obsolete because of advances in computer and other technologies. Schmidt made a string of other inventions that were ignored during his lifetime and remained unpatented.

Schmidt's relationship to the one key woman in his life, the German student Johanna, is evidence of his status as a loner. There is love, but there is also rejection. Perhaps these are echoes of the life of Kross himself, who was married three times and would no doubt have suffered some of the agonies and ecstasies that he carries over to Schmidt. In some respects, especially emotionally, Schmidt remained the willful and taciturn boy he was at the time of his accident.

This multilayered book thus tackles a large number of questions involving the interplay of the self and society. But there is also the direct historical dimension. Estonia's future hung in the balance from the first democratic movements around 1905, via the Russian Revolution of that year, until full independence in 1918. And it was to remain a sovereign country for only just over twenty years, until it was once again swallowed up by the Soviet Union after World War II. Bernhard Schmidt lived to experience only the first fifteen years of Estonian independence between the wars, but events preceding independence haunted him.

This historical dimension also plays a role in the very writing of this novel. In 1987, when *Sailing Against the Wind* was first published in what was then the Estonian Soviet Socialist Republic, it was by no means certain that Estonia would emerge relatively unscathed from ruins of the Soviet Union; the monolith collapsed only a few years later. The novel was written in a society that was still heavily censored in regard to recent history, and it is therefore interesting to note that although the repression and totalitarianism mentioned in it was that of the German Nazis, Kross was always very skilled at making sly allusions and digs at the way the Soviet Union itself was run. Not everything attributed to the Nazis was so very different from the actions of Soviet politicians, soldiers, and bureaucrats.

One of Schmidt's minor inventions beyond the field of astronomy is a boat whose paradoxical technology is symbolic of his attitude to life. This somewhat pointless invention is very dear to Schmidt; it occurs in his dreams and is mentioned periodically throughout the novel as a leitmotif. It is a vessel in which wind power, picked up by vane above the boat, is transferred by means of gearing to a propeller in the water. This, theoretically at least, means that the boat can perform maneuvers that appear to go against the laws of physics. The boat moves by means of that propeller in the water against the very wind that is powering it. The Estonian title of the novel, *Vastutuule-laev,* refers to this boat that sails against the wind, but the title is untranslatable into English.

I end this short introduction by quoting the brief dedication that Kross scribbled in Estonian in the copy I used while translating: *"To Eric Dickens, making no claims on him to translate this book. 20.11.88."* Well, over twenty years later, I have finally done just that and translated the book after all!

Eric Dickens
Uppsala, Sweden
January 19, 2011

PREFACE AND ACKNOWLEDGMENTS

This preface has three aims. First, to attempt to identify the genre of the book. Second, to explain in a few lines how it came about. Third, to thank at least the most important of the very many people who helped me when I was writing it.

So, the book you have just opened is not a biography of Bernhard Schmidt, either in the scientific or popular scientific meaning of the word. If you stretch the term a good deal, you could call it a "romanticized" biography. But it is a novel above all. Which means principally that historical and fictional events achieve equal status between these covers. For instance: my conversations in West Germany with people who had actually met Bernhard Schmidt (and I did talk with them there) are as real as my exchange of ideas with Eerik Schmidt—now known as Erik as an adult abroad—on Mallorca (travel to which proved to be too complex an undertaking, so I never went there). But: some of the exchange of ideas with Erik Schmidt did take place via letters and telephone calls, beyond the fictional dimension of the book.

It is therefore a novel. That I only dared to write because of a number of circumstances. In an interview in [the Soviet Estonian cultural weekly] *Sirp ja Vasar* (*Hammer and Sickle*) I was asked whether there were still people in Estonian cultural history about whom you could write novels from the biographical angle. In a reply that was not meant to be taken too seriously, I listed ten people about whom you should, let alone could, write biographical novels. The tenth name I mentioned was Bernhard Schmidt: "an oversensitive, exceptionally shy loner from an island village who finds himself quite alone in the Germany of the 1920s and 1930s with his memories of pebbles and jellyfish along the shore of the island of his childhood, quite alone in the increasingly insane maelstrom there, quite alone with his one hand with which he polishes, without wearying, without compromise or subjugation, lenses and mirrors to bring closer the stars of the heavens."

That somewhat romantic tirade happened to be read by doctoral student Peeter Müürsepp in Tartu, who had already made great efforts to introduce Schmidt's name in popular scientific magazines. He wrote to me. Wondering when I was going to start writing. I replied with some hesitation. He looked me up and began to get me interested in the subject. In his typical unselfish way, he would bring, over the next few years, all the material he could lay his hands on to my writing desk. So Peeter Müürsepp is the first person I must thank here. But I extend equal thanks to the staff of the Bergedorf Observatory for their help. Especially Professor A. Wachmann, who was kind enough to give me access to his surprisingly large collection of Schmidtiana. And, of course, Bernhard Schmidt's relatives, in the first instance Erik Schmidt, as mentioned above, for his letters and telephone calls. Bernhard Schmidt's niece, Dagmar Siitam, in Tartu for a number of family reminiscences, which she shared with me in a generous manner. And dozens of people in Tallinn, Hamburg, Helsinki, and [at the observatory at] Tõravere, who took the trouble to hear my questions and thus shared my concerns for a shorter or longer period of time. I must thank Dr. Seppo Kuusisto from Helsinki for referring me to invaluable archive material covering the background to Bernhard Schmidt's last years. I would like to thank the doctoral student of physics Uno Veisman for his descriptions of what became the many technical details in my text. And likewise academician Jaan Einasto for his encouraging words, which were few in number but nevertheless boosted my self-confidence significantly during the time I was writing this book.

Jaan Kross
Tallinn, Estonia
November 1986

SAILING AGAINST THE WIND

1

TWO YEARS HAVE PASSED SINCE THEN—I HAD JUST ARRIVED BACK from Lapland—and we were standing in the city park under the glass spheres I had hung up in the trees to check my mirrors, two hundred meters from the workshop (the police had got used to them over the ten years that had passed since the war and now tolerated them). We were standing in the dusk of that July evening and I took your hand, a smooth, soft hand, strong and large for a woman's, large and fatefully familiar, and I did not have to look at its back, as the evening was now too dark—with its small bunch of freckles. As with the Pleiades, termed the Sieve, at first you see ten or eleven stars, but on looking more closely you see some five hundred. I took your hand in mine and said: "Johanna, I'm going to Hamburg. For good." And before you had time to cry out, "Goodness me, then I'll have to pack a suitcase and come with you," I said: "But you are not coming with me." (Not, "You are not coming along just yet," simply, "You are not coming with me.") "You will stay here, in Mittweida."

You took hold of my hand and said, quietly: "Very well."

Two years have passed since then and I have done a lot of thinking. You do of course know that I had several reasons for doing what I did. And I have asked myself a hundred times what the proportion of these reasons is. Sometimes this question seizes hold of me when I'm working. I sit there in the chilly cellar of the Bergedorf Observatory tramping the pedals and polishing the rotating mirror by hand. In painful concentration. From the center out toward the edge and from the edge back in to the center. Sometimes with my eyes fixed on the job, sometimes even shut. So that I can feel every irregularity of one-hundredth of a millimeter with my fingertips (the only such fingers in the world . . .), and suddenly ask myself:

Why did I do this to her?

What percentage of my decision was determined by the fact that Professor Schorr offered what was more or less sufficient independence? Or did my decision have nothing at all to do with that? Of course it didn't. How could I be thinking so illogically! If my reason was only because Schorr had offered me that opportunity, I would have taken you along . . . That is to say: What percentage of my decision was derived from the fact that I also wanted to be independent of you? Because of what we can call my grand ideas, one of which I had begun to implement especially. Because of that? Or simply because I am twenty years older than you. Or, 20 percent of the reason is because I am relatively old, while 80 percent is because of *it.* Because I am an invalid. And it was high time that you found yourself a man you could start a family with. At least find yourself such a man who could carry your sacks of coal into the kitchen (you didn't have an electric stove in Mittweida) and could move the wardrobe from one wall to the other, as any wife would wish . . . I would of course have risen to such a challenge. It would have been merely a minor technical problem. Small pieces of felt under the feet of the wardrobe. A strong hook attached to three points by wire. Something I could knock up in my workshop in a couple of minutes. And then the cautious sleigh ride across the floor. But you do nevertheless need a man who can drive a car. With me you would have to spend a lifetime behind the wheel. Which you did, after all, do, didn't you? I didn't find it demeaning. I was above all that. I was quite above such matters. It was even rather pleasant. You looked so fine behind the big yellow steering wheel of that clapped out old Opel.

So why, despite everything? To set you free? Or to free myself from you? Please forgive me for asking this so bluntly. But I am not asking you, I am asking myself. And yet I have no clear answer to this clear question. Our mirrors ideally reflect mist. We ourselves reflect our ideas very mistily. You see, *der höchst wortkarge Sonderling* is making such a play on words that you might ask who could make them wittier . . . And do you know, Johanna, it was to escape such thoughts that I went off on that voyage to the Philippines. To take pictures of the corona round the sun, that too, of course. Taking up Professor Schorr's kind offer. That is clear. Because those photos of the sun I took in Lapland had come to be recognized as the best ever taken. So that was also why I traveled to the Philippines. But for another reason at one and the same time: to escape having to answer my own question.

Because I thought that it would leave me alone while I was out there. I would travel away and it would remain behind. In my cellar workshop. Like a question mark drawn with a fingertip in the glass dust of the polishing bench. Or in the residences of the observatory, in my bachelor pad. Like a sheet of white paper slid under the green cartridge paper of the drawing board. On which has been scribbled your profile: a pretty little Greek nose, full lips, and smooth hair combed straight back from your forehead, curling at the neck. Or I thought that the question would at least leave me alone in Land's old restaurant. Like a superfluous line drawn on a beer coaster in the pigeonhole at the counter, where I myself keep track of what I have drunk. I've employed the same method here with Land the landlord as I used to do with old mother Mimmi back there in Mittweida. But the question did not leave me be even then. Quite the opposite. I had an alarmingly large amount of time to ruminate on the matter. What else is there to do on a long voyage by steamer nowadays? Apart from lazing around.

I remember how, as well as all the lapping of the sea, we would travel out during my boyhood days, every autumn, with the pilot boat from Naissaar to Aksi for my great-aunt's birthday, with Father, or later on Uncle Frans, and Mother, and August, and sometimes the girls as well. A little later on, I was already on equal terms with the crew. Until my accident. Sometimes the sea was really autumnal. And then, with sails unfurled, a brisk northwesterly, in the spray, holding one's breath, the waves coming ten foot high over the side, with the prow of the boat sometimes hovering in midair (and one's stomach reciprocating)—that was what you could call a voyage. At any rate, those thirty or forty kilometers seemed more like the sea than this voyage of mine halfway round the world.

I said, lazing around. It is a sleepily humming seven-thousand-ton hotel that is sailing along here. Gibraltar. Port Said. Aden. Colombo.

Luckily, our *Münsterland* was largely a freight vessel. Though it nevertheless carried a few dozen passengers. Apart from Baade and me. Indeed. Our expedition was, on that occasion, traveling so far afield that they couldn't afford to send more than two men. By comparison, Lapland was in Hamburg's backyard, and on that expedition two years back there were eight of us. But they sent only two off to the other side of the world. So I said to Baade, "Well, I do understand, I suppose everything is relative." They sent eight from Germany to Lapland, and three from Estonia: Öpik, Livländer, Simberg. To the Philippines they sent two from Germany and none at all from Estonia. In Estonia, it presumably didn't enter their heads to send anyone that far. But nonetheless, I said to Baade, because of Germany's impoverished state, they've not even sent enough to make a whole ape—instead of four hands, we have only three between us! Anyhow, luckily other voyagers were thin on the ground. We got a two-person table in the dining room. So during the whole voyage I practically didn't need to introduce myself to anyone or chat and make small talk. But what was the point of it all? We were on our way. The instruments had been packed away. We couldn't make any observations or measure anything. No chance of doing any work in the cabin. Just imagine—one and a half months, two times over. Scribble a bit. Calculate. Otherwise all there was to do was take pointless walks through the ship's corridors and along the deck. Stare down at the wake, as if this would help speed the ship up. And on the voyage out between Ceylon and Penang, we were not only tormented by the boredom and the heat but a storm arose too. Baade was laid low for three or four days. I didn't become seasick and tucked in heartily in the virtually empty dining room. But because of the rocking motion it was nevertheless difficult to move around and they didn't serve soup and the plates of steak almost flew over the edge of the table. Even though they had depressions in the table that were intended to keep them in place. Anyway, between meals I simply lay on my bunk and read, which I never normally have time to do to that extent. A couple of things from the ship's library, Wells's *Time Machine* and whatever else there was. But every time I put the book away in the drawer of my bedside table (it would have fallen on the floor otherwise), my question, that is, *your* question, sprang to mind. Should I have treated you as I did? And it was an utterly pointless question to ask, whether in my cellar at Bergedorf or on the Indian Ocean. Seen from your point of view (through my eyes) my deed had been almost, damn it, heroic. But on the other hand, an act of abject egotism. From the angle of my *work*—well . . . the devil knows. But *one* idea did pop up in my head while the storm was raging. Somewhere between the Andaman Isles and the Malacca Strait.

We were traveling as cheaply as possible and this meant that our cabins were on the bottom deck. That is to say, they were right above the hold, where our expedition equipment was stored in fifty-two reinforced crates. Such a quantity that I was forever worrying how we were going to cope in Manila and on the island of Cebu. In the ports there were bearers, fair enough, the main thing being how careful they would be, but we would keep an eye on them and things would move forward. But at our destination we would have only a brief while to find assistants. And how we would—with our team consisting of three-quarters of an orangutan—well, that will come to light later.

At any rate, our cabins were located far down on the starboard side on the waterline, and with the storm blowing from the south the waves more or less covered my porthole. So that my cabin was, by turns, dark and light, dark and light, dark and light. The dark periods lasted some seven seconds, the light ones around five. During which time the wind blowing across the ship was so strong that as soon as the porthole rose above the surface, water ran down the glass, forming for a moment a second layer of pane on the porthole itself before it was dispersed in the air. And at the same time the porthole appeared to bulge inward ever so slightly. In reality, the twenty-five millimeters of porthole glass wasn't of course bulging at all. But the thought suddenly flashed through my mind as to what form a correction lens should take that would compensate for the fatal fault of telescopes—spherical aberration. I said that this thought *flashed* through my mind. By chance. Well, not of course entirely by chance. Because I had been ruminating on this problem for several months. Every day, during the earliest hours before getting down to work. And during breaks. And as I fell asleep at night after fulfilling the tasks I'd set myself for the day. And in effect, any circular piece of glass would have been enough to give my thoughts a shove. I naturally realized instantly that the lens I needed had to be a good deal thinner than that of my porthole, but I was sure at once about the profile of the surface that would face the mirror. And you can imagine, maybe from your own experience, that I would be endlessly goaded—until I had found a way of checking my ideas. But that would be quite impossible before returning to Hamburg. And I was obliged to put a brave face on it and carry on chugging my way on to Manila. And to let Baade, when he had overcome his bouts of seasickness, expand on how he was so nervous about all the work he had left half finished, and how my phlegmatic Estonian character was such an excellent defense against such nervousness.

On the morning of the twenty-eighth of March we reached Manila.

The large ocean port is on the edge of a grand bay that also forms the estuary of the river Pasi right through the middle of that one-quarter European and three-quarters Asian city. The higgledy-piggledy shops and the confusion of automobiles, rickshaws, and bicycles stretched out right up to the foot of the cranes at the port. Some officials from the German consulate and a few gentlemen from the Manila meteorological station received us there. It turned out that our equipment would be loaded onto a river steamer that was said to be moored in that same estuary of the river Pasi, but at the south port, which was a couple of kilometers away. The men from the consulate and the meteorologists wanted to take us straight to the hotel. They regarded it as quite normal that we would spend a few days looking around the city, *et cetera.* Because in their eyes the eclipse was *so* far ahead in time. In other words, they proposed that our equipment be put in storage at the port and that we travel out to Cebu a week later. The small steamer *Mactan* would be setting sail again, but this time round the steamer would be setting off the very next day, and we wouldn't make that.

Baade was quite in agreement with the idea, but I was opposed to it. I felt that hurrying along now would shorten my time waiting to get back to Hamburg. I convinced Baade (right in front of the other gentlemen, which I realized later wasn't very tactful on my part) that he could not imagine what sort of country we were in now, and that unexpected delays could crop up on the way, and time-consuming and unforeseen problems could arise as we set up the equipment. So in the end they all gave in. We decided to spend the night on board ship. The gentlemen from the weather station got hold of a truck.

The bearers, pleasant boys with yellow faces and flashing eyes, appeared from nowhere, winches began lifting our crates, some onto the quayside, some straight into the truck. I don't know how much Baade paid for all of this, as I had asked not to be involved in money matters. I do so only when it is unavoidable, that is, when my own money is involved.

That same day I traveled three times in that vehicle, the following day six, along quays and streets one kilometer to the north over a stone bridge built by the Spaniards and along the northern shore to the river port where our *Mactan* was waiting. The automobile was a Renault dating back to the Great War; its rubber tires were as hard as wood, and it leapt along the potholed roads like a wild boar. Once we reached the *Mactan,* our crates were winched up onto the deck, and when I had croaked enough at the bearers in English, German, Swedish, Russian, and Estonian, it was to be hoped that our equipment was on board in a more or less complete state.

After lunch I strolled around the town a little. I walked through the Spanish and Chinese quarters. In these parts of the city it was quite plain to see how the American way of life was beginning to outgrow that of both the other cultures. And if the spirit of the country was to develop sufficiently, you never know, something approaching an indigenous Filipino lifestyle could even take shape. Quite evidently, such a brief stroll did not allow me to become any more acquainted with the area than, let us say, by leafing through an album of city views. So I will admit: philosophizing about the Philippines would be against my wishes. I don't really know anything at all about the islands. Such reports as journalists come up with are always hearsay and twaddle. And if there is a country that I do know anything at all about, it is Germany, where I have now been living for almost twenty years in a row. And Naissaar, of course. Whose product I am in terms of both chemistry and tradition. As for the Philippines, it has to be said that I got to know more about it by reading a couple of books back in Hamburg before coming here than from the dark, gray walls of the Spanish old town and the smell of cooking oil coming from the tiny Chinese eating houses.

In 1898, taking advantage of the war that had broken out between the United States and Spain over Cuba, the Filipinos pushed the Spaniards out of the country with the help of the Americans. Four hundred years of colonial rule were at an end. But it soon transpired that the Yanks had not only helped the Filipinos because of their beautiful coal-black eyes. The United States also needed a base in this part of the ocean to support its fleet, and now sat on the Filipinos—as Uncle Frans from Naissaar said—with its ass on their faces, instead of the Spaniards. This seemed almost normal to the outside world: if the Filipinos had been under a foreign yoke up to then (the republic that had lasted a few weeks in 1898 was not worth considering), they would in the future need someone else to rule them instead. And Spain ceded the country to the victorious United States in a peace treaty.

Naturally the United States did find support among the local populace. As always happens when money is involved. And the Americans stayed put despite all the uprisings. And remain there to this day. Although they have disguised their colonial presence with the trappings of quasi-autonomy. As Herr Heckermann from the local weather station confirmed, President of the Senate Manuel Quezón could expect the Americans to let him become president of the whole country. And why not? Those working as meteorologists are specialists in forecasts.

On the evening of the twenty-ninth, I was obliged to be social and sit with Baade and the other gentlemen at a Chinese restaurant on La Escolta Street and eat trepang soup and swig rice wine. But when I asked Herr Heckermann, a quiet man with a black mustache, born from the liaison of a Dutch father and a Bisay mother, what sort of weather he forecasted for the ninth of May, he replied through the tinkling of the tambourine group:

"The month of May, second week, on the eastern shore of Cebu—dear, dear, dear . . . I will tell you: it is not possible to tell. Anything can happen. Still, clear, springtime weather. The wind blowing from the northeast. A temperature of ninety-five degrees. Or summer weather. Wind from the southwest. Ninety-four degrees. Or cloudy weather with the rain coming down in buckets. But the situation could also be just right for the first typhoon, which comes as spring changes to summer. On the ninth of May on the shores of Cebu anything is possible."

"But the probabilities, Herr Heckermann? The statistical likelihood, going by your experience?"

"Three times thirty-three point three, Herr Professor."

This "Herr Professor" business was a long-term bluff, a random title that has stuck to me for a good while now, and continues to be applied ever more frequently nowadays. Every time it is used it causes, well, not inside me, but in the atmosphere immediately around me, a mixture of acute embarrassment, of disappointment, shame, and proletarian pride all rolled into one. People around cannot fathom that a man with one hand could possibly be a craftsman—which is what I am. He has to be a professor!

We went off to the *Mactan* that night, and early the next morning the journey continued.

I have to say that I managed, during that trip, to discover how boundlessly large the small isolated world of the Philippines really is. Perhaps approaching such, what shall we call them, distant giants has been a relatively intense experience because of my career. Anyway, not only in the case of astronomical matters but also in more worldly things, I often have the feeling that the islands *open themselves up* in some strange way before those that approach them, and possess their own worlds of detail and space. Not only, let us say, Naissaar. That, certainly. As, to an extent (a ridiculous yardstick, whose ridiculousness I feel so clearly that it makes me smile wryly and doubly), as a yardstick for other parts of the world. Not only is it my island. But also, let us take as an example that translucent jellyfish out there in the waters of the beach between the rocks at Kabelikari, in the waters of August already grown chilly. With purplish, starlike veins, like some spiraling mist. That grows to the size of the Milky Way if you penetrate it by using the appropriate microscope.

And now we on our good ship *Mactan* were penetrating deep into an archipelago of some seven thousand islands.

Johanna—I would be a fool if I started describing all of this in detail. First, you know *how little* I like describing things. And second, I won't ever get to describe it all to you when I am here in Hamburg and you are in Mittweida. When I have just stepped outside of the Ollen Klinke bar and taken a seat on a bench at the beach by the ramparts by the sluice, eyeing the black water and the lit up horizon of Hamburg that has been ruining our photographs of the sky to the northwest. And the overcast sky that promises to be cloudy even tomorrow, so that any photography of the sun or stars both at night and during the day will be rendered impossible. In a word, when I am here and you are there. Let the distance be what it may. It is in fact a mere speck. A crumb, as they say on Naissaar. Three hundred and fifty kilometers as the crow flies. In light-years—virtually zero. Wait a second, let's calculate. One light-year, I don't actually need to calculate, it's in my memory, is 9.46×10^{12} kilometers. And we now have to divide that damned 350 kilometers by that number. This comes to naught point . . . and at the end we have that be-e-eautiful round number thirty-seven. With a point between the thirty-seven and one, two, three, four, five—yes—ten naughts. My distance from you is 0.000000000037 light-years. Forgive me, such calculations are simply rather crazy. You have said that to me on a couple of occasions. As for me, I don't really remember what I replied to you, but I am now replying: forgive me, but I'm only doing this present calculation as a joke. Because the ease with which I can make it is foolish in itself. Even better than Hannes from Uude. Who was he? My grandmother's nephew, Johannes Klamas. From Estonia. From the island of Aksi. Born 1847. Don't unfortunately know the date of his death. A simple fisherman. Who was regarded as a little nutty because of his knowledge. Because he knew by heart how many pickets there were to each garden fence, how many logs in each wall and planks on the floor of the main room. And how many times the word *yes* appeared on specific pages of the Bible, and how many times *no.* And all these figures and many more besides he was able to multiply and divide with ease. So it runs in the family, and in terms of light-years you are right next to me. Even nearer than that. But what's the use, as you have, by now, already become Frau Brandt. The wife of the honest, accurate, and diligent bookkeeper Werner Brandt. And becoming his wife seemed to me, for one fleeting moment, to be your true joy in life.

Hmmmmm.

And then we went deeper into the archipelago of seven thousand islands.

The distance from Manila to Cebu is more than 800 kilometers of earth. Of water, actually 0.000000000085 light-years. And as we had sailed out of the Bay of Manila and turned to the east and arrived at the sound between the islands of Luzon and Mindoro, we found ourselves in a huge area of sea within the archipelago across which we were proceeding on our eight-hundred-kilometer voyage. Our small vessel, once painted white, and now with a mottled rusty hull, a hundred passengers on board, a dozen Europeans in the first class plus some Filipino plantation owners, and down below the other ninety or so people representing an inscrutable section of the local population, was chugging along at a speed of ten knots on the miraculously calm sea, sailing in an east-southeast direction. The blue sea glittered and the clear sky promised the best weather possible in which to view the eclipse. The islands came and went, the straits narrowed and widened, to such an extent that rocky shores would stretch almost to the horizon. The sea inside the archipelago was itself divided up into separate seas: to the northwest the largest one, the Sea of Sibuyan, in the middle the Sea of Visayan, and to the southeast the Sea of Camotes, which was in fact already the strait between Cebu and the Leyte Isles.

The landscapes, inasmuch as we ever saw any, reminded me most of what I had seen (and these are not that many) of last year's groups of islands and fjords on the Norwegian coast. But only to a small degree, and only at a certain middling distance. Farther away, the islands of the archipelago rose larger and were relatively young volcanic heaps of odd formation, whilst from nearby vegetation of a tropical type could be made out: palm groves, rain forests, mangrove swamps.

Nevertheless, the landscape of the former and partly still active volcanoes gave the archipelago its distinct character. For me, coming from level country, they were pretty enough, but somehow alien, and, as I come from a part of the world quite lacking in seismic activity, they feel, subconsciously maybe, a little dangerous. The ground would shake several hundred times per year on those islands. We had, by the way, detailed maps with us and on them some features were more clearly visible than in nature itself. We laid out our 1:1,500,000 map of the Philippines on the sundeck of the first-class section of the ship so we could follow the voyage from island to island. I think that the whole of the Sea of Sibuyan is in fact one huge inactive crater with a diameter of some 120 kilometers; within its midst is the 200-meter-high cone of the secondary crater, that being the island of Sibuyan itself.

On the first of April we docked at the island of Cebu, in the capital of the same name.

Professor Schorr had sent our letters of introduction on beforehand. The deputy director of some Hamburg firm (Meyer & Behn—no idea what kind of firm that is), a Herr Moll, was already waiting in the port. This Moll, with short gray hair, but with the appearance of the German silent movie actor and film director Harry Piel, had a great deal of local experience and was an almost unbearably fussy man. His first task was to get us installed in our hotel. Well, by European standards, it was not exactly a luxury hotel. Maybe such a thing simply did not exist in the whole of the town of Cebu—but maybe the firm of Meyer & Behn had quite precise information about our financial state. Because our hotel was no slum hostel either. It was quite near the harbor and turned out to be a large two-story wooden bungalow set among palm trees, in a garden with goodness knows what kind of other trees.

The three of us ate our dinner there in the half-empty dining room, and despite our weariness we discussed the plans for the next day. Herr Moll promised to get us transport, and at ten o'clock (I had suggested eight, but Baade preferred ten) it would be there by the steps. We wanted to drive round the island along the coastal road and pick a good vantage point. Actually, the gentlemen from Manila had already chosen a suitable area; two villages, or, if you like, settlements, some fifty kilometers to the north of Cebu, and we had to decide which of them was the most suitable: Catmon or Sogod—initially we knew nothing about them beyond their names. And going by the names I would have chosen the first—if it is allowed to choose for such an idiotic reason. Because the name Catmon sounded rather herbal to me, and it later struck me that this was because it sounded like *cardamom,* which is called *kardemon* on Naissaar. While at the same time the name Sogod suggested swamps and bogs. Such silly ideas can sometimes flash through the coolest of heads.

After the travails of landing in the morning and the day spent loading and walking, when the heat of the day was some ninety-three or -four degrees Fahrenheit, and then, after the tambourine music at evening meal and the weary but urgent conversation, I felt that it would be hard to get to sleep and my dreams would be troubled. Before rising from the table I took a good swig, what Uncle Frans would call a nightcap, of Johnnie Walker, a bottle of which Herr Moll had ordered, but I knew it wouldn't help.

My room was a box with whitewashed walls and a low ceiling. Two square windows with slatted bamboo blinds, a few wicker chairs, a writing desk made out of some reddish wood, which was already quite knocked about, although it could hardly have been used for copra deals and games of whist, or for counting the money for rice wine and whores. Herr Moll had told us the copra barons and their lackeys would come into town to do business and celebrate. Be that as it may. The barons in the more exclusive hotels, and the dealers here. And in my room there was also a bed, wide enough for more than one person, with a carved headboard, but entirely without a footboard.

I took off my jacket, whose armpits were drenched in sweat, and with a laughable delay it struck me (as always under such circumstances) that I could have left it off all day, in which case I would have sweated only half as much, but I just hadn't paid it any attention.

I stripped naked. I even took off that knitted black sock (I cannot really call it a *glove,* can I?) that covers the stump of my right hand so that it isn't so obvious. (Johanna, do you remember what we used to call my sock? Course you do: in our private language it was my condom. And you didn't want to believe that it was called that only in your presence. You pulled such a face to demonstrate that it didn't matter to you, but actually it did. And you could have believed me, because it was true.)

I had a wash behind the plank wall in the shower corner with its cement floor, under the tepid raindrops that emerged sparsely from the showerhead, then pulled up the blind at the foot end of the bed. Maybe I could get some cool air from outside. But the suffocating blackness was no better than the air of the room itself. So I lowered the blinds again and lay down on the bed.

I am not very tall, only 179 centimeters, as you know, but the bed was unexpectedly short. In order not to keep rubbing my head against the headboard—I'm balding quickly enough as it is—I rested my feet against the wall beneath the window. The plaster was unexpectedly and pleasantly cool against the soles of my feet, and I lay there waiting for sleep to come, though I knew I would not doze off. I knew from experience what to expect.

Over the years, over the space of thirty-five years, and more than a hundred times, maybe two hundred, I have lived through this. So that I'm actually no longer afraid. Falling, which I can sense before it happens, the sudden paralysis in a state halfway between waking and sleeping, and everything happening again in half sleep, quarter sleep. Because of the repetition and knowing what is going to happen, it has become completely abstract. Like a faded photo instead of the event itself—but a compulsive photo nonetheless. And a photo in which alongside what is already long familiar, there is something new. Usually something minor, absurd, unreal, something that never happened; and the mechanism whereby it has entered the world is something that I do not understand.

And then I'm there at the edge of the forest lying on my stomach among the junipers and bilberry bushes. In my gray faded quarter sleep something astonishingly living, strangely brightly colored, has appeared. I get the feeling that I am remembering each and every wet green bilberry leaf and the dark-pink flowers of the juniper against my face. And that I can feel the warm breath of Klaamann's lad at my neck. As through the scrub we watch the large reddish boulder on the forest path some twenty paces away. The path produces a vista straight from the heart of the island, cutting along the southern edge of the mast pinewoods and emerging on the flat ground near the sea to the west. The boulder is lodged between the two walls of the forest right in the middle of the path. A clump of rock I picked out myself. Picked it out because the side facing inland is almost smooth, as smooth as any natural rock can ever be unless it is crystal itself. So that it sticks out of the withered clump of moose hemp facing the sea at an angle of almost exactly forty-five degrees. At an angle of forty-five degrees, that much I do know about ballistics, a flying object flies farthest.

We stare out through the bilberry bushes and the iron tube that is ten inches long and an inch thick and is positioned in the vista on the smooth sloping side of the large boulder and is pointing out toward a clearing and the sea. I welded the end of the tube shut in my shed with Uncle Frans's blowtorch. (I am so keen that the experiment will succeed that I am saying father Frans instead of stepfather.) I then fixed a cone-shaped hat on the end of the tube to reduce the air resistance. To fill the pipe I carefully measure and mix gunpowder and guncotton. The gunpowder comes from the seal guns of villagers and the guncotton from their store for blowing up rocks, which I have cadged thimbleful by thimbleful. The speed of the explosion of the gunpowder is four thousand meters per second and that of guncotton seven thousand meters, that I know. I know that if too much guncotton is used in the mixture, it won't fly farther than on previous occasions—forty, fifty, eighty meters. But if it is just right—and it has to be just right—then this time it will fly as far as the Vallimägede hills, maybe even as far as the strip of beach. In which case—I am not yet sure whether to call my tube a *rocket,* a new type of rocket to be used as an improved method of rescuing people from ships that have run aground, or a new weapon against enemy vessels should they dare to approach Naissaar. Presumably both, once it exists. God knows.

But why hasn't there been a bang yet? Why not yet? We are almost choking, the Klaamann boy and I, as we hold our breath and wait! No, no, the fuse has probably gone out. Although it was a nice piece of hempen cord and carefully soaked in paraffin. But the sand and the moss and the gunpowder have grown damp from the drizzle this morning. The fuse has no doubt gone out. And I must go and check it. Me, quite obviously. As it is, after all, my experiment. The Klaamann boy only happens to be with me here. Although he is some five years older than me and has reached the age of twenty. He doesn't understand a thing about mechanics and chemistry. What they say about me, on the other hand, in the village is that . . . Even if for God, if He exists, all that me, me, me . . . No, there's no way out. I have to get up and go and have a look. And what could be the danger? Practically none. If the mixture is right. And if you approach the tube from the side, the last bit at least. So that the exit flame, should there be an explosion, would pass by anyone getting near. The only problem is that coming from the side means that I can't feel the fuse with my fingers.

I jump to my feet. I run the twenty paces over to the tube and throw myself to the ground. My movements are exaggeratedly easy and spry due to my excitement. But I am not afraid. I can see the fuse as it winds over the moss toward the boulder a little to the right of my right hand. I take hold of it. It crumbles to black soot in my fingers. This means that it has gone out nearer the tube. At one level of memory my movements are light and swift. At another, leaden and stiff. In the latter memory I move toward the tube with horrible effort, crawling, in the way that you crawl away from a train that is about to run over you in a dream. Or toward the train. So that what must happen, will happen.

Then I am on all fours next to the boulder, in the lee of the boulder. I stretch out my hand—my left one, as I remember—and take hold of the fuse as it rises out of the brown moose hemp along the boulder. The string crumbles to soot. Strange—I am thinking—there's only a meter to go to the tube. That means it must have burnt right to the end, then gone out. There is, practically speaking, no other alternative. The other possibility—that it is still burning somewhere along that meter—is just too unlikely. It is a hundred to one against, a thousand to one against. At any rate I wait a further twenty seconds. That covers the speed a fuse would burn over the length of one meter. Now the chances of an explosion are one in ten thousand. (In all truth, I cannot tell whether I thought in such elaborate terms in reality, and how much is a mental construction in hindsight. But what I am thinking is: be careful, sure. But my lad—if this turns to cowardice, what sort of inventor will I ever become?) I get up from the ground. I just have to beat that crucial moment of danger, that tiny moment of danger, to it. And show Klaamann's boy, show myself, show the world. No way out. I seize hold of the tube in my right hand. Interesting: the fuse crumbles to soot. That means that it has burnt right up to the tube? And gone out *there*? Impossible! I immediately take a look . . .

I do not hear the bang. I do not feel any blow, any pain. Just a hideous instant of light. Then darkness. And in fact this moment is beyond a leaden wall of a dream repeated a hundred times. Except for one thing: the awareness that my heart now quails, and a stab of pain flashes through me from my heart to my balls. Yes, the explanation I get, immediately, an instant later when I come to, is the Klaamann boy's chalk-white face over me. I can see him clearly, as my left eye is completely OK; my right one is covered in blood, though I don't notice that yet. I can clearly see the Klaamann boy's face, white with shock, his tousled hair and trembling jaw. And then—this I do remember—I stretch out my hand, maybe to pat him on the shoulder and say, "nothing wrong, Juhan, everything'll be all right," or perhaps, "sorry, my fault" . . . Something of the sort. And then I see: my right hand is still hanging by a few bloody tendons and strips of skin to my wrist. And this lump, poking out from the blood-covered sleeve of my jacket, lacks the thumb and the first two fingers. I refuse to understand. And nevertheless understand that I have lost a hand. Unredeemably. For as long as I live. And this realization causes a stab of pain from my heart to my balls. And still does. To this very day. Every time I remember. At whatever level of memory. Especially when the levels of consciousness cut across one another, my light and swift waking memory with that other one, diffuse, dream leaden, and grievous. Even now. A stab of pain. So that I wake up. This time in the heat of my dark hotel room.

For a moment this seemed to be an escape from under the fateful concrete road roller of memory. But human beings are ungrateful creatures: a minute later the humid heat began to become oppressive. So I stretched out my hand to where I remembered the bedside table stood. To switch on the electric lamp.

Johanna, do you remember how I would sometimes make things up? Things that never happened. Or, to be more precise, things that have happened, but partially and slightly differently. I'm sure everyone does, so me too. A little fantasizing, to be more interesting to you. And by the way, you would find a good explanation for this. No mere tactful explanation, but the right one. An example? Well, I told you when we first met that before coming to Mittweida I had been a student at the Chalmers Institute in Gothenburg. To a certain extent this is the truth. Later on it came out that I had not studied there for three semesters, as you had been led to believe, but rather for three weeks. But you said, with a strange smile on your face, so that I remember your words: "Oh Benn, given the terrifying precision you demand from your work, it is only natural that in other matters you must otherwise feel a little bit *free.*" But right now I'm not fantasizing. I have indeed just had my third glass of korn at the Holtenklinke bar. So as to become just a little free, when it comes down to it. After more or less working night and day for three weeks in a row. And what happened back then in that hotel in Cebu was in no way fantasy. Why should I make it up? When you are at a distance from me that can be measured in light-years. It happened exactly as follows.

I had angled the bedside lamp in such a way that the light didn't shine straight in my face. It shone on the window, on my feet, and on the wall surrounding the window. And widely to either side of my spread toes pressed against the plaster wall. I saw: right in the middle of the windowsill, on the lowest slat of the bamboo blinds, on an axis that formed an extension to my own body, some twenty centimeters above my toes, something was moving. Something black and rather hard to identify from so odd an angle. Until suddenly I realized: it was a scorpion.

I have to admit that I belong to that type of human being who thoroughly loathes spiders and anything vaguely resembling them. I do not know what brand of atavism this is. I have even tried to investigate the matter, but could not really be bothered to root out the literature about the phenomenon. And there is probably not much to find. I am a little ashamed at my disgust for these creatures. As it seems a little womanish. I have noticed such things principally in women. Young girls will scream with horror should a garden spider crawl across their hand. I of course manage to overcome my disgust on every occasion. But it is undeniably present. If unexpectedly I see a wasp crawling over the back of my hand, I let it continue to crawl around undisturbed, and I interpret its courage as a sign of trust, and try myself (though this may sound a little ridiculous) to instill trust in the creature. And enjoy the feeling of mutual trust. But if it is a spider, or even a daddy longlegs, I need a second to get a grip on myself and overcome the urge to kill it, and I finally blow it soberly off my hand. And my disgust is quadrupled in proportion to the size of the creature. But the scorpion on my windowsill, which I saw from an unusual angle, was twelve or thirteen centimeters long. Such a creature affects you perversely, half insect that it is, by its very size. I carefully scrutinized it for a moment. It had positioned its upper body with its face, if you like, in my direction, although it is true that I could not make out its eyes in the black mass from that distance. Its body was largely obscured by its left foreleg or claw or pincer. In general, it gave you the impression of a small model of a bronze warship. Which I had once seen goodness knows where. A naval vessel from the time of Ulysses, broken in half. Four or five pairs of legs or oars and a high tail curled forward like an ancient prow. Then the ship made incomprehensible oar movements, made a strange three-centimeter leap and ended up on the edge of the windowsill. I am no specialist, but I am pretty sure that a sting from such a tail would not necessarily kill a human being, though it could do so.

Well, I overcame a certain amount of shocked paralysis and made a choice of movement somewhere between the slowest and quickest possible. To the advantage of a slow one. I had no idea how far the creature could see beyond one and a half to two meters, and how it would react. We know nothing about the psyche of such creatures. We understand less about it than we do about the sign of Scorpio. At any rate, I moved my hand quite slowly toward the bedside table and picked up my open pocketknife, with which I had just been paring my toenails, without so much as turning my head. It was very sharp and had a very rigid blade. A penknife, as they would have said in the olden days. My great-grandfather Jakob had made it in his own little smithy on Naissaar, and I was given it for my tenth birthday by my father before his death. And if there was anyone who could defend himself against a scorpion with the knife, it was me. Yes, I don't know how dangerous this creature was to me, but I was ten, or even a hundred, a thousand times more dangerous to it. I had repeatedly carried out all sorts of hand exercises for five years in a row. Including playing the violin. Which I gave up. Because when I had fixed the bow to my stump with a clamp I invented, I could play the "Roslagen Waltz" and "Keeping the Beauty of My Country" as well as they would be played at a village dance, but I could play nothing more. So, gritting my teeth, I had given up playing the violin. But knife throwing was something I had practiced endlessly. From a distance of about one to twenty paces. With all sorts of knives. Including table, kitchen, hunting, and fishing knives, even the sort you flay seals with, Finnish *puukkos* that have between two- and fifteen-inch blades, as could be obtained on the island, plus pocketknives or penknives with all sorts of blades, shafts, and weight. I had made millions of throws. And to this day my hand will faultlessly pick out the balance point, where to take hold of the knife, and the force needed to hit any particular target.

I raised my hand slowly up to my left ear, gripping the knife blade between my thumb and index finger, aimed . . . and hesitated. The scorpion, as it was sitting there, was an infinitely uncertain target. Its legs were very thin, its body seen from the front was only twenty millimeters wide, and it was some distance in front of the blind. I would no doubt hit him. Despite my awkward throwing angle. But the throw would be no more powerful than its insignificant weight.

The knife would simply brush aside the creature and fasten somewhere between the bamboo slats. I cannot say whether I thought this at the time or later: the scorpion will be brushed aside and fall off the windowsill—or even leap from it, because it is a hellishly swift creature—and land on my naked foot, and inevitably sting my big toe out of sheer fright . . . So I hesitated for a moment. And then something unbelievable occurred. Ulysses' semi-bireme made another lightning move. I couldn't follow what happened, but suddenly it was no longer on the horizontal windowsill but rather on the wall, on the white plaster right in the middle of an equilateral triangle whose tip was the middle of the edge of the windowsill and whose two lower points were my big toes. It was now in the ideal position to hit: the knife would pierce the front part of its body, which was sufficiently broad, some twenty millimeters in width, and nail it to the crumbly plaster wall. I maybe imagine for a split second, as the tendons of my hand tensed, how the stricken scorpion would try to sting the shaft of great-grandfather's knife, smoothed with use. But I still delayed. And presumably for another reason. Because I realized: something about this creature was different from what it should be, different from other scorpions. It took a couple of seconds for me to realize what this was. It was not symmetrical, as they tend to be—and it took a further second to realize why: its right claw was missing. And then I found myself still hesitating, and understood why. Because a crippled man feels shame at the killing of a crippled creature. Our deformities (I realize how comical it sounds—using the word *our* for me and a scorpion—I'm not even a Scorpio, I'm an Aries), our deformities united us. I realized that we were both cripples from an ideal point of view. And that we would have to live with, and forgive, each other. This was grand, mind-blindingly idiotic rubbish (well OK, even nowadays I daren't use the term "idiotic"), yet a mind-blindingly sweet moment as well. I don't know what it really was. Anyway, I put the knife back on the bedside table. Quietly. But not as quietly as I had picked it up. And not without turning my head. Because the next time I looked, the scorpion was gone.

Ha-ha-ha-haa. The moment of revelation was past. I rummaged around in the room for a whole hour. Not in order to kill it but rather to frighten it out of the room. I pushed the wardrobe aside, moved the bed, and turned over the mattress. It wasn't there. And although

I—though I cannot really say other than *we*—although under the influence of *our* recent encounter, and perhaps of the stresses of the day, the intolerable heat, the plethora of impressions, the tiredness and the whiskey, I believed for a brief moment that absolute faith in the scorpion would create around the believer a bubble of inviolability so that the creature would not sting (in the way that faith can move mountains), at the same time I couldn't help smiling, in my European way, at the impossibility of both absolute trust and faith. So I left the bed right in the middle of the room and the electric light switched on just in case, and slept deeply until morning only because of my extraordinary weariness.

But nothing more unusual happened in Cebu. The next day we traveled through the area in the north and did not choose Catmon; we chose Sogod instead. It is situated fifty-six kilometers to the north of Cebu, almost by the seashore. Off the Camotes Sea, cooled by a pleasant trade wind, and linked to Cebu by a road, which Herr Moll confirmed to be one of the best in the area for car travel. Anyway, by driving carefully, we managed to get our equipment there in one piece. Although my backside did at times take the brunt of the journey.

Seen from afar, Sogod is a real postcard idyll: the massive old church, a Catholic one of course, the center of the settlement, the villas of the planters, that is, a few white bungalows, and so on, all under coconut palms; all around the gray and brown shanties of the locals, their steep yellow thatched roofs among fields of maize and tobacco of various shades of green, to the right the blue sea, to the left the cultivated slopes of the interior of the island, which rose up into the hills that became mountains in the distance. From nearby the settlement was a pretty run-down and higgledy-piggledy place, swarming to an unbelievable extent with half-naked Bisay children, plus the buffaloes, small cattle, and hens of the villagers. So at first all you could do was imagine what a sea of mud the tropical rains would turn the purplish lanes full of hoofprints into.

I do not know whether the local school had been specially cleared for us or whether their local summer vacation had already started, but we had the run of the place. It was in effect a wooden shed consisting of two classrooms plus side rooms. We turned one of the rooms into my workshop, the other into our living quarters, a third into the store. Our observation post was the schoolyard, whose exact location was 10°45' latitude and 124°0' longitude.

Nothing more. We were obliged to mix our own concrete for the three bases for our equipment. We set to work with due care. The four Bisay boys that Herr Moll had sent us proved to be skillful beyond expectations. We mounted our instruments on the concrete platforms on the eighth of April. By the twenty-second, our observation post was ready. Apart from the final adjustments. By the way, we had planned to also take some extensive photographs of the Milky Way as seen from the Southern Hemisphere for a week or so before the eclipse itself. But nothing came of that. As if by witchcraft, the sky would cloud over at around six or seven and only clear after the regular morning thunderstorms. So all we could do was to wait for the ninth of May and nurse all our hopes and worries for the weather on the day of the eclipse. Oh yes: then the Americans came to visit us.

Their expedition consisted not of two, but, I believe, of twenty men, and they were to take their photos of the eclipse at Iloilo on the island of Panay, 150 kilometers to the west of us as the crow flies. And when I say twenty men, that is a modest estimate. You could just as well have said two hundred. Because the Americans came to the sea roads at Sogod on a cruiser, and there were certainly two hundred men aboard. The crew, in their blue-and-white zebra shirts, rowed the scientists ashore, and for two hours our schoolhouse and observation yard rang with the loud conversations of the Yanks. Their speech is, I must say, so hard to understand that I can hardly comprehend the fact that I have read so many scientific tomes in the English language and, in my opinion, have understood perfectly well what was written.

Then the Americans had a look at our observation equipment. And in this context, one of them sticks in my memory. Although I never did find out what he was actually called. Maybe Link or Flink or Hink. And I didn't go and ask him, "How do you spell it?" A middle-aged man with a thick pink neck, fair hair in a crew cut, and white eyelashes. He eyed our horizontal mirror with its fifty-five-centimeter aperture and especially its adjustment settings, which I had thought up on our expedition to Lapland, and asked:

"But why did you bring this plaything all the way from Hamburg? Can you really do anything worthwhile with it?"

I said: "You can always play with it . . ."

But Baade asked gruffly and in a businesslike manner whether the gentlemen happened to have seen our photos of the sun taken in Jokkmokk a couple of years previously. Seen the photos? Of course they'd seen them. They had even studied them intensely. That same Drink or Prink then said:

"To be sure! They're the best ever taken!"

And so Baade curled his somewhat short upper lip and, to my embarrassment and triumph, announced, flashing his broad teeth:

"They are, aren't they? But they were all taken by Herr Schmidt here and using this same equipment."

Whereupon this same Mr. Flink cried: *"Incredible!"* and offered me a cigar, which I refused.

In the end, the Americans drank a toast to us in whiskey on the veranda of the schoolhouse, and offered us some as well (the zebra-shirted sailors or the cruiser's galley boys had brought along crates of ice and soda water). Then they went on their way, and Baade began to expound on his impressions of our guests. With me, for want of better company, although I did not comment on his commentary. Meaningless chatter, when all's said and done. A person can have *thoughts* about such matters. The daftest thoughts, if they amuse him. But why utter them aloud? So I listened to his words in silence. Except for one occasion. I said:

"Dr. Baade, it wasn't really necessary to rub their noses in it by telling them that the Jokkmokk photos were taken with the same equipment. It would have been sufficient to let them think we were playing with toys out here."

I have to admit: I was not entirely sincere in saying this. In fact, it was a lie. False modesty. It was perhaps even an attempt to fish for more praise of my equipment from Baade. Clearly, my soul was still in need of such. Because, in fact, despite the embarrassment Baade did flatter my ego by praising my work in front of the Americans. But I immediately received my just desserts for my insincerity. Baade said (he himself as sincere as could be):

"No, no, my dear colleague. It was absolutely necessary. Don't you understand? It was necessary for the reputation of German science!"

And I'm afraid that my mouth fell open in astonishment. No one had ever said to me, nor had I ever myself—and I mean never—thought that. That in Baade's eyes I was a *German* scientist. And not only in his eyes. I felt that something inside me jumped up and started protesting. But at the same time I understood that from his point of view it was perfectly true. Because what nationality was I with regard to my science? When I had lived and worked in Germany for almost thirty years. With breaks on Naissaar and in Tallinn, true enough, but mostly in Germany. And with German buyers and German institutions paying for my upkeep. And with German scientists doing research with my lenses and mirrors—Schwarzschild, Vogel, Schorr, and others—only Germans. Apart from a couple of amateurs, one in Pärnu maybe, one in Gothenburg, a couple in France. The main thing is: Whose national did I want to be as a scientist? And that question was not an easy one to answer. I had lived in Germany almost eighteen years on a Russian passport, and ten on an Estonian one. Because of my Estonian passport I had traveled from Mittweida to Berlin during my most intensive period of work, to Eduard Vilde—that author had just recently been appointed Estonian ambassador to Germany. They made out an Estonian passport for me there on Hildebrandstraße without much ado. Or it would be truer to say: they made it out to me after a great deal of ado. As the old gent—well, he did seem to be in his sixties, though I don't know exactly when he was born—the old gent deigned to chat to me for a whole hour, so worried and agitated was he. About who I was and what I was doing in Germany and why I specifically wanted an Estonian passport. And I explained. And asked a thing or two for my part. Since I was from Naissaar by birth and Naissaar was now part of the Estonian Republic, as my mother had written to me in so many words. So it was absolutely natural that I should be an Estonian citizen. When such a republic had been born under such unexpected circumstances. But it also interested me what sort of state it was and what it wanted to become.

It struck me, as far as I remember, that the old gent had some problems with this, something he didn't want to discuss with a complete stranger. Instead, he leaned back in his office chair, peered at me through his oval gold-rimmed pince-nez (a large, peaceful face, but with a nervous complexion and a graying mustache), and said:

"Ahah, you come from Naissaar. You see. I have also been to Naissaar. Just the once. But it was a memorable occasion."

And then he told his tale. About how he, as a twenty-one-year-old, accompanied a troupe of Tallinn German Theater actors to take a trip *in die Grüne.* By sailing boat from the Kalaranna harbor. Young men with stiff collars and mustaches and young ladies in padded dresses. A dozen or so people, bottles of wine, *wurst* and *butterbrod.* He said: "You will know this yourself. Naissaar was not in those days one of the most popular venues for sightseeing trips. It was quite unknown to city folk and rather a place of fantasy for most people. But that was the very reason that the actors had chosen it. Theater folk always have rather fanciful ideas. Especially when they are mere amateurs and feel the obligation to make an especially original impression."

He carried on talking, about how they had landed at the Lõunaküla harbor in the south and sat on the rocks by the sea to enjoy themselves a little and then walked the seven or eight versts through pleasant pinewood scenery and taken lunch at a farm somewhere in the village of Põhjaküla in the north, he didn't remember precisely where, then toward evening started having a party. Vilde said: "You yourself will understand, sir. Why should such a group of young people need to find such an isolated spot? Because of romance. Especially as Sofie was present, with her auburn hair and green eyes. Let's call her Sofie . . . Who was known to one of our actor friends (let's call him Feldmann or Bürger) from the school of needlework in Tallinn." Anyway, this Sofie had laid the table for the young gents—I'm not sure whether in the farmhouse itself or in an adjoining building—and then sat with them for a while at table and listened, her green eyes looking at the tablecloth, the evening light on her auburn hair, and her pronounced cheekbones (as I seem to remember), to how Herr Feldmann or Herr Bürger declaimed poetry. Maybe Vilde uttered witticisms himself. Because it wasn't a Vilde that went for a walk with the gentlemen along the eastern shore to the big deciduous wood. But a certain Herr Walden. Yes, indeed. That was the sobriquet that Vilde used when acting at the Tallinn German Theater. And on that occasion on Naissaar as well. In truth I have forgotten details of his story. But when he told it (and if I remember rightly it more or less got as far as challenging either Herr Feldmann or Herr Bürger to a duel), when he mentioned that, I began to catch the drift of his story. After all, they were actors, weren't they? And that wood where they were walking was the garden of the Danish king. And those young men whom he wanted to be rid of were playing, the one Rosencrantz, the other Guildenstern. He, that is to say, young Herr Walden, had not played Hamlet, that is quite true. And young Vilde was miles away from that role, as far as I can judge matters. But now in his later years, he cobbled together chance motifs from his youth so skillfully that it was a joy to listen to. If I remember rightly, the name of the village elder was also briefly mentioned in the tale. No, it wasn't Claudius. But Klaus or some such name. And indeed, Klaus from that robber's island of Rävasaare was the village elder during my boyhood days. So I thought with amazement: Why hadn't Vilde polished up this tale to form one of his well-known short stories? That would have become more important than some of his other ones. But maybe he had done so and it was now in one of his collections. As I'm not really acquainted with them.

And I also began thinking: some older men like to look back on their younger self as more problematic than it in fact was. I personally think in quite the opposite terms. I hope I am not making myself out to have been so naive in those days as to be a more problematic figure now that I'm in my fifties. To anyone who would claim that, I would say right out: "My dear fellow or lady or whoever, up yours!" For what indeed are problems in the context of personal or private life? They are too vague to start blabbing on about. *Scientific* problems are ones I understand—as I realize that they can be solved in a systematic way. Well. In the case of Cebu, we couldn't solve them in that way either. Because when they began to arise everything was already messed up.

The weather had turned during our week of waiting, becoming worryingly unstable. The approach of the rains was in the air and by afternoon the humidity tended to be ominously high. But some days were radiantly sunny, and on the morning of the ninth it looked as if that day would be one of them.

During that last week, two professors from Manila University had come to our assistance. Hyde and Melchor. Neither had any experience of astronomical observation, but they were pleasant enough young guys and eager to learn. So that from morning onward our big guns were adjusted to perfection, which I checked myself with great care, and we were ready for battle, ready to shoot.

The eclipse was going to begin at the local time of 2:26 P.M. At about one o'clock the sky was, I would say, nothing to worry about. Just a li-i-ittle bit hazy. But by two, a glittering rainbow-colored halo had formed around the sun. Hardly noticeable, but unmistakably there. Owing to the increasing density of water droplets at cirrostratus level. No one else had noticed it, and I spoke to no one about it. But I had the feeling that our attempt would result in failure. The total eclipse was estimated to occur at 3:45 and forty-eight seconds. For the next eighty minutes or so the sun was free of cloud cover, but cirrostratus clouds formed here and there and the sun was veiled, something that was hardly visible to the naked eye, but a damned hindrance to photography. This was the case during the first minute of the eclipse. The five of us stood, sat down, jumped up—Herr Moll had also come to help us—each behind his instrument. We held our breath and took photographs with each telescope. The main aim being: to record the formation of the eclipse as it crossed the sun's inner corona, as this was the most significant band in terms of solar science. Our instruments clicked at regular intervals, all around us a curious violet-gray ashen dusk that would soon reach its peak. An unreal darkness, where everything loses its contours at the same time as every single trembling leaf seems easier to distinguish than by the light of day—or, well—even of you cannot see them so, at least they appear as individual. When not staring into my ten-meter telescope and making photos, I noticed a group of young boys from Sogod had sneaked up to the plank fence of the schoolhouse and now and again peeped over it with their lilac-gray faces to see what we were doing. We were, after all, something of an attraction for the villagers. At the same time old men and women and some of the children had got to church in good time and through the open doors the *Miserere* could be heard, played on an asthmatic organ in this night in the middle of the day. To whose chords people were praying to the Lord so He would stretch out His hand and prevent *fear* from overwhelming them. And although my thoughts merged with this chorale (hoping He would hold back the wall of cloud, which was moving toward the moon and the sun from the west), it was to no avail: during the second minute of the total eclipse the thickening cirrostratus cloud finally swallowed the moon and sun altogether. At the end of the eclipse (this occurred about four and a half minutes from its beginning) the sun was blotted out, as if by loathsome witchcraft, by a dense rain cloud. So we were unable to observe the end of the eclipse. At which point we pulled the tarpaulin sacks over our equipment as the rain came down.

Baade later wrote, I don't know whom he was comforting, presumably himself, that the haze caused by the cirrus clouds had indeed affected the photographs in a very negative manner with regard to individual parts of the outer corona of the sun, but that we had nevertheless managed to get perfect details of the inner corona. Hm. Maybe other people need comforting in a disaster, be that as it may, but I cannot allow myself to be comforted. So I shall say out straight: the photos of the inner corona were no more than satisfactory. In other words, they might as well never have been taken. But I do admit that things were easier for me than for Baade on two counts. First, it was not me, but him, that had financed the whole enterprise and set up all the foundations and funds, so that we had at least fulfilled a good deal of our project. And second, I was by now only interested in my mirage seen in the porthole on the Andaman Sea, namely, my glass correction plate.

The next week, in the ever more frequent summer showers, we dismantled our observation post and packed up our equipment. On the twenty-second we were transported back to Cebu. On the twenty-eighth we boarded the *Dardanus* in white torrential rain, and two days later landed in that same type of rain in Manila. Hapag's brand-new *Duisburg,* launched the year before, now took us home via Hong Kong, Singapore, and Colombo. At thirteen and a half knots, an entirely normal speed for such a class of vessel. But still deadly slow.

■ □ ■ □ ■

2

"SO, YOU WOULD LIKE TO WRITE A NOVEL ABOUT BERNHARD Schmidt?"

The man with the lively face of a seventy-year-old, but who is in fact over eighty, drums his fingers on the table next to his glass of vermouth.

I nod.

Our conversation is taking place ten kilometers to the south of Gernsheim, among the vineyards on the banks of the Rhine, in a garden where the wrought-iron portal can be seen over the rhododendron hedge. You cannot see the nameplate and the bell from here. On the nameplate is written: FRIEDRICH KELTER, DR. RER. NAT. But the wrought-iron bow over the gate can be clearly seen. From inside the garden the letters appear in reverse: SOLNEKLOW ALLIV. From the outside, you can read: VILLA WOLKENLOS.

"And why ever not," my host smiles his well-shaved, sinewy red-complexioned smile. "For us Schmidt has, when it comes down to it, become a kind of—how shall I put it—mythological figure."

"A myth is a myth," I reply, "but you have met the real, living Schmidt. You knew him. For that reason, I . . ."

"Yes, what do we mean by 'knew'? Superficially, of course. And only *him,* not his *life* to any extent. There is a difference. Especially for a novelist. I saw his life only inasmuch as to doubt whether there is any subject matter for a *novel* in it. But then again, I am after all only a businessman. And a bit of a physicist. So that I have no real acquaintance with your *métier.* Beyond the cliché"—he stirred his straw around the ice cubes and took a swig of his Cinzano—"that a skillful author can cobble together a novel about the life of just about anybody."

I offer the opinion that specialist skills are not, in this particular case, necessary. At least not if the gentleman could help me by way of his memories of Schmidt. Which ought to be all the easier, since his memories and those of his father form one whole, and as far as I am aware his father had a favorable attitude toward Schmidt. So would he now not like to . . .

"Yes-yes-yes. Favorable is rather a modest way of putting it. Look, my father was not a man of feeling. He was an industrialist. And a professor, that as well. But his title was not awarded by some university for academic work. He had received it from the Prussian government for services rendered to science and industry. Principally for the organization and running of his own enterprise. The Kelter firm was a notion in itself. What does, let us say, the name Zeiss mean? Very efficient production, of course. But *mass* production. Items that required individual solutions, ultraprecise and large objects, scientific equipment, but not only that, things that could be used by astronomers or just as easily by defense; you understand, such things were ordered from Kelter's. We were a relatively small firm. But established in our field. One hundred fifty employees. Many of them hand-picked engineers. The most accurate Kärger lathes for grinding and polishing. At those lathes sat the most experienced master craftsmen available. And at the head of all of them was my father. On first-name terms with them all. He had been to America and lost his Prussian rigidity. So even some of the workers would *tutoyer* him, some of the more senior Social Democrat foremen. No more, but no less either. I can confirm to you: there was a fine patriarchal atmosphere in the best spirit of old Berlin. Educated technicians and skilled workers, I would say an aristocracy of workers, working hand in hand. Indeed: *that* would be the stuff of a novel! But do forgive me. You come from *over there.* You will not be interested in what industrial relations were like somewhere else in the world before your Lenin came along."

I admit: "Do forgive me, Dr. Kelter, but you are so right: what interests me at this moment is in the first instance Bernhard Schmidt . . ."

"Yes-yes-ye-e-s!" cries Herr Kelter, half bursting into laughter in his eagerness, "I do understand: novelists are oddballs—forgive my plain speaking—and are interested in oddballs. Because your Schmidt was undoubtedly an oddball himself."

"Do tell in what way." I switch on the tape recorder with a questioning gesture. He nods, indicating that it does not trouble him at all.

"Well, maybe because he lived in such a hole as Mittweida for thirty years. I could have understood had he been a philosopher. Whose world is in his head. In such cases it doesn't matter. Like Kant's fifty years in Königsberg, Husserl's twenty in Freiburg. Or if he'd been a novelist himself. Such people don't care in what surroundings they do their fantasizing. But a *technician.* I can understand that two hundred years ago such a blind devotion to the individualism of the craftsman would have obtained results. But in the twentieth century? When technology depends upon contacts and information! How could a talented technician—nowadays they even call him a genius—bury himself in Mittweida for thirty years? I can think of only two reasons for this. And neither of them does him any particular credit. The first: inertia. Hanging around where he had happened to end up. This would simply be due to a provincial inferiority complex; if you come from one peripheral place, you don't make any effort to get out of another. The other possibility: a blind feeling of superiority. I am Bernhard Schmidt from Naissaar, I don't need any of your Berlins or Munichs. I will settle wherever I want and do my job; sweat, struggle, and polish my way to the top. Till all of you begin to look me up . . . Wait, wait, wait. I can see from your face that you are growing boundlessly irritated by my cogitations. But you know from your own experience of the world that these two elements are indeed present in human nature. Never of course in a chemically pure form, one or the other. Always in a practical mixture. And besides and by the way: I know nothing about the mentality of people over there. That is for Sovietologists to study. But I do receive the impression that in your case there is a lack of our type of objectivity, scalpel sharp and at the same time—if there is a reason for it—an apologetic, immediate, somewhat clumsy and bantering critique. Where you come from, criticism is either a matter of damning something or praising it to the skies. And Schmidt ended up, in some strange manner, being counted among those who are praised by people living over your way. Is this not so?"

"Herr Kelter, my answer would not be of any importance to you. Because you do not intend to write either a treatise on Sovietology or a novel about Bernhard Schmidt. For that reason—if I may—could you not describe for what reason, and under what circumstances, you made your trip to Mittweida?"

"Listen, it was—I would think it was in 1925. Yes. The early spring of '25. I remember that the inflation was over and Father had managed to save his factory. Not *all* of German industry had disappeared into the pockets of the likes of Stinnes. We had started erecting a new main building, We had received our first orders from the state. And then it entered my father's head to go and have a look at what sort of man this Schmidt really was."

"So Schmidt was already a concept by then?"

"Well, not that so much. But before the war he had made some surprisingly well-constructed pieces of equipment for the Potsdam Observatory."

"And your father went down to Mittweida in the spring of twenty-five to get a look at Schmidt?"

"Precisely."

"Perhaps also to invite him to join your firm?"

"No-no. Not that. Or only if he were to prove particularly suitable, if you see what I mean."

"And you traveled with your father?"

"Yes. I was studying physics at Berlin Technical University at the time. Second year. And was helping my father with the firm. With a couple of projects. Correspondence. And on business trips I acted as his secretary. Cheaper and more reliable that some paid outsider."

"And then?"

"You know, I haven't a clue what Mittweida is like now, in Herr Honecker's day. But then, in Herr Ebert's day, it was a depressing provincial hole. We booked a room with added cockroaches at the very best hotel and went in search of Schmidt. We had his address. And became convinced all the more, on the way to his place, that there really was nothing of interest in that town."

"Well, it did have a famous technical college. Where Schmidt had also studied . . ."

"You know, if Mittweida is a seventh-rate hole, then its technical college is, shall we say, a fifth-rate seat of learning. It was only better than the town itself to that extent. Are you not acquainted with it? It was really just a vocational school by today's standards. With regard to what was on offer there. OK, a little more pleasant, as all educational institutions were in those days, but really just a vocational school. Of course, the greenhorns in the first class now learn the basics of quantum theory. In those days they learned two times two. In those days Adam Riese was still a respected man. And the results there were—I mean relatively, you understand—better than now. But as for Mittweida Technical College—it produced specialists of only middling professional ability. They were given engineer's diplomas. But that didn't make them engineers with an academic education. As for Schmidt, he didn't even have any such diploma in his pocket."

"Are you sure of that?"

"Absolutely. My father later checked his papers personally at the office of the technical college."

"With what aim?"

"Hmm—quite simple. He wanted to get to know Schmidt. And acted with typical German *Gründlichkeit.*"

"And then?"

"Well, as I said, we had his address. It was relatively near to the station. On Wilhelmstraße, if I am not mistaken. A shabby three-story rooming house from after the war. The front gate hung crooked. On the ground floor some kind of communal kindergarten. Noise and voices through the open windows. A narrow flight of stairs, smelling of onions, up to the top floor. Where there stood in the murky doorway some kind of lady with buffed hair surrounded by the petit bourgeois smell of naphthalene. You could see from her face that her lodger didn't like visitors. And besides, her lodger wasn't at home. Was likely to be in his workshop. Or maybe not. As the woman said vaguely. We let her describe the way there and went in search of his workshop. It was some three or four hundred meters farther up the road. And, by the way, Schmidt's whole life had been contained in those three hundred meters for all of thirty years. The rented room. In the next street a vegetarian eating house called the Sanitas. And his workshop. Behind that an observation post. And right next to his workshop a restaurant called the Lindengarten. So in the very literal sense of the word, thirty years and three hundred meters!"

I don't bother to correct his claim, and point out that the distance between his observation post and where Schmidt lived was some six hundred meters across Mittweida. But I do say: "Herr Kelter—at least before the First World War he did have a car, which would enable him to . . ."

"What would that enable him to do?" Herr Kelter cries out, and pours me another vermouth in triumph. "A few odd trips, with the help of friends. Because he couldn't sit at the wheel himself. And that was indeed *before.* Then came the war and he was interned. His friends too. As the citizens of a hostile power. When he was set free came the postwar distress. Not a time for car trips. And then came the postwar chaos and the inflation. He sold his car for five hundred billion marks and received three loaves of bread for it the following week!"

"Did he tell you that personally?"

"No-no, not personally. Not to me. But someone had told this to my father. Anyway. We then arrived at the door of his famous bowling alley cellar. I remember bleak concrete walls and muddy cellar steps. Father knocked a number of times and tried the door handle. No one answered and the door was locked. One of the residents came down the stairs and offered the opinion that Herr Schmidt might be at Bretschneider's, that is to say the Lindengarten restaurant. That was said to be his *Stammlokal.* So my father and I went there. It was a small provincial town bar. But spotlessly clean. The landlady was wiping the counter with a cloth and eyed us as if to size us up. No, Herr Schmidt had not been seen there that day. If he really wasn't in his workshop, then he must be at his observation post. The landlady went with us to the door and pointed to an allotment across the road.

"'There, to the left, you can see his tubes and other contraptions.'

"Behind the raspberry bushes two small wooden huts began to emerge and between them a telescope, presumably one with a thirty-centimeter aperture, a solid piece of equipment. But underneath it there wasn't the usual support made of steel tubes but rather some strange homemade wooden tripod. The huts were locked up and the plywood chair behind the telescope was vacant. We went back to the restaurant. Herr Schmidt had not turned up. We asked the landlady if he could perhaps be at the vegetarian eating house. She said that he never went there after five in the afternoon. He would go there between one and two o'clock—those days that he ate lunch, she added. Father decided to take another look in the bowling alley in the cellar. We went up to the door. Father knocked for a long time and shouted: 'Herr Schmidt! Can you hear me? This is Professor Kelter from Berlin. I would like to meet you . . .' But there was no reply. I said that maybe he was crouching inside, as people had told us that such things had happened. Father was sure that he couldn't be in his workshop: 'If he were there, he'd have opened up at the name Kelter.'

"We decided to go to the hotel—it was near the station, and it meant retracing our steps down that same street along which Schmidt's life of to-ing and fro-ing took place—anyway, to go to the hotel and have a late lunch. But halfway along I remembered the cockroaches and suggested that we go back to the Lindengarten to eat. Maybe Schmidt would turn up there. We turned around and walked in the direction of Frau Bretschneider's—and would you believe it—Schmidt was already sitting there! So now there was no shadow of a doubt: he had been in his workshop the second time we knocked and shouted after all, but had not opened the door.

"We instantly recognized him by his right hand and Father went up to his table to introduce himself."

"But Herr Kelter—your first impressions of Schmidt when you first saw him in real life were . . . ?"

"Well, he looked younger than he was. At that time he was already forty-five, but I would have taken him for under forty. Because of his thinness and an element of translucence. As one sees in TB patients. Though I doubt that he suffered from that disease. And his face was, I would like to say that it looked like what he was—the face of a stubborn peasant who had become an intellectual. Pale, rather high cheekbones. A skeptical, maybe even sensitive mouth. A little ginger mustache. Very close-cropped hair of an auburn tinge. A straight triangular nose. Gray, relatively deep-set eyes, but slightly bulging, staring. Thin eyebrows. But such eyebrows belonging to a person with whom it is difficult to argue."

"Herr Kelter—I have to say, you have an excellent photographic memory. From only one or two visits . . ."

"Well, you know, I have seen his photo often enough. In Father's study there were pictures of all those Frauenhofers and Abbes in a row on the wall. And later of Schmidt as well. But what I also wanted to say was: what people say about his being sloppy about his appearance is only partly true. At least according to my observations. Though people do tend to dress up when they are going to be photographed. But I don't think that Schmidt had done so to any degree. Because I am talking about my own memories. I'm prepared to wager that he had just come straight from his work to Bretschneider's. His suit was, of course, neither new nor elegant. That is true. Some cheap off-the-peg dark-gray suit. A little dusty, no doubt because of the particles of ground glass, and quite creased. A number of people have mentioned the crease in his trousers, or lack of it, his trousers that bagged around the knees. But it wasn't so bad for Mittweida. Maybe because there was some woman in his life. But what I want to say is: there was a hint of what could be termed proletarian elegance in his clothing, something that struck you immediately—he wore a cheap knitted tie and a very clean white shirt with a stiff white collar. And his shoes were polished to perfection, despite the foul April weather."

Herr Kelter raises his glass with his right hand and puts the straw to his lips. Then he remembers another detail, as clearly the idea of a photographic memory has enthused him unexpectedly. He raises the index finger of his left hand and takes the straw out of his mouth:

"And, by the by, he had a size thirty-nine neck, but the clean collar that I mentioned just now was a forty-one or even a forty-two. Ha-ha-ha-haa."

"But Herr Kelter—do you remember what his hand was like? Did you shake hands?"

"Yes. Well, it was a bit of a mismatch. As is every handshake between right and left hands."

"But anything else? You no doubt paid the pressure of that handshake some attention. As it was rather an unbelievable hand—for someone with your professional knowledge."

"Oh, listen, I said to you right at the start: I don't indulge in mythologizing about Schmidt. Not even now when there are others who do. And all the less in those days, when the myth did not yet exist. And when I was a young man, in my—how shall I put it—most unmythological time of life. So I didn't notice anything unusual. A normal, rather delicate, nervous hand. As far as I remember. Yes—

maybe I did receive the impression that it was a sensitive and very thin-skinned hand. But that would have been more than natural."

"And how did your conversation go?"

"As I said, Father introduced himself, mentioned that we had traveled to Mittweida specifically to meet him, and asked permission to join him at the table. He gave it. Not with exaggerated respect, but anyway. He had in front of him half a glass of schnapps and half a cigar resting on the ashtray. Father asked if he could order him anything. He spread his fingers in the air and refused the offer. For him—nothing more. By the way, with that one hand of his he did more gesturing than he did speaking, being a man of few words. Father asked him if he would even refuse vegetarian hors d'oeuvres. He refused. Father asked him what he would like to drink, and ordered a bottle of korn for us at dinner. Although he never drank the stuff himself. Schmidt allowed us to fill his glass from the bottle. And then Father began his conversation with Schmidt."

"But even before that—do tell me Herr Kelter: What was it that really drove your father to this?"

"Curiosity. Above all. Because Father simply could not believe what people told about Schmidt. That these extraordinarily precise instruments he had constructed in Potsdam and elsewhere could be made using such primitive equipment. And by a man with only one hand. As tools, he was rumored to use some strange things he'd cobbled together from wood and tin. Plus an old pedal-driven lathe. Plus lumps of glass and pieces of chamois leather. But his accuracy when at work was—hmm—almost the same as with our newest Kärger lathes . . ."

"Almost as good? Or almost even better?"

"Mmmmm—you know—sometimes the one, sometimes the other."

"And what was talked about, on that occasion?"

"Well, during his life Father had learned to approach people in a variety of ways. And he had quite some *Menschenkenntnis.* But in the case of oddballs, his experience in this field wasn't really of much use. Nor do I want to in any way idealize my father. He could err when choosing his approach. He could exercise judgment using unchecked data. Imagining he could somehow allow himself a degree of improvisation as he was steered by the psychological instincts of an experienced man. In Schmidt's case he presumably thought that he should not push things in the case of this provincial and, as the Germans say, fall *mit der Tür ins Haus.*" In order to win confidence it was necessary to beat about the bush in that good old-fashioned way. So he began by saying that we, the Kelters, are to a certain extent also Baltic Germans—ha-ha-haa. I hope that my then twenty-year-old facial expression was sufficiently opaque. So that Schmidt did not notice my surprise. Because all the Kelters are from Brandenburg and we have nothing more in common with Baltic Germans than one aunt who got married to some forest steward in Courland and lived out her days in Mitau. But Father never got the chance to expand upon the theme of Baltitude. Because Schmidt blew his cigar smoke in his face—not on purpose, of course—and said:

"'We've got Baltic Germans in Estonia, a pretty unpopular bunch.'

"Father said: 'That is unfortunate, of course. And for someone who has a rather sensitive disposition such intolerance can be a burden from time to time. So I can understand you completely when you say that you moved to Germany because of local intolerance . . .'

"At that point, Schmidt took his cigar from his mouth and said: 'Look, I'm not a Baltic German! I'm just one of those—one of those local intolerants, if you wish.' So Father could do nothing else but utter an *Ach so!,* with a longer *oh* sound than usual, and saved his skin by bursting into laughter. After Father had put his foot in it, things got a bit embarrassing, so I interjected: 'Herr Schmidt is, as far as I know, from Naissaar—*von der Insel Nargen bei Reval, nicht wahr*?'

"Father seized the moment—he did of course know this fact himself—and steered the conversation to how those that lived by the sea, and especially those from the islands, had strong characters. And so on. Not too chatty, but in a well-considered way, almost taciturn, so that his aim was obvious only to those already in the know. Incidentally, the fact that Schmidt hailed from Naissaar—*seine Nargennarrheit*—was well known among his acquaintances. And was, you know, also quite obvious in the stories about him. When you phoned me and said you wanted to talk about Schmidt, I looked in our archive (luckily we managed to save it when the old factory burnt down in 1943) and went through the papers referring to our Schmidt. His *Insel Nargen,* his *Narreninsel,* as I could put it, keeps coming up in Schmidtiana to this day. Oh yes! His obituary—some fifty years ago, there was a one-page obituary in *Astronomische Nachrichten,* written by Professor Schorr—mentions Naissaar twice. For Schmidt's hundredth birthday five years ago a scientific conference was held, and in his two-page speech the vice chancellor of Hamburg University—the names of the other participants escape me—well, he too mentions Naissaar twice. And so forth. Apart from that, on the gravestone that colleagues had erected, the word 'Nargen' is, at all events, inscribed as his place of birth. I would like to ask: Why do people who know nothing about it keep mentioning his island in connection with his name? And I would say this: because he himself kept mentioning it ceaselessly. Although that ceaselessly is relative, isn't it? Because, you understand, relative to his extremely reticent nature, his Nargen refrain was very noticeable. Or audible, if you like. This, his hobbyhorse, his hobby isle if you like, had been mentioned to my father by several colleagues, and so Father exploited this fact at once. He explained that we, the Kelters, were also islanders to a degree. Which made me think that, well, damn it, what is he basing that assumption on now? We don't have anything to do with islands except for the fact that we have rented a summerhouse on that island full of hares in Lake Schwerin . . . But that was what Father had in mind. He didn't need any more than that! And I can testify: he spoke entirely objectively and convincingly about how he had visited that island, and how being there had helped him solve scientific and organizational problems, and how he had found a fresh approach and increased concentration out there. He added, modestly: 'Nevertheless, we didn't have the rush of the sea under our window, as you of course did, just the lapping of the lake. And were even in the middle of autumn, stumbling over late summer guests on our island. Yes, despite everything, I do very well understand your attachment to Nargen. Especially when I think how that slight addition to individualism that an *island* can offer has inspired my own imagination. Yes indeed. So that I have my island to thank for my lively imagination . . .' Such unexpected associations came quite naturally to my father. And then rushing forward to the point he wanted to get to even more so. In this instance all the more so because Schmidt—I feared that Schmidt would start smiling all the time my father had been talking—Schmidt had listened to Father's island fantasia through his cigar smoke not only without smiling but even with a favorable mien.

"Father pushed aside his plate of gnawed *rinderbraten* that he had now finished and poured Schmidt and himself a glass of schnapps. Frau Bretschneider brought us coffee, Father raised his glass to Schmidt, they chinked glasses, and after that Father put his cards on the table:

"But—Herr Schmidt, all that I have told you now is indeed the result of a lively imagination—but I can't fathom yours. Even though I am a specialist at a, shall we say, somewhat more theoretical level than yourself, or more practical, no matter, I'm a serious specialist, if you see what I mean. In spite of all that—or perhaps because of it, I cannot make you out.'

"Schmidt took a puff at his cigar and remained silent. Father said:

"'You will ask in what way. I will tell you. Look, those of your achievements that have become well known—let us select from them the most minor ones, such as *correction work,* astronomical mirrors, things made by large firms that you have polished to perfection—I cannot imagine that they have been done in the manner that some people say. I mean, using the most primitive equipment you could ever imagine. Some ancient lathe and chunks of glass. On the other hand, neither can I believe the opposite stories: that you have discovered some hitherto unknown way of computation and polishing. So, Herr Schmidt, would you like to explain to me where your secret lies?'

"Schmidt's mouth was hidden behind the fingers holding his cigar, so with the best will in the world I could not see whether under that little mustache a smile had formed or not. He thought for a moment:

"'What secret could there be? The equipment is old. But the method is, of course, new.'

"'Oh yes?' cried Father in genuine amazement. 'This is a most mysterious business! Do explain. What does this new method involve?'

"I have already mentioned that we had heard that Schmidt was unwilling to let just anyone into his workshop. Especially strangers. But Professor Kelter's name was of course not unfamiliar to him. And Father's interest in his method seemed so damned genuine—and indeed it was, was it not?—that Schmidt thawed out. Well, this was not entirely unexpected. You can imagine that genuine interest from a well-known expert and the hidden expertise of a hermit could come together over a glass of spirits. Schmidt beckoned to Frau Bretschneider:

"'Put three korns on my bill for this evening.'

"'But I've only brought you one, Herr Schmidt,' the landlady insisted.

"'I took two glasses from Herr Kelter's bottle. Take them off his bill.'

"Father tried to dispute this. Schmidt had already risen from the table: 'If you want to see, come and have a look.'

"Schmidt led the way. Father paid the bill hastily, and as he passed the landlady he slipped the bottle of korn into his pocket. Schmidt's cellar was in the adjoining building. A minute later he unlocked the door to the former bowling alley and switched on the electric light.

"A long, low room. More or less as you would expect. A bowling alley, about one and a half meters wide and a dozen or so long, as is usual, filling most of the room. On the dirty plaster walls hung star charts, rolls of wire, chronometers, instruments of unclear function, some sort of blueprints for lenses, mirrors, and reflectors, rather sketchily drawn, a number of propellers of greatly differing sizes made out of wood or tin, some clearly from boats, others from wind machines, and two old straw hats. The alley itself had been sawn obliquely in two through the middle. A section about a meter wide had been removed, forming an aisle of sorts. The front end of the bowling alley, you understand, had been raised on low feet to about forty centimeters in height. So that this area formed a huge long workbench, strewn with instruments, books, and drawings. On the lower half of the bowling alley there were a number of contraptions whose function was obscure and had no doubt been built by Schmidt himself, but not for polishing, that much was clear.

"Father asked on what grounds Schmidt had chosen this rather odd room as his workshop. Schmidt explained that he had a number of preferences: the low rent, plenty of space, and the fact that the bowling alley provided a more or less horizontal working area.

"Father said: 'But an annoyingly low temperature.'

"'But a low and *level* temperature. If the radiators are turned off. That is the most important condition for precision polishing,' said Schmidt.

"He strode into the nether regions of the room and pointed to a large shelf on the wall. On this shelf lay, in rows but not exaggeratedly neatly, chamois leather cloths and chunks of glass of several shapes and clearly different hardness and quality.

"'There you are,' said Schmidt in a somewhat naively victorious voice, 'my instrumentarium.'

"'And that is really all there is?' asked my father.

"'The polishing lathe as well, of course.' Schmidt indicated the pedal-driven lathe standing in front of the shelf.

"Father cried: 'But that thing's surely fifty years old—if not something dating back to the time of Spinoza!'

"'It is indeed,' said Schmidt, 'a good fifty years old. But I have myself given it precision.'

"Father looked around in disbelief, then straight at Schmidt. Because the reply sounded absurd to him. And to me. So my father asked once again:

"'And that really is your whole instrumentarium?'

"'Yes. Plus, of course, my main instrument,' said Schmidt—you know, the tiniest hint of a cheeky smile appeared on his face. 'But that is much newer. It is forty-six years old . . .'

"'And that would be?' asked Father.

"Schmidt said: 'This,' and thrust his sole hand rather impolitely under Father's nose.

"But my father was, of course, not in any way insulted. Because Schmidt interested him too much, you understand. So that he began to laugh and said:

"'OK, OK. That instrument, naturally. But every master craftsman has one, some of course a little more precise than others. The main question in such cases is nonetheless the *method.* You told us that you have discovered a new method. Tell us of what it consists.'

"Schmidt looked Father straight in the eye, pursed his lips, and I couldn't judge just how serious or flippant his reply was going to be. He said—as I remember—something like this:

"'The method is, of course, new. Or actually, very old. The oldest there is. But it is seldom put into practice.'

"He fell silent and Father was at him again: 'This is all damned interesting. So what is it?'

"'The thing is that I ask the glass.'

"'Ask it—in what way?'

"'I ask the glass. Whether I am moving in the right direction, or going astray.'

"'*Ach so.* And the glass gives you an answer?'

"'Huh-huh.'

"'And then?'

"'Then I do what it says.'

"Father burst into gales of laughter: 'And in what language do you speak to it?'

"Schmidt smiled a wry smile, but I observed him closely and it seemed to me that he almost felt genuinely bewildered:

"'Mmm—I hadn't thought of that . . . Glass language . . . Or Estonian, maybe. Yes, surely, in Estonian,' he said with rather childlike eureka joy.

"Father laughed: 'It must be a very mirrorlike language!' He took a seat, as if at home, on the edge of the workbench and began to put concrete questions to Schmidt: well, for example, was it true that he, Schmidt, was, as rumored, capable of feeling zonal aberrations of some thousandths of a millimeter on the surface of a parabolic mirror? Schmidt confirmed this. Father said that, excuse me, Herr Schmidt, but I do not believe you. Schmidt went to the other side of the workbench and opened two or three large drawers. In the drawers lay concave mirrors of various dimensions—from fifteen to thirty centimeters in diameter.

"'Take your pick, Professor. These are the work of the Goerz glass grinders. Pretty misshapen, the lot of them.'

"'OK,' said my father, 'I'll take the one in the middle. And what are we going to do next?'

"'Take hold of this etalon. You will test using the etalon and note down the deviations. As with a target. Clock time and points. And an estimation of the size of the deviation. When we've found them. I will check by hand. And I will write down my results separately. Then we will compare notes and check the results against one another.'

"And would you believe it. They spent a whole hour slogging away at that mirror. That is to say, Father slogged away with the etalon for a whole hour. And did of course find five or six small deviations."

Herr Kelter begins to put more ice cubes into his own and my glass. And I ask myself: Is he working up strength for a major confession or a major denial? Then I can resist it no longer:

"But what about Schmidt?"

"Ah, well. It was like this. When Father was ready, Schmidt walked up to the table and pushed a blank sheet of paper in front of me: 'Young man, write this down . . .' You understand: he hadn't got a free hand to do so himself. He placed his hand on the mirror. So lightly that it seemed as if he wasn't even touching it. Like someone juggling plates while not touching them. He was of course touching the mirror. But very, very lightly. And began, with three fingers together, maybe only the middle ones, to describe a spiral from the center outward. Clockwise. He was looking down at the plate, but I got the impression that his eyes were in fact shut. While doing this he muttered the details that I had to write down: 'Eight points, eleven o'clock to half past one. A bump up to two hundredths of a millimeter . . .' And so on. Altogether he found—as I seem to remember—eleven deviations. Then he and my father measured the exact deviations with a micrometer. And compared the depths and heights of those found. Well, there's no point lying about a scientific truth. If you can call such an odd phenomenon that. Schmidt's results were more exact than my father's."

I put my glass of vermouth down on the table and say—and the words come out with more force than I intend:

"But Herr Kelter—this is the mark of a genius!"

"Oh, there's no need to use such grand words. It was far from being the work of a genius. But in its own way it was very nearly perfect. That it was. You know, if you transfer these powers of his to, let us say, a musical level, he had perfect pitch, *very* perfect pitch. But no more than that. Did you know whether Beethoven had perfect pitch? Or didn't have? You don't know? Nor me. Because it is of no importance. And besides, we both know that later he couldn't hear anything at all. But still remained Beethoven, didn't he. So Schmidt's powers are not such a big deal. But he did impress my father a lot. You see, he was a self-made man who had acquired his education in middle age. He was an old practitioner. He had in fact begun where Schmidt had ended up now, from a single room. He didn't of course start hopping from one foot to the other at Schmidt's performance. But said instead: 'Herr Schmidt, I have to admit that this is very impressive.'

"I said at the start that my father was not a man of feeling. That he was, in the first instance, a businessman. And in general this was true. But on the rarest of occasions he would make an exception. Or some primitive inkling of feeling would make some exception in him, to be more precise. Well, for instance, at Christmas every year, he would send some small sum of money to the junior school he had attended as a boy. And on occasion he would take steps in the direction of charity when something reminded him of his own childhood as an orphan or impecunious youth. And Schmidt's case seemed one of these occasions that reminded him of such things. Schmidt's odd sovereign and refractory nature was quite different from that of my father—but they had something in common. And compared to my father he was a relatively young man, some twenty years his junior. So Father could well have felt a protective attitude toward him. Besides, Schmidt's pretty vile living conditions were plain for all to see. But his manual skills were manifest. As well, to top it all, the fact that he was an invalid came into the equation. To my father, with his strong and somewhat ruthless character, Schmidt had something of . . . something, you know, of the repugnance and attraction caused when you see an injured bird. Anyhow, I detected in my father's voice—once he'd admitted that Schmidt's little act had been impressive—that he had become, well, slightly moved by him.

"But Schmidt himself looked at his pocket watch from Grandfather's days and said (although he didn't need to apologize to us) that he was now, unfortunately, in a hurry. That he had arranged to meet someone at home at eight. Well, Father thanked him politely for a most interesting opportunity, as he expressed it, to get a brief look at his work, and so we all stepped out together onto the street. We were going the same way, he to his home and we to the hotel further down the same street.

"Father strolled along ahead with Schmidt, and it strikes me that I heard their conversation quite clearly. Father asked Schmidt one or two details about his uranostat. Schmidt explained. Father asked something else and explained something for his part. Schmidt cried out, 'No-no-no . . . !' and by now we had arrived at the gate of the rooming house. Schmidt said: 'Wait, I'll explain,' looked round in a rather perplexed way, and then said:

"'OK, come up then.'

"We went up the familiar stairs to the familiar door to his room. When Schmidt unlocked the door and we stood in the hall, which smelled of naphthalene, the door to a room opened and the landlady with the buffed hair we had already encountered stepped out. You'll be happy to hear, my dear novelist, that I've found her name in the archive. My father received a letter from Schmidt before our trip to Mittweida. And it happens to have survived. Along with the envelope. On it is written 'c/o Frau Knechtel.' Authors tend to think that alongside a free imagination, such exact details, as in police records, are of importance. So, there you are: Frau Knechtel, Wilhelmstraße, No. 6. Anyway, Frau Knechtel stepped out into the hall and announced that Fräulein Johanna had come seeking Herr Schmidt and promised to return later. Schmidt then asked:

"'Haven't the children come yet?'

"Frau Knechtel said no, not the children, not yet. Yes, specifically 'the children.' *Children* were coming to visit the confirmed bachelor and stellar optics expert Schmidt! You can imagine the scene: suffer the little children to come unto me, and they shall see the heavens—or something like that. Slightly modulated, with 'the heavens' instead of 'heaven.' That would be acceptable to you too, wouldn't it? Anyway . . ."

Herr Kelter, in a fatherly way, forgives my rather narrow views regarding the kingdom of heaven and my excess of sympathy for Schmidt, tops up our vermouth glasses, and continues:

"Anyway, we stepped into Schmidt's room. The room was as you would expect. Quite spacious, but of course shabbily furnished. And I must say, in an unbelievable mess for someone who worked with precision instruments. And if you imagine that the room of a person whose workshop is only five minutes' walk away would be of quite a different character, not so much in terms of wealth but of function, that a workshop was for work and a home for coziness, then, in Schmidt's case, you would be greatly mistaken. His living room was nearly as much of a workshop as his bowling alley in the cellar. The only thing missing from the living room was the lathe and the shelf with glass for polishing. Only bare walls with blueprints, a drawing board, and even some dismantled amateur telescopes and their parts, a table strewn with books, sketches, drafts, calculations in random heaps, and in the middle of all this a quite large, quite worn, plush armchair. And at the back, behind a screen, a bed.

"If I remember rightly, Schmidt didn't ask us to sit down in the first instance. He pulled a sheet of paper out of a drawer somewhere, held it in place on the table with the stump of his right hand, and made a lightning sketch with his left hand of his uranostat. Then he started to explain to my father its principle of rotation. I followed the explanation standing in between them—via my father I knew all about minor sensations in this field, but some specialists had written that this was supposed to be an exceptionally accurate instrument without peer. The problem was roughly this: while observing, you had to move the telescope in accordance with the movements of the heavens. The sky moves absolutely evenly. But it is damned difficult to get a telescope to move at an absolutely constant speed. The object of study always ends up getting nudged out of focus. Schmidt's uranostat solved the problem in an idiotically simple manner and resulted in, practically speaking, absolute uniformity of movement.

"'And by what principle do you get it to work for you?' asked my father.

"'A water reservoir with throughflow,' replied Schmidt. 'When the level of the water moves, the speed does too. When the level stays the same, the speed stays the same. It's very simple to build.'

"'And did you really get the idea,' Father gave a cough, 'as people say . . .'

"'Yes,' said Schmidt, 'from the water tank of the toilet.'

"Schmidt explained to my father how he determined the movement of the earth by the corresponding movements of the apparatus—but I saw that Father was no longer giving him his full attention. Then Schmidt stopped talking and Father thanked him again, as he put it, for his little enlightening lecture, and it was then that Schmidt noticed that he had not offered his visitors a seat. He showed Father to the armchair and pulled a stool out from behind the screen and asked me to sit down on it, until I found another for myself and left the first one for him. We were now sitting at the more or less free end of the table and with a most matter-of-fact look my father put the bottle of korn on the table.

"'I noticed that this was your brand. But maybe we can get a cup of coffee from your landlady?'

"I remember: Schmidt became childishly embarrassed for an instant. He mumbled something to the effect that using the landlady's services was not part of his rent agreement and he had not used them up to now. At any rate, he rose from his seat reluctantly. He wanted to, or didn't want to, go and ask his landlady for the coffee. But Father prevented him from leaving the room and said simply:

"'Herr Schmidt—if you will allow me, I'll arrange for . . .'

"Father went into the hall, and through the door we heard him talking to the landlady. Something that would work in such a situation: that he was Professor so-and-so from Berlin. That he had already had the honor of talking to the lady earlier that afternoon. That Herr Schmidt was a younger colleague of his and very well regarded. And he, the professor, would be boundlessly grateful to Frau Knechtel if she would make Herr Schmidt and his guests a small pot of really good strong coffee. 'No-no-no, please take them!' could be heard as he clearly pressed some mark notes into the landlady's hand. And would the dear lady bring the pot, three cups, and three glasses to Herr Schmidt's room. 'You know what Herr Schmidt's like. He's too modest. He didn't dare to ask you himself.'

"I don't remember," Herr Kelter continues, "what we talked about for the next quarter of an hour. Then Frau Knechtel brought in the pot of coffee. Quite excited and waggling her bottom in her willingness to please.

"When she had left the room, Father opened the bottle and poured our glasses full himself. Well, he added a few appropriate words about how nice it was to make Herr Schmidt's acquaintance and they downed their glasses. As my father was present, I only wet my lips. In those days, that was the only thing a twenty-year-old boy could do in polite circles. When my father filled their glasses again, Schmidt said that *as an exception* he could allow himself an extra glass. It just happened that that very morning he had sent something quite unastronomical to the Patent Registry in Berlin—a new design for a wind-driven engine for boats. Father thought that Flettner had already built something similar, but Schmidt said very self-confidently that his engine was quite different from Flettner's, and much better to boot. I remember him saying that Prandtl himself had added a glowing attestation. But he added, almost grinning, 'I won't, of course, obtain the patent. And this will be my eighth attempt . . .'"

Herr Kelter returns from his reminiscences to the present day, and explains: "Maybe you have found out why he didn't get the patents. I'm not so sure myself. One was, anyhow, something he was negotiating with Junkers about—a telephoto lens to be used on cartographers' airplanes. Another was, I think, a gastroscope. Some kind of flexible tool for use by doctors. The patient would have to swallow it and the doctor would then take a look at the inside of his stomach. A third was some kind of precision screw. A fourth was, of course, his uranostat. A fifth—I don't know whether it in fact merited a patent. Hardly. It was what you might call a home periscope. Not for peeping through roofs, but for looking downward. No not for the police to use either, ha-ha-haa. His relationship with the police was a little on the bad side. Some clever farmer from Frankenau who had grown rich on moonshine had ordered such a device. For some strange reason he lived in the loft above his cowshed. Schmidt's device would make his life a good deal more comfortable. He would switch on the lights in his cowshed at night and would look through the device, which was on his bedside table, to see if all twenty of his cattle were OK—which were chewing the cud, which sleeping, which lying down, which calving—surveying the whole scene without having to rise from bed. Apart from the uranostat, that must be the only device that was built after the war for which Schmidt actually got paid. And he said, out of bitter experience:

"'I'm afraid that even if I get the patent for my wind motor—I will receive the same meager rewards as with the seven previous ones for which I applied. Because there are no more buyers for that than there are for my astronomical junk.'

"Father said: 'Yes, Herr Schmidt, your experiences are exactly the same as mine were in my youth—an inventor who needed independence above all else is constantly dependent upon chance occurrences in the most ridiculous of ways. It's a tragedy. I know.'

"Schmidt looked at my father for a long time, with what I felt was an almost agitated expression, then concentrated on lighting his cigar and said, 'I am seriously thinking of selling all my junk to a secondhand stall at the market, and starting all over again . . .'

"I would love to have known what the new life would have consisted of (and it would have been handy for an author to know), but as I remember, we never got to hear. Because Father said all of a sudden: 'Herr Schmidt—I have a proposition to make. Come and work for Kelter's!'"

Herr Kelter Junior takes a bitter almond from the crystal bowl on the table, the first during our conversation, and pops it into his mouth.

"Father's suggestion was quite unexpected, so I remember it quite clearly. I was the future boss of the firm. And I remember that the idea of Schmidt working for the firm did worry me. Not because he would become too great an authority, as you might imagine. But simply because I could sense his willful character. He had, of course, achieved more in optics than I had at the time. So any feeling of rivalry was not entirely alien to me. I remember Schmidt getting to his feet at Father's suggestion, in roughly the same way as he did when rejecting Father's suggestion for dinner—or as if he was drawing someone's attention to something with all five fingers—and at that very moment Frau Knechtel knocked on the door and announced that *the children* had arrived.

"Behind the landlady's back stood three or four lively schoolboys of folk school age, ten or twelve years old and moderately badly behaved. Instead of quietly going on their way after what she had just said—Herr Schmidt has got guests from Berlin!—they demanded to have a word with *Uncle* Bernhard: they had an appointment with *Uncle* Bernhard. And Uncle Bernhard did not set them an educative example. Instead of packing the children off, making apologies to us and giving what was, after all, a very serious offer on our part his full attention, instead of doing that, he invited them in and almost apologized *to them;* you understand: as you can see, I've got these visitors, but we'll manage even with them here.

"It turned out that Schmidt organized lessons on 'getting to know the sky' for children from Mittweida and nearby. And, by the way, not for payment, but in order to get them to 'develop their knowledge of astronomy.' So things went exactly as I have described: suffer the little children to come unto me, that is to say, he was this century's astronomical Christ *par excellence.*

"He agreed with his young disciples that they would meet at ten—and the time was already past half past eight—which gave him and my father (I myself didn't count) just over an hour. The disciples were to congregate at ten—not at Gethsemane, but at the gates to Hetzger's garden. They would go in and he would shown them Saturn's rings. If I remember rightly.

"And when the classically small, or actually quite large, act of temerity had passed and the boys had gone and Father had returned to his proposal—for he was of a consistent nature and once he had decided to do something he would always come back to it—he still didn't receive an answer. Because right then Schmidt's Fräulein Johanna marched right in, knocking at the door but not waiting for an answer."

"Oh! . . ." I can't suppress a cry. "So you also met Fräulein Johanna! But this is priceless. So I'll get to hear what your impression of her was."

"I don't really know," says Herr Kelter, "what role she played in Schmidt's life. We heard—or rather had already heard, that despite his handicap Schmidt was rather keen on women during his first years in Mittweida. Whether this was despite his handicap or just because of it, we shall never know. Later, and by the time we were visiting him in Mittweida, that young lady was more or less his common-law wife. What her surname was is something I regretfully do not know." Herr Kelter gives a smile of apology. "Schmidt didn't send us her address and it can't be found in the company archive. What was my impression of her? . . . Well, a curvy brunette with rosy cheeks. In those days maybe twenty-five or twenty-six. A little tall for Schmidt. Almost his height. She was quite tall for a woman of those days. Though she wouldn't be taken on by any basketball team nowadays. A pleasant lively girl wearing a cheap blue costume and a pair of worn street shoes. With, no doubt for Schmidt's sake, quite low heels. But otherwise a *perfectly ordinary* woman. A typist at the county council or similar. You know, some quite outstanding men have had very ordinary wives . . ."

Herr Kelter looks me in the eye. He is watching my expression in the way a victorious old fox would—and raises a didactic finger. "No-no, do not draw the conclusion that I am trying to heighten Schmidt's unusual qualities by making her so ordinary. Some quite outstanding men have very ordinary wives—but that is only half of it. The other half is that ordinary men also tend to have ordinary wives. But anyway. I don't remember why Fräulein Johanna dropped in. I got the impression she was bringing him an evening meal, some cabbage stew or something similar. What is perhaps more important is my impression of how Schmidt treated her. No-no, in quite the usual manner, of course. He even introduced us to her and her to us. But during Johanna's half-hour visit Schmidt did exhibit some measure of boyish restlessness. He was, like a little boy, ashamed at the arrival of the girl while strangers were present, and at the same time her arrival brought with it, how shall I put it, a kind of worry mixed with joy. Whereas the girl treated him with a somewhat motherly pride, a proud motherly solicitousness. As with a childishly clever child. Whose mother does of course think he is a genius. As mothers always do. Johanna drank a cup of coffee with us but refused a schnapps. Schmidt had, I think, shown off to us a bit with his schoolboys, without actually saying anything, that is. But with Johanna he was uncertain. At the same time as the girl herself—I have to say—seemed to be *showing off* to us, however subtly, how at home she felt at Schmidt's place, and with Schmidt in general. Despite this behavior that verged on the tactless, she did give the impression of pitying him ever so slightly melancholically. I don't know whether you can understand me. It was only a fleeting impression. Which I have warmed up for our present conversation. Then the girl left and I have never met her since. And a few years later she also vanished from Schmidt's life as far as I know—when he moved to Hamburg, first temporarily, then for good. Anyway, there we were, the three of us once again in Schmidt's Mittweida room, when my father returned to his offer:

"'Herr Schmidt, I am still waiting for your answer.'

"The interruptions had given Schmidt time to weigh his reply, so that he put his cards on the table forthwith. And I do have the impression that he tended in general to be a man of few words, though maybe not *so* taciturn as myth would have it; but now his words sounded well formulated and came out with some rapidity:

"'I will agree on one condition. That the firm pays me two hundred new marks per month . . .'

"Father interposed: 'Two hundred and fifty.' From which I saw with surprise just how much getting Schmidt for himself now meant to him.

"Schmidt repeated: 'Two hundred marks a month, but that my status remains someone in voluntary collaboration. The firm shall not impose on me any concrete responsibilities.'

"'How do you mean?' my father wondered. 'That would be most unusual. My firm does not have anyone in what you term "voluntary collaboration." You will receive two hundred marks a month and the position of junior engineer. And when you have worked your way up, there could be a position as senior engineer in it for you, and three hundred and fifty a month. Despite the fact that your engineer's diploma is only from Mittweida Technical College.'

"'No,' said Schmidt, 'I will not take upon myself any type of responsibility for what Kelter's produces.'

"'For what reason? Aren't Kelter products good enough for you?' asked Father, both surprised and shocked.

"'Do you really want to know?' Schmidt asked, for his part.

"'I most certainly do!' shouted my father, not without a slight challenge in his voice.

"Schmidt said: 'OK. When it comes to mechanical polishing, Kelter's is undoubtedly one of the best. But all such firms and all their Michels and other lathes are, when it comes to precision polishing, mere barley mills. I am prepared to come to this agreement with you: I continue to work on my own. But over the year I would *choose* which of your orders I would fulfill, taking suitability into account. Under the brand name "Bernhard Schmidt Kelter." And for that you will pay me two hundred marks a month.'

"Father yelled: 'You mean without any obligation on your part and with no checks by the firm?'

"Schmidt said: 'With the necessary trust by both parties.'

"Father said nothing, swallowed the temptation to tell Schmidt to go to hell, and smiled. Then he said:

"'Herr Schmidt: normal responsibilities, discipline, a working day eight hours long. The brand name "Kelter." But the title "head of construction" and four hundred marks a month.'

"I saw Father lick a tiny bead of sweat from his upper lip and look at Schmidt, eyes narrowed.

"Schmidt shook his head. And do you know, it seemed that the rogue was actually enjoying the situation. When I had collected a few details on him on my father's instructions before we set off, I was told that sometimes on a Sunday before the war he would travel to Dresden to bet on the horses at the hippodrome. Before the war he would at times have a little money. In short, he must have had something of the gambler in him. And now it struck me in a flash that his little ginger mustache jerked in what must have been the somewhat rambunctious joys of gambling. All the more as Father rose to the challenge:

"'Five hundred marks a month!'

"Schmidt shook his head. I trod on Father's foot under the table. He pulled his foot free and pushed mine aside. Perhaps I had intuited the possibility of such simple outbursts, but I had never experienced such behavior before. Father shouted:

"'Hell and damnation—how much do you think you're really worth?'And when I tried to pull at his sleeve he shouted at me: 'No! Don't you try to lecture me! I want to see what this young man (notice that he called Schmidt a young man) . . . what this young man himself thinks . . . Six hundred!'

"Schmidt shook his head. And Father shouted, 'Nine hundred!'

"Maybe you, as a writer, will be able to find some subtle psychological reason why my father missed the intervening hundreds without jumping straight to one thousand. I was quite sure that Schmidt would shake his head for the fifth time. So sure that I didn't even look in his direction. But I did watch Father's face, reddened and sweaty from awkwardness and worry. Even in those days he already suffered from hypertension. And then, can you imagine, Schmidt said suddenly, in a fairly low voice, but very cautiously:

"'Agreed.'

"I was thinking to myself: Is this scoundrel playing on the fact that Father is an old-fashioned Prussian whose word is his bond? Schmidt *could* well feel that Father would foolishly be forced to stick to his word. And I myself cannot know whether indeed Father will do so—and if he does, Schmidt really is a psychological blackguard. But no. To my joy, my father proved to be a good deal more flexible than I had feared. You know, his experiences in America had helped a lot. He was silent for only three or four seconds. Then he burst into wails of laughter, whereupon he said, his voice almost under control:

"'Listen here, Schmidt . . .' He said: Schmidt—forgetting the Herr. It was patently obvious just how angry he was, when, for reasons of common sense, he was now forced into retracting what he had just said. 'Listen here Schmidt—you didn't seriously think that I really meant what I said when I raised my offer, did you? Ha-ha-ha-haa!'

"And I have to say: Schmidt wasn't a fool. He reciprocated with a dry volley of laughter:

"'No, Professor. Did you seriously expect me to accept your offer?

That you would be able to buy my independence for nine hundred marks a month!'"

"And," Dr. Kelter adds, "take note: he didn't feel obliged to mention that to put nine hundred a month straight in his pocket—if indeed Father had paid him that—really would have been a really dirty trick. But as for Schmidt, he was in fact telling the truth when he said that he hadn't taken Father's offer seriously. He may have even said that he wanted to see how my father would react. But Father, the silly old kindhearted fool that he was, did tell an untruth. When he confirmed that the offer was only a joke. Because at the moment he cried out nine hundred marks he really was prepared to pay Schmidt the sum."

Dr. Kelter eats a bitter almond and takes a sip of his vermouth. "Anyhow, as far as I remember, we drank no more schnapps after that. Father looked at his watch and declared, rounding off the conversation, that it was now time for Herr Schmidt to go and attend to his young disciples. Schmidt agreed instantly, in an almost discourteous way, and we said our goodbyes. That very evening we traveled back to Berlin and I saw no more of Schmidt for more than ten years."

I now say: "But you did meet him once more at Bergedorf?"

"Yes. A few months before his death."

"And when may I hear your impressions of *that* meeting?"

"Hmmm. Phone me next week."

"Just one thing: by that time he had already invented his coma-free telescope. Tell me: Would you not say that on the strength of that invention he *really was* a genius?"

"Oh, goodness me," cried the doctor, almost with vanity, "why do you plague me with that word? Very well. I shall admit: he *was.* In the way that—not quite in the way that a blind hen finds a grain of corn—but let us say—a one-eyed rooster, who pecks and pecks and pecks till he finds a diamond. Ha-ha-ha-haaa . . ."

3

I SHOULD THINK ABOUT MY PLATE. MY CORRECTION PLATE, IN FRONT of which I got to work as soon as I returned from Cebu and put my suitcase in the corner and my coat on the peg. I came running down the stairs, opened the door of the workshop, locked it behind me and breathed in the cool smell of the oil paint and the linoleum of the cellar. I had the feeling that I was a dolphin (I've seen such creatures in glass cases innumerable times at Hagenbeck's)—a dolphin who has been dragged around in the dusty air until it can hardly breathe, and who has finally sneaked back here—here to the pool of my own home. Back in the water. My own water.

For three weeks in a row I only came out of the water for four or five hours sleep. Someone would bring food and cigars to my workshop. Thank goodness there is a shower room and a toilet here as well.

Once before the war and before I got to know Johanna, I happened to hear some famous poet giving a lecture in Dresden. I don't remember his name, maybe Hasenjäger or something similar. Nor do I remember how I ended up going there. Dragged along by some bluestocking or other. But the lecture was titled "On Inspiration." Overblown of course and a little bizarre. A self-important little man, with long hair and a broad black bow tie. Like the Italian who sells ice cream on the corner of the Gojenbergsweg. And this poet explained theatrically that a poetic idea should on the one hand have the inspiration of the gods, and on the other should have—something like this, anyway—*eine nietzscheanisch übermenschliche Eingebung*—

I can't really express it in our language. At a superficial level it was pretty painful to listen to. But there was a grain of truth in it. Oh yes. Also concerning the birth of a *technical* idea. Because the birth of a technical idea is not at all rational. Or at least it doesn't always need to be. Or, for the sake of truth, let us narrow the claim down even more: the birth of *my* technical ideas doesn't always have to be a rational one.

I cannot tell what serious scientists would have to say about this confession. The most serious among them would give a wry smile. Because of their own experience in these matters . . . And now suddenly that disturbing feeling again, that anxiety-laden feeling: Where do I get this belief from? That serious scientists think like I do. Who am I compared to serious scientists? Oh, I do know, and anyone who knows me even slightly will also know: a village boy with half an education, maybe a quarter. Yes—in the cold and incorruptible light of day: the eternal amateur. A hopeless amateur, a mouse who has got caught in the cage of amateurishness and whose spur is no longer an unusual surfeit of technical ideas—what sort of ideas could I have in any case, when I do not possess enough knowledge, for example an in-depth study of mathematics, when all my ideas are the inklings of an autodidact, the fruits of the sick urgency of the amateur—all except my manual precision, except my craving for fame? And when the urge to invent is due not to a surfeit of ideas (as some of my semi-educated friends would like to convince me) but simply my physical disability? An eternal amateur, God, this is even a documented fact. In my desk drawer lies a sheet of paper, so real that I needn't bother to pull it out—a foolscap sheet of top quality Watman paper, yellowed, but written in indelible neat technical handwriting: *Hiermit wird festlich bezeugt, daß der Studierende des Mittweidaer Technikums Bernhard Schmidt in Wintersemester 1901 zum vollberechtigten Ehrenmitglied des Technischen Dilettantenclubs daselbst angenommen worden ist*—by the way, this is perhaps the only organization to which I have ever belonged! And added to that, this is the sole qualification that I have ever possessed—and it is simply a joke.

But I should get back to thinking about my plate. Because that really does exist: a plate made out of French glass with ideal characteristics and polished almost to perfection. A lens, to wit. Like an ice floe of salvation (the one on which I floated back to the beach as a ten-year-old out near Kabelikari—Charles's chapel was in fact almost a trapezium and hardly transparent), my correction plate—like an ice floe of salvation, on which to float above the depths of self-destruction . . . God knows . . . But I now want to return to the rational and irrational aspects of the birth of that plate.

I remember quite clearly the two phases of that idea. Actually two flashes of lightning. The first—which arose from wetness and the porthole drying out in the storm on the Sea of Andaman. I remember intuiting, grasping (I don't know what it was)—I suddenly *knew* that the lens, practically a plate, that would correct the cometary aberration had to be a few millimeters thick. (By the way, the trapezium-shaped ice floe that brought me back to land at Kabelikari was not, relatively speaking, any thicker.) And I knew immediately what its surface should look like. I didn't grasp this fact mathematically, but my inkling was so clear that when Baade had recovered from his seasickness I told him about it. A very unusual occurrence for me to start babbling on about something like this to colleagues. Of course this was the fruit of partly subconscious mental effort continuing for a whole year. Whose elements were brought to the surface in a flash. Whereby the logic of this fusion (I underscore this in the face of all pure rationalists)—this logic of fusion itself occurred beyond my consciousness. I do not know whether it was beneath my consciousness or above it. Due to a quite small element of sympathy-despite-everything for the gods of inspiration, I should like to think that it was above it. If that means anything.

The second flash of lightning occurred right here in my cellar. One and a half days after I had sat down, lit my cigar, and pulled the blank sheet of paper toward me. The whole business had once again advanced with difficulty during my Philippines trip, partly consciously, mostly consciously of course, but with some thinking down at another level, from where it suddenly broke through like a surge into my consciousness. Suddenly I was aware: the profiled side of my correction plate had to be polished to form a point of rotation whose meridian curve would have to be a fourth-power parabola.

I can now say:

I managed to finish one such plate two nights ago. One such plate exists in this world. After that I slept for twelve hours. But the existence of one such plate does not even solve half the problem. Even after I checked it and found that it worked. I mounted it onto the thirty-centimeter aperture telescope at our observatory and took five photos. Luckily, it was a Sunday. I fetched the keys to the laboratory and developed my own photographs. Simply so as not to confuse the lab staff. I have to say: despite the fact that I have the childish tendency to entertain a maximum of expectations (and behind these are thoughts filled with pessimism), the pictures came out better than I had dared to expect. A slice of the heavens, completely without distortion, completely free of comae, and sixteen degrees wide. I have an inkling of endless opportunities, crazy opportunities. But although the question has been solved, the actual solution does not yet exist . . . That's how things stand. If I were to describe everything to the uninitiated, it would on the one hand sound like a foolish boast, on the other like a hopeless lament. But that's how things stand. Only the two or three people most knowledgeable in these matters would believe me. For instance Schorr, who has followed my work from far enough away and close enough as well.

The fact is that the plate I have polished to perfection deviates so minimally from being level that it requires a devilish amount of precision when making it. May the good Lord forgive me, but it is true: just now in the world there is no one but me who can produce such a plate. The problem does not lie in the necessary knowledge but rather in the technical execution. No one else has the required sensitivity and precision.

So I ought to start thinking about my plate. Until I have discovered a simplified method of production for it, a method that is available to all, I will remain a wizard whom no one believes, as his wizardry cannot be tested in any laboratory.

Oh damn and blast, I should be thinking about my plate, but just can't. Now that it actually exists, it no longer blocks the path in my consciousness to my *second* problem.

I thought that I could escape this second problem in the crude old-fashioned and depressing way. I got on a tram and traveled to the Reeperbahn.

I remember, in 1924, how I had left the madhouse of inflation that Germany had become and gone home to Naissaar till that insanity had subsided, and went off to Tallinn now and again. August had come home from a long voyage abroad and was staying a while over the fall with his family on Naissaar. When I arrived once again at the harbor, so that old man Kühn could take me into the big city, August yelled, so that the others in the household could hear, that "our Bernhard must still have some fiancée over there in Tallinn, 'cause he keeps on sailing there so regularly, so faithfully, and in such bad weather." And I muttered, though with a little more bravado and louder than necessary: "What d'you mean fiancée? It's just a matter of y'r regular old gun cleaning, nothing more."

I dealt with this matter in a purely mechanical manner. I got it done by barmaids somewhere out by Kompassi or Kuke Street way, in an old house and with no psychological complications. I say with no complications, except for the fact that I had already got to know Johanna. But at that level, our acquaintance could not yet bind me. Or maybe it could have? Or even should have. If I had been a man of a more serious disposition. A man of a *purer* disposition. Hmm.

Johanna was a slip of a girl when we first met. Not really such a young slip, as she was already seventeen, as far as I remember, and in her last year at Mittweida High School.

I had returned from the internment camp. Had been back in Mittweida for a year or so. Where else was there for me to go? The war was over. The armistice had been signed. The kaiser had gone into exile in Doorn. The revolt in Berlin was over. But the old world nevertheless lay in ruins. Only a few of its elements remained intact. My room at Frau Knechtel's place. I again had the old roof over my head and tried to adjust myself to new worries. Standing in line for potatoes or bread (lines for meat were luckily out of the question due to a shortage of meat) I tried to work out how I could earn my next sum of money, which was all the time losing its value, so that I could stand in such lines. With regard to people's interest in astronomical optics, it seemed to me at the time that I had had a ridiculous dream about the subject. So I mended all sorts of equipment, a couple of movie projectors, a couple of chronometers, a couple of amateur microscopes (as far as I know, there were no amateur telescopes in the whole of Mittweida at the time), plus quite a large school microscope as well. At the same time, I unpacked my crates of observation equipment up in Frau Knechtel's attic, which had luckily survived the war, and Hetzger the gardener, an affable old man, promised to set them up on his plot of land again. He had chopped up only one of my two observation huts during the war to heat the water for his ersatz coffee; the other had remained intact. I went over to the girls' high school on the invitation of the teachers for their microscope, which was needed in science lessons. Those now matriculating had been skipping on the street as small girls the last time I had seen them, and I recognized them neither then nor now. But in this small town there were one or two girls who nevertheless remembered their *Linsenschmidt.* Maybe a girl from the junior school had even joined my instruction classes in astronomy. At any rate, when three girls from the top class came over to me at Frau Knechtel's in order to lug the newly mended microscope back to the schoolhouse, girls who were quite unknown to me and had the eyes of does, they asked me whether I would maybe agree to show them the stars in the sky in Hetzger's garden one evening.

If I had said no, it would have meant that I was afraid of the girls. That for starters. Second, although there was no hope of ever making astronomers out of any of them, refusing them would also mean the end of what used to be my regular habit of teaching astronomy. And third, this was the first time any interest had been paid to the starry sky in this postwar period that I was aware of. Why would I refuse? Even though I had before given lessons principally to children. I said that I agreed.

Two evenings later, a dark, moonless, starry November evening with a light frost, the class came at around nine to Hetzger's garden. Well, standing before twenty nearly adult girls, I did feel a little odd, I cannot deny. I would have felt more at ease had their female science teacher been with them. And four years previously, before the war or maybe even only a year ago, before Germany completely collapsed, in the Mittweida of the Prussian Germany of the kaiser, the teacher's presence would have been the only way possible. But as I have said, the old world had recently fallen apart; only a few of its minor elements remained intact, and the duty of the girls to invite their science teacher to the *Linsenschmidt*'s lessons about stars did not prove, as it turned out, to be one of those elements. And what does it matter? But I really did feel a little uncomfortable nonetheless.

They came into the garden and I had them take a seat on the steps of the pavilion. I have to say that the sum of their fragrance (against the background smells of the compost heap of the Hetzger graveyard flowers) was stimulating. So that we could see what we were doing,

I lit the outside lamp hanging on the wall of the observation hut. Their small, slightly bleary-eyed and chilly faces as they hunched up there under their drooping hats and in their turned-up collars.

I had to say something to them, and this wasn't easy. I couldn't talk to them as if at a kindergarten, nor too scientifically, and these were the only two ways of explaining things that I really knew. I had to improvise along some middle way, and by fits and starts I managed. I told them about the Milky Way as a galaxy. Round about one hundred billion stars in a kind of lens shape, which had an average diameter of around a hundred light-years, and was some fifteen light-years thick. I had them raise their faces to the sky and look more closely at the misty dregs. And I told them to imagine that the earth, their vantage point, was actually somewhere in the middle of it all. I mentioned in passing the accident that befell Hera when suckling Heracles, according to the myth, and whence the name of the galaxy. And added, while fixing my gaze on the serious face of one of the girls (she was one of the original three who had come to my room) and no doubt wanting to make her laugh:

"But by the way, a knowledge of astronomy can have various uses. For instance, one of you may one day travel to Greece. I've not been there myself, but I would gladly go sometime. One of you will go there and see on the street a sign saying *Galakteion.* And will know right away that this is not an observatory to study galaxies but rather—what?"

No one answered. Not even the girl with the serious oval face to whom I had largely been addressing my remarks about traveling to Greece. I was slightly disappointed and gave the answer myself:

"A milk shop."

After that we looked at the most interesting parts of the galaxy through a telescope. I drew their attention to the clusters of bright stars beyond the archer Sagittarius and the bright strip from the Swan to the Centaur. They could only look through the telescope one at a time and occasionally I myself would cast a glance through it to check. So that I would in turn feel against my cheekbone the cool flush of their faces. When the girl on whom my gaze had for some reason fallen stood at the telescope, I explained to them all, though mostly to her: in practically the whole of Europe our galaxy is known as the Milky Way, as it is in German—*die Milchstraße.* But on the island that I come from in Estonia, Naissaar, in the Baltic Sea, it has the name *Linnutee*—meaning *Vogelstraße.* Because the Estonian language imagines that this is the route taken by each migratory bird as it flies to the south in the autumn, and returns along it in the spring as it finds its way home.

I can still feel, at least now, ten years later, how that girl stood there at the telescope and bent over it for a second time, and how her hair brushed against my temple.

Two days later a letter was delivered to me at Frau Knechtel's. A small blue and pink envelope that smelt faintly of eau de cologne from a handkerchief carried in a woman's handbag, and in which was a piece of paper on which was written in childishly distinct lines with the assuredness of an adult:

> Esteemed Herr Bernhard Schmidt,
> May I come by your place on Friday evening at seven o'clock? I am in pressing need of answers to a number of questions with regard to the study of astronomy.
>
> Thanking you in anticipation,
> one of your listeners yesterday evening.

She was thanking me in anticipation—so I could not be out at seven o'clock on Friday evening. And furthermore I just knew that this had to be that selfsame girl to whom I had explained that galaxy the Milky Way. And it was her, Johanna.

She arrived punctually at the appointed time. And not alone by way of postwar bravado, but with a friend, as provincial decency prescribed. She was with her benchmate Hilde. But she did not do what a more scheming and more theatrical girl would have done in her place: she did not try to push the rather angular and freckled Hilde to the fore to talk with me while herself pretending to play second fiddle.

She placed her hands, markedly large for a girl, but with beautiful slender fingers, decisively on the edge of my desk and set out her business. Very calmly, very clearly, although a light blush gradually spread across her face, no doubt because I simply listened and did not in any way encourage her. For what was there for me to add? When it wasn't clear to what extent her tale was serious and sincere—or on the other hand a refined female ploy. When I didn't understand it at all. When I still don't really know to this day . . .

She was the daughter of a schoolmaster and hailed from a village some twelve kilometers to the north of Mittweida. Her father had fallen at the Battle of Valenciennes ten days before the armistice. But it had been her father's wish, a sufficiently rare one for a German village intellectual, that his daughter escape the vicious triangle of the *kinder-küche-kirche* routine and receive a university education. And Johanna wanted to start studying physics at Berlin University the following autumn. Specializing in astronomy and cosmography. To my question as to why just those subjects, she made me smile at her childish sincerity: because it had been her father's wish. For one. Because her father had considered astronomy and cosmography as the most independent of subjects. And I must say that at that point I began to sympathize with her unknown father, who would now be lying in some mass grave near the river Schelt. And second, she herself. Johanna herself agreed with her father. So that the fortunate coincidence of the wishes of her father and her own meant that she wanted to become a teacher of cosmography and astronomy. And she was now asking me for advice as to what she should read, over and above what was taught at school during this last year of hers, so that she would get some basis for her studies in Berlin right from the start. That was the first reason. The second one (and this surprised me by the fact it was so well thought through, but even more because it was so unexpected): she was not at all sure, even if she were to succeed in her studies in Berlin, that she would immediately find a post as a teacher. In the long run she would, no doubt. But initially, with no contacts and patrons, this wasn't so sure. School boards, were, it was said, still reactionary institutions here in Germany and would therefore still, and with mathematical precision, regard a female teacher as a weaker candidate than a male. University studies would in any case put a severe financial strain on Johanna herself and even more on her mother. Her mother being a bookkeeper in a draper's in some such village as Erlau or Crossen, earning no more than a hundred marks a month. So that she, Johanna, would have to first of all obtain some professional qualifications, so that during the period of her university studies she could earn her own keep. But she thought (and this was the link in the chain of reasoning that surprised me the most) that it would be more sensible if she were not to train as a laundry seamstress or shop girl, but instead tried to study something practical linked to the subjects she herself had chosen to study, that is, astronomy and cosmography. Let us say she had chosen to become a pianist, and as long as she had not yet made a breakthrough in that field, she could make ends meet by working as, say, a piano tuner. And now she was in the fortunate situation that in this very same Mittweida lived—she could not claim this from personal experience, but she had been told about it—one of the greatest masters in the field of astro-optics in the whole of Germany. That is to say, me. And her, Johanna's, question was now this: Would I agree to teach her how to polish optical glass?

I asked her whether she thought that a glass polisher was a more competitive career in Germany than a schoolteacher. And she replied that undoubtedly it was. As cosmography and astronomy were sciences, and in science women were not considered capable of having a say in things, only at the high-school level at the very most. Glass polishing was, however, an art, and in the arts women were considered to be somewhat more competent than in the sciences. But the main thing was that many people considered glass polishing to be a form of handicraft. And in the handicrafts, prejudices against women were supposed to be weaker.

I do not know myself quite why I went along with her suggestion. An inability to say no is not one of my innate qualities. I have throughout my life been able to refuse, in quite an abrupt manner, seemingly interesting proposals that have been put to me but that were either pointless or tedious. Maybe I really did want to make the attempt to school this girl to become a good polisher of glass. Or, lord knows, maybe that was a mere background factor—maybe my spirit was whispering to me in the foreground: here is your chance to finally get near to someone of the female gender. Something of quite a different order to those pathetic gun-cleaning exercises. Genuine close contact without which a man's life lacks something essential, however much a man might deny its importance . . . God knows. Anyhow, I answered Johanna, shrugging my shoulders slightly, that we could give it a try . . .

I did not start lying to her. I said that I myself was, for the most part, self-taught, and with regard to preparatory studies for university, I should first like to obtain further information. And so I did.

I ordered a copy of the very latest "Mitteilungen für Studierende" from Leipzig, and spread out on my desk in front of her the syllabi for astronomy and cosmography and the corresponding area of physics, a list of staff, and the recommended reading for students of the first grade. First we made a choice from among all of this, which required a good week's intensive work on my part. After that we agreed that Johanna would come two evenings a week to my workshop and would receive practical instruction. I showed her how to use etalons and micrometers. I showed her how to get the polishing lathe to rotate, and put pieces of various types of glass in her hand and explained how to work with them. And most important of all: I taught her to listen, during her work, to her own hand, that is, to follow the reactions of the surface as it was being polished as carefully, as subtly as she could. The way I put it was: listen to the language of the glass. When she had questions relating to the books she was reading at my suggestion, we discussed them together.

What sort of pupil was she? Well, I have to say that she did not possess any brilliance with regard to improvisation. But she had a woman's consistency of action. And a woman's thoroughness. So her quiet progress with the mathematics, physics, and optics taught in the first year of university was as expected. Only the precision of her reactions at the polishing lathe left something to be desired. I had perhaps expected greater things from such an attentive and observant girl. But maybe I was expecting too much of her. Clearly I was.

Incidentally, the whole question of payment very nearly put an end to our relationship. I could not allow myself to be paid for my efforts, as I knew in what straitened circumstances she lived. Ultimately we found a solution: she would become my assistant at the workshop. So, for instance, there is a little of Johanna's work in the uranostat that Schorr ordered from me for the Hamburg Observatory. She succeeded pretty well with operations of a secondary or tertiary level of importance: she would saw the supports made out of wood and veneer them to an almost acceptable level of precision, then cleaned and varnished them. And so on. And did all of this quite tactfully. Without drawing attention to the fact that such manual tasks were a good deal easier for her to carry out than for me to do. At any rate, right up to the late spring I did not entertain the slightest suspicion that her willingness to learn had—let us say it straight out—the covert aim of getting close to me. Not the slightest suspicion, even in connection with the present she gave me on my forty-first birthday.

I have always neglected my birthdays in the most chronic of ways. During my childhood, my mother would always keep count. Whether it was August's, or Olga's, or Berta's, or mine, there would always be a bunch of juniper or pine twigs bound to our chair with a red ribbon on our birthday morning. And when the face of the birthday boy or girl had been washed and they had come to the table, Mother would place her hand on their head and wish them a happy birthday. Then the rest of the household would do likewise. And the birthday child would get, next to their plate of porridge or their anchovy sandwich and cup of coffee, a slice of bilberry cake baked by Mother. Presents were given only on even number birthdays. But I do remember a fantastic book that Mother gave me when I was ten, and another for my sixteenth birthday. The fact that she gave me what she did for my tenth birthday is, looking back on it, something of a miracle. This was during the time that my father lay dying. It was a hardback with gold letters on the spine, several hundred pages long with pictures, some in color; a book acquainting the reader with the latest technical advances, titled *Das neue Universum.* She gave me a similar one, except it was five years newer, six years later. I remember this second event with great clarity. Mother had already bought it the previous autumn, during the time that I was recovering at the Free Hospital after my amputation. When she handed it to me on the morning of my birthday the following March, I asked her when she had bought it. The strait was blocked with pack ice and no one had been able to reach the city for several weeks. Then she told me that she had bought it at Kluge's bookshop in Tallinn the previous November. And I understood her train of thought very well. She had of course noticed—we had talked about such things for several years—how the first book had interested and excited me. How I had learned the first elements of knowledge from that book and had, up to the time of my accident, been a boy keen on technical matters. For several years running. Which the whole family and even the village knew and were convinced of. All those cameras and spyglasses and other things I had made myself. My accident had destroyed all of this at one blow. It was as clear as clear could be: What kind of technician could a boy who lacked his right hand ever become? A technician had to be handy.

And I remember: I was lying there about a week after the amputation at the Free Hospital. The first high fever was beginning to subside, but Mother had come every day and sat for long hours at my bedside. Then Uncle Frans came on a visit. He did of course already know what was up with me. He had just piloted his umpteenth ship, a Dutch one, into harbor and had got twenty-five rubles in his pocket, plus a bottle of gin on top of that. Mother was sitting on a chair at my bedside and reading aloud from a book to me and, in effect, to the other eleven patients in the ward. Then Uncle Frans marched in wearing his jackboots smeared with pig fat, peaked skipper's cap in hand. He sat at my bedside. He smiled at me with his red lips through his pepper-and-salt beard in sympathy and sadness, and pushed a large bag of caramels in my direction, then said:

"Now we'll have to think what the boy is good for in the future. I've nothing against him getting an education. I have even thought that if he wasn't so silent, as if he had fallen on his mouth, he would have the makings of a clergyman . . ."

"But that wouldn't suit him at all!" laughed Mother, rejecting the whole idea.

"Oh, I do understand that it wouldn't suit him," Uncle Frans conceded discontentedly, "for how would he cope with waving his arms about at the pulpit or doing things at the altar—when you could see from afar that he was a man whom the Good Lord had punished severely?"

I do not really know whether Mother actually believed what she said to Uncle Frans, or whether she was just saying it for my sake. I have the impression that she looked all eleven patients in the eye first, all of those who had been listening attentively to her reading and were now listening with interest to what was being said. Yes, Mother seemed to look them all in the eye and say, whether she placed the responsibility on herself or perhaps on me or even on the Lord. She said, and I will remember this as long as I live:

"Frans, we don't know if this was a punishment. And if it was, then it has been inflicted on me rather than on him. For what evil could the child have committed? Perhaps God did this to *spur him on . . .*"

"How d'you mean spur him on?" asked Uncle Frans with that element of curiosity in his voice that I was familiar with from his way of checking my mother out during conversations with her. Because

Uncle Frans had realized that my mother moved in her thoughts in regions that he, Uncle Frans, could never aspire to reach.

"Perhaps in this way," said Mother slowly. "The Lord wants to force him to redouble his efforts. So that he will develop quicker than he would have done otherwise."

When I asserted just now that I will remember my mother's words as long as I live, that really is the case. Nevertheless, her reply popped up in my memory only later, I don't quite remember when exactly. At the time, in the Free Hospital ward with its dirty bluish-gray plastered walls and the smell of iodine, I was mainly thinking: How is it possible that Mother does not know—but how could she know—that I most certainly had committed a sin? That piece of corrugated iron with which I made the nose cone of the rocket that exploded—that iron I had stolen from Uncle Frans behind his back . . . But what sin could *my mother* have committed—so that she thought the punishment could have been intended for her? And I continued along this train of thought: funny, when it seems as if Mother is teasing Uncle Frans and he is uneasy (and this had been happening more and more of late), then I don't blame my mother for teasing him, and Uncle Frans's clumsy and forlorn mellowness becomes almost a sympathetic trait. But when Mother's expression suddenly stiffens at the same time as Uncle Frans becomes overriding and demanding, then I don't rush to defend my mother, no, not at all, I am now too big a boy, I just want to get away from Uncle Frans and from Mother too. Be that as it may. What I was racking my brains about was actually how it was that I received the second volume of the "Universum": Mother had bought it for me when I was lying in hospital and gave it to me for my sixteenth birthday. In order to support her belief that the Lord had a plan to urge me on to use my strengths. But what I actually wanted to bring to mind was what Johanna gave me for my forty-first birthday.

After I left home, my birthday was celebrated only for a short period. At technical college the eighteen members of our amateurs' club, the Franconians, had the custom of commemorating and celebrating one another's birthdays. But not to any greater extent than walking up to the birthday boy in the corridor of the college and shaking his hand. Also, in my case one of the slightly older students and a quite unofficial honorary member of the club congratulated me. And in the evening, several bottles of beer would be drunk at Frau

Bretschneider's. Afterward, when we had ended up in prison or internment camps at the outbreak of the war, our lives went in different directions to such a degree and I heard no more from them, so that Johanna's birthday surprise was all the more surprising. She turned up after lunch on the eleventh of April at Frau Knechtel's rooming house, flowers in hand, and reminded me that it was my birthday that day. I wondered at the time why the hell such a nice girl had to bother with such trivial tokens of convention. But I could not avoid expressing my thanks to her for her attentiveness. She borrowed a vase from Frau Knechtel and filled it from the kitchen faucet. For some time now I had put up with such small familiar gestures. I have to say: I put up with them, smiling at my helpless protests and with just a tiny bit of enjoyment.

When Johanna had made room for the vase on my desk and placed the flowers—three yellow roses—in it, she sat down next to me at my desk and put a sheet of paper under my nose:

"Look, Herr Schmidt—I got this for your sake."

I felt the chestnut-colored hair and smelled the smell of clove soap. I had known this smell from long before, yet had ignored it.

"What is this, then?"

It was a certificate issued by the Mittweida police authority that Johanna Krüger had obtained a license to drive an automobile.

"Ahaa," I said with light irony and more or less indifferently, "you are of course adding to your technical education. Not bad. But in what way will it be useful to me . . . ?"

"But your car is just standing there and isn't being used."

This was perfectly true. At least to a certain extent. My Opel, my Nõbu Nette—Cousin Nette—as the Franconians had dubbed it, was now sitting for a fifth year in the garage of the technical college. When I was interned in the autumn of 1914—as a citizen of a power inimical to Germany, and one with telescopes and mirrors was an especially suspicious person—I had managed to leave the car in the hands of the technical college people. Inasmuch as the fee for the garage was covered. When I returned, no one took any interest in my car. Oh yes, it was still there. It was said to have been driven for some thousands of kilometers in the meantime. That was only natural. And it had to stay in the garage under the same conditions. Thank goodness. I was in no hurry to sell it. As the value of money was falling by the week. And besides I had a kind of personal relationship to that car. A strange one that involved the memories of prewar trips to the Rhineland, Switzerland, Austria, the landscapes of the Tirol, the Bay of Genoa, concerts by Bruckner at the Vienna Philharmonic, the most grand impressions on this earth that I had (my impressions by way of my telescopes are another matter, of which we shall not speak here)—and besides all that my relationship to this car had a curious ambiguity: it was my car, my object of pride, my slave, it had to be subjugated to me—but it wasn't; it always required subjugation by a third party . . . Oh damn, I couldn't myself do a thing with that car. As I had no driver. And because private persons could only get hold of petrol via speculators and at an astronomical price.

"Well," said Johanna, "you have no use whatsoever for that car. Your friends are scattered all over the place. Herr Grünfeld and whoever the others were. The ones that used to drive you around. You told me about those trips once. But now the young gents at the college use your car for driving practice. I know all right."

Interesting that at that moment I was jealous of them. Of a stranger. Or strangers. Not because of the driving practice in my car, but because Johanna knew of the excursions. At the same time, I was unable to find out anything more about them. All quite stupid, of course.

"And then I decided," Johanna continued, "that now there ought to at least be a driver for you. And now there is . . ." She folded up her driving license and put it back in her handbag. "I can drive you anywhere you want. No-no, I will be getting a trip myself in this way too. That really pleases me. You just have to say. Of course, during school hours I cannot be available. But it will soon be Easter, and I'll be free for a whole week. Well, not the whole week. I do have my duties to Mother. And then we'll be breaking up from school at the beginning of June. And I won't be leaving for Berlin until August. So we have two months during which to make some longer trips!"

Nevertheless, we didn't make that many trips during those two months. But already by Easter, a few days after my birthday, I showed her the garage at the college and ordered the car to be brought out, as Fräulein Krüger would be helping me with it. And when she sat for the first time at the wheel in my Nōbu Nette (though it was by now quite a battered Nōbu Nette) and me next to her, we traveled to Dresden at my suggestion and ate lunch there. It was simply impossible not to take up the offer. As Johanna was really excited about the idea of driving a car and showing that she had it under control. And she could handle it pretty well.

On a couple of occasions during the school term we visited that same small Dresden restaurant to have dinner, and once we did not return to Mittweida until ten o'clock at night—this too would have been impossible for a high-school girl in the petit bourgeois atmosphere of prewar Mittweida, but now, after the war, when strange things were part of the prevailing morality—now it was no more than a mildly piquant episode.

At any rate, there was not the slightest trace of piquanterie between us. I was not of course so blind as to not have thought about such opportunities during our trips. I believe that the little restaurant we visited even had upstairs rooms for day-trippers like us. Or indeed for quite a different sort of customer. But I switched off my thoughts about any such developments.

I decided: any relationship with this girl could bring down a fateful dependence on her. It would so change my life that I would have to begin behaving like a different person. And I no doubt thought, above all: I have no idea how she would react were I to try to enter into such a relationship. She might look at me, her face flushed, or indeed pale, burst into tears, scream, whisper, whimper, I don't know. "But my God, can it be true that the sincere wishes of a young girl to get educated could lead—even in your case, Herr Schmidt—to her teacher's bed . . . ? And I had no idea whether she would necessarily mean *in your case, Herr Schmidt,* but rather . . . Because what she could also mean was: in the case of such an honest, decent, and dependable man such as myself. Or she could even mean: for someone as old, it would be unheard of and quite unsuitable for such a man as yourself, Herr Schmidt—and not only for me but for any woman, in the case of such a cripple as you, Herr Schmidt, to . . ."

Maybe I was to a certain extent afraid of Johanna's reactions. But I was also afraid of tying myself down. And that was the primary reason. Absolutely. Because otherwise my curiosity and desire for fun and for self-esteem would in the end have made me walk on thin ice.

No-no, the inescapable quality that a man needs from a woman is something he has to obtain without tying himself down. But if I had sought such solace in the case of Johanna the chains would have been inevitable: everyday personal contact, the total loss of independent privacy, and even in the best instance the anxious necessity to adjust—although I did also understand: in an ideal situation, a practical one of course, in the ideal instance, allowing for a number of reservations, it would be easier to imagine myself with Johanna than with anyone else. Perhaps for the reason that with her it would be possible to have an intelligent conversation about the technical constants of the concave mirror on my lathe and maybe about the opportunities open to spectral astronomy of the future. To converse intelligently about such things, so that it did not become sheer *Mache,* small talk, a naked game of understanding, but rather a serious and uplifting discussion. And yet all of this could not entice me. Because a relationship with Johanna would mean nothing less than marriage. The only way for such a girl. Not in the sense that she would not, under any other circumstances, allow any intimacy between us. I imagined then that she would allow such things, and later experienced that this was so. Marriage would be the only way for her because of her serious attitude to things in this world and—damn it—my seriousness in relation to her; these two contradictory or parallel truths just didn't allow for such things. Her seriousness lay, beyond her weakness for car trips and visits to restaurants, in one very serious aspect, namely, her morality, based as it was on the old Lutheranism of a village schoolmaster's family from Saxony. While my own, well, I wouldn't dare measure its depth, but its origins, the origins of my seriousness, were something I could pin down. This was the islander mentality, especially on my mother's side, a concerned or worrying nature that was sensitive and strict, proud and a little anxious, half worldly and half religious. Something like that. Not that I am entirely sure. But what I did know for sure was that I was unsuitable for marriage. To Johanna, or to anyone else. Neither my nature nor my habits nor, if you were to use that rather pompous expression, my understanding of the cardinal values in life (and thinking of such things is painful enough, damn it) were suitable. Yes, I had said as a joke at the table of the Franconians, or at my colleague Ackerberg's place, when those same Franconians, amateurs and engineers plus young Frau Ackerberg, had tried to tease me for a second time and asked me whether I would ever get married; I had replied, and very politely, given the young lady's presence, the expressions that race through my mind right now are not exactly polite ones—I was thirty-five or thirty-six at the time—that the sum total of so many vectors needed to be synchronized and I would for that reason desist. When such a wise man as Voltaire is said to have noted that getting married before the age of forty was too early. Or I had, on other occasions, replied in less polite words, saying yes, sure, I'll get married some day, but not until I need a nurse to care for me . . .

Up to the time she left high school, Johanna limited our car trips to two to Dresden, and even in the summer we didn't go on particularly long drives. Except for one trip in July when we went to Dessau. I went there for my work. By way of an acquaintance in Dessau I was hoping to find French glass of prewar quality at the Junkers factory. And I decided: Why bother traveling by train when there was a more interesting way to travel at hand? And to some degree the thought that Johanna would be in Berlin a month later, and perhaps move permanently out of my orbit, also egged me on. And the thought that not going would simply be a sign of fear. Fear of her and of myself. But all in all, the whole thing was perhaps merely crossing a little narrow bridge when I really wanted to swim across.

Johanna was enthusiastic. We would have to leave early in the morning and be back before nightfall. We left at seven and Johanna got up a pleasant speed. Only when traveling through the intervening towns of Grimma and Delitzsch and wherever did she drive at forty kilometers per hour; mostly she clipped along at fifty or sixty. And I have to say that on those stretches where she bowled along at seventy, so that the wind in the open car ripped my tie out of its tiepin and flapped it around my neck, were the parts of the journey I liked most. We chatted about all sorts of things. But only about *neutral* matters. As always. I remember that we talked about the Northern Lights. She had some idea of their physical and optical nature. But had never seen them. I had seen them on Naissaar during my childhood, every blasted year, I would imagine. Very interesting and powerful in November, in the village of Põhjaküla or, to be exact, the woods near Põhjaküla, known as Karu-Jüri, that is, Bear George, when traveling to visit Grandfather and Grandmother, and the children, after much nagging, were allowed to stay for two or three days. I may have seen the Northern Lights there a couple of times, or only once, and the rest of the time elsewhere. But I always feel that the heavens throughout the autumns and winters of my childhood were filled with the lights I saw at that specific spot: blue swords flashing in strange silence above the black pines and dark sea from the Virbu naze to the horizon in the north. Or motionless rows of silvery organ pipes over the northeastern sky in an arc from Flensborg to Hallikivimaa.

So I told Johanna about these organs and sword fights mixed in with particles of the sun that made the atmosphere glow at a height of some five or six kilometers—green and red from the oxygen, blue and violet from the nitrogen. And I remember when we had already passed Oranienbaum and were driving into Dessau that I said to her: on Naissaar people believed they could actually become such phenomena. The Northern Lights were nothing other than a rainbow caused by the feasting of souls that had sold themselves to the devil. This was all simply the glow of their red horses and the flash of their iron sleigh runners. I said: "Ah yes, I even once saw an old man on our island who could turn himself into the Northern Lights." And Johanna turned away from her driving and toward me with such a strange twinkle in her eye that I immediately felt afraid that she would drive off the road, and I was filled with the joy of the street urchin at the idea that she no doubt thought that I myself could turn into some part of the Northern Lights and join those who had sold their souls to the devil.

And what happened between us there in Dessau? That is what I want to stress: nothing at all. Not as yet. We were there about three hours. Johanna parked the vehicle in front of the front gate of the Junkers office building and waited for me in the car. But the German punctuality had slackened a good deal since the war. Old Pregel, the head of the department, with whom I had made an appointment by phone, was not there. It turned out that he had not yet returned from Berlin. He would be arriving the next morning. I went back to the car in two minds about what to do. But Johanna said, as if it were quite self-evident:

"Herr Schmidt—if you have to be here tomorrow, then we're here already. I can stay that long. Let's have a look around for the day and see the sights. And in the evening you can go to a hotel and I can stay with the sister of a schoolmate of mine. You remember Hilde? Well, her sister. And her husband. Her husband is a draftsman. Also something to do with Junkers. They will be only too glad to put me up for the night. And we'll drive back tomorrow. When you're ready with everything."

And this was decided so smoothly that I could do nothing but assent to the plan. With a certain amount of reluctance, that is true, a certain amount of recalcitrance at the fact that a strange girl was deciding over my life, but with a smile of wry pleasure nevertheless. And with regard to Johanna's decision about our night quarters—me here, she there—this made me smile with great relief and yet a tiny twinge of disappointment as well. But it was, of course, how things had to be.

We ate lunch at a small restaurant on the Mulde, looked round the castles of the dukes, drove the three kilometers north and had a look at the Elbe in the summer sunshine and the large river port that, with the coal dust and smell of oil and the barges loading and unloading, seemed to be trying to stretch its limbs and wake up from its suspended animation. Next we went to look at the Cranach paintings in the Marienkirche back in Dessau itself. I would myself of course have preferred to take a look at the famous Junkers workshops where they assembled the all-metal planes. But maybe my friend the head of the department would be able to arrange that. And as he wasn't there, I wasn't going to start speaking to his deputy about the matter this morning. Because I was afraid of asking for favors that would be denied me. Such nos are horribly humiliating. So although I caught a glimpse of the Junkers factory buildings on the outskirts of the town several times, I avoided looking in their direction.

In the evening, Johanna drove me to the hotel and then went off to her friend. We agreed that she would be waiting for me at ten o'clock the next morning in the car outside the Junkers office building. By then my glass procurement should be over and done with. I didn't go there myself at nine but was already at the office by eight and got hold of Pregel there. And the glass I needed right away. Oh damn, Pregel ought to have known how much I wanted to see the all-metal airliners and acquaint myself with some details of the F-13s. Because the gadget I'd been sweating over recently was intended for that very aircraft: for a cartographical periscope (I had already worked out how to make a one-hundred-degree viewing angle!). But I knew that the firm had a penchant for revealing as little as possible to the eyes of outsiders, even things that were no longer secret. I have said that Pregel *ought to have had* an idea of my interest, but he didn't bring up the subject of showing me the planes. And I refrained from asking. And was standing, ten minutes later, out on the street, with a five-kilo lump of glass packed in corrugated paper box in my hand. There was still one and a half hours left before Johanna would arrive. I decided to walk to Hilde's sister's place, as I knew her address.

Incidentally, when I say that nothing happened between Johanna and myself in Dessau, this is in *one* way true, that is, regarding our coming closer together. But with regard to *growing apart,* something fateful nearly did happen.

On the street, rather empty as it was of people and vehicles, I immediately spotted our Nõbu Nette parked in front of a house. Johanna's classmate's sister, a real twittering type, let me in to the small flat smelling of ersatz coffee and babies. I understood immediately that she knew of my existence and that didn't surprise me. As Johanna must have talked about me. That was not the point. But Johanna was not there. She had gone to the shop to buy, I don't remember what, maybe a new pair of stockings to replace her worn out ones. And the woman of the house offered me a cup of the ersatz coffee, whose smell had greeted me at the door. Her husband had gone to work, the child was still sleeping in its hammock, and this twenty-five-year-old calf-eyed, snub-nosed, and freckled young woman was sitting across the waxcloth-covered table from me and started a conversation. And I must say: customs and habits can vary a hell of a lot from country to country. In Estonia, especially on Naissaar, such talk between people who had just met would be unimaginable. But this stranger, who I didn't know from Eve, with her calf-eyes—well, the ancient Greeks regarded it as the greatest compliment to remark on "cow's eyes" when describing women—anyway, she rolled her eyes and twittered away with great gusto.

"Ooh, Herr Doktor—I've heard so many nice things about you from Hilde—do take a little condensed milk for your coffee. It's really nice. French stuff. They handed it out to Junkers staff last week. Only for the office staff, and, by the way, Karl got four tins of it. It's already got sugar in it . . . It's so nice that for Johanna, Hilde's very best friend, you understand . . . I'm so happy for her. And I'm not worried about anything. Almost nothing, anyway. Except for one thing . . . Herr Schmidt . . . Johanna is so fascinated by your knowledge and your experience of life and maybe other things, that she allows you to do anything you want. But you yourself, Herr Schmidt—you should not allow yourself to do anything at all with her. Not for some while, anyway. Such things don't happen in decent families here in Germany, you understand. *Over here,* we consider it right that you should get married to Johanna. No doubt about it. Herr Schmidt, it's for Johanna's sake I'm saying all this. Johanna is from a decent family. And out of respect for you. You are a very respectable gentleman and a clever one. Only, do forgive me, but it is the most clever men that do not always know what they ought to do . . ."

I didn't get to ask her whether she wanted to act as Johanna's go-between, or what. I couldn't ask as I didn't know how to say it in German. Or whether the Germans even had go-betweens.

At that point Johanna returned from the stocking shop and stepped into the kitchen, where we were sitting drinking our coffee, and the young woman, with her back to Johanna, raised her finger to her pursed lips, and made a painfully familiar sign to me, as would a kitchen maid indicating: keep your mouth shut.

Johanna cried out: "Oh! You're here!" In a completely happy, surprised, and open voice, and I explained in a relatively hushed voice how I had one and a half hours to kill and so I had decided to seek out her lodgings. Johanna went into the room next door to put on her new stockings and the lady of the house whispered to me:

"Herr Schmidt—don't for God's sake tell her what I've just said to you . . ."

I mumbled back: "Of course not," and thought to myself: things have certainly been said. I won't say anything to Johanna. *Can't* say anything to her. But what I *think* is something I cannot be responsible for . . .

Johanna was back in a minute. She thanked her hostess for letting her stay the night. I picked up my glass package. We said goodbye to the young woman and drove off.

But even from what has gone before it is evident just how hurt and annoyed I was at Frau Fröhlich's words—you see, I even remember the name of that snub-nosed individual—and it is equally evident just how important Johanna had nevertheless become for me. Because while she was sitting next to me, carefully and riskily, unconsciously and vigorously turning the steering wheel, I felt, as I sat on the black imitation leather upholstery of the Nõbu Nette, as uncomfortable as a magpie who had stepped into bird lime. No-no, that poor girl, that straightforward child was of course in no way to blame . . . But was it really true that . . . ? *What* could she be guilty of? She had presumably not recruited Frau Fröhlich as a go-between. Of course not. But she must have said something to Hilde. And must have let something shine through there in Dessau just now, which should not have been revealed . . . And I have to admit: from then on, right up to Johanna's departure for Berlin in mid-September I was unable to relate to her in a free and easy way. As free and easy as we had been before. Not even when she came one afternoon to Frau Knechtel's to say farewell and made some tea in Frau Knechtel's kitchen and we ate up all the pickled sprats with herbs from Naissaar that my mother had sent through the post in a large tin can. Just wasn't able. For a short while I thought that now, at any instant, I will be able to reconcile myself with her—for she was in no way responsible for the tactless chatter of the silly woman, as she was indeed a greater victim than I myself. Yes, for a short while I thought that soon the crust of whitewash that there now was between us would fall away—especially when I noticed just how good Mother's sprats tasted . . . But at the same time I realized that I was unable to get over this, and now that, within a few hours, she would be going to the railway station and away on the train, and start a new life completely away from me, it was now too late to change . . . I don't know whether she had noticed my withdrawal those last weeks. Now and again I felt (or thought I felt) as if she had, but I thought it too intimate a question to ask. God knows. At any rate, we said farewell in the cool way that friends do. She thanked me, stammering a little, for the way I had helped her with what she had achieved. Turned and left. I heard the door to the flat shut, and wrestled with myself for a moment—should I go over to the window and watch her emerging from the front door below and wave to her when she looked around—or stay put at the table and look over some plan for a concave mirror—I wrestled with myself and won (or lost, maybe) and stayed put . . . And God knows, but it was perhaps at that very moment, as I forced myself to stay put, that I decided to move to a new place as soon as possible . . .

Though hardly that. Maybe I simply decided to wait and see what she would write to me from Berlin, and act accordingly. So that if her letters suggested that there was still something to wait for, then I'd wait. But if not, I would leave this wretched country. Probably that was the sort of thing I decided. At the same time as trying to convince myself that I regarded Johanna's departure with relief, as a release from an awkward situation. But with human decisions it is like with scientific ideas: whole years can pass between conception and execution.

During the winter of 1920 to 1921, things gradually got even harder, but even in the most bleak minutes I would find some work to tide me over. And my demands really were minimal. So minimal that I would sometimes hope: the time just *had to* come when the observatory once again received money so that the equipment could be renewed. So that I would be guaranteed not only enough for me to scrape by on but also enough of an income to allow me to carry out experiments I had planned long before.

During the first year of her studies, Johanna sent a couple of brief and hopeful postcards: she had found a suitably cheap room in Berlin. She had received the grade of *Ausgezeichnet* for her first physics exam. In the spring, when I thought in passing that she would be back in Mittweida for the summer vacation, which was quite a pleasant thought, if a little burdensome, a letter came from her saying: she would have to spend the summer working at an optical firm in Charlottenburg—and would Herr Bernhard Schmidt in Mittweida send references that she had received tuition from Herr Schmidt . . . I remember reading this amidst the smell of onions fried in margarine that was seeping into my room from Frau Knechtel's kitchen, and thought: what a funny old mess everything is . . . I am living here in this modest dwelling almost without work—and she has got work in the capital on the strength of my reference. From me—and maybe I did hope that she would return for the summer—she was asking for a reference that would offer her the opportunity not to come back. And here I am, agonizing whether or not to send her the reference—also for a second reason (and principally maybe for this second reason), that is, I wondered what she had actually learned from me. Even though there was no real question of serious learning. And I do not know which of the arguments weighed heaviest, and which remained in the shadow of the other. Perhaps the most decisive factor of all was the fact that in that split second when I had almost refused that service to her ("Dear Johanna, you yourself will understand, that the little that I explained quite unsystematically is too little by a long chalk to . . ."), at that moment I asked myself: But who had I myself actually learned from? So I thought damn it and put it in the mail. And she got the job and didn't turn up that summer in Mittweida. And this was a good thing in several ways. Because I admit: to some extent her presence had disturbed me. Well, if not otherwise, then at least regarding the gun cleaning that I practiced now and then with the misses of Dresden. I went to Dresden because if I had done such things in Mittweida, it could happen any minute that someone would bump into me on Wilhelmstraße or Schillerstraße. Or would walk up to me and ask me for a cigarette when I was sitting and relaxing in the Lindengarten. In a word, Johanna did not turn up during the whole summer. And it was when autumn was at hand, and everyday concerns so many, and I owed Frau Knechtel three months' rent, and my various jobs had come to an end that I decided to give up my Nőbu Nette. I didn't have a driver anyway and chance came to my aid when I wanted to sell her. If you can regard the contribution that chance made as aid.

The idea of selling the car came really from the technical college. They made the suggestion that I sell the Nőbu Nette. Partly because the college needed it and partly to cover the rent for the garage. I had nearly agreed. But suddenly imagined, indeed saw, how my car would come bowling along the worn and potholed black cobblestoned surface of Wilhelmstraße, and behind the wheel would be some complete stranger, and she, Nette, would *look at* me with the round nickel eyes of her headlights. And I imagined a number of variations on this theme, but always with more or less the same feeling that I was meeting a girl who was for sale, but who luckily did not exist here, with whom I had slept, whose father I could have been, but whom I had rejected and abandoned, and whom I was ashamed of. And this vision prevented me. And yet the idea that I could get out of my penury with Nette's help, and for quite some space of time, was too insistent to ignore for such a trivial reason. So in the spring I sold Nette to a Leipzig *Raffke,* a greedy type, for five hundred thousand. When I went to look at her, now already sold, in the garage at the college—the *Raffke* had not yet sent his driver along—it did still seem to be a pretty good car and got rid of at too low a price. And I went and stood by her front mudguard and ran my fingers over the left headlight's nickled frame, and felt, all of a sudden, that it was moist. And I just had to smile at the fact that I had been startled by what were the most ordinary drops of condensation due to the humidity of the air.

From Johanna's postcards it transpired that her mother had fallen ill. Not so ill that she required her daughter's presence every day, but ill enough not to be able to work at the draper's account's department and to need her daughter's financial support. So that Johanna had broken off going to lectures and gone to work for the firm with the resounding name of Blümers Spezialhaus für Schuloptik. Now that people were being laid off right, left, and center, and were forced to close down due to a lack of orders and raw materials, she could be glad that Blümer's was still allowing her to earn her daily bread. So she didn't come the next summer either. But in the fall, the fall of 1922 that is, she came nonetheless. One gray October morning she stepped inside my workshop, where there was no activity taking place and no heating. And looked such a sight that I leapt to my feet and asked:

"Johanna—where have you just come from? What's the matter?"

She had just come from her mother's funeral and had to take the evening train back to Berlin.

She was very thin, with bags under her eyes, and had clearly been crying. I offered her a seat. Her mother had died of some pancreatic disorder, and she had only found out about how serious it was when it was too late, so she had not seen her alive. I asked her whether she was managing to more or less eat properly in Berlin. Times were such that this was a common question. She said more or less. But that she already had to pay two or three hundred marks for the canteen lunch at work. I said:

"But Johanna—your place here is absolutely free right now!"

She began to argue: "No-no-no . . ." I picked up my gastroscope from the workbench—the first and initially only one of its kind in the world as far as I know—a device that looked like the head of a tapeworm with five lenses and a tiny electrical bulb mounted onto a flexible metal tube and a system of mirrors—pressed it against her stomach just above the navel, switched on the lamp so that her blouse was lit up for a radius of five centimeters and looked down the tube.

"I can already see what's wrong: you're starving!"

"How can you *see* that?" she asked in astonishment.

I started laughing: "Through this tube I *would be able* to see everything. But you would have to swallow it first. So that was just a joke. I can see with the naked eye that you're hungry. Listen—do you still remember my mother's sprats?"

She did. And I put the umpteenth tin of sprats that I had received a few days ago on the workbench. After a short pause, while she still felt herself a stranger, Johanna boiled water for the tea on the spiral hotplate. I started slicing a gray, sawdust-like loaf of bread—and said suddenly, rather to my own surprise:

"Johanna—I'm now quite a rich man. Well, to be more exact: the rumor of wealth is of course nonsense. But I sold our Nette for five hundred thousand. And I still have more than half left. I could with absolutely no difficulty give you one hundred thousand. So that you could buy yourself free from Blümer's and take the exams you planned in the spring. And I was thinking—given your thrifty nature, as far as I am aware—that money could free you for a whole year to pursue your studies. And with a bit of luck you could have your studies finished in—let's say three and a half years—this would not be impossible in my opinion . . ."

She began shaking her head, her mouth still full, and said, even before she'd managed to swallow her mouthful:

"Herr Schmidt—thank you very much. Very, very much. But I can't accept. Because if you are thinking of this as a student loan—I have no prospects of ever paying it back."

I cried: "But no . . . !" And she continued:

"But if you were to think of it a gift—well, then this would be even less acceptable." And when I started up with "But why?" and "How can it be so?" she said, wondering why she had to explain it all:

"Herr Schmidt—for a man like you it should be especially clear that I would lose my independence toward you. And that cannot be something you would want. But do you know what? I would be very grateful if I knew that—that in a real emergency—not now, not now, but when I have no other choice—that I could ask for a loan from you of let's say one or two thousand."

I was most willing to lend her that sum and that is what happened. One and a half hours later I walked her to the station—and thought as I strolled beside her: I wouldn't have done this previously. Why am I doing it now? Aha, I know: previously she had not just arrived from her mother's funeral, but it was from there that she was coming today . . .

Johanna traveled back to Berlin, and over the next two months my two hundred thousand melted away like snow in spring. Unnoticeably at first, then under my observant, uncomprehending, and wryly smiling gaze ever more quickly. Actually, I had been aware of how the value of money had plunged ever since I asked the waiter at the Sanitas one morning to put a portion of asparagus salad in the fridge for me until that evening, and that I would pay immediately for my breakfast and for the salad later. But he said that it would be better to pay for the salad now as well. I asked why. Did he not know me? Wasn't I a customer who came there every day? And he said:

"Because, Herr Schmidt, by this evening the salad will cost 140 marks instead of the present hundred."

After that I cut out the currency exchange rate tables from old newspapers over the past month and lay them side by side on my table. And I remembered—and this was almost a shock to me—a week before Johanna's latest visit, the first of October, one American dollar was worth 1,632 German marks. A week later (I didn't notice the change over that week as I was fully occupied with the model for my gastroscope) one dollar was worth 2,162 marks. And now, on the third of November, the price of one dollar was 4,561 marks. So in the space of one month the buying power of the German currency in your pocket had shrunk by two thirds. By the way, when it became clear that the whole of my 200,000-mark capital had been worth around a hundred dollars in early October (but living in my own little world I hadn't noticed just how far the mark had fallen)—well, after that it wasn't exactly very shocking to realize that my savings were now worth no more than forty dollars. It was more amusing than anything else. And the joke or the drama, or actually the tragedy, just kept on growing. And that was only the beginning. At the end of December and during the first few days of January the mark became one seven- or eight-thousandth of a dollar. And at that point something happened in the world that was much more interesting than the German mark. In Russia, 130 versts away in the town of Tsaritsyn, at the Akhtuba Station, as the papers wrote, a unique meteorite had fallen. What sort it in fact was, I never found out, but it did grip my imagination for a while. Because they wrote: the meteorite was sticking up a few meters out of the ground where it had fallen! This seemed to run counter to the idea that it was a meteorite, given the huge velocity and mass as it fell to earth. But then the French occupied the Ruhr. The newspapers reported that in Düsseldorf and Essen and wherever else it was, French tanks were rumbling along the streets, and on the roads along the banks of the Rhine whole divisions of the French army were marching. In one week the value of the mark fell fivefold to forty thousand marks to the dollar. And at the Lindengarten tavern workers from technical workshops and the cigarette factory and from Die Alte Hoffnung lead mine would discuss at the schnapps table at around seven in the evening who the hell was responsible for all this. Soon they would be arguing so loudly that Frau Bretschneider let her own kitchen boy bring my bottle of korn and cigar to my living quarters. During which time I managed to achieve a perfectly clear photo with my periscope with a field of 115 degrees, but could only keep body and soul together thanks to the fact that my mother illegally sent me several thousand marks' worth of banknotes in Estonian currency, which the Mittweida branch of the bank in Saxony would initially exchange for notes with numbers ten, then twenty, then soon twenty thousand times larger printed on them . . . Because in the meantime the decline of the mark had been temporarily halted at one two-hundred-thousandth of a dollar, and it stayed there until April. I do not know what trick the government used. But then the tale became even more absurd. Having your hair cut would soon cost as much as let's say a small suburban villa before the war. And not only that. I went to the barber's on Freibergerstraße, looked at the price list on the wall—today up to two o'clock, sixteen thousand marks, after two, twenty thousand. I went in to have my hair cut and handed the barber twenty thousand. But he stretched out his hand and, looking away, said:

"Erm—Herr Schmidt—you may have a German name but you're a foreigner, aren't you . . . ?"

I said: "Well, Herr Lohmann, you have cut my hair for twenty years—but you are right—a foreigner I am."

"Then you have to pay at the rate for foreigners."

"And how much would that be altogether?"

"Altogether—sixty thousand."

And suddenly, everything in this country had grown three times more expensive than for a German citizen. Then came the demonstrations. Then they started shooting at demonstrators. On the Augusteplatz in Leipzig, there were around a hundred dead and wounded. Then people ransacked shops and there were strikes and a growing risk of starvation. And little by little the whole of the economy became paralyzed. To the accompaniment of small arms and machine-gun fire. But I was, well—a foreigner . . . ? Amid the increasingly apocalyptic catastrophe that this country was facing. I *was* of course a foreigner. And was both unemployed and broke. But I had to stick it out for a month or more. Taking the idiotic decision to stay put until the mark had reached one-millionth of a dollar. And maybe with the secret hope that something so phantasmagorical could never happen. Ha-ha-ha-haa. By July that unbelievable event was at hand. I sent Johanna a postcard of one and a half lines (which I remember, as it cost thirty thousand marks in stamps), stuffed a loaf of bread (costing one hundred fifty thousand marks, if I remember rightly), a few lenses, and a cut-throat razor into my briefcase, and for my last three million I bought a train ticket to Stettin. Captain Siimann, a friend of my brother August's, took me to Tallinn on his vessel the *Thorsten,* and let me go on board without a ticket. By the second or third of August, I disembarked at the Kaupmehe jetty in Tallinn.

But I really must now start thinking about my correction plate. I mean to say how, well, not just any old bungler, but at least the average optical glass polisher could grind one of my correction plates. Because this plate of mine would then, after all, be something more than some unique object of the-devil-knows-what provenance. Only then would it be a technical reality. At least for the world at large. And then—damn and blast—I wouldn't have to shudder inwardly as I still do when I remember with what kind of self-esteem I stepped ashore in Tallinn six years ago.

Because that was one of the most humiliating experiences I have ever had.

Twenty years previously, I had embarked at that same Kaupmehe jetty. After having clocked up four classes of the village school on Naissaar and worked as a telegraphist at the Tallinn coastguard station for eighteen months. Where they took me on, let's face it, because they felt sorry for me. Thinking that I would soon realize how incompetent I was for such work. But as they themselves realized as time went on (and they noticed quite early on), by some miracle I could nevertheless get the equipment to work and never deviated one millimeter from the message in the telegram. And then that brief year at the Volta factory. In the draftsmen's office. Where the same occurred: let the poor boy sit at the drawing board, as he is so keen to get there. And then, what do you know, they noticed that given his lack of experience, he was doing exemplary work. He could manage to hold his ruler and set square with the stump of his right hand while wielding his pencil, pair of compasses, and drawing pen perfectly well with his left hand, with more dexterity than many an old draftsman with his right. His handwriting was admittedly a little odd, but evenly written, like printed letters. He produced his drawings as if playing around, but they were nonetheless a good deal more accurate than was necessary.

Oh, the heady days of youth . . . When enough such observations reached my ears, sometimes indirectly, sometimes directly, and I myself had experienced the same thing in my own work, I began to think that anything was possible. I don't know how much my mother really believed in me, or to what extent she convinced herself that her boy would get where he wanted—but she gave me the fifty silver rubles that she had saved, and Uncle Frans did likewise. And then one August morning in 1901, with a light bundle in my hand I climbed aboard the *Nemrac* at the Kaupmehe jetty, and thought: Edison, Ericsson, Eastman, Niepce, Nobel . . . And my propeller sail, with which you could sail with the wind or even nearly straight into that same wind, seemed to more or less be ready and could take me through all winds. As well as my automatic rudder (roughly the same as the one Flettner is said to have invented some twenty years later), which I had in reserve so as to enable me to negotiate every reef . . .

But now I was back there. With not the slightest scrap of fame clinging to my name. That tiny glimmer of recognition that seemed to be growing among experts before the war—had been swept away, had gone out, been forgotten . . . Not a bent penny in my pocket—yes indeed!—in the literal sense of the expression: I buy the ticket to Naissaar with the fifty Estonian marks I've borrowed from Captain Siimann as we said farewell. I come—with empty pockets, in jacket and trousers worn to rags, a loose collar washed under the faucet in the cabin with the last bit of soap, so that it is still damp around my neck, and weak at the knees from a year of undernourishment . . . In my briefcase, as I mentioned, my cut-throat razor, and a few sketches for my uranostat (as if I thought that I would find anyone in Estonia interested in it) and a few small lenses and five or six *Schleifschale* (I don't know what they are called in our language)—so that *if* I were to find work here polishing optical glass I would at least have the basics handy.

I walked along the harbor street of Sadama and the tediously bright flagged limestone pavement of Suur-Patarei Street and the lumpy cobblestones of the Miinisadam—the Mine Harbor—and I thought (and felt how my thoughts were physically affecting me): so is this the way that a hunter of fame returns home—with his poor empty stomach along with the meager catch of sprats belonging to his not-all-too-beloved Uncle Frans? Can you imagine any more embarrassing fiasco?

The *Sextant,* a small ship used for placing buoys, and which connected Naissaar with the mainland, was to sail in half an hour. You could see ten or so people standing on deck. I went into the cabin near the prow to avoid their gaze. It was empty, but very stuffy. The porthole had rusted shut as if welded and I couldn't open it. But I preferred the stuffiness in here to the gaze of passersby on deck and the questions of those getting on board that my arrival would no doubt have given rise to. A quarter of an hour later, now out at sea, and I thought: this little ship will never again set marker buoys or reach any harbor. Because right now, right now under the burden of my feeling of suffocation, my feeling of humiliation, all the rivets will loosen and it will sink to the bottom of the sea. I could feel quite directly how a feeling of no escape was pressing on my eardrums. I heard how the cabin was creaking from the pressure on its white-painted iron walls and I *saw* how the porthole began to bulge outward because of the terrifying pressure of my feeling of humiliation . . .

But hell and damnation—No-no, that time in the cabin I must have passed out and came to when the ship began to slow down at the approaches to Naissaar harbor. But hell and damnation—what I want to say is: *this* would have to be the solution. Now! Right here in the cool and secure cellar—if not at home then at least in the secure cellar in Bergedorf . . . The solution: glass as thick as your finger, at a specific change in pressure, will cause even relatively thick glass to deform in the necessary manner . . . So that it will be deformed to *the necessary extent,* then it can be hoped that . . .

No, now I do not have the time. I shake out the ashtray into the sink and run out of the workshop. I am hardly capable of remaining faithful to my habit of locking the door behind me. Then I am standing at the door of the workshop of our precision mechanics and our technical store. The door is shut. No one about as yet. Oh damn, I pull my watch out of my pocket: it is only twenty to eight. Very well. I'll be back at ten past eight. The storekeeper Grote and Meister Schmidt, Paul Schmidt, that is, my namesake, will be there. And I have the list and sketch I drew up in half an hour of the things I need. No, not everything can be found in the store. As I need an iron, a cylindrical vessel made of steel at least 6 millimeters thick, 200 in height, diameter 340 millimeters, that should have a thickened upper edge, and that edge, 20 millimeters wide, must be polished completely clean and completely level. The vessel must have a tap and a manometer. And a valve to allow tiny amounts to be released. Such a vessel. And also a very sensitive air pump. For which I need a pedal construction. That my hand can be free to work. And a hose that fits the pump and the taps of the vessel.

Well, I have of course sold my soul to a certain extent here in Bergedorf. If not in reality, then theoretically nonetheless. Inasmuch as I gave in to Schorr and started working here. But I am nevertheless only *a voluntary collaborator,* no doubt the only one of his kind in the whole of Germany's system of astronomical observation. A voluntary collaborator who receives no fixed salary, but can do what he wishes, and as much as he wishes. On the proviso that he does more or less sensible things. But thanks to that dependence—because it is dependence to a certain extent—thanks to that dependence Grote will in one moment come away from his filing cabinets and into the store to see if what I need is available, and Schmidt will be scratching his neck, bent over my sketch with a very diligent look on his face. Because I know that Schorr had said to them: "Everything that Herr Schmidt wants must be carried out swiftly and in the best manner possible." But Schorr is a professor, an academic doctor, and the director. For Grote and other types of good Germans that is the same thing as God himself.

Things are sorted out to this extent: the vessel will be constructed, the manometer exists, the pump will be obtained in Hamburg. But despite all this: not before tomorrow at three o'clock. Quicker than that is, unfortunately, quite impossible.

I find fault, grumble at them, even bawl them out. I ask: Why the hell is their store as empty as a gypsy's tobacco pouch? And why does the workshop work at such a slacker's pace? Oh hell, I feel ashamed of being like this, but we just haven't got the time!

They put on an expression indicating that they have understood me but that nothing can be done any quicker. And all there is left for me to do is to put on an expression that I have understood them. And in all truth I do understand is that however minor the things I need are, no one would get them quicker than they would. The best thing for me to do is to return to my own workshop and stretch out on the old sofa with its springs poking through and again think over exactly *how* I am going to tackle this problem. And ask myself: Does the result still feel as inevitably real as it felt for that instant when it sprang to mind *in a flash*?

Incidentally, I have long ago noticed in myself something maybe peculiar to me, maybe common to mankind in general, but it is in any case something that almost follows the rules of nature. If I divide up my decision to do something, into let us say into three levels of intensity—weak, middling, absolute—then in the case of the middle intensity things always end up like this: the more I try to concentrate on this decision, the more I try to think it through, the more I try to clarify it for myself, the more the temptation grows to cast it aside, play for time, procrastinate or simply commit things to memory. And conversely: the more I try to put off focusing on something for a short while, think about something else, the more I am assailed by this problem that wants to sweep all else aside. Anyway, why do I not mention the weak and absolute decisions in this context? Because in the case of the weak decisions, the swings have very weak contours. But the absolute decisions are, in my terminology, such sudden rushes of thought that they require the minimum of effort and have in any case already given me such a crack of the whip on my neck that no thought of avoiding them ever arises.

In a word, tomorrow at three o'clock they will bring the necessary equipment and assemble it on my instructions. I send them off with my thanks then lock the door. And check—this could take several hours—whether my intuition was right or not. If it was, then—very well. What it means is that I now have enough time to think through my experiment. But now I'm simply going to bed. And as I wait for sleep to come, I will ponder upon what then happened that morning six years ago . . .

4

EVIDENTLY I DID PASS OUT IN THAT CABIN. FROM THE STUFFINESS, THE misery, or an empty stomach. I don't really know which. And only came to as the vessel slowed down and from the noise as the engine went into reverse.

Through the porthole a strip of coastal sand could be seen, beyond that the forest; and in front of it in the sea, the concrete jetty with its plank roof—an insolently large building that was erected here right after the war and that I was seeing now with alarm and apprehension, seemingly for the first time.

I let the ship dock and waited. A dozen or so voyagers had stayed on the sunny deck for up to the one and a half hours that the voyage had lasted. No one had stepped inside the cabin at the prow. I watched them disembark through the porthole: they were, thank goodness, all strangers to me. Except for one whom I only just recognized from twelve years before: old Villem from Sõrve. In those days he was already a little unkempt, a youngish man, still vigorous enough, his eyes sometimes serious, sometimes glittering—but now, suddenly, a decade or so later, he had become a veritable skeleton, his face covered with pepper-and-salt stubble, a face like an old, sick, and gray hare.

The quay was deserted and no one emerged from the sheds nearby as I walked along the deck of the *Sextant* under the gaze of a couple of very young sailors and down onto the alien quay, and began to walk past the alien sheds and the even more alien barbed wire enclosure in a southerly direction, that is, toward home.

After my previous home visit one summer twelve years ago I had received a few brief letters from my mother. Then nothing for four years. Then, after the war, letters and food packages. The latter, however simple, were, against the background of the semi-starvation in Germany, pretty luxurious (consisting of sprats with herbs, dried whitefish, and crispbread). The letters that accompanied them were not much by comparison. Nonetheless, I had managed to glean from these letters a brief glimpse of the fact that in the spring of 1913 Russian officers had turned up at the summer houses on the edge of Lehtmetsa, some with their wives, others without, then the land surveyors, the engineers, and the first builders of barracks, so that the island bustled with construction and fortification work. Some of the old men had raked up ancient memories from their great-grandfathers' time suggesting that similar things had happened before—Vallimägi, the ruins of the old five-pointed fortress, a stone's throw from our yard, was clear evidence of this. And the old men muttered that according to what people remembered nothing good came of it all for the inhabitants of the island, and no good would come of it now either. But some younger men had simply smiled and been enterprising enough to bring calves and beet and carrot seed from Tallinn and had expanded their plank huts and vegetable patches. Because they could do good business with the new folk, who seemed to have money: sell them vegetables and milk and meat. Besides the fish that they would automatically start buying from the islanders. Which was much to the advantage of the island dwellers. They would no longer have to take their sprats and herring and pike all the way to market in Tallinn, where the fish wholesalers made the profits.

So that was that. But on the twentieth of October 1913, the islanders were summoned to the schoolhouse at Lõunaküla in the south of the island. Little more than 150 people in all. The Russian governor of Estonia had arrived in person with his adjutants and gendarmes at the new jetty in a couple of warships to address the people in the schoolhouse. A blue-uniformed brass band played the czar's anthem to the silent populace so that the low ceiling of the building reverberated with the sound. The governor had stepped up to the schoolmaster's worn and ink-stained desk and made a speech. And I thought as I read my mother's letter: what an honor for that shabby piece of furniture, before which I myself had stood for four years when being tested by old Klaamann on my arithmetic or scripture . . . Mother wrote: a general with a Cossack mustache. That is to say, Major General Korostovets. The same one about whom more political jokes were told all around the *gubernia* than about anyone else. So that one or two stick in my memory: he is supposed to have suffered from severe headaches and in the end traveled to a hospital in St. Petersburg to have the cause of the pain identified. There they had sawed the top of his skull open and put his brains in an enamel dish. At that very moment, an order came from the czar that Izmail Vladimirovich had been appointed governor to Estonia. Whereupon the general had risen up from the operating table and stood to attention—he could not receive orders lying down—and then stormed out and off to Tallinn in order to receive a list of his duties. His brains were left behind in the enamel dish. And no doubt the people of Naissaar remembered this brain joke when listening to the governor's speech. Because the governor said the following: by decree of the czar, Naissaar was to become a *link*—a vital link—in the powerful chain of fortifications named after Czar Peter the Great that would be built around Tallinn in order to defend the city of St. Petersburg. This would be a great honor for Naissaar. But such a little island could not do justice to so great an honor if it was filled with a population of civilians. So the island would be cleared over the space of two months of all civilians. And this would be carried out in the usual manner, that is, for the benefit of the local population, so that it could be said of them: by this decision they have been blessed with good fortune. First: the state will buy up all farms at a just price and pay in pure gold. Second: all will be given new land befitting their way of life and habits in a suitable place, that is to say on an *island,* the Isle of Muhu, facing the Väike Väin, the Small Strait. The sea will be just as wet, but much quieter and with more fish stocks than here. Third, and this was the most important point of all: in exchanging their present bleak and semi-barren location for a much more pleasant one they will have the pleasure of doing the czar and their native land a noble service, which is the duty of every decent subject of the realm.

From my mother's letter it was not clear how the inhabitants of

Naissaar responded. I can only surmise that they would have sniggered up their sleeves at the general, then weighed up the matter with much worry later on and come to the conclusion that abandoning one's home is the hardest of hard decisions to make, however high the compensation. Whereupon some of the more thoughtful men had nevertheless suggested that a couple of those present be sent to Muhu to reconnoiter and see what sort of land was being offered there.

At the end of April, when the sea was free of pack ice, the governor was back. He considered that the construction work, albeit suffering from delay, had moved forward. But it was unheard of that the islanders were still on Naissaar. And entirely unheard of was what happened at this second meeting at the schoolhouse. When the czar's anthem had been played and the governor, grim on this occasion, had barked at them that the entire civilian population must be off the island within the space of one month, old Berg-Andres had stepped forward and declared in the name of the assembled gathering, his face pale, as I imagine, and beads of sweat on his forehead from the strain of his task, and said quite quietly too, although in a firm voice: the people of Naissaar were not taking up the offer of land on Muhu. Because those lands consisted of nothing more than crunching gravel and soggy bog. And the so-called sea was, there near Väike Vain, only a mere three-foot deep, so that—the governor did not allow him to finish, but jumped up and yelled:

"Then go to hell, the lot of you! Anyone who is not off the island in two weeks' time will be clapped in irons, face a military tribunal, and be sent to Siberia! Dismissed, quick march!"

By the way, my mother did not write about such things. This last piece of information was sent to me by August in the spring of 1914 from Sweden. After that, only a few fragments of news reached me from home. Until Mother's first postwar letters said a little bit more. The forced clearance of the island was only half complete when the war broke out. The last families were expelled over the space of twenty-four hours. Mother and Uncle Frans and the then fourteen-year-old Ester, my half sister, among them. August was aboard ship and my full sisters Olga and Berta had left home several years previously and were living, the former in Borgå with her Finland-Swede Wallenius, the other in Tallinn with her husband, surnamed Blees. These last two, Berta and her husband, had managed to obtain a flat in the Kalaranna district on Suur-Patarei Street and helped Mother and Uncle to make ends meet until the compensation money for the forced clearance of their farm, Jaanipere, reached the old folk. Despite the war, the Russian Crown Office paid them, whether at the correct rate I don't know, but duly in gold rubles. With that and some chance jobs—I don't remember exactly what—they managed to survive the German occupation. Up to the time that the new Estonian government began to sell off the farms on Naissaar alienated by the Russian government, their former owners enjoying first refusal. If the former owners did not buy them back, or were not interested in doing so (which was usually due to a lack of money), then the government would sell them to entirely new people. Let my relationship to Uncle Frans be what it may. Some of his traits and behavior are what they are, but he is nonetheless more attached to Naissaar than the average islander. And that is quite significant. So that Uncle Frans and Mother were among the first to move back to Naissaar. I can imagine that some of the money used to buy back Jaanipere came from what they themselves had saved up from that sale at Russian prices, but the sons-in-law did indeed add to the sum. Because Mother did write that they had to pay fifty thousand Estonian marks for the purchase. This was quite a big sum for four and a half hectares of stony ground, when you think in what state the buildings and outhouses had been left in the spring of 1919: doors hanging crooked on their hinges, leaking roofs, broken windows, the windmill knocked off its pedestal, and the sauna, the one that had caught fire, burnt down as a result of my photographic experiments twenty-five years previously, but had been rebuilt—had now burnt right down to its blackened cornerstones. But Uncle Frans would not have been Uncle Frans, and even less so my mother my mother, had not they immediately begun to rebuild and restore Jaanipere, as much as they were capable of doing. A year or two ago August sent some photos of home that he had taken with the camera I left behind, not my very first one made of old spyglass lenses and an old harmonica, but a later one that was a little less primitive. You could at any rate see from the photos: the house itself was now in tip-top condition, and by the porch the first violets were blooming in a well-weeded flowerbed. And the second photo, which showed the inside of the house, was even more telling. The floor was covered with a large rag mat. At the coffee table in the middle of the mat sat Mother and Uncle Frans and the neighbor Jakob Schulmann from Kopka and old Frans Rosen from Valli, a relative of my mother's, and Auntie Leena plus a row of unfamiliar faces. They had Mother's flower-patterned coffee cups in front of them, and in the middle of the table stood a piece of my mother's dowry, a large silver-edged glass bowl, which we at least considered to be made of crystal, and which could well have been, and was filled with what looked like cumin buns made the way Grandmother used to make them . . . In the Germany of two years ago, a starving country, I could clearly imagine what they smelled like . . .

And that morning two years later, and now six years back, I had reached the smell of those home-baked buns halfway. With my self-esteem as it was. So I didn't intend going *straight* to Jaanipere. Especially as I found that right from the sheds in the harbor I stumbled upon something quite unexpected and incomprehensible in the sand dunes of Naissaar—a railroad track. I knew from Mother's letters that one was supposed to have been built. But the tar smell of its sleepers and the shine of the metal rails on the edge of the pinewoods were nonetheless quite alien to me.

I stopped amidst the young pines at the edge of the gravel road and eyed the sleepers and rails of the fortification railway, as if it were a dragon that had encroached upon my home woods. My feeling of alienation surprised even myself. I had never shown much interest in, or liking for, railroad technology. But had the due respect of a technical man for them. How could I on occasion have regarded the renewal of boat engines as a favorite problem-solving pursuit—and at the same time have despised the most important mode of transport on dry land? Stephenson's first steam engine fifty years before my birth, the opening of the railway traversing the United States some forty years later. Siemens's first electric locomotive in the year of my birth, the first turbine locomotive by the Brothers Ljungström almost on my fortieth birthday—I really was a child of the railroad era—but here, in the woods, through the hillocks of juniper where there are said to be the graves of French sailors from the Crimean War, here where I have stood feet apart in knee britches looking out over the sea and pretending to pilot the shipping, or lying on my stomach in the darkness of night, my heart to the ground, waiting fearfully for French wraiths to emerge from the grave—here the presence of a railroad line was sheer temerity . . .

In order to avoid the tracks—and clearly also in order to delay my arrival home—the idea arose in my mind to drop in and see Harbor Villem. So as to let the man who made claims to be the wizard of the village and has boasted of being a soothsayer put me right as to what had actually happened on Naissaar while I'd been away. So I turned off the old road to the net shed at Noodamaja, but one kilometer later ran again across the accursed rail tracks and then, before the seal cove at Hülgekari, across the remains of the concrete bunkers of the huge collapsed gun emplacement that they had recently tried to blow up, as if the bones of the earth, the knee joints of the earth, had been ripped away from the body of the earth and been left to bleach in the sun. Nearby was an abandoned hut. And not until I had passed Villem's sauna did I realize that this indeed was his house, his hovel, dubbed the cabbage sauna. I turned round and entered Villem's yard. The door was hanging crookedly on only one hinge, the wind blew through the open window gaps. Nettles and mallow were growing on the doorstep and had not been trampled by human feet. I walked through the porch into the living room. On the windswept floor there were only a few scraps of blue wallpaper and dust. In the kitchen corner on the tiny rusty iron stove lay a broken earthenware bowl. A massive, dark-green, almost black bowl. It had broken into four pieces, as if it had sprung apart by a small amount of water left in it as it turned to ice. For some unknown reason one quarter of the bowl had in turn broken into a couple of dozen smaller gray-edged shards. But I nevertheless recognized that bowl. Or it would have to have been an exact replica that I thought I recognized.

On the evening in 1896 before I left Naissaar and moved to Tallinn, on the evening before, Auntie Leena had dragged me along, without the rest of my family knowing, to Villem's sauna. She had put a half liter of Blue Neck vodka on the table in front of the owner of the hovel and there we had sat, the three of us. Auntie Leena, Villem, and me, in that same room as now at a small round table that was, of course, no longer there. In the middle of the table had stood that very same glazed bowl, dark green, almost black. Villem had poured all the vodka slowly into the bowl and looked into my future by the flickering light of the petroleum lamp. I remember:

"Long, long, long roads," he muttered in what I remember to be a slightly tipsy whisper, and pointed with his black-rimmed fingernail at unseen lines in the shining surface of the vodka. And I thought: rubbish . . . What kind of long roads are they, when I'm going to work as a telegraphist in Tallinn harbor . . . "But always alone—always alone. I cannot see girls around you," murmured Villem, looking into the bowl. And I thought: thank goodness for that. It would be all I need for him to now start attributing to me stories about girls in the presence of Auntie Leena—although the idea was nonetheless a little exciting. "And you will climb high in life, I'm telling you," explained Villem, "changing all the time—dark empty spaces and dark narrow staircases or whatever they are. But further into the future—things simply sparkle! It is the glitter of gold, the sparkle of coins, what else. Just look at the glitter at the bottom of this bowl! Soon ten times, twenty times more than with ordinary people . . ." And I thought: I certainly need that. Why not? And it isn't completely impossible. Because if I manage to actually build my propeller sail and get the patent for it and all the boats in the world begin to use it—then I would be earning serious money . . . Oh, what an observatory I would then have built on Naissaar, on Kuningamäe—the King's Hill. Or Suurmägede—the Great Hills! I would have to weigh up which spot I would choose.

That same broken bowl.

I put my briefcase down on the floor and picked up one shard a cubic centimeter in size and slipped it in my pocket. If for no other reason than to be able to laugh at all those others who had laughed at me. *If* for no other reason. Then I went back outside and now took the quickest route to the village. And straight through the village.

Half the farms seemed abandoned, some even in disrepair. But people were still living in a good half of them. Here and there in the yards some old man or woman could be seen who stared at me. From the yards of the Küüns and Säki-Leena, the Luthers and old man Eelias. But none of these present people were familiar to me, nor me to them, no doubt. But I called out in a loud voice: "Tere!" and "God dag!"

The houses seemed grayer than before, the bright Swedish reddish-brown paint more faded and patchy, and the village somehow more squashed up than before. So that I was already walking along the grassy knolls of the Vallimäe ramparts, then into our yard and the house itself.

I don't remember the first words I exchanged with my mother. But I do remember then sitting at the table covered with flowery oilcloth, my mother having grown curiously old, yet being curiously the same as always, so that I couldn't decide which she really was as she took sprats pickled with onions out of a black iron pot and set them in front of me, spread butter on a slice of bread, and said:

"Our Frans was wondering, judging by what is written in the *Päevaleht,* how it is possible to survive in Germany given the crazy prices they now have there."

And I said: "Well you see, there wasn't any work anymore either. At least not for me."

Mother said: "You've been as thin as a rake all your life. But now your face really does look like a goat's hoof. So you can take it easy here. As long as you need to. There'll still be bread for you on Naissaar."

August was said to be on a long voyage. To China or Japan or some such place. But Uncle Frans came home that evening. It turned out that Jaanipere farm now owned a motorboat. With its six-horsepower Bruck motor, running on oil. In that, Frans went out from the Lõunaküla harbor with a crew of four to go fishing. Out to the fishing grounds of Nisumadala and Naamanimadala, that is, Wheat Shallows and Naze Shallows. By now he was fifty-eight years old and his tread was noticeably heavier than ten years previously, but his eye was just as sharp and his words ditto:

"Well—hello, Pänn! What kind of miracle has brought you home?"

He shook hands, his paw roughened by the scales of fish, sat down across from me at the dining table, let Mother put some food in front of him, and then showered me with questions. Slightly mockingly, almost in a friendly manner. And then in passing, slightly full of himself and his mouth full of sprats:

"Some people I know in Tallinn pointed out your name in some stargazing rag or other. I don't remember the name of the paper.

Didn't understand either in what connection it was. But it was your name—*Herr Bernhard Schmidt zu Mittweida.* I told mama that—look, here's . . ."

I did, thank my lucky stars, not start listing for my stepfather a whole load of German publications in which my name could have been found, this one or that one. Nor did I start asking in what connection I was mentioned, as a photographer of stars or in the context of some observation instrument or other . . . I can thank my lucky stars that I didn't attach any importance to the fact that my name had been mentioned. Because the old man peered at me over the bowl of curds and asked forthwith:

"But how does it work with them—are they paying you for it all?"

"You mean for the fact that they mention me? Course not."

"Well," said my stepfather, almost relieved, "I always imagined it was some boast of yours that they wouldn't even waste one penny on."

We put up loyally with each other. In my first week I simply took walks around the island. And I have to say: it was a fantastic week. I went all over the place. From Veskikari in the south to Virbu beyond the northern lighthouse. I stood in the woods near Storkärr and watched how the marsh gas bubbled up through the algae-covered waters between the rushes. I wandered, with ferns up to my chest, through the steeple-high pinewoods at Suurmägede. I felt the bark of the pine trees with my hand, sometimes as smooth as silk, sometimes as rough as stone. I listened to the waves standing on the red rocks of the Järvesaare naze. I jumped from rock to rock as far as I could out to sea, and stood, my mouth open, facing the wind from the south as it splashed the spray into my face. And felt that this, my island, was the safest place on earth. My return was like returning to the womb. And yet at the same time what I saw around me constantly ripped apart this feeling. The metal snakes of the fortification railroad track, half abandoned but ineffaceable, cut my very own, my pristine woods, to pieces. On Hülgekari, Klaose, Kõrve-Toomas, Mustmetsa the gun emplacements stood whole or blown up, but in any case enormous chunks of concrete that were impossible to get rid of had their huge, rusting, ten- and twelve-inch guns pointed at God knows what target. Above the sinister new harbor, among the pine trees, lurked the empty barracks in barbed-wire enclosures, where four years previously terrible things were supposed to have taken place. People would answer: "Why ask? We don't really know either. We weren't on the island at the time. Nobody was on the island at the time. But those sandy mounds beyond the barbed wire—they are said to be the graves of the Red sailors. How many? You can go and count them for yourself . . ." I had crept back into the womb. But the war had raped my mother.

And during the whole of my sojourn on Naissaar, I swung between two opposing poles of feeling, that of security and that of an inevitable defilement.

Half of the farms were occupied, half of these by new people or strangers, but the other half by the original occupants, at least by name. Because I could only more or less recognize those that were middle aged; the older people had aged beyond recognition—apart from those closest to me, quite naturally—and the children had grown unrecognizably big. I asked myself how much of this was an illusion on my part—I had after all seen Harbor Villem come to the island with me on a boat, yet his house was devoid of dwellers. It turned out that Villem now lived in Mädasadama, in the house the Blekmans used to live in. But when I had learned that, I thought: Will I bother to go there? Because what did I really have to say to him? Instead, a week—maybe only four-five days—later I put my old bench and its vise, used for woodwork and other things, in Uncle Frans's back shed in order. And began to mess around with it. In the outhouses and attic of Jaanipere I found the cartridge cases of artillery shells of various calibers. Some of them had had their ends sawed off, some still had them, some I set aside to be used as the tubes of rockets some twenty-five years ago; the majority had been picked up from what was left of the ammunition after the war, on the principle that sooner or later every item could come in handy on the farm. In the same way, a whole lot of other material could be found in the boxes and drawers in the barns and sheds of the farm. And as my project developed, I was obliged to use similar junk from further away than home. I just had to stomach passing the time of day or chatting with people as I met them, and started with the nearest neighbors. I visited the Freibergs and the Rosens, relatives of my mother, and the Luthers and old Mats, that is, Mats Matson. I tolerated their more or less inquisitive questions, replying as briefly as courtesy allowed (as I wanted at all costs to avoid giving the impression that I had become proud—all the more as I had so little damned reason for being so), and asked their permission to have a look in their boxes and crates for old iron scrap. Each farm had its share of old clocks, adjustable oil lamps, bicycles, sewing machines, especially ones made by Naumann or Singer, as we did, and of course boat engines, all set aside just in case they might come in handy one day. But inasmuch as they were not useful right now, I received the things I picked out for nothing, sometimes accompanied with a slightly embarrassed look on the faces of their owners. Embarrassment because they had collected such utterly useless things, as a magpie might do.

Then I managed to collect material around my workbench that I felt might come in handy and set to work. Using three lenses that I had myself polished to near perfection, of eighty, eighty, and forty-five millimeters in diameter (which I had transported in chamois leather cloths in my briefcase), I mounted them on a cartridge case and made quite an ordinary but in its own way perfectly serviceable little telescope. By the second evening of work I had the feeling that this could make an admirable average amateur telescope. After work I read, in that same shed and by the light of the petroleum lamp, a number of newspapers that always arrived in the evening with the fishing boats returning from town. At least during summer and inclement weather. I also collected the latest newspapers from my room, insofar as they had not already been put to use for other things, and leafed through them.

In Estonia, the new government under Konstantin Päts had been established for about a month. I couldn't be bothered to read the names of the ministers. What importance did they have? Salted bacon cost fifty-eight marks a pound at the Tallinn market, and ham, sixty. Well, that was because the currency used here wasn't *German* marks. And the American record altitude of 34,183 feet made by Macready had now been beaten by the Frenchman Sadi Lecointe at 35,116 feet. This record still had the potential for being topped. But by how much was anyone's guess. This was in the case of propeller-driven planes. There had been workers' riots in Saxony. From the Lenbach villa in Munich someone had stolen . . . (Who was Lenbach? God knows. Hang on, now I remember: a society painter. Cheap and famous. Died a couple of decades ago. Yes, that's right). From the Lenbach villa someone had stolen paintings to the tune of ten billion marks:

works by Cranach, Holbein, Hals, and Teniers. Would any of those painters have had the money to buy an equivalent painting made some century before their own? Hardly. Every day in Germany now they were printing some eight thousand billion marks' worth of banknotes. And to save time, they were now only printed on one side of the paper.

On the eighth of August one U.S. dollar cost 1,654,125 marks, the next day 3,308,250 marks.

It would seem that the bottom had fallen out of the bottle that was the value of the German mark, so there was now nothing to stop the bottle from running empty. There was an actual speed and an actual acceleration to this process and *something* had to be governing it—but did anyone know what? Hardly. At any rate it was interesting to see how far such madness could go. When would the hundred million mark be reached? Could this really happen, now that they were talking about the resignation of the Cuno government and the arrival of Stresemann as chancellor? At least Frau Knechtel, as far as I remembered, believed in Stresemann. But what importance could you attach to such faith?

As opposed to my usual practice, I started with the look of the telescope. I thoroughly cleaned the inside of the copper tube with Sidol. I painted the inside black with stove-iron paint, and varnished the outside rather ridiculously with an eye to its use. The Rosen boys, lads of fifteen or sixteen, could of course have done this work for me, and were only too keen to help their uncle home from abroad. But I hadn't a penny to reward them with, even with caramels or other sweets. And I didn't dare stack up any credit with them.

I was quite likely reminded on several occasions during this work of mine that Johanna would have been very handy to have around to perform such tasks.

With ends of tubes and brass rings, using a suitably sized screw, I made the objective and the reversal lens for the main body of the apparatus. Even the lens itself. My device was more or less intended for amateur observation of the moon and the planets, so the work on it was at a level at which the upside-down nature of the image would still disturb the viewer. When the eyepiece, which could be moved on brass runners, had been mounted, I could note the general measurements: aperture 75 millimeters, length of focus 1.2 meters.

And then, just for fun, as a challenge, by necessity and chance I made one more device. It was a chance piece of equipment in that old Mats Matson happened to find in his house a forgotten theodolite left behind before the war by some land surveyor or other; the tripod, the horizontal ring, and the meridian arc, all of them with a light layer of rust or verdigris. From our own house and some other place I managed to get hold of two identical ivory knobs, from sewing machines no doubt, plus five or six perfectly suitable cog wheels. I polished all of these things till they were spick and span and put them together to form a telescope plate, and I attached to this a very stable adjustable horizontal and vertical device.

I packed this whole thing into a wooden crate that had been intended for ten-inch artillery shells from the Luther manufactory, or similar, in which I had added laths to support the contents. This crate was scoured with emery paper both inside and out and coated with varnish, and on the lid was the small inscription in black capitals: BERNHARD SCHMIDT, MITTWEIDA.

I believe it was on the seventeenth or eighteenth of August that I sat down at six in the morning at the boat harbor among the flatfish crates that August Küün had on his boat. It was windy and the sky was gray and the sea seemed to be brimful of water, as it sometimes is in late autumn, but rarely in the month of August. I had to protect myself from the spray behind the cabin; by the time I arrived at Kalaranna in Tallinn I was so soaked that I was glad we had arrived early (it was a little after seven), and while August emptied his crates into wagons I spread my jacket out on the aft of the old boat to let it dry out.

At nine o'clock I lifted the strap of the shell crate onto my shoulder. August had managed to sell his fish for thirty-five marks a pound, and received the money for them and followed me into a few shops. We wandered along the shore and past the gasometer, to our left were the sleepy goings-on of the flea market, to our right the allotments along the foot of the old city wall. We marched through the Great Coastal Gate into the city itself. August went off on his own to get some fishing tackle and I went along to Mr. Amos's shop on Jaani Street.

By European standards this was a perfectly average optician's, by Tallinn standards a first-class optical equipment store. Because, as the newspaper adverts proclaimed, and as could be seen from the shelf displays, apart from spectacles you could also buy microscopes, opera glasses, both of a binocular and monocular type, barometers, thermometers, massage equipment, and cut-throat razors. And among the three or four people behind the counter I spotted the proprietor immediately. This was a youngish, somewhat fish-faced man with mousy pomaded hair, parted and combed neatly. And I felt that direct contact, a frontal attack, was particularly distasteful. And was only possible because the alternative would have been to fall back on Uncle Frans's charity, such an idiotic form of dependence, when I didn't even have money for cigarettes (so that I had been without a smoke for a whole week). I heaved my crate up onto Mr. Amos's counter. Mr. Amos eyed my stump with amazement, as people so often look at it, and he was just opening his mouth, no doubt to order me to get that great big crate off his glass counter, when I, beating him to it, said:

"Mr. Amos in person, I presume . . . ?"

"Yes, I am. And you are . . . ?"

"Schmidt. Mr. Amos—do you have any telescopes?"

Mr. Amos had of course sized me up and expected that I would be buying the cheapest pair of spectacles, with lenses of about plus 1.5 diopters. But now we were suddenly speaking about things a hundred or so times as expensive, so he replied most obligingly:

"Yes. Of course. We have very good Zeiss telescopes . . ."

"What model?"

"The FA 102."

"And how much would one cost?"

"That would be sixteen thousand marks. Without a tripod. The tripod costs an additional three and a half thousand."

"I see. If you could bring it here and show it to me . . ." I pointed to the counter in front of me.

"Yes, one moment." He beckoned to the senior sales assistant and gave him the order. Two minutes later they had placed an elegant seventy-centimeter-long black telescope and tripod on the counter.

I said. "Very well. Now point it at something—through that open window. Let's say—at the marketplace—at those women selling butter. There, by the wall next to the market hall. And then bring them into focus."

Mr. Amos carried out this small request personally. He adjusted the eyepiece and pointed the telescope at the market, until the butter sellers' stall some 150 meters away could be seen quite clearly.

"There you are, sir . . ."

I cast a fleeting glance at the telescope. Ten or twelve times magnification, but the marketplace had quite blurred edges and, beyond that, some vague figures of women and a yellow mass could be seen.

I turned toward Mr. Amos: "That telescope has a seventy-centimeter focal length, illumination of one to four, and twelve times magnification. So that the FA 102 is a nice little toy. Do you have any more powerful telescopes?"

Mr. Amos shrugged his shoulders: "No. We don't just at the moment, there's very little demand for them . . ." (He was so apologetic that I almost began to feel ashamed of myself.) "But we can order one right away!" (Thank goodness, his zeal wiped away my shame.) "Yes, Zeiss can get one to us within ten days. I have their catalogue here . . ." He started rummaging in a drawer. "We can check the price . . ."

I cut him off in his eagerness: "I don't actually want to buy a telescope from you. I want to sell you one."

I really hated what I was doing. But to avoid a situation that would have been even worse, I opened my crate and lifted my telescope and tripod onto the counter. People say that despite my handicap of having only one hand, I manage to do such things with agility and aplomb. Maybe they exaggerate, but there is some truth in what they say. At any rate, in my whole life I have never knocked anything over. In some fifteen seconds my telescope was on Amos's counter and focused. And at that moment I could see the old butter-seller woman in the market with two pegs in her hand, a piece of wire between, cutting a chunk of butter in two, and a young lady counting out coins onto a saucer. But by that time Mr. Amos had managed to speak for ten seconds:

"Oh, no-no-no-no. We don't buy from private individuals. We buy from factories. And what is this thing anyway? No doubt some piece of do-it-yourself equipment. Or what? I don't understand. No-no. Take the thing to some secondhand shop. Go to Tarumaa's on Sadama Street. People tend to take that sort of stuff there . . ."

I *really* hated doing this. But deep inside this horrible feeling was just a tiny little hint of the joy of victory. I said:

"Mr. Amos, Tarumaa buys and sells things secondhand. He doesn't have the slightest idea about optics. You are an optician. Have a look through the telescope."

And Mr. Amos had a look. And another. And yet another. And adjusted the eyepiece slightly. And turned the focus knob. Then let his watery gaze roam over the brass plate on the lid of the crate:

"We-e-e-ll. Bernhard Schmidt. I *have* heard about that firm. It's a very small one."

He hadn't heard a damned thing about any firm.

I said: "Yes. A very small one. But a very good one."

He asked: "You say that your own name is Schmidt? Are you, er . . . related?"

"No. Just a coincidence. I'm the Estonian rep."

"Ye-e-es. Well, if this instrument were to be of interest to us—how much would it cost?"

I said in my most matter-of-fact voice: "Forty thousand."

"Oh, no-no-no-no. Such a price is out of the question."

I felt even worse now. But my pleasure at a good fight and victory overcame my distaste. I said:

"You'll sell it within a year for at least fifty thousand. And you don't have to pay warehousing costs. But if you really are not interested, I could always go to Viidik's . . ." I made as if I were going to put away the instrument. Mr. Amos asked:

"Have you already been to Viidik's?"

I said. "No. I started with you. I thought that a larger business would have a wider set of customers. But it's often the opposite way round."

"Listen, wait a minute," said Mr. Amos. "What are the specifications of this instrument?"

I told him the truth: "Depth of field 1.2 meters. Magnification forty times. The objective—as you will have noticed—is achromatic, triple, using French flint glass. Best quality. Meunier."

"Mmmm. Whether it's best quality or not—we would pay twenty-five thousand for it."

I was disgusted by what I was doing. But my playful spirit had been aroused. I began to loosen the wing nut that attached the telescope to the tripod:

"You know, Mr. Amos, I will first go and see if Mr. Viidik has a broader outlook that befits a specialist than you have."

"Well-well-well-well," laughed Mr. Amos in a falsetto. "OK. Twenty-eight thousand."

Ten minutes later, I had sold the telescope to Mr. Amos for thirty-five thousand and let his assistant count out seventy newly printed greenish-brown five-hundred-Estonian-mark banknotes for me.

We had planned to travel back from Kalaranna at two o'clock. But when I had looked for Ackerberg for a couple of hours on Liivilaia Street without finding him and had a quick meal in an eating house and arrived at the fishing harbor at one, it turned out that the boat was not going to sail after all. August Küün was sitting among the other fishermen who had pulled up their boats onto the shore, was holding his cap on his head in the wind with the palm of his hand, and explained to me through the noise of the waves: the sea was riding so high that the waves were splashing right up onto the jetty. And that you could see this with your own eyes with no explanation needed. And it was also obvious that had the fishermen not pulled their boats up onto the shore they would have been smashed to pieces against that selfsame jetty. In such weather there was no question of setting sail. It would be a miracle if they could get away even the next morning. So August and I took a walk back into town. Or, in fact, we let the northwesterly blow us back, and by the time we had reached Pikk Street it had started to rain. We stepped inside a small café. Then we ran through the rain to a few shops in search of some fishnet yarn for August. And when we'd got that, we ate dinner. I remember that a bottle of beer was exactly the same price as a pound of plaice. Where August then went off to I don't remember. The rain was coming down in buckets and stopped me from going very far. So I turned up my coat collar and went from one bar to the next, led by the signs that followed one another in quick succession. I did not order more than a glass of cognac, a cigar, and a coffee at each of these stops. And saw, if I was sitting near the window, how the wind was ripping at people's clothes on the street and turning women's umbrellas inside out. And how the raindrops ran down the windowpane in parallel lines. As if the windows were being whipped by strings of glass beads.

I did not of course become drunk from a few small glasses. I never really got drunk in the true meaning of the word. What could I have managed to achieve with the trembling hand of a drunkard? But I could certainly relax with one glass after a hard day's work. And this was enough for one or two German ladies to regard me as an alcoholic. One of Frau Knechtel's friends asked her every time she came past for coffee—and I've even heard her say so myself: *"Und wie geht es mit deinem sympatischen Quartalsäufer?"* "How's your friendly binge drinker getting on?"

Well, OK, three or four glasses. But these do liven you up to an extent. So in the evening I did end up in a certain part of the harbor. First in a restaurant, a spick-and-span little joint. Was it on Sauna Street? And wasn't it called Kelnerite Klubi—The Waiters' Club, or something similar? So first in the taproom, then by eleven in the lounge, at a small empty table in one of the booths, near to the little band—a women's band—next to the guitar player—that is to say, she was next to me when the band took a break, and I had clearly been looking sufficiently in her direction. And then off to that brunette's bed. Which was quite nearby, maybe on Müürivahe Street where the watchmen used to live (I don't know Tallinn Old Town that well), under the eaves. She herself, Iira was her name, was supposed to be the daughter of a captain who had perished in Yudenich's army. When I woke up the next morning she was already boiling the tea water on a primus stove and wanted to fetch me white or brown bread from the baker's. What was she like . . . ? Well—*ordinary.* Or maybe not entirely. Which of us is? As she stood in the middle of the room pulling her dress straight, she stopped and said:

"But you must be an officer. In which war did you lose your hand—fighting against the Germans or the Reds?"

I said from the bed: "Go and get some bread. Then I'll tell you . . ."

"And you make sure that the water doesn't boil over . . ."

And went out. Her somewhat worn youth was gone. All that was left was a whiff of cheap eau de cologne. I jumped into my clothes, put a fifty-mark note on the bedside table under the edge of the cloth, put out the primus, and fled.

It was nine by now, and the public sauna was likely to be open. After asking the way a few times I found it and scrubbed myself down in the empty bathhouse. I felt very ill at ease when I thought of Iira. Not only because of my escape, but also because of *where I had fled to.* As if I was, on principle, better and purer than her. Hm. Relatively speaking, I had entered the world of the stars with all my lenses to a lesser extent than she had with her bar guitar playing, or the world of love with her body. Or at any rate no more than she. Nevertheless, the ladles full of warm water on my back were pleasant, almost salvation.

At three o'clock August and I set sail from the jetty at Kalaranna. The sea was somewhat calmer now, but still quite choppy. We arrived home, more or less wet through from battling with the wind and the waves, at about six. That same evening I handed over (in the presence of Uncle Frans so that he wouldn't start telling tales about me behind my back) twenty thousand marks to my mother. And said (so that Uncle Frans could hear) that the cost I had incurred with my stay in her house would be covered until the end of the year.

"Goodness gracious me," said my mother in protestation, "what kind of expenses have there really been. Those bird portions that you've been eating. And this is an enormous sum of money! Remember this isn't your German money that you need so much of."

Uncle Frans pouted his still-red lips and simply said: *"Ska vi se, ska vi se,"* and this meant nothing at all in these circumstances, apart from that he was trying to rise to the occasion, but wasn't really sure how to do so. In such situations he would always say something in Swedish, something that didn't quite fit the context.

So in this way I survived the autumn on this lucky and luckless isle. Doing some fairly meaningless job, alternating with walks through the empty woods and along the deserted beaches. With regard to what could be termed my work, I brought back from the appropriate shops in Tallinn paper, especially greaseproof paper, of varying thickness and strength, but more important, thin tin plate and a few odds and ends, and started to experiment with things I had done as a schoolboy: the effect of wind on vanes that had various profiles. In order to find the most efficient shapes for propeller blades under various conditions. Soon, a dozen or so ever-changing vanes were whirring and whirling on the edge of the roof of the shed, and they glittered and glimmered there, some affixed horizontally, others vertically, stuck to pieces of tin piping. Because I had been mulling over

Flettner's idea for a wind-powered motor for a decade or two until I finally abandoned the whole idea for that rotor in the spring of 1925. But then, in the autumn of 1923, old men on Naissaar said that Smith's Bernhard—yes, they all now called me Bernhard (in itself a perfectly normal and pleasant name—but nonetheless a little alien and saddening—only old Mats Matson with his eighty years would keep on calling me Pänn), anyway, Smith's Pänn wanted, using his propellers, to get the shed at Jaanipere to lift off the ground and fly to the moon with it . . .

When I grew tired of vanes and propellers, I clambered up the wobbly rungs of a ladder onto the roof of our stable to the platform with the chest-high railing and looked out over the sea with a spyglass, watching the ships as they sailed home and wondering which it would be our family's turn to pilot into harbor. The responsibility for this task went in a clockwise order round all the farms on the island. So that when Frans-from-Valli, who was two ahead of us, had received his ship to pilot, one or another of us boys, that is, August or me, would climb up onto the roof with the spyglass to watch the next ship to pass. And when the ship before ours was passing, that is, when Ambrose's Janne had received his, then whoever was holding the spyglass would yell: "Hey, our turn now!" Whereupon Uncle Frans would put on a tie and take the pilot's flag from the drawer and thrust it into his pocket. And the watchman up there would keep an eye on things. To see when the next ship would approach through the strait displaying the sign that a pilot was needed. Because such signs could take on different forms and you therefore had to keep a good lookout. And besides, apart from fishing, piloting was the principal way of earning your daily bread on the island of Naissaar. The pilot received one ruble for every foot that the ship extended downward under the Plimsoll line. Plus a bottle of the best foreign schnapps. But as people only drank the strong stuff on the island during large family feasts, and then only in moderation, there were all kinds of schnapps and gin to be found in our pantry for every occasion, even though there was no shop selling liquor on the entire island. The German ships would raise their flag in the foremast, that is to say their black, white, and red tricolor with white edging, while other ships would simply put up their national flag, always on the foremast of course, or, according to international custom, which has now changed, the flag denoting the letter *G,* that is, a yellow and blue one with six vertical stripes, but at night simply a light signal from that same mast. Anyhow, when such a signal was spotted, the one holding the spyglass would shout: "Our ship ahoy!" and Frans would pull on his jackboots and, in the appropriate weather, that is, almost always, his oilskin and set off for the harbor, usually along with August. Once in the harbor he would fix the blue pilot's flag with a white square, or the letter *P* for pilot, to the stern of the boat and August would raise it above the sail. Twenty minutes later they would be sailing somewhere between Vallikari and Veskikari and Frans would be winched aboard while August took our boat back. Frans would arrive in Tallinn by evening and the next day would come home on one of the island fishing vessels, a whiff of gin on his breath, but as sober as a judge of course, holding some tasty morsel wrapped in a paper bag. These pilotings became adventurous and exciting when such ships picked up a pilot from Naissaar and it turned out that the ship was sailing to Riga and wanted to be piloted via the island of Osmussaar or Põõsapea headland or through the neck at Hari and Viire, that is to say, through the Muhu Strait down into the Gulf of Riga. Such ships would pick up their pilot from Naissaar and only let him go in the port at Riga. So the pilot would return by train and arrive only some two days later. This route formed a major source of income for pilots from the village of Lõunaküla in the south, at the same time as Põhjaküla in the north would deal with ships to St. Petersburg and receive assignments from everywhere in the Gulf of Finland and right up to the western end of the sea canal to Kronstadt.

But by now the stand on which the spyglass rested on the upper platform had rusted and been abandoned and one end of the wooden railing had come loose at the corner. So if anyone were to lean on it without noticing, they would fall head over heels. Uncle Frans still went out for a catch; fish was needed for food, as was the money from selling it. The pilots were now organized in a pilots' union, and anyone wanting to join would first have to pay in some capital deposit. And when Uncle Frans had scraped together the sum, maybe with the help of August and his sons-in-law—he was still no longer able to scrape the weight of years off his shoulders.

So there I was standing on the upper platform, looking out through the swaying black pine branches toward the towers of Tallinn on the horizon to the left and the white horses on the autumn sea, clutching the railing. I *had to* keep a grip on it. Because a two-handed man could afford to fall, while if a one-handed man fell he would make a complete fool of himself, risking a fall merely to have a look out at the horizon.

I came down from the watchers' platform and went for a walk in the woods. Not of course to the harbormaster's house to ask the young sailors with their blue cockades for the latest news, not of course to the casino end of the officers' mess to chat with the girls at the counter. Nor of course in the direction of Lehtmetsa, where on Sundays you could hear the brass band playing to day-trippers from Tallinn and the throb of the polka and the *pas d'Espagne.* But into the woods, away from the railroad track that scarred the body of the island, away from the concrete constructions and the open sores of the trenches. I strolled past Stenmalmen, where there was said to have been a harbor during the Viking era. I don't know why anyone would have needed to situate a harbor among all these huge boulders and cliffs. I did, of course, stumble upon the railroad. I fled to Põlendiku. I wandered aimlessly over stretches of soft bright-green moss and dark-purple heather, under the giant pines and through the patches of ferns that grew to chest height and whose leaves, which had become a rusty color, rustled on touch as if made of one-millimeter-thick tinfoil. I let the west wind sweep over me on the beach at Akerskareli and Rävasaare, so that I got gooseflesh not only on my skin but also right into the marrow of my bones. I walked home describing an arc around an artillery battery beyond Klaose. I felt that I had gained in courage and patience from my dialogue with the wind and the open spaces. But then, when I had reached the outskirts of the village, I saw the stables at Jaanipere and the buildings come into view, and the dozen or so vanes turning on the roof of the shed in one corner of the yard, and a feeling of paralyzing depression seized hold of me:

Jesus Christ—what tools and opportunities were not available to serious scientists! Prandtl in Göttingen had all manner of wind tunnels and similar instruments at his disposal as well as aerodynamic weights. And what about the turbine researchers in Greifswald? What equipment, laboratories, assistants they had—one institute after another . . . What was I compared with all that? With the inflation, the flood of intolerance that wafted even out of my cellar there in Mittweida—and now here on the island in this tumbledown shack with my childish, ridiculous little wind vanes—trying to invent something that the doctoral types in their laboratories had not managed to do . . . To express the situation with merciless tranquility: a pathetic and hopeless enterprise, turning one's heart cold with the sheer hopelessness of it all . . .

And yet, on the island and its worn and violated ragtag existence—I nevertheless felt at home and secure. When I walked in from the silent cold moonlight of November into the lamplight of the room and sat down at the table and looked at the face of my mother, now once again her own eternal and unchanging face, when Mother poured me coffee from a small copper pan and I opened the newspaper, I glanced from this distant vantage point, this undisturbed elsewhere, at what had happened in the world:

During the past few months the flight of people from Estonia, mostly to America or Russia, had increased markedly. At the Royal-Bio movie house they were showing *Sodom and Gomorrah.* The aftermath of the Communist revolt was making itself felt in Hamburg. In Aachen, a month previously, the Republic of the Rhine had been proclaimed by separatists. As the *Päevaleht* noted, German industrialists Stinnes and Co. were trying to carve up Germany in order to salvage their property. Dr. Schwalbe wrote an article that appeared in several different newspapers about prostitution in Tallinn. German firms were offering pages full of all manner of goods from, metaphorically speaking, baby clothes to caskets, pins to locomotives—but not everything! Firms dealing with glass offered mirror glass, industrial glass, decorative glassware, luxury glassware, crystal, vases, pitchers, plates, sets of crockery, chandeliers, ornaments, everything—but not one item involving *optical* glass. Presumably they already knew that no one in the country would need such things. Hitler (who was that, now?) had decided to march on Berlin (from where?). But on November 6 one dollar cost 421,080 million German marks on the Berlin stock exchange . . . So that the madhouse was continuing unabated, spiraling downward at an ever-crazier speed. Things had clearly got so far that even people used to dealing in large numbers had to first visualize such sums. Wait, wait, wait—let's see. I fished out a German mark, postwar and made of iron, that I happened to have kept in my vest pocket, goodness knows why, probably to use as a screwdriver because of my lack of tools, and put it before me on the table. It was oxidized black and twenty-three millimeters in diameter and about one millimeter thick. So, if I put this on the table on front of me—or, to give it a more solid base, on the concrete floor in front of me (there were more than enough such floors nowadays on Naissaar)—and then stacked up similar marks on top in a tower, it would need one million marks to be one kilometer in height . . . Mother had gone to bed, Uncle Frans had been sleeping in the back room for ages now. I put out the light, pushed aside the net curtains at the window, and looked at the full moon in the northwestern sky. It was, as far as I knew, some 384,400 kilometers away. So that to buy one dollar I would need as many marks as would reach to the moon . . . I looked with open eyes at the greenish light of the moon. I know that anyone looking on would have said that I had a blank look in my eyes for several moments, because at that moment my attention was taken up by dividing a millionth of the price of the dollar by the distance of the moon in kilometers—and arrived at 1,095—from the earth to the moon and twenty-seven thousand kilometers farther on, traveling straight through it . . . That was the height that a tower of one-mark coins would have to be to buy one dollar.

A couple of weeks later—in the Modern movie house in Tallinn a film was shown entitled *The Miracle Worker,* and at the theater called the Kirev Mask the danceress Sent M'Ahesa gave an oriental dance soirée. In Berlin, the price of a pound of butcher's meat had risen by another billion. At the commercial college in Tallinn there was a literary evening to mark the tenth anniversary of the death of the poet Juhan Liiv (that name I had in fact heard before). And Hitler (even this name I had seen in the paper two weeks previously) had tried to stage a revolt in Munich, but the revolt had been suppressed and he was now in prison along with Ludendorff. This was, in itself, a strange occurrence: because General Erich Ludendorff was a famous name. If not for the fact that he was the chief ideologue in Germany during the Great War, then maybe because he was the brother of the astronomer Hans Ludendorff. Hans Ludendorff had already been the director of the Potsdam Observatory for a couple of years now and one of the leading experts on variable stars. But now General Ludendorff was being mentioned in the papers *after* Hitler. Even though Hitler was a completely unknown figure. But thank goodness, as Mother was wont to say, thank goodness that the name Ludendorff, although applying to the brother, was not in the first place associated with a reactionary revolt. Anyway, by now on the Berlin stock exchange the dollar was no longer worth 1.1 times the distance to the moon if calculated in German marks—but rather *eleven* times that distance.

On Naissaar, however, the sea continued as before to splash against the cliffs. The autumn wind whined as it had always done through the village and along the boat strand, past the coastguard building with its faded plank walls and between the low ramparts of the Old Fortress covered in sea grass, although the gusts were now mixed with the scurry of yellow leaves and flurries of snow. And across the black sound there was in the evening the distant glow of city lights. One dollar would still, as always, buy somewhere between ten and twelve pounds of plaice. So in comparison to the whirl and tumble of a writhing world, Naissaar was an unreal, secure place to be. Or rather: compared with the reality here, the world beyond had gone crazy and was almost the stuff of unreality.

Before the sea froze over and even before snow fell in the harbor, I visited this unreal outside world beyond Naissaar on a number of occasions. Well, yes—one reason for going was gun cleaning, that too. But what I found more interesting was this: I looked up the Ackerbergs at their apartment on Liivilaia Street in Tallinn. Stout Jakob, having grown even stouter, with his wild mustache, his wife, Julie, and their daughter, the lively little Karin, who had by now grown unrecognizably into a fifteen-year-old young miss. Jakob worked as an engineer in some forestry company, his wife taught courses in German, and Karin was attending the commercial college. It was a peaceful, established family. When they first met me after some ten years' absence they were pleasantly attentive. Jakob wanted to get together with all of our old Franconian student mates—Grünfeld, Nõges, Johannson and the rest were said to all live in Tallinn—but I stemmed his eagerness. Why go to all the trouble? I didn't want to be the cause of all this. I was quite happy to just sit with Jakob, smoke a cigar and have a glass of cognac, and hear what he had to say (though I already knew what to expect): it was quite pointless trying to find work with stellar optics in Estonia. They made nothing here in Estonia beyond glass lenses for spectacles. The only possible institution that might on occasion need some piece of equipment was the observatory in

Tartu. But their budget had been cut to a minimum. So there was not much to be hoped from that quarter either, though Jakob did promise to get someone he knew to ask Professor Rootsman. And I thought to myself: what law or curse always seems to hold sway so that (and this was not the first time for me) someone's *opportunities* are scaled down in the same proportion to any increase in their *power* to achieve anything? Any other work in my particular case was out of the question. I had glanced at the jobs vacant and jobs offered sections of the newspapers over the course of the autumn. Here and there they did indeed need farmhands and maids, janitors and shop assistants, warehousemen and cabmen. Even waiters, circus artists, and ballet dancers were sometimes advertised for. But when it came to anything mechanical, services were being offered—for cleaning and repairing sewing machines, typewriters, and tills. There was clearly some demand for such purely mechanical work. Among advertisements by those seeking work you would also find ads like this one that sticks in my mind: *Dear Businessmen and Company Directors! Please give work to an experienced bookkeeper who is, however, an invalid (no left hand) . . .* So that any other technical work within the optical field would be hard for me to offer. I do, of course, remember how Schorr in his usual blunt way told me what Vogel had once said to him. In those days, Vogel was the head of the Potsdam Observatory. And he was the first serious scientist I ever dared to contact. When I finally realized that my qualifications from Mittweida were sufficient, in my own estimation. So that in the spring of 1904 I sent him a letter. And a couple of years later, Vogel mentioned to Schorr the impression that the letter had made on him: "Clumsily printed handwriting, like someone who has never learned to write properly. I had no idea that he was writing with his left hand. And as for his grammar—full of the most basic errors. *Erlaube mir die Frage ob Ihr vielleicht für Spiegelteleskope interessieren . . . möchte in eigenen interesse mal sehen was sich mit einen Spiegel fotografieren lässt, wenn es montirt ist . . .* Signed: *Bernhard Schmidt, Mittweida . . .* Damn and blast! A German who writes German like that had to be someone who was completely uneducated! I couldn't imagine that he would be an Estonian." And Vogel had relegated me to the hopeless group of amateurs that wrote now and again to the observatory offering their services, unaware of the difference between their own standards and those of the observatory itself. And it was only by sheer chance that he had seen the postscript: *Beifolgend ein Mondbild mit einem 50 cm Spiegel aufgenommen und Sternspuren mit ein 38 cm Spiegel*. . . (Well, my German was even worse then than it is now.) And it was out of sheer inertia that Vogel opened the enclosed gray envelope and cast a glance at the photos within—and had not believed his eyes at first glance. Because the photos, both of the moon and the traces of stars, had clearly been taken by an expert with an exceptionally good telescope. And Schorr in turn had, after the death of Vogel, held me in painfully high esteem. But this had not helped me in Germany, given the disintegration going on all around there. And unfortunately it helped me even less in Estonia.

So I went back to Naissaar and played with my vanes until the snows came with those winds filling the port, and I got stuck there. With the last sailing of the *Sextant* before the strait was filled with pack ice for several weeks at Christmastime, August arrived back at his winter quarters accompanied by his young wife.

This Johanna of his was a dear young woman. A dear young lady would be a better way of putting it. And the fact that her name happened to be Johanna too was obviously slightly thrilling for me. August had become a gentleman over the last ten years. Johanna's skunk collar and fur hat with peacock feathers did not surprise me one bit, as I was seeing her for the first time. But young August's homburg and satin lapel overcoat, not to mention his walking cane, were quite new to me. He had always liked being a neat and tidy young man, but he had now become a rather fine fellow. A captain for sea voyages, no less. Early in the war he had become the captain of a steamer called the *Nargen,* and it had plied a triangular route between Tallinn, Naissaar, and the island of Aegna during the time the fortifications were being constructed. But he was then sent all the way to Vladivostok to join the merchant navy out in the Far East. At the end of the war he had ended up in China and had now sailed home under the British and some other flag via Singapore and Ceylon. And when the two of them, August and his young bride Johanna, had traveled from the harbor to Jaanipere (on the narrow-gauge fortifications train almost all the way to the village) and set down their suitcases in the living room, the customs post labels from goodness knows which ports were still to be seen. And when they opened these suitcases the fragrance of Shanghai and Colombo and London wafted out of them.

I remember that Johanna gave Mother, that is to say her mother-in-law, a morning coat made of embroidered silk. So that Mother touched her daughter-in-law's hand uncertainly and said: "My dear child, what will I, an old woman, do with such a gorgeous garment . . ." But then Johanna pulled a pink flask from one of the suitcases and spread a little pinkish cream on Mother's hand (so that the room was filled with the fantastically sweet and fresh fragrance of lavender), and said: "Look, this is also for you and will soon make you hands smooth and soft, so that . . ."

While Uncle Frans put on the Scottish pullover, and said to himself and to August about the bottle that August had brought, from which he had poured in a trice some whiskey into my glass too: "This here Englishman's jersey will keep an old man like me nice and warm."

So in retrospect it is embarrassing for me to remember that when I returned home after ten years' absence I brought nothing at all for the old folks back home. And I must admit: I did not even convince myself 100 percent when I thought, while sipping August's, now Uncle Frans's, whiskey: For them, such things hold a special meaning, but I feel that they are all quite meaningless, when compared with really serious things . . .

Also quite meaningless but natural was the fact that August and Johanna then moved into the adjoining corner room where I had been living, and I moved up to an empty one under the eaves. This had once been the boys' bedroom at Jaanipere and had a pretty functional tin-plated stove. I lit a fire in it. So that the large window looking out over the sea soon thawed and became beautifully clear. Then I fetched the spyglass stand from the observation platform on the stable roof, polished it free of rust, and set it up by the window. I affixed to it the old sea spyglass through which we had once watched the ships for pilot services. So that when I opened the window a little as dusk fell, and poked the device out into the evening air, I could see the whole sky above the lights of the city in the southeast all the way across to the winking of the lighthouse at Suurupi in the southwest. There was nothing much to actually *see* with such a telescope from that vantage point. But I still remember a picture—which I had seen in some boys' book or other—of a red Indian who, while a hundred or so men were looking in vain for him by the river, was hiding on the bed of that same river and breathing through a bulrush stalk . . .

Quite meaningless and natural (or important and still natural?) was maybe what happened one frosty January morning. As if August and myself transmitted telepathic signals to each other. In order not to upset my mother, I had gone to eat meals with the family at the appointed times. So that we were drinking morning coffee together at table: Mother, August with his Johanna, and me. Uncle Frans had been away for three or four days. Despite his sciatica and his age he had gone seal hunting on the ice in the west with men from the Mädasadama harbor. We rose from the coffee table and I went up the stairs to my room, in a bad mood mostly because I was being fettered here for the whole winter and worrying about a problem that had plagued me for several weeks now: I had, in Uncle Frans's presence, declared that I would cover the costs of my housing until the end of the year. But now the end of January was at hand, and I had no more than a couple of hundred marks left of the money that Mr. Amos had sent me. I had received several letters from Germany, but of course not one cent. By the way, Johanna, my Mittweida Johanna that is, had written to me. The Blümer workshop in Berlin had shut its doors and Johanna was back in Mittweida or Crossen and was trying to make ends meet with her mother's market garden. So no one was sending me any money. Quite the reverse: Johanna wrote that she had met Frau Knechtel, and she had been sad that I had left Mittweida, leaving her with a gas bill for seventy million German marks . . .

So I went up to my room in a relatively depressed mood to scribble down on random scraps of paper calculations to do with concave mirrors or look through the window that was half iced over to watch how the bullfinches were flapping their wings in snow-covered junipers at the edge of the garden. Before I got down to work, I heard that someone was ascending the creaking stairs and I just knew this had to be August. And it was. August, who really did closely resemble me in appearance, so this was not simply what other people pointed out. Anyway, among all the sons and daughters of our family he was the one whose mentality was closest to mine. Though he probably didn't realize this himself. Because I had, of course, never said this to him.

August sat down on a stool at the table and came immediately to the point. Which showed that his years at sea and his role as captain had affected what was really a shy nature.

"Pänn—I want to ask you how it's going with your money."

"I've got shit-all."

"Just as I thought. And you came back from Germany with empty pockets . . . Mother did tell me that you pulled some miraculous trick in Tallinn and sold something for a lot of money . . ."

"Well yes. One telescope. To Mr. Amos. I had brought the lenses with me from Germany. But I haven't got any more lenses left."

"But this time we're pretty well off . . . when it comes to money. So . . . here you are . . ." And he laid a bundle of banknotes on the edge of the table. "There's two hundred dollars here. I hope you're not going to be so foolish as to refuse it."

August looked at me with what was an almost pleading expression. And I wasn't such a fool as to refuse it outright. But I *had to* be able to retain some measure of folly and independence:

"August, I don't know what opportunities you have as a captain. But I do know my own needs. So that . . ." I had by now counted half the notes in the bundle. "I will be able to manage on a hundred dollars from now until the autumn. So you take back a hundred, and I will be very grateful for the rest. I'll pay you back when I can."

My authority as elder brother was deeply ingrained in August despite his career as a captain, although I was only four years older. In turn, he muttered, almost in gratitude:

"OK. You know best, I suppose . . ." And he pushed the money I had returned back into his pocket, with no further attempt to thrust them into my hand.

So that's what happened. I exchanged my dollars in town for Estonian marks, gave half to Mother, and lived at home for the next few months. In April, August and Johanna went off on a ship, and the summer was at hand. And I didn't rightly remember when it was that I saw in the paper that in Germany the so-called *Rentenmark* had been established and one fine morning one billion German marks was now the equivalent of one new mark. I have never bothered to study how such economic black magic can be done. Because it cannot be anything other than black magic. All those de- and re-valuations, what are they really? Fairground fiddles. A stroke of the pen that, in reality, alters nothing, no value is added. All that arises is an agreement at a certain point in time to play the game in the belief that something will actually emerge from the conjuror's top hat at the stock exchange. And since the world entered into this game with the

Germans (on the condition, of course, that they ceased the occupation of the Rhineland, etc.), the Germans themselves played along with a sigh of relief. At the end of the month of August a letter arrived from Mittweida via old Kientz. This old man, a former watchmaker and a steady hand (though only when not affected by his glasses of korn from the previous day), was someone I remembered in a positive light due to his reticent nature and objectivity. After Johanna had gone off to Berlin, he had been able to help me with some small jobs, inasmuch as I obtained any. Now Kientz was writing that both Schorr in Hamburg and Pregel in Dessau wanted to get in contact with me owing to some orders or other. So that precisely thirteen months after my homecoming I dismantled my propeller vanes, which had been whirring on the roof of the shed since the spring, and took one last stroll down to the burnt woodland at Põlendiku.

That walk was in itself half of a departure. And for that reason, both still being around and having gone away were very tangible. So that by remaining and having left I had the feeling of being at a third level. And this almost hurt. Every needle on the young pines at the edge of the burnt woodland seemed to exist individually. Each burgeoning flower of the heather was like a personal question.

I was already on my way home through the woods at Põlendiku when it started to rain. One of those long showers in early September that pour down in buckets from a low sky and threatens to last for hours, judging by the banks of cloud coming in from the west. So I had to take shelter in a nearby farm until the rain at least eased off.

As I emerged from the pine coppice near the cabbage patches of the Mädasadama harbor area, my jacket was wet through. I had already passed Tagavälja, where Uncle Julius lived, and, yes, had even reached the Styrmans' farm. But I didn't have any business there. There was a new owner. Someone called Juhan Lillevars. And at the next farm, Samuel Ambrosson's old Samos, there now lived Kaarel from Konka. Whom I also did not know any more than having passed the time of day with him on a couple of occasions over the past year. So I passed by there too, my steps hastened by the rain. And so I was now at the gate of the Blekmans' farm. A farm that they said now belonged to Trollen—in Swedish, the troll—and who was called the vodka soothsayer in Estonian. With reference to what the owner Villem from Sõrve would get up to.

"And a good morning to you," said Villem from his doorway, in which he was standing.

"Hello," I replied—and felt that I ought to say something more (a feeling I rarely have), so I said: "Well, well. You were the last person I met on Naissaar those twenty-five years ago when I left. And the first person I wanted to meet when I came back. But haven't bumped into you up to now . . ."

Villem squinted at me out of that yellowish-gray face that, on close inspection, had grown old, his hair and beard now dappled with gray. He said:

"And now I am perhaps the last one you'll meet. Come out of the rain."

I stepped after the old man into the house. A higgledy-piggledy murky bachelor's home. About which it had been said that he bored holes in the corner of the living room, and washed his clothes by pouring a bucket out onto the living-room floor and later sweeping the water into the corner.

"Well, what's it like living in your new house?"

"New house, old ways," grunted Villem. "They threw me out of my old one. Even before they threw us all off the island. The old sauna was meant to form part of the foundations of a gun emplacement and was going to be knocked down. But it wasn't. It was simply plundered and left to rot. So that when I returned I couldn't be bothered to renovate it. What sort of life would that be—living in the shade of the cannon barrels over the roof. This house was standing empty . . ."

I said: "When I was last at your place—there at Hülgekari, you remember, with Auntie, we brought a bottle of vodka with us. But this time I haven't . . ."

"That little problem can be remedied," said Villem. "Take a seat."

I sat on a stool, and Villem took a seventy-five-centiliter bottle out of the gray-painted cupboard. He said:

"*If* I am at all able to see into the future for such a faraway place as Germany . . ."

I should have said: "Villem, leave off. Stop bluffing with all that stuff. You can't really tell fortunes." I should have said: "Villem, I just happened to be walking past. I didn't come for any of that. The thought never entered my head. You must understand. Even that time previously, I only came because I was dragged along by my aunt.

Now it's me who's the stargazer. That you must know." Instead I said to him:

"Wait, sit down. And explain something to me."

He brushed aside the remains of his dinner, put the bottle on the table, and sat down. I continued:

"Ever since I was a child, I have heard people say here on Naissaar that you spoke to the Russian czar once in your youth. Is there any truth in the tale? Or is it just empty talk?"

And at that same moment I made the decision: if it is all rubbish (which it of course is), I will also reject Villem's ability to look into the future. If his czar story is true, then let him carry on, and I won't feel embarrassed about rejecting his tale, but I will be embarrassed at wasting his time.

"Quite true, of course!"

"Ah-a-haa! So where did this happen? And when? And how?"

"When? When I was doing my military service. Where? In Kronstadt. Boys from the islands like Saaremaa were put in the navy. On a small sloop, the *Lebed,* which had been refurbished to serve the steamers. The czar wouldn't come over for such a trifling vessel. But they had a big parade quay built in the harbor. And the czar came to have a look how the construction was progressing. Unexpectedly, of course, but a courier did nevertheless manage get there on horseback to warn us beforehand. So we were ordered to stand at attention and wipe our brows clean of sweat."

"Which czar was it?"

"Alexander II. In the spring, about a year before they did away with him. And he arrived in an open carriage and said: *'Trastuite matrooosy.'* And we said: *'Traayuselaayuvaas-imperrratorskvltsvo!'* That was some sort of imperial greeting."

"And then?"

"Then he walked on and drove off."

"But your conversation?"

"Well, that was it."

"And you call that talking to the czar!"

"What else could it have been? He looked me straight in the eye and said 'Hello' and I stared back and said the same, but more drawn out. Right into his eyes and mouth. There wasn't a yard between us. What do you think it was, then?"

And I burst out laughing. No doubt more uninhibitedly and loudly than I would have wanted. And I thought to myself: God Almighty—what else was this but a conversation between Villem and the czar? At any rate, I slid a couple of one-hundred-mark bills across the table to Villem and said:

"OK. Open your bottle and let's hear it."

And right now I am thinking: no doubt the discoverer of Nova Persei and consultant to three German observatories, *und so weiter,* simply wanted to hear what Vodka Soothsayer Villem could have to say about the future . . .

I gave him a little time to settle down and looked aside in embarrassment. He lit the petroleum lamp and pulled a black shawl across the window wet with rain. I asked:

"Have you got that shawl ready there by the window for the sake of your tricks?"

He said: "It's been hanging there since the time that there were soldiers living here and the windows had to be blacked out for fear of German Zeppelins."

Then he poured the vodka into a black enamel bowl and went and sat opposite me at the table. And although the bowl was a new one, the old man's tale was much the same as five years previously:

The same: long-long-long roads, toward the north, the south, west, and east, especially the east. Naturally, I didn't contradict anything he said. I didn't say, look, my dear fellow, not even my brother August sails any longer to the Far East, let alone me. Only to the west. As far as Mittweida. What long-long-long road is that—compared with voyages or journeys undertaken by the average man from Naissaar? Then he talked about money. Gold. Which I would receive heaps of. If it *were* gold that was shimmering there somewhere in my future. But it couldn't really be anything else. If only I understood how to seize hold of it. In a word, his repertoire was unchanged over a quarter of a century. But all of a sudden his bushy eyebrows drew together and he gazed fixedly into the black vodka mirror and cried out:

"Hey listen—there's a woman waiting for you there! Yes, really! Do you know about this yourself? A woman—or a girl—I can't see which. But a very pretty one. That I can see. And isn't she there somewhere on the periphery of that, that, that stargazing you indulge in . . . ? Yes, and she'll be your woman, if she isn't so already."

Villem got so excited that he almost started speaking in rhymes. But I didn't feel that what he said had any particular influence on me, that I had been electrified and that a thunderstorm was raging within. To dissect it as with a scalpel: I did maybe feel a little shameful excitement within. And a certain regret as to what kind of fairground psychologist lurked inside Villem's mind—*a girl on the periphery of my stargazing activities.* On the island itself, I had avoided all relations with women that year. Though people in the village knew full well that I occasionally sailed over to Tallinn for such matters. I mean to say that people knew that women nonetheless played a role in my life. So that, by the logic of our village, I was bound to have some serious woman in my orbit out there in Germany. And where else would the likes of me (over forty, a scientist and a hermit, an invalid) have found one—except *on the periphery of my own stargazing activities*? How cheap the train of thought behind Villem's eyebrows, bushy as chaff . . .

I do not of course wish to say that Villem's thoughts inspired me in any way. Not even in a fairy-tale way as you can read elsewhere: How can this be made to come true? I mean, how otherwise ought Vodka Soothsayer Villem's words be made to come true? Ho-ho-ho-ho-o!

But—at least with hindsight: they did come true nonetheless.

Ten days later I was, with my last forty dollars in my pocket, back in Mittweida. And the day after my arrival Johanna popped in at Frau Knechtel's (which she had done on one or two occasions over the past year) and asked whether she had heard anything from me. So when I emerged from my workshop at nine in the evening, Frau Knechtel was there to meet me with a bored yet crafty look. I understood that she wanted to start explaining things to me and rushed past her with a *Guten Abend!* and a *Schon gut, schon gut.* I hastened my way up to my room and shut the door behind me. And there, at my desk, sat Johanna reading a book by the light of my green-shaded reading lamp—Volkmann's practical guide to lens optics, which she had taken down from the bookshelf. She rose on my arrival:

"Hello . . . Herr Schmidt! And do forgive me for being here. Frau Knechtel encouraged me to wait for you." She paused for a moment, and, as I did not reply, continued: "But I haven't been waiting long. You see, the coffee that Frau Knechtel has made for me is still hot . . ." She lifted the cozy (black velvet with a hem of glass beads) off the steaming coffee jug. “In your Estonia, you were no doubt pampered with real Brazilian coffee—and all we have is roasted oats—but still . . .”

I muttered: “Well, miss, this is rather a surprise . . .” But for some reason I was overcome by laughter. She was there at the desk so unexpected and fresh, and I surprised myself, as her presence did *not* bother me; nor did the offer of coffee (whether Frau Knechtel had a hand in making it or not) strike me as an importunate act. I said, or rather heard myself saying:

“Johanna, do sit down. It would seem that you are, or that fate is—and you never can tell which—that *someone* at any rate worked out just what I would like at this very moment: a cup of hot coffee, ersatz or not. And with it your company. Which is entirely real.”

We drank a cup or two of the hot oat coffee and Johanna coaxed me into talking about Naissaar. And I started chatting away. In this room, which Frau Knechtel had somewhat tidied up before my arrival, but which was still full of old tools and smelt dusty, with its view of the windows set into the gray façade of the building across the street, where the lamplight of peoples' lives glowed in those windows as in a beehive—in that narrow dusty room it was nevertheless pleasant to describe to Johanna the way, for instance, that Alpha Cygni shone in an idiosyncratic way in the northern sky over Naissaar. In the midst of it all, I remembered that I had an untouched bottle of korn hidden away in the wardrobe. And it was still there. So that I put it on the floor and, holding it between my feet, pulled out the cork. As I always did. I filled two tiny spirits glasses, let Johanna touch it to her lips, she refused anything more, drank mine up and continued with my tale. Oh yes. I drank a couple more glasses and talked about the smell of the fishing nets, and the structure of the swirling spiral mists reflected in jellyfish, and how baby seals cry when calling their mothers—and goodness knows what else. Until Johanna said:

“Listening to you, I have to ask how someone coming from an island can manage to live here in Mittweida.”

And I said—or in fact heard myself say:

“Johanna—I'll tell you how: only if you help me to do so.”

Johanna looked at me with surprise in the stark light of the table lamp and said quietly:

“As far as I'm concerned—forever.”

And I put out the lamp.

Now it seems to me: as a schoolboy would have done. But I'm still glad I did so.

I can say with equal justification that I don't remember anything of what happened then and that I remember every last detail. One or the other. Depending on which attitude I start out with. Because I related to what happened in two different, not to say opposing, ways: the photographically exact picture of a slightly sad, slightly ironic bystander, by way of which I remember fine details and a dreamlike and excited urge, striving for something indefinable and vague, but painfully attractive. So I remember the buttons of Johanna's blouse between my fingers, their polished edges and the radial pattern of their center as I undid them, and my vaguely rueful thought: everything is inevitably a variation on the same theme . . . That thought, unbroken like the iron rod that measures the depth of a well. And around it, well, how should I put it—a somewhat rash, bubbly, hopeful darkness, in which *this time,* everything had to be new . . . I remember grabbing her round the waist with my left arm, with the right, as much as there was left of it, round the hollows of her knees, carrying her behind the screen to the bed (because of the street lamps you could see right into my room). I remembering thinking while doing this: a good job that Frau Knechtel gave me a set of new sheets yesterday and made the bed . . . Then there we were, stark naked in bed. We had managed to get through the part of undressing surprisingly smoothly and without noticing, where (at least with regard to prudery) otherwise both keenness and resistance can generate ridicule. We were stark naked in bed. I had kissed her mouth for some while, her throat, her breasts. And she was just as thirsting for it as I was. But I had not yet penetrated her, as I would already have done long ago with my usual women. Because with her, this somewhat enigmatic young girl, I wanted to be—how shall I put it—*gentle.* Although I had up to then regarded any playfulness as something childish, as play is in general. Although I did not know then—Lord Almighty, I don't even know today—how you actually had to behave to be gentle in such circumstances . . . And then came the fantastic moment, that indescribable instant . . . I was right above her flushed face and glittering eyes. I stroked her cheek with my left hand, supporting myself on the elbow of my right arm and thought to myself: now I'm going to enter her,—and at that same moment I saw the stump of my arm on the pillow next to her. Well, I was too used to this to say that it traumatized or hurt me. All too practiced. And yet—maybe instinctively—I shifted my point of support and hid my arm under the pillow. Probably I didn't even notice myself. But I saw that Johanna did. My movement of shame. She gripped my arm and pulled it forth, slowly and without my being able to resist. She raised it to her mouth and kissed it all over. At the edge of a scar, the severed nerves can be surprisingly sensitive, but I felt no pain. Then she covered my mouth with hers and pressed the stump onto her sex—and I did not know whether to freeze with shame or melt in the bliss of liberation. She squeezed my arm with her thighs and squeezed until I was conquered and she had reached her climax. Only then did she invite me to enter her.

You can think what you like about all this. But there was something there. Something—and for fear of which should I avoid using the right word?—at least for me there was something *uplifting* in that moment. Though maybe also something degrading. One thing at least was sure: from a certain night in September 1924 I had the feeling that my relationship with Johanna was happy, fateful, and lasting.

■ □ ■ □ ■

5

. . . BUT WHY IS DAD SUDDENLY WEARING A TIE?

As a rule, he doesn't wear one. When he's mowing the hay for the cattle behind the schoolhouse and is gripped by a fit of coughing, so that he leans on the shaft of the scythe and produces his dry long drawn out uh, uh, uh, I can see the tendons in his thin neck stand out through his open shirt collar. Mother assures us that the coughing is because of the pollen from the grass, but we seem to notice him coughing at other times too. And when he is sitting at his bureau in the village hall and is writing in the ledgers, his shirt collar is buttoned up, but he doesn't wear a tie. He only wears one when he is sitting to the right of old Ambrosson and to the left of old Berg and in front of the bureau is standing some villager demanding his legal rights in a settlement of debts. Then Father wears his striped black and gray tie that he bought in town. But his badge of office as village bookkeeper he keeps in the bureau drawer. And I have heard the odd man in the village grumble about why the government should have given Smitt's Karl a medal when he can't be bothered to hang the thing round his neck on its ribbon.

But anyway—going on a Sunday stroll in Tallinn, me in a clean shirt and wearing knickerbockers, but Father without a tie and wearing suspenders—that is something rather odd. There is an inappropriate foreboding in this act. But I can't be bothered to think about it. I deliberately avoid pondering on the fact. Because right now we are walking past the port in a crowd of people growing denser all the time, in the direction of—goodness—the *circus*—the Ciniselli Circus! And I just can't bring myself to ask Father if it is appropriate to go to such a place of entertainment in shirtsleeves, without a tie and vest . . . And then we are already standing at the red ticket kiosk. From the ticket window an old woman with the face of a hundred-year-old chimpanzee is smiling at us (I've seen her before somewhere, but can't place her), and Father buys me a ticket and presses it into my hand. I do of course notice that he doesn't buy a ticket for himself and am afraid—that he is going to leave me at the entrance so that I will have to go to the circus alone. But my urge to get in is so great that I don't mention it, as then he might say: "Well, don't go then . . ." And I am keeping quiet all the more because when I accept the ticket and clutch it in my sweaty palm, I look back and see: Father is strangely enough standing there at the ticket window *barefoot*—while the rest of those buying a ticket are wearing patent leather shoes, or at least recently polished ones. So I now understand full well that it would not be appropriate for Dad to follow the crowd of people—and I wave shyly and briefly to him. The mass of people moves on and sweeps me forward and Dad has gone. But I am now inside the circus with my ticket and must be allowed to see all its wonders. Suddenly I am standing in the strange church-sized marquee at a narrow curved table. The table is standing at the edge of a large circular piece of ground and forms a segment of say twenty degrees at its edge. The swarm of onlookers, although already thinner than previously, is standing in groups along the outside edge of this long table. On the table stand small vodka glasses in a row. The glasses are transparent. I can't count how many there are, maybe fifty, maybe more. From the right end, about two-thirds of the glasses are empty, but at the left the other third are filled with red, flavored vodka. A clown with a white face and lilac blotches indicates to the crowd to raise their glasses and taste the vodka and I think: *children* shouldn't be doing this. At the same time, I see in the mirror that shines there on the wall: me wearing the Chalmers Institute peaked student cap, dark blue with yellow stripes, and a *Vatermörder* collar and a black propeller tie. So that raising my glass is not a problem. But I don't take a sip nevertheless. Because I see an elephant riding around the outer ring on a tiny bicycle with rubber tires. The elephant itself is of normal elephant dimensions. So that the bicycle must be bigger than it seems. It has its hind-leg paws on the pedals, its front paws on the handlebars and is holding its trunk in the air. As it pedals in a clockwise direction and passes the inner side of the long table, where stand a handful of onlookers including me, it snatches the first of the filled glasses of red vodka with its trunk, and pedals on with the empty upturned glasses balanced on it. But I want to ask what this really means (and I don't even know why I should think that it has any significance beyond the ordinary). Those people standing around me watching the elephant know no more than I do. But I remember the white-faced clown, he's *from here,* he ought to know. I start looking around for him, but he is nowhere to be seen. So I decide to ask the elephant. He must surely know. He is said to be a particularly wise creature. So I bend down, crawl on all fours under the table and slip out the other side. Then I think: it would be interesting to know whether I should be ashamed of myself, as this is humiliating, or should be proud, as this is a unique discovery. À la Columbus's egg. When I emerge from under the table and am on the stage, the stage no longer exists. That is to say, it still exists, but has changed entirely. There are two wooden stairways facing each other. Forming the contours of a pyramid of stairs in the air. I look up both the left and right ones, and climbing smoothly up each stairway are two sea lions, a large gray male to the right and a large gray female to the left, both trained to balance a glass sphere—about one foot across—on their noses. I want to run up to them, but my feet are glued to the ground. I want to cry after them, but not a sound emerges from my mouth. I want to shout: Listen, you hairy fish! Don't climb up there! When you get to the top, Uncle Frans will let off his old seal gun! . . . And make sure you don't climb up there with those glass spheres! If you've got glass spheres the police will come and arrest you right away for spying. You are sending signals with those spheres to enemy submarines . . . With great effort I finally get my feet to move, but I am already somewhere else: in a long, dark, green corridor made out of material that looks like papier-mâché. And along the corridor into a hall of mirrors. And then a stroll through the hall of distorting mirrors. So that I see myself on all sides as an unrecognizable giraffe or giant louse or hippopotamus. Whereby, for each step I advance the giraffe images change into lice and the hippopotamuses into cars or vice versa. But on the back wall of the hall is one central mirror. And this renders—I don't know how I know, maybe silent loudspeakers are sending the information through the ether—this mirror renders the strangest distortion of all. Despite a shiver of fear down my spine I want to see it. But I cannot reach the mirror. Because in front of it, with his back to me, some unknown figure is standing. At first glance it seems to be a sea lion—or even several of them—that have climbed up the ladder and got past me in some miraculous manner. Then I understand that the elephant is standing there, and has stepped down from its bicycle and has managed, against all expectations, to traverse the papier-mâché walled corridor. It is standing on its hind legs, and as I approach I get the impression that it is spitting onto the mirror and wiping it with its trunk. And then I suddenly understand: it isn't an elephant. It is a god who looks in a comical way like an elephant, the god of success, Ganesha as people call him, whom I have seen in a Tamil temple in Colombo, I don't quite know when. Maybe recently, maybe when I was in short trousers. The elephant-headed and four-armed Ganesha is standing before the mirror and is polishing away with its four arms and his trunk. I want to ask it whether it is doing this to get rid of aberrations, or to make it even more perfect. But before I can open my mouth, it grasps its left tusk—it hasn't got a right one, it is one-tusked—it grasps hold of its one tusk, snaps it off, and taps it against the mirror, knock-knock-knock-knock, and looks over its shoulder at me with its elephant eyes and yells: "Herr Schmidt—don't you understand: *an aberration removed is an aberration perfected, Herr Schmidt . . .*"

Knock-knock-knock-knock. "Herr Schmidt . . ."

I wake with a start and look up at the gray oil-painted ceiling of the cellar and similar walls. I'm completely awake and in the place I should be. But the knock-knock-knock-knock continues, and Ganesha is calling cautiously outside my door:

"Herr Schmidt . . ."

I jump up from the sofa, hurry across the linoleum-covered floor in my socks, and open the door. It is Grote and Schulze with the equipment I have ordered.

They have packed it all in a plywood crate with two handles, and now lift it up onto my worktable. Everything I ordered is there. There is a steel cylinder, 340-millimeters in diameter. Its upper edge is 20 millimeters thick and perfectly polished. When it comes to things like this, it is Grote with his dark-stubbled chin who is a man of precision, even though he may behave in other circumstances like a coarse bumpkin, and can, according to rumor, be argumentative too. The tap and the manometer have been mounted where they should be. Even the vacuum pump is in place. This is a miniature one, no bigger than a car battery and brand-new. Schulze unpacks it proudly from its tissue paper:

"Just brought over from Hamburg especially for Herr Schmidt."

There we are. I can link the pump up to a pedal. Finally, they take out of the crate the hose that will connect the pump to the cylinder. The hose has steel thread ribbing so that it doesn't get nipped shut by the pressure of the air outside when the air inside begins to thin. Well, I will have to get them to do one or two more minor jobs for me. Not least with regard to pulling the hose over the end of the tube. When the diameter of the hose has been chosen very exactly (and it has to be exact)—then this requires a good deal of effort on my part. And other things. But I won't ask either Schmidt or Grote for help, as I can't abide having too many assistants when working. If I really need to, I will look up Wachmann. That tall boy is well enough brought up to do what I want and not start asking why this and why that. As he is here partly as a stargazer but also to an extent—well—as my assistant. I am altogether too incomprehensibly *unordentlich* for his German sense of order. From the point of view of his coevals, I am simply too old and too old fashioned. Both with regard to my trousers and my habits. And also my uncertainties regarding *der-die-das* and *des-dem-den,* which undermine my authority. So my skill, inasmuch as he notices it, is not defined by him for what it is but rather in accordance with *how Herr Professor Doktor Schorr has recognized it to be with his mien of a genius.* And so forth. What I do know is: he lets show with some vague aspect of his behavior that he cannot take me completely seriously. Especially after that damned piece of misfortune that I experienced back in early spring . . .

I had been sitting in "*Zu den drei Eichen*" as have been doing forever and a day. I left there at three in the morning. And discovered as I reached the iron gate to the observatory grounds that I didn't have my key with me. Damn and blast! It was my vanity that had caused all this! Before going to the bar I thought that my old trousers were just too shapeless and stained with ground glass and pitch. So I had pulled on my new pair of trousers and left the key to the gate in the pocket of the old ones. But the night watchman shuts the gate at eleven at night.

I had been polishing the extra mirrors for our large telescope night and day for two weeks and got it finished, and had therefore received three thousand in banknotes from Schorr's bookkeeper and shoved the money into my pocket. That evening I'd got talking to three Elbe bargees in the White Swan and then moved on to the Eichen. There I told them all about Naissaar and how the westerly storm would lash the landscape at Järvesaare, and now, at the gate, I was three sheets to the wind. But as they say, a heavy cargo makes the soul light. So I decided immediately not to press the doorbell next to the gate. Why bother the night watchman? I can go along the iron railings to a spot right across from our block (why there, I do not know) and climb over the railings. So I went to the left along the outside of the railings until the white plaster wall of the block peeped through the trees. All the windows were of course dark in our block by that time, so I climbed up. The railings were two meters high, so not much to speak of. First a stone foundation of about half a meter in height, then railings with spikes on top, not more than three meters in all. I climbed up and got to the top. But when I slid down something went a little wrong. The spike of one of the railings went through the collar of my overcoat and I remained suspended there, about a meter from the ground. Rather unbelievably, but true nevertheless. My weight was supported by the armpits of my coat. They cut into my own armpits a little, but I wasn't particularly uncomfortable. And all of a sudden my head was filled with laughter. So I guffawed, then decided: now I must consider my plight objectively and make a choice: Attempt to climb up and hope the spike slips out of my coat collar? Or attempt to reach the buttons of my overcoat with my left hand, open them. and try to fall out of the coat? I tried to weigh up which of these methods would require less of a struggle. And I was in no hurry. Silence reigned in the park, on the street, and throughout Bergedorf. It was a perfectly clear night and at least eleven stars of the Pleiades could be seen with the naked eye . . . Anyway. Then I heard Wachmann give a cough:

"Herr Schmidt—are you alive?"

I asked: "Hell, why should I be dead?"

And he said in his delicate, somewhat mocking manner: "At any rate, your present position is a trifle unusual . . ."

Whereupon I asked: "According to what you know from experience, do dead men hang from railings more frequently than living ones? Which set of stellar statistics suggests that?"

They both chortled at that (Wachmann had the night watchman with him, or to be more accurate the night watchman had Wachmann with him), and as they started helping me the night watchman said:

"Herr Schmidt, *I* found you here and—if you will forgive me—I thought at first glance that you were dead and ran to fetch Dr. Wachmann . . . But it now turns out that you were only sleeping . . ."

Wachmann climbed up next to me, pulled me up out of my overcoat, and asked: "How on earth did you end up here? Did you climb over the railings?"

I replied: "No. I jumped down from the moon. Cyrano de Bergerac's eighth trick. But I misjudged it by an inch. There is clearly a repellant force emanating from buildings of the institute. A minimal one, but a force nonetheless."

Then my feet were on the ground again, my overcoat back on my back, and I said: "Gentlemen, I thank you, of course. But I do wish to stress the fact that I did not summon your help."

Since then—as I feel it—Wachmann has not taken me 100 percent seriously. He is of course a gentleman and has never spread rumors about my little misfortune. But when we met in the observatory library at around dinnertime he really did have to control himself to suppress a laugh. And a certain strange quiver appears at the corner of his mouth when he speaks to me. Well actually . . . this quiver occurs partly because I am old fashioned and half educated. And too fond of the bottle and other things. Of greater importance in this quiver is a young boy's self-defense mechanism . . . Yes. His defense against my flights of fancy, which are hard to follow and seem irrational to him. Although he admires them nevertheless. Ha-ha-haa. If it isn't the case that this explanation is not in turn my own defense against the superiority of decent society. He being the son of a professor and all that . . . The devil knows.

But despite everything, I would rather look up Wachmann than start talking to the mechanics. Though it is best of all to be able to do things by oneself. And I do so, of course.

"Alles Notwendige da, meine Herren. Herzlichen Dank, Herr Grote. Danke schön, Herr Schulze . . ."

They leave together, with a look partly of being secretly satisfied that they are my fellow conspirators, and partly guilty that they were getting out of having to take any more trouble and leaving the rest to me. And I lock the door behind them.

So there we are.

I pull off my jacket, stretch, and take a deep breath. Then I lift the shiny vertically striped cylinder up onto my workbench and fix it right in the middle of the disc. The next task will be to link the cylinder to the air pump by means of the stiff hose. Pulling the hose over the end of the tube will require some twenty minutes' work and will mean that my armpits will start sweating, but using a couple of pairs of tongs I will manage and will fix the ends of the hose where they should be by means of two tin bands.

The air pump is tiny, the sucking cylinder has a volume of 1,500 cubic millimeters, just as I asked. Because my experimental cylinder is, after all, quite small too, yet the air must be thinned as gradually as possible. As I asked, the pump has a flywheel for the transmission. And now I am linking up the transmission belt to the wheel of the pedals. The pedal construction is a kind of tool for all seasons. Made out of the base of an old dentist's drill. So that it can perform all manner of secondary rotation movements. If you regard the rotation of the lathe itself as the primary one.

Then I take out from its box the rough lens for the correction plate. This is a 360-millimeter diameter disc of flint glass, which is five millimeters thick. I cover the polished edge of the cylinder with a thin layer of pitch and place the lens on the cylinder.

OK. It's now in place. I loosen my tie, unbutton my collar, and gradually press down the pedal of my dentist's drill. The air pump starts to suck and I follow the reading on the manometer. It moves by one-hundredth of an atmosphere. In other words—the thing works.

I stop pumping and take out my spherometer from the crate. This is the only piece of equipment I have constructed myself. It consists of a tripod on whose middle axis hangs a freely adjustable rod. The bottom end of the rod is fixed to a plumb of adequate weight. The top of the rod is higher than where the legs of the tripod meet. Cogs are fixed there, so that when the rod moves up and down other cogs are set in motion, and they in turn move indicators on different scales.

There are three dials. The first shows whole millimeters, the second, tenths of millimeters, and the third, hundredths.

I put the feet of the micrometer on the edge of the cylinder and the plumb to a central position. And gently resume pumping. Five minutes later the manometer shows that the pressure in the cylinder has dropped to 0.71 of an atmosphere. At the same time the plumb of the micrometer has dropped by 0.43 millimeters. If the calculations I did this morning are correct (this is based on Hooke's law, the general properties of the glass plate and its elasticity when exposed to even pressure)—*if* these are correct (but this is two-thirds mathematics and one-third intuition)—*if* these are correct, I have to carry on pumping until the micrometer reads about minus 0.94 millimeters. So I carry on pumping. Very slowly. Very carefully. Expecting at any moment to hear a dull cracking sound indicating that the lens has broken. But there is no cracking sound. The plate *holds.* And in ten minutes I have reached 0.94. I shut off the cylinder and stretch my limbs. I go to the toilet and smoke half a cigar. I return, take the micrometer off the plate, and loosen the hose from the tap on the cylinder tap.

There we are, then. I prepare the necessary amount of abrasive paste in the sink and apply it cautiously to the plate. I lay the polishing glass on top, at first this is a disc 360-millimeters in diameter, and start work. I have to polish the underside of the plate that has bulged due to the air pressure so that it becomes flat again. So that the lowest point of the bulge is level with the whole of the surface again. When that has been achieved, I have to wait and see what our Lord has in store for me . . . Will He act in accordance with my continued calculations following Hooke's Law as I am hoping? Or has He got a calculation of his own up his sleeve . . . ?

Well, what awaits me is five or six hours of routine toil. This will, of course, be able to be effected mechanically in the future, nor do I want to disparage such methods. I do, in general, regard mechanical polishing as a vulgar method, but this particular operation is simply too straightforward for me to get annoyed if it is done mechanically. Quite the reverse: I am testing it now in order to find the simplest method possible. Except that now, this first time, I am doing the work by hand on principle.

And so I set the snail wheel of the lathe at two revolutions per second and work on the glass that has to be polished and that has been adjusted more to slide round than rotate, with movements that direct the polishing glass, that is to say, with tiny clockwise movements in the opposite direction to the revolving plate. And *listen*—via the glass and my hand doing the polishing—to what the glass is whispering to me. Listen, in the hope that I am not taxing the elasticity of the plate too much and causing catastrophic tensions within it that would result in the glass suddenly breaking with a dry crack. Listen to the friendly whispering of the glass as it accepts its treatment with tolerant surprise, with welcoming amazement . . .

Listen to the ever gentler whispering of the glass for hours on end. Rinse the plate clean of abrasive paste and follow the expansion that the polishing belt has achieved. Prepare the next batch of abrasive paste, grayer than the last, that is to say a finer batch, and work on, with the bitter taste of two, three, four, ten half cigars in my mouth, my stomach reminding me now and again of its state of emptiness, then falling silent again, and a little higher up slight pangs of the hope of victory alternating with the fear of disappointment.

. . . In fact, I should be entirely beyond the fear of disappointment. Thanks to the experience I have gleaned. Or rather—thanks to the experiences that I have to a large extent picked up myself. Principally the experiences of various discoveries. And maybe most of all in connection with one recent thing that has never become either an invention or a discovery. That has never become more than an embryo of hope. But the loss of this hope (or the liberation from it—both words would ring true) was nevertheless ridiculously painful.

As soon as I had come to from the chloroform in the operating theater at the Free Hospital and saw what had happened to me, I began to think about an artificial limb. Well, not perhaps during the first hour or, more likely, half hour. Then I was presumably too *shocked* by the whole event. But the vitality of a fifteen-year-old is naiver than naive and stronger than strong. So I started to think about an artificial hand even before Dr. Kobzarenko, the man who had sawed off my hand, had begun to comfort me with the idea of one. And in recurring bouts of thinking, I have thought about artificial hands to this very day. Sometimes even after thinking about that central disappointment that I see in my mind's eye. Sometimes even after that.

In the hospital, even during the first week there, I asked my mother to get me pen and paper. She did so. I began practicing drawing with my left hand. My right arm was still bandaged up and hanging in a sling. I drew on the bedside table using its rough surface with all the stubbed-out cigarettes and the bread sliced up on it. Initially, I felt horror at just *how* clumsy I was with my left hand and I began, when the initial paralysis of shock had subsided, to exercise my left all the more assiduously. At first I did not draw complicated things such as ships or trains or other things still beyond my powers, but instead drew simple geometrical figures. The sheet of paper was fixed to the bedside table by four thumbtacks and was soon full of squares, rectangles, triangles, and circles. Until a gleam of hope began to glimmer through my rage at my own clumsiness. Because the straight lines I was trying to draw began to become more or less straight and crossed more or less where they should. The rough surface of the bedside table, which I could feel with the pencil point through the paper, made me think of—I had by that time read a little about famous men—the pebbles in Demosthenes' mouth when he was wrestling with his stammer . . . Learning to write with your left hand actually required much more effort than learning to draw with it. But I am thinking now about drawing. One of the first things (following my geometrical figures) that I first began to imagine, then draw, was a hand. An artificial hand. As I imagined it. During my second spell in the hospital, I finally got some idea what it would be like in this way:

Mother substituted for a doctor on Naissaar. She was the midwife for the women from Lõunaküla and Põhjaküla. And she would even bind the larger wounds when someone was injured. Everyone came to Mother in the case of more serious injuries and diseases. She had to decide whether to continue to nurse them herself or send them by ship to a real doctor on the mainland for treatment. When a storm prevented people from sailing to the city, the whole job fell on Mother's shoulders. And Mother did not carry out these tasks only because she had learned a little when serving as Dr. Krause's nursing assistant in Tallinn after she had left school on Naissaar and there was no one else qualified on the island. Nor for the small tub of butter that she would receive for her work or the twenty kopecks, or even a silver ruble, that people would press into her palm as recompense. No, she was also carrying them out as her calling. Because she was suited to the task. And was aware of her suitability. I was at first too small a boy, then too big, for anyone to let me anywhere near births. But I do remember her dressing old Abram Berg's leg. While chopping timber, Abram Berg had given himself a nasty chop on the knee with his axe, and had managed to drive back on his wagon, which, as luck would have it, was standing nearby, and by lashing the horse had reached our yard. I don't remember who helped him into our house. But I do remember Mother's face as she cut away the old man's bloodied trousers around the knee, and ripped up a sheet into strips to stem the flow of blood from the artery so that it wouldn't bleed so profusely, and tried to push his kneecap back into place, then bandage the wound and send me to the Bergs' to get a boat ready to take Abram to a doctor in town. Yes, I remember to this day how Mother's very young, very narrow face was radiating concentration and almost glowing with it.

Mother had that same kind of face when she had been summoned home halfway through the church service, and came running into the living room and saw my shattered hand, and immediately began to wash and bandage it. She ordered Uncle Frans to get a boat ready in the harbor to take me to Tallinn. Exactly that same look of concentration.

But in the Free Hospital, after the amputation, she tried to have as little as possible to do with my wound. She asked Dr. Kobzarenko to keep me in the hospital for at least two weeks and left the bandaging to the doctor and the nurses. But a few days later she did what I asked: she went to that same Dr. Krause where she had worked before getting married, and where she had even been on one occasion with me, and asked him for what I wanted: to bring the first volume of the big Brockhaus encyclopedia to the hospital. And during the second week, after taking the first one back, the second one. As I had got it into my head to leaf through all sixteen volumes during my stay in the hospital and learn useful things from it. In that second volume (I remember it was the 13th edition, printed in 1882) I found an article on Götz von Berlichingen, i.e., the Man with the Iron Hand. The three-column biography didn't interest me a great deal. Apart from the fact that he had lost his right hand at the Siege of Landshut and that it had been replaced with an artificial one made of iron. And that next to the text there were remarkably exact modern drawings, eight in all, of the iron hand. At the time I did not think that this was something odd, merely a vestige of German hyperbole with regard to *Gründlichkeit.* At the time I thought it stood to reason that they *had to be* there. What especially fascinated me was the fact that the knight's right hand—and it was his *right* hand, both according to the text and the drawings—worked extremely well. It was written there word for word that thanks to the iron hand he could wield a sword to good effect.

There you could read: its mechanism affords the following movements—the fingers can, four at a time, or one by one, with the natural pressure of the hand, adopt whatever pressure you like. By pressing Button B they all jump back to the straight position. The thumb can likewise be pushed inward and by pressing Button E can be straightened again. The hand itself can be bent at the wrist and maintain the rigid position adopted. And so on—the buttons, springs, bolts, pins, cogs, rods, brakes, joints, rotors. Numbered and marked. I did not get a complete understanding of this hellishly complicated construction. And besides when I, twenty years later, just before the war, was driving around with Grünfeld and the Nōbu Nette-mobile in the hills of southern Germany, we dropped in at Jagsthausen Castle, where that hand of Berlichingen was kept at the time. For a small tip, the museum guard took the hand from its display mounting so we could get a closer look at it. Well, it is no *miracle* as such. It is made of quite ordinary tin and iron that, despite oiling, has rusted here and there. About one and a half kilos in weight. The work of a craftsman. But the thing is not so far from a miracle either. When you think that it is over five hundred years old . . . Yes, in the days I was at the Free Hospital in Tallinn and practicing drawing it was exactly—and I noted that to my surprise—exactly five hundred years old. And that same Berlichingen had lost his hand as a fifteen-year-old! So that object maybe fascinated me even more. Because only some ten years later did I happen to find out that I had read the Brockhaus entry wrong, and that he had lost his hand when he had been ten years older than I had imagined. At any rate, I decided there at the Free Hospital to build a similar hand for myself. Even better than that one. Because since that time five hundred years had passed and steamers and the railroad had been invented, electricity had been discovered, leading to the telegraph, the telephone, and so on. All of which technology could help when constructing a modern artificial hand . . .

As my amputation scar was healing slowly, Dr. Kobzarenko, a

friendly man who had been an intern at the Kharkov University Department of Surgery before coming to Estonia, added a week, then another, to my stay at the hospital.

When we sailed back to the island at the beginning of November—Uncle Frans brought us home in his own boat—my wound had not yet healed completely but was a good deal better, and the main thing was: I had drawings of Berlichingen's iron hand in my inside jacket pocket. Not completely accurate ones, unfortunately. Only as good as I could manage. But accurate enough, in my opinion, for a skilled craftsman to do something with them. I also of course had in my pocket a copy of the description of how it worked, taken from the encyclopedia.

For understandable reasons, I didn't manage to build such a hand, or an improved version. Because I soon realized (or maybe knew right from the start) that I wouldn't be able to cope with it. At least not while I was an invalid in the double sense of the word, inasmuch as I had only just started learning how to use my left hand. And using the tools available in Uncle Frans's home smithy, which were the only ones I had access to.

When I, by the way, take a break at my workbench from trying to anticipate the reactions of the glass, my favorite pursuit is to anticipate (and think about with hindsight) the motivations for human actions. Including my own motives for doing things: Where does the *real* motive for my actions shine through? And what does this *real* motive consist of? Is there always something there amidst the flock of subordinate motives and arguments for and against? (When you look at them all, you do see that they constitute a whole flock . . . ?) Where does self-deception begin when it comes to motives? Where does this game of deception begin vis-à-vis others, where in relation to oneself? What is the significance of contradictory, or often *parallel* motives . . . ? I think that even if I avoid answering such questions in more detail—because we usually cannot answer most of them—it is still worth my while to raise them. At least to a *small* extent. In fact—why should they be of less value than the whole of our knowledge of astronomy? Because the equivalence of the micro- and macrocosmos is an age-old idea. And we have hardly penetrated the mystery of ourselves any more deeply than we have the starry heavens. We are trudging along the same path in both cases. With the exception of course when we—hell and damnation, it's all painful for me, but I will follow the train of thought right to the end—with the exception that if I manage to polish to perfection this disc I am holding, so that my correction plate becomes an everyday object . . . Because it then nudges the balance between microcosm and macrocosm. Has to nudge it forward—at least temporarily—to the advantage of the macrocosm . . . As our telescopic horizon will open up—by how much? At least twentyfold. OK. God be praised that no one has noticed my blushes . . . The thought struck me that I didn't (and still don't) know why I gave up the idea of constructing an artificial hand as a sixteen-year-old. Because by that time I had in fact worked out the details of its construction. Presumably I began to grow afraid that the hand would weigh too much. To realize that I couldn't reconcile myself to wearing a two-kilo lump attached to my stump, which despite everything remained free as a bird. That what I would gain from this burden would be precious little: maybe the clumsy ability to grasp medium-sized objects, but only by using the other hand to press the buttons on the iron hand. Maybe also the ability to chop firewood—with the risk of chopping myself in the knee like Abram Berg. I am, by the way, still idiotically sensitive when it comes to seeing such things in my mind's eye. I threw aside the leather sheath that I had designed to use with a violin bow (this was in fact a more unpleasant event that I would rather not think about right now), and concentrated on training my left hand. And I can say this: it succeeded much better than I had expected. Within about a year, I was writing quite legibly with it, I could draw better than some boys could with their right hand, and to my family's surprise I could tie and untie my shoelaces. *Et cetera.*

So that my first dreams of an artificial limb subsided, partly because I recognized my lack of opportunity, and partly because of my high demands. But after three or four years, they rose to the surface again. When I was already working at the Volta factory. I did pretty well there with my draftsman's work. And from the reactions of onlookers I did so too with a number of everyday tasks: buttoning my shirt, trousers, jacket, collar, and overcoat, getting matches out of the box to light my *papiross,* even when I was making minor astronomical observations with my homemade telescope from the attic window of my rented room near the factory. I could manage all these things perfectly well. The observations I sent to the *Astronomische Rundschau* in Germany were published on a number of occasions. But I had noticed at one or two of the parties that were held by the men from the draftsmen's office that my stump, covered as it was by a black silk sheath, did upset the odd damsel. As a nineteen-year-old you are damned sensitive to such things. At any rate, I suddenly began to long for an artificial hand with pleasantly bent fingers and a white glacé glove.

I had no doubt noticed a few advertisements for artificial limbs that appeared now and again in the Tallinn daily, the *Revalsche Zeitung*. And the thought that a hand made of pear wood and rubber and whatever else would be four times lighter than Berlichingen's hand would not leave me in peace. So I removed the lenses and abrasive paste from my workbench—I mean the one I had at home—and messed around for a couple of weeks in my rented room on Prii Street with rubber tubes and pieces of pear wood. Until my eagerness ebbed away or evaporated, I don't know which. At any rate, it became clear to me that even the lightest and most glacé-covered artificial hand would be a *dead* object. And that the few practical tasks I would have liked to carry out with it could only be achieved using a living hand. And that an artificial hand would be no less upsetting to finicky young ladies. Especially in such circumstances as when you take off your jacket and its sleeve no longer conceals the supporting strap once you are in shirt sleeves. When it came to the crunch it wasn't worth carrying around a dead hand.

No. Instead I concentrated on improving my left hand's ability, and artificial limbs no longer interested me for the next fifteen years. So that when the idea arose again in my mind, it was only in the negative sense. A few months after, Europe, with its crazy head, had turned itself into an invalid factory, and the papers and magazines started to come out with the weirdest of advertisements. For obvious reasons, I noticed them more than ordinary readers would. And not only the text but the pictures as well.

One fellow with a working limb that resembled a hook was pushing a wheelbarrow, and thanks to his artificial limb he was laughing too. And the text read:

> German soldier, you who are a hero from the battle front and who have now come home an invalid and who thinks that you must now let others do your work for you—you are mistaken! Professor Meyer's brilliant in-

vention coupled with the German precision of the Müller Company will restore your working hand, whose powers are no less than the hand you have lost! Furthermore: the Müller Company has a number of advantages over your former hand:

It is afraid of neither heat nor cold!
It does not ache when it gets tired!
No knife can make it bleed!
No hammer can hurt it!
Not even the hardest toil can give it blisters!

Almost saying . . . my poor old German friend, you who have not managed to lose your natural hand—please put it in the way of a piece of shrapnel or even a circular saw and cut it off at the elbow. So that the Müller Company can have the pleasure of offering you a much better hand instead . . .

I pushed aside such pathetic rubbish. Until suddenly—and this was some years later, which just shows how indifferent I was to the problem—I happened to hear about *Sauerbruchs Hand—die willkürlich bewegbare künstliche Hand des Professors Sauerbruch* . . . Yes, I happened to see this in print, but this time it was not accompanied by vulgar advertising. Only some solid articles that had at least been signed by people of the rank of professor. So it was only natural that I browsed, then started to read such things. And it turned out that:

Sauerbruch's hand was also made of rubber, leather, wood, and metal. A dead foreign object, of course. But it was claimed that it had one unprecedented quality—it could be moved at will by the wearer. Not by pressing buttons with your real hand, as had been the case with all artificial hands since that of Berlichingen—but rather by the power of the muscles still present in the stump of the amputated arm.

Purely at the level of technical prowess this was such an interesting concept that I ordered a copy of Sauerbruch's book plus articles about his invention. Sauerbruch had, in 1918, moved from his post of professor in Zurich to Munich, and this in itself commanded one's respect—from the well-off tranquility of Zurich to the hunger and chaos of postwar Munich. Why? Presumably because Germany was crawling with war invalids and therefore offered him many more wounded specimens than Switzerland did! Invalids as raw material to improve his invention? Or invalids as human beings who needed his help? God knows. Even if it was the former motive that counted, the only one that counted, Sauerbruch's arrival was still a notable step . . .

In the town of Singen in southern Bavaria a whole hospital and operating theater had been built to develop and implement his method. Articles were written about the between two and three thousand operations carried out there and the advantages of the artificial limb. Doctors who themselves wore Sauerbruch's artificial hand were supposed to have been able to give injections and use analytical weighing scales. Some organist or other was said to have continued to be able to play the organ. Not to mention professional people with fewer demands on their limb such as civil servants, businessmen, and the rest. In one brochure there was a facsimile of a text written with an artificial hand: perfectly legible, individual, natural lines, a couple of them in strikingly elegant handwriting.

I have to admit: all of this went to my head to a certain degree. I was proud of the achievements of my left hand after my twenty-five years of training. Rightly so, as I still think. However small the number, there were people who knew about the precision with which I carried out polishing work with that one hand. Nevertheless, the ideas generated by Sauerbruch's hand went to my head. This could happen, as S's principles on which his invention was based were generally applicable, while its application was entirely individual—just as all solutions are that affect people. So that the efficacy of the result would naturally depend on the nature and extent of the original injury. And by that measure, my injury was among the easiest to compensate for! Sauerbruch was said to have attached working hands even to short stumps of the upper arm. But all I had lost was my hand and my wrist, and I still had all the muscles in my arm. And as I consciously used my right arm as much as possible when working, these muscles could not have atrophied to any significant degree.

I did not need such a hand for my basic work. I had exercised the use of my left hand beyond such needs. But in the area of some ancillary tasks, some secondary movements, another hand, even if it were clumsy when using a pair of tweezers would, I can imagine, save 15 to 25 percent of the time used. And that in itself would be a wonderful gift.

I can no longer assess to what extent my interest in Sauerbach's hand was affected at a deeper level by the existence of Johanna. Or to what extent it was my dream of a hand in a glacé glove that had been reawakened. At a higher level I could say with regard to how this all affected our relationship: not one whit. But at another level, a lower one that involves vanity and a yearning for perfection, Johanna's presence did enter the equation. I remember such an instance:

I am standing in my room, up there in Frau Knechtel's rooming house, looking out of the window and can see—when I glance over my shoulder—how Johanna is sitting at my desk among all sorts of junk and looking at Sauerbruch's book about the artificial hand. She is leafing through it and looking at what, for the layman, are rather off-putting illustrations. I ask her:

"Well, Johanna—shall I let them make one for me?"

And she replies:

"My dear, that is a decision you most definitely must make for yourself." She rises from the desk. She walks up to me. She looks at me—how should I put it—with *transfigured* eyes. She says: "It's not necessary for me." I want to say something, but she interrupts me (something she otherwise would never do). "Wait . . . I have something to tell you . . . Listen to me. I would be exaggerating a little—if I were to say that I love you more as you now are than if you had your other hand. That would be exaggerating. But understand this: it would be nearer the truth than you imagine. So regarding that thing," and she gestures toward the book—"you have to decide what is best for your work . . ."

I put Sauerbruch's book in my briefcase and went off to Singen to see what would happen there.

The idea central to Sauerbruch's method is to, as it is termed, channel the remaining muscles. In such a case as mine this would be done as follows. A rod would be inserted into my arm and would emerge at the appropriate spot. The rod would pass through the extensor and would be more or less at right angles to the bundle of muscles. The channel that has been created with the rod is widened using increasingly larger instruments, which Sauerbruch (or maybe surgeons in general) terms "dilators." When the channel is wide enough, a square piece of the skin and the subcutaneous tissue of the arm is cut open at the entrance to the channel. This must be joined near the opening to a sufficient extent that blood supply is not cut off. The square of skin that is cut away along three and a half sides is rolled up into a tube, the outside surface turned inward, and the edges are sewn together along its length. This skin roll is drawn up into the channel and is sewn at the opening in a circle to the surrounding skin. After healing, the muscle has two openings lined with outer skin. When a similar channel has been created in the contracting muscle, fixing rods are placed in the channel. These are placed at right angles to the length of the arm and are raised or lowered a few centimeters in relation to how intensively the muscles are contracted or relaxed. As the motion of contraction and relaxation are opposed to one another, the movements of the fixing rods are doubled. From the ends of these rods that protrude outside the skin, metal wires run along the length of the arm to the fingers and thumb of the artificial limb. By pulling these threads you can move four fingers contra the thumb, or two fingers at a time contra the thumb. A third channel to turn the hand was not necessary in my case, as I could turn my arm as a whole. So my operation would be a relatively simple one.

Dr. Hammer at the hospital in Singen confirmed this. He was a surprisingly young man with sleekly combed reddish-blond hair, and I was sent to him for consultation. I also talked to patients who had undergone the operation and were now exercising their limb. Those patients to whom the doctor introduced me praised the operation for its positive results and were satisfied with how quickly they got used to the device, in two or three cases *very* satisfied. At any rate after eating lunch I returned to the hospital from the guest residences. To chat with patients I had picked out myself. There were about forty men who lacked either one or both of their hands and they strolled around or sat on benches. For an outsider the sight would be quite shocking. Some wore hospital clothing, but as the weather was hot most were walking around in their shirtsleeves; their artificial limbs, the dark-brown color and various holes that looked odd and reminded one of skeletons, were mercilessly exposed with all their straps and wires. As had been the case during Dr. Hammer's demonstration that afternoon, all those I saw were instances of more fundamental amputations than my own. So they were patients whose two hands were artificial, but who somehow seemed, despite the tragedy of their situation, rather scurrilous. I do not remember who the hell it was that wrote about the so-called three-dachshund effect (i.e., one dachshund is normal, two is on the verge of comic, while three is hilarious).

Anyhow, this group of maimed men did invoke a kind of untoward hilarity—I really hoped that behind this reaction there was *no* cheap joy at myself being the least crippled of them all by comparison.

My state of being less of a cripple did at any rate create an immediate element of tension. I tried to remain composed, overcame my inhibitions about talking to people, and went to sit down on an empty stool near two men and struck up a conversation. Both were war invalids, one about fifty, the other half his age, both with artificial limbs up to their elbows. Both having lost both arms. I only noticed this once I had taken a seat.

"What is your profession?" asked the older of the two.

"A polisher of glass."

"Ah well, you can carry on polishing your glass. Whereas I *was* a watchmaker. What am I now? They promised a miracle with those fucking forks, but I just can't get them to work right."

"Paul likes *moaning,*" said the younger man, turning toward me. "In fact you can have lots of fun with them. I've told you this already, Paul." And he turned back to me, as it was new for me.

"Three weeks ago our master tanner came back from Murnau. He was a former NCO and a factotum in the military district. The same chap that sent us to the front straight from secondary school. In September 1918, you understand. I saw him again now for the first time in six years. In the bar. I go there for a drink now and again. You can't chase the ladies with these claws . . ."—he stretched out his wooden arms—"but you can hold a beer mug in them. In other words I'd had a few. And he clearly had too. Anyway, I'd drunk enough to start telling him the truth. But that started him off, of course. He'd been in Munich, or wherever it was, come from some course or other, and he recognized me and had already heard about my hands. So he shouts: "Hello there—you're our hero!"

I said: "I'm not so sure I'm a hero. But one thing's for sure: you're a cunt." And so we started yelling at each other. For a couple of minutes or so. Till words failed him and he pulled a knife on me instead. That bastard wanted to stab me in the gut. I stretched out my right-hand club and he sank his knife into it. But the joke was that the knife went in between the skin tube and wooden block and the wires. Look, there's the knife hole where he stabbed me! Ha-ha-ha-ha-haa! He thought it was hurting like hell and I was pissing my pants. So he started pulling out the knife. But I felt like a bit of a joke. And the second he pulled out the knife I walloped him one with my right-hand club. I've still full strength in my upper arm. And the club is as hard as flint. He got it three times. The second and third times with his neck against the wall, so the blows went home. I then pulled the knife out with my teeth and went my way. There he lay—and he's shitting teeth to this day. I only noticed when I got home that he'd severed the motherfucking channels . . ."

Paul gestured slackly with his arm—and he'd certainly never have been able to do that without his Sauerbruch—he shrugged his shoulders and said:

"And I'm telling you what I've already said: you should thank God you've come to this hospital. And won't be going back home. Your tanner no doubt belongs to one of those gangs—the Rossbach gang or whatever their name is. They'll do you in round the corner if you strike back."

"Well, well, well. I'd like to see that happen," gloated the younger invalid. "And after that load of crap you've just uttered you're going to be checkmated by me!"

And indeed: between them stood a board with chess pieces in a half-finished game. The younger one stretched out his right artificial hand, gripped hold of a white knight between his artificial thumb and two artificial fingers, and set it down on some square or other, f6 I think it was:

"Check—and your rook is also in danger!"

"Your channels have healed, it would seem," I noted.

"Fuck knows . . ."

"Healed or not," muttered the older man, who went by the name of Paul—and with a similar artificial hand lifted his king out of the line of fire—"they wipe the pus out with cotton wool every day."

"There's not been any pus there for three days now. They still itch a bit though."

I sat with them for over an hour and observed the other patients in the garden out of the corner of my eye. And as to my conversation partners at least, my impression was this: without their Sauerbruch arms they would have been entirely helpless and couldn't even perform the simplest everyday tasks and would be totally dependent on the help of others. Even now they needed such help. But to a lesser extent. Others helped them with the hygiene of their muscle channels and keeping their artificial hands properly fixed and in trim. Even allowing for Paul's grumblings, he could still move chess pieces, use a knife and fork, and dozens of similar movements. This was almost a *miracle.* Paul said to me:

"Your injury is child's play by comparison. You carry on polishing your lenses so that they glitter. And they can give you a right paw that you can play the piano with. What's the problem . . . ?"

At all events, when I went back to my guest room I felt a little embarrassed and was perspiring from the stress of it all. In the morning I found myself back in Dr. Hammer's surgery:

"How much would all of this cost in my case?"

He let me take off my jacket and roll up my sleeve. Yes, in my case it would be easier than average to cut channels, that was true. I see, optical polishing? We-e-e-ll. For that I would need an artificial limb on three axes, the very best hand they could make. Plus a work limb with three exchangeable attachments: a screwdriver, tweezers, and pliers. And where did I lose my hand? And when? *Ach, auf der Insel Nargen. Ja-ja-jaa*—there where German troops were *too* . . . Oh, not in the last war? In 1894! During your boyhood days? A homemade explosive device!

"Pfff . . . You see, we practice humanism here in the broadest sense of the term. But differentially. This is of course inevitable, you understand. So that when it is a case of an invalid who is not a *German* war veteran—who is not covered by the war validity fund—it would cost—if the individual is a *German*—around one and a half thousand."

"And if the victim is a foreigner?"

"Oh, you know—in such cases we prefer payment to be made in dollars. But I can get back to you on that. I imagine that we are talking about a sum of let's say two thousand marks. We can only give the definitive price once the operation has been carried out. And it would depend to an extent on your satisfaction with the whole procedure. And we are of course *most adamant* that you are satisfied."

I remember taking a walk through the vineyards near the town trying to arrive at a decision: first—almost impossible costs, the unpleasantness of the operation, the loss of time, between six weeks and two months, plus the limitations of having this foreign body attached (which you could ignore to an extent, but it also made the whole thing pointless). Second—the artificial limb for working with its three attachments was not particularly suited to my needs (because of the ever-changing stages of my work, I would have to change attachments every couple of minutes). But on the other hand, that sleek-combed Hammer also promised that the ordinary, hand-shaped limb could carry out precision movements and powerful ones, at any rate nothing less precise than doctors with such a limb were said to carry out when administering injections. And it would nevertheless be, damn it, some kind of *victory* . . . And then I would no longer have to be the cause of all those half-secretly turned-away faces, their concealed stares when they saw my stump—even when walking on the street with Johanna—no longer . . . Because a hand in an ordinary glove of some ordinary color would not be noticeable.

I went to Dr. Hammer's five o'clock surgery and asked him to book me a time for the operation the following week. I said that I would be traveling to Mittweida to obtain the two thousand.

All of a sudden, the somewhat cold-blooded and businesslike doctor said almost gushingly:

"Herr Schmidt, I can offer you a pleasant opportunity, a very pleasant opportunity: we can do your operation for half the price. And what is more: we will do it for half the price of that of a German invalid. So that it won't cost more than six hundred marks. Certainly not more than six hundred."

I wondered: Do I really look so pathetic? And asked:

"Why such a . . . reasonable offer?"

"Oh, simply out of gratitude. For the opportunities that are then opened up for us."

"I'm not sure I quite understand . . ."

"Herr Schmidt—I owe you an apology. Your name is not particularly uncommon. And you did say: a polisher of glass. I did not associate you with stellar optics. But in the meantime, I have received some information. You see, if you personally become one of our patients, then things written about the Sauerbruch hand can always mention, and with perfect veracity, that Bernhard Schmidt polished his stellar optical equipment using a Sauerbruch hand . . ."

I didn't even have the time to cry out: "But look here . . . !" before he himself corrected his choice of words. "I mean to say—that would perhaps be the wrong way of putting it—but let us say: 'Bernhard Schmidt's famous stellar optical equipment has been polished *with the contribution of* a Sauerbruch hand.' Don't you think? The *contribution* is after all beyond dispute! There's no way out of that one! Ha-ha-ha-haaa!"

"Yes, yes, no way out for me. Quite true." I bared my teeth in the same way that he was baring his. And left Singen. Never, of course, to return. Because God Almighty, I had never allowed the Zeiss, Goerz, or Kelter firms to do business on the strength of my hand. Although they would at times have dearly wished to do so. What damned right did Sauerbruch's hand have to muscle its way in there? And in such an accursed way that it couldn't be denied that it contributed to my skills. In a way my work would be taken out of my hands . . . In the future people would claim that my achievements had been made *partly* with Schmidt's hand, and *partly* with Sauerbruch's. And no poor devil would bother to ask what percentage of Schmidt and what of Sauerbruch there was in all this. Oh, I could well imagine how my colleagues in industry, the mechanical grit grinders that I am standing in the way of, would change their attitude if I were to give them the opportunity by using a Sauerbruch. They would soon be talking in unison—maybe not entirely in unison but in that direction—that Schmidt did not achieve his degree of precision *despite* his Sauerbruch hand but rather *because of* it . . .

Was this all in fact because of my oversensitivity, foolishness, idle fancies? Maybe it was. Maybe, by such logic, I should have stopped using my pliers and hammers and lathe! As they too were not physical parts of me. They too were foreign bodies . . . Be that as it may. I felt unable to act in any other way. That same evening I was sitting on the train leaving Singen. And slung all my revivified ideas about an artificial hand clothed in a white glacé glove away somewhere—down the railway carriage toilet hole . . . To this day it is impossible for me to say which battling and contradictory motives were at play then: the desire to increase my capacity to work effectively, the wish to avoid the visible signs of my disability, the horror at the way such an artificial limb would invade my sovereignty, the disgust at using it as an advertising prop, and last but not least, maybe—the fear that made me instinctively run for cover after my accident. The fear of experiencing another trauma, which the operation would inevitably have meant to a certain degree. But despite everything, my triumphant refusal still left a bitter taste in my mouth.

The word *bitter* has reminded me that the half cigar I have just tossed down the lavatory is the twentieth since this morning, and on an empty stomach it feels as if my mouth is tanned with cigar smoke.

I place my spherometer back on the disc, which I have rinsed clean of paste under the shower, and I am convinced that the absolute depth of the center remains unchanged, but the edge of the plate has thinned by 0.94 millimeters. I remove the spherometer, spread an even layer of water across the plate, and place it on the checking disc. I watch the water flow away between the plates like lakes, pools, rivers, streams, and fords. Until not a drop is left. This means that the water on my plate has not found any uneven patches.

Now I have to start polishing. I feel I ought to go and eat something, but that would require a good deal more patience than I can muster. Besides, God Almighty, it's nearly one o'clock in the morning! I would only be able to obtain some asparagus salad via the back door of Land's—but the visit to the bar would take at least half an hour—there and back again. So I open the wall cupboard and pour myself half a glass of cognac from the half bottle there. Half a glass is, at this moment, both a necessary quantity and the only one possible.

And then I carry on. I put my can of pitch on the electric stove in the next room to warm up. I bring the tin of red polishing emulsion up to the lathe, put the paintbrushes in a row from the finest to the coarsest, and adjust the polishing plate to 360 millimeters in preparation. Now the pitch is warm enough to use. I take the little tin and sniff it. Inside is a mixture of pitch and resin and it has a warm, curiously double fragrance of the old peat stove blended with that of pinewoods in springtime. My nose can always detect the right temperature: I pour a suitable amount of the polishing pitch onto the middle of the disc and spread it out over the whole disc with a ruler like cream on a cake. I press a crisscross network of lines into the pitch with the ruler. This all goes very smoothly and I enjoy the fluency. I cover my correction plate on top of the air-expulsion cylinder with red emulsion from the tin. A hundred thousand tiny red spiders spread out across the bright gray surface. Then I take hold of the polishing plate by its two opposite edges with a pair of tongs designed especially for this purpose, turn the disc, and place its pitch-covered side on the surface of the correction plate that is waiting to be polished. I wait for four or five minutes until the polishing plate has sunk evenly into the layer of pitch. Then I start up the lathe—still at two revolutions per second—and start off. But now it is no longer a question of circular movements but rather of straight strokes.

I am working semi-automatically. So the twenty movements per minute across the plate and changing the pitch every half hour become almost mechanical. Only adding the red emulsion with a small paintbrush, stroking the top layer, that is, the finest layer of the emulsion, is where my active participation keeps on increasing. At the same time as this work process is diminishing in its other aspects, sinking down to the first level of dreaming.

I carry on working, and in so doing select random thoughts, after what principle I cannot tell, but in the hope that some of them will linger for a moment and offer some interest when I twist them and turn them, well, even polish them . . .

. . . How great a thinker am I . . . ? Apart from playing around with a number of rather basic technical ideas, I simply don't have the stamina for thinking. Everything is really boastful improvisation. Merely sententious voids—that have emerged during minutes of relaxation. On the strength of which a few kind fools have begun to look on me as a philosopher. For example, that same young man—Wachmann. At every opportunity he will now quote what Bernhard Schmidt is supposed to have said about his own hyperindividualism. "Only one human being on this earth is worth anything. Because once you have two such men there are bound to be tensions. And with three you will have intrigue. And with ten—conflict. And a hundred would mean war." Ha-ha-ha-haa. I could well have said that in some breezy moment. Why not? Because it is by no means a lie.

But in general I am no great lover of philosophizing. Or at least not that we so lightly call philosophizing, that is, ratiocination. Of course we can say that every human being asks himself questions now and again. Someone dealing with the heavens no less than others. In fact, more than some others. Let those who believe differently stand eye to eye with infinity, night after night, and *not* ask anything. But once someone asks, he is also trying to provide an answer. That's only natural. To answer as profoundly or childishly as he is able.

I have posed questions about all sorts of silly things. And answered them for private use. Question: Does a ninth planet exist? Answer: very likely. I wait every day for someone to discover it. Given Lowell's calculations that he made long ago. Question: Do the canals on Mars exist? Or as Schiaparelli suggested some fifty years ago, are they optical illusions? And not only him. I did too. All those times I saw the canals? Presumably. Everyone who sees canals on Mars is suffering from an optical illusion. Otherwise you would have of course to draw the conclusion that . . . And so on. A load of rubbish that you at first find no answers to. But that which has gripped me most when catching a glimpse of the heavens . . . (You just can't describe it in rational language! The very expression *catching a glimpse of the heavens* sounds as if it is dripping with pathos! But OK. Let it be.) What has seized me and given me a light sense of intoxication—I will say what it is: *the contrast between me as a mere speck of dust and the infinity of what I can grasp with my mind.*

And then—the most constructive thought alongside all those things that seize me as I look into the heavens, a thought that is almost one to build a system out of, though there has never been time in this world to develop such a system or put it to the test. In a word, against the background of Darwin's starlit heavens. Or let's put it this way: first, there are signs of gravitation both on this earth and in the heavens. A comparison of such observations would suggest that gravitation is a universal law, a cosmic law. Second, there are a whole range of observations made from Earth concerning *development* stemming from geology via chemistry and biology. To me, Darwin is providing me with its biological phase. There are no observations from any other quarter. Except for one important circumstance: the lack of proof to the contrary. The lack of proof to the contrary, also to the extent, however infinitesimal, that we have had access to the elements that make up a meteorite. Now, can we draw two conclusions from these two things: that given observations from Earth, and the lack of evidence from elsewhere, that there is a cosmic law that states that things move from simple structures to more complex ones, from simple elements to complex compounds? The devil knows, maybe there is. But maybe it is possible to conclude this at least in the sphere of living creatures. Perhaps only in the form of a hypothesis . . . If the emergence of life on Earth is not merely by chance—but what do we mean by *chance*? I know that others have different answers, maybe better ones, but I would say this: chance is governed by laws and it is unlikely that the whole bundle of reasons would coincide in time and space. Yes. But what degree of unlikelihood is there when it comes to the emergence of life? The five or six miserable elements necessary, plus a suitable temperature . . . A temperature of let us say between zero degrees and a hundred—while the range of temperatures within the cosmos stretches from absolute zero at minus 273 Celsius to six or seven thousand degrees. If you take into account the surfaces of stars. And then those five or six elements from the ninety or so that exist. Adding the fact that their number has increased slightly over the past few years. Hafnium and rhenium, and whatever the rest are. But it is unlikely that more than ten or twenty more will be added to the list. In the cosmos, the likelihood of these elements being found together by chance—carbon, hydrogen, nitrogen, oxygen, and so on, and with a temperature of between one and a hundred—this chance is *inescapable.* You can even calculate mathematically what this chance is. And it turns out (I'm almost bursting out laughing, but I cannot permit myself to do so because then my polishing plate would jerk and the layer of polishing pitch would grow uneven)—what I am saying is: if everything is like that, then you can think in, fit in a single thought into the whole mechanism of the world, its whole living nature, whatever you want to call it, the whole universe. Because if what has happened on Earth, that is, the emergence of living material and its development into thinking material, sentient material, if this is all governed by laws—*then we know the meaning of life! The meaning of life is to perceive life itself!* That mess of moss that arose two billion years ago on the surface of the rocks of the earth is the way the universe is trying to become aware of itself. And then come the jellyfish, and the fish, and dinosaurs. And me. This is all an attempt by the universe to create something to look at itself with, such as, for instance, an eye. And a brain as a means to process the information it receives. I am the eye and the brain of the cosmos . . . Thank God that no one can read my thoughts, because these would be blasphemous ones: me as the eye and brain of the universe . . . And even crazier: me polishing away at a sharper eye, as if it were a commission from someone . . . Briefly: existence is a game by the universe played in order to become aware of itself. Agreed. And that's how it is from my perspective of being able to embrace an infinite amount of thought. From my speck-of-dust perspective, this is a serious idea. More than I can understand . . . And in this way it turns out that even harmony is contained within my system in some unbelievable way . . .

But even more incredible is that my polishing activities—polishing a new and sharper eye for the universe—are now, my hand tells me, *finished.*

Suddenly, I am wide awake, so awake that I see everything with such great clarity that everything else subsides: the avalanche of ash that is weariness, the painful shoulders, the dull ache in the small of the back, the doziness from the monotony of the polishing, the shooting pains in my knees, and the taste of gall and cigar nicotine denoting an empty stomach. I switch off the lathe. I wipe my face with my damp hand. I can feel the stubble on my chin. It is five o'clock. For one fleeting moment I wonder whether it is five in the morning or the afternoon, and then realize it is the morning. I then take off the polishing plate, fetch some sponges, and let the shower water run. And I rinse my plate, my (ho-ho) eye-of-the-universe lens clean of its tarry afterbirth. I dry it off with great care. I aim the lamp at it and across it and look at it from both angles with an 8x magnifying glass. The surface now seems to be ideal to all intents and purposes.

I struggle for ten minutes trying to get the air hose onto the vacuum cylinder. My face grows slightly sweaty, the lack of food and my impatience make me perspire more easily than otherwise, but now the hose is in place. I go over to the wall cabinet and pour out a glass of cognac for myself. I drink the whole glass in small tasty gulps, right there where I am standing.

I return to the workbench and sit down on the stool, move the switch on the vacuum pump from *aus* to *ein* and slowly open the valve tap. The air from the hose enters the cylinder with a light hiss and the manometer moves from 0.221 to 0.227. I make sure that the cog on my dentist's drill is set at maximum. This means that the pump will be working at one-hundredth of its normal speed. And then I start pedaling. Pedaling and watching the manometer and, most important of all—the plate.

I have placed a couple of two-hundred-watt bulbs on flexible cables about two meters from the lens and the cylinder, one to the right, the other to the left. My hand is now free and I switch the lamps on and off. So that the side of the plate facing the lamps will not heat up too much. The lamps are hanging in the same horizontal plane as the plate, and the light will immediately reveal the contour of its surface.

My pump is letting air back into the cylinder at the rate of three times 1,500 cubic millimeters per minute. I could presumably increase the rate quite a lot without any risk that the plate would crack. But let it work slowly for now.

And now I must be able to see, as they say—what God is doing.

About ten minutes later, I begin to notice, in other words, imagine I notice how the plate is bulging. Then that it is bulging especially in the center, and that the strip around the edge and the central area form a slightly concave belt roughly as wide as one-third of the radius. At four minutes past six the manometer shows exactly one atmosphere. I stop pumping and open the valve tap. My armpits are sweaty. My pulse is pounding at nearly a hundred. My plate is ready. And I realize that if I now stand up abruptly I will have to grip hold of something so as not to fall over.

But I do not yet know whether my plate *is* exactly how I expected it to be. I do not yet know whether it will work . . .

■ □ ■ □ ■

6

"WELL, AT THAT MOMENT IN TIME UNCLE BERNHARD DIDN'T YET KNOW IT, *but we've now known for fifty years: it worked perfectly, right from the very start. Inasmuch as we onlookers can judge from the outside and by hindsight . . ."*

The son of sea captain August Schmidt, that is to say Bernhard Schmidt's nephew, Erik Schmidt, looks at me merrily over his whiskey glass with his round silvery-blue Naissaar eyes. Yes, he has to be taken as someone from that island. Because he was born on Naissaar, although on his mother's side, whose maiden name was Karro, sometimes Karo, his line stems from Torma or Malla or wherever. And our conversation takes place on an island, not unfortunately on Naissaar, but rather somewhere very far away: beyond Spain, on Mallorca, in the city of Palma de Mallorca, or to be precise in its northeastern suburb, which is called, very functionally, *Establiments,* that is to say, "Stay-Put-Ville" or similar.

We are sitting in the home of Erik Schmidt and his Swedish-born wife Kerstin, a white two-story stone edifice with a flat flagged roof in the middle of a garden with St. John's Bread, mandarin trees, and almond trees, in the restful shade of the interior of the house on this sun-drenched Mediterranean island.

I am not going to start asking Erik Schmidt about the course of his life after he, as a nineteen-year-old, left Estonia with his mother. He has at any rate been living on Mallorca for twenty years and has worked principally in the tourist branch, has also run a hotel, but has now been retired for a number of years and occupies his time with what he has always considered his calling: painting pictures.

A month ago, he returned from Toronto, where he had an exhibition. Before going to Canada he had finished an altarpiece for Palma's Swedish church—six meters in length—which he is keen on showing me.

"Sure, it's here in Spain, sure it's been done for the Swedish church—but for me there's a tinge of Estonian culture in it nonetheless."

Of course. By all means. But above all I want to talk with my host about his uncle.

Incidentally, there is no lack of the cult surrounding his famous uncle in his home. But why should there be? Quite the opposite: as long as there is no place in the world that commemorates Bernhard Schmidt (apart from his grave in Hamburg and a tiny little museum room at the Bergedorf Observatory), while there is still no Schmidt museum in Tallinn, or Tartu, or at the observatory in Tõravere, then a few objects that remind people of him can at least be found here at *Establiments.*

On the wall of Erik Schmidt's study there hangs a portrait of his uncle Bernhard. This is the only large oil painting ever done by my host, and is of course done from a photo, because the old, fading memories that the nephew had of his uncle would not suffice to construct a painting from. And what is hanging here is, in fact, a duplicate of the one he painted some ten years previously. He tried and failed to sell it in Estonia and therefore sold it to the Palomar Observatory in California instead.

"That observatory—well, you know this yourself—played the most significant role in making Uncle Bernhard posthumously famous. Professor Baade moved there from Bergedorf in 1931. By that time, Uncle Bernhard had completed his coma-free telescope and Baade knew how it was constructed, as Uncle Bernhard had described it to him. And following the joint decision made by Baade and Hale—fame came posthumously, alas, not only for Bernhard but for Hale too—the pride of Palomar, the *Big Schmidt,* was born. And as far as I know, Uncle Bernhard's portrait now hangs on the wall of the room where they operate the Big Schmidt, and looking through the glass partition wall—from the portrait's perspective—there is a seven-meter-long somewhat curved silvery-gray whale, or rather a sea lion with a broad backside and its nose gazing up at new galaxies . . . But what you want to know is something about my uncle himself."

Erik Schmidt was sent all my questions beforehand by mail and has had time to neatly systematize his replies:

"You see, my immediate personal memories are pretty minimal: those that are more or less clear to me are from the autumn and winter of 1929. My father was then the captain of the *Nautic* and made sea voyages, between Scandinavian and British ports, I think. I was on Naissaar with my mother, at Grandmother and Uncle Frans's place. And then Uncle Bernhard came back home from Germany. What I remember visually is: a tall thin gray-haired man, pacing along Grandmother's multicolored rag runners from one room to the other, then to a third, and back to the first. Maybe he wasn't actually so tall, but I was a four-year-old toddler at the time. I also knew that Uncle Bernhard was the most famous member of the family, and such an item of information will have increased his stature in the eyes of a little boy. Well, because of his defect, I was very curious to see his hand, and I remember clearly that when he used to pace the rooms in this way, or walked along the road on his way to the boat harbor, he would keep his right hand behind his back and would stroke his chin with the fingers of his left, as if feeling whether stubble had grown there or not.

"Another group of memories are things I heard my father tell about him. First and foremost about their common childhood days, which can be divided up into two types: *before* and *after* the accident. Whatever. A third group were all those things that the family told about his later years.

"So my personal memories are summed up by: a tall man in a gray suit walking on Grandmother's bright-colored mats. And if I now move on to *my father's* memories then I would like to say something right from the start, as you happened to mention something about the *myth* surrounding the fact that he was a man of few words. I have to say this: my father maintained all his life that Bernhard really was an exceptionally reticent boy. And was so both before and after the accident. He would answer his mother with a yes or a no. His stepfather with hardly even that. And would always be vanishing off somewhere. To do his own thing. And only very rarely, when he was doing something together with the boys of the village—that is, something the others could be useful for—would he give them a whole lecture.

For example, when he was testing his gunpowder-driven model motorboat in the Capernaum Moat. What was the Capernaum Moat? It was some old—how shall I put it—archaeological dig. To the west of the Lõunaküla fortifications. I think they had once started excavating some kind of moat around the old fortress but had never got farther than the southwest corner. And even in my childhood there was still a little water at the bottom of it. But in the days of Bernhard and his father, forty or fifty years earlier, it could be anything up to three-foot deep. Why the biblical name? That I really don't know. You will have to make do with your own explanation, that is, that maybe there was mud at the bottom that the villagers used to cure their rheumatism. And that someone mixed up the story of Christ healing a servant at Capernaum and the stories in which people sought relief from their aches and pains in the pool at Bethesda. No-no, I've never believed in such things!

"But there in the Capernaum Moat, Uncle Bernhard, when he was thirteen or fourteen, tried out his gunpowder boat along with the other boys. I don't know exactly, but I can imagine that the model was about one meter long. He has lit the fuse at the water's edge—it was set up in such a way that the gunpowder would not explode all at once, but would instead burn gradually and therefore propel the boat forward. And the model was emitting a fearful hissing sound as it sailed along, and the village boys were watching from both sides of the moat, holding long poles in their hands in order to push the boat back on course down the center of the moat. My father mentioned that this was one of the few times that Bernhard had explained things, shouted, and given orders in a loud voice."

And then he told of one more episode. "But my father had been the only witness on this occasion. This was a couple of years after Bernhard's accident. Maybe even earlier, only a year after. Because eighteen months after the accident he was already working in Tallinn as a telegraphist."

Erik Schmidt puts down his whiskey glass with a dissatisfied look on his face. "You know, if I'd have known I was going to be telling these things to someone who was going to write a novel about him—I would have asked my father a lot more details. But that time—well, Bernhard had built some kind of machine. My father had explained: an electricity machine. Some kind of dynamo, presumably. Which he had knocked together in Uncle Frans's outhouse. But it was at any rate an enormously large and heavy device. With a particularly large and heavy flywheel to which a cranking handle was attached. When this was turned, of course by hand as they didn't have a motor, then the machine was supposed to produce electricity. And the current would light up a bulb."

I ask: "Had he bought the bulb or made it himself?"

"Yes," says Erik Schmidt, and pours us both another whiskey—"when you ask that, I have to admit: I do not know. I never thought of asking my father about it. Or I've forgotten. But now I feel that it must have been one made in a factory. Such things already existed. Whether in Tallinn is hard to say. But they did exist. Around 1896 or 1897. Edison and Swan and some others. And I get the feeling it had to be quite a large bulb. So the boy could hardly have made something like that on his own. Not having access to an air pump, for one thing. Because there was hardly likely to be such a thing on Naissaar. And then Bernhard had, one autumn evening, at what was perhaps the time of year when the nights drew in early, invited my father to his shed . . ."

"Would he allow his brother in there at other times?"

"It would seem not," says Erik Schmidt with a smile. "It tends to be like that with an elder brother and a younger one. My father was only fourteen at the time. And maybe Bernhard was underscoring his superiority in some way. For obvious reasons. As Adler has explained, hasn't he? But my father was tough, tougher than Bernhard, and he could easily crank the handle. At least more than Bernhard could. And then Bernhard had muttered as he pointed toward the device with his chin:

"'You see. There it is. Now we're going to see whether it works. Grab hold of the handle and start turning.'

"And so they turned, until the sweat ran. Bernhard along with my father, inasmuch as he could with his hand. Occasionally, Bernhard would jump away in order to look at the lamp, then cry in a hoarse voice: 'Keep turning! Keep turning!' Then a moment later he would jump back to his place next to his brother. And my father was already completely out of breath, and who knows how many times Bernhard was bent over his lamp for the umpteenth time, when he suddenly yelled:

"'I've done it! That's enough! Stop!' Then he stood, arms akimbo, jutted out his chin, and said: 'Yep. Schmidt's machine has given a flash of light.'"

"So he'd managed to get his lamp to light up?"

"If it actually did light up," says Erik Schmidt, "but it at least glowed for a moment."

"And your father saw it with his own eyes? That would at least require—how many volts? About fifty at least. For such an old-fashioned large lamp. Don't you think? And pretty good wires and plugs. OK, why not. It's always possible. If your father actually saw it . . ."

"No," says Erik Schmidt, "my father didn't actually see it. Because Bernhard was bent over the lamp, so he was blocking my father's view . . ."

I have to admit: I want Bernhard's experiment to have succeeded; I want the fact he saw the lamp light up to be beyond dispute. If his brother August said he'd seen light with his own eyes, that would be beyond dispute. I feel my tendency to cultivate myths rising, but hasten to help Erik nonetheless:

"That means—that your father didn't actually see the lamp, but the boys were messing around with it at dusk. So your father will have seen a glimmer of light behind Bernhard, or the light reflected in his face . . ."

"No-no," says Erik, "my father didn't see a thing. The glow was clearly too brief for that to have happened. But Bernhard did see it. He'd been working hard to build his machine for several weeks and he had expended as much effort on it as he always did. He saw the filament glow for a fraction of a second . . ."

I now feel a little embarrassed at my haste a moment ago, and ask in a more probing way than I actually want to:

"But maybe Bernhard wanted to see that brief glow so much that he simply imagined it. We do, after all, know that the barrier between reality and expectation—reality and great expectations—can fall away more often than we tend to notice in everyday matters. For example . . ."

Erik Schmidt interrupts:

"That's true, that's true. But now I must say one thing. Bernhard was such a boy, right from the start—I must repeat: I was hearing this from other members of the family, and principally from my father—

Bernhard was such a boy, and remained such a man all his life, that he did not allow himself to harbor any type of illusions. He despised illusions. He despised them with quite a savage bitterness. With an intolerance that had stacked up by way of his painful experiences . . . In fact . . ." Erik Schmidt looks helpless for a split second, then tilts his glass to the right and left within a millimeter of flowing over and continues with a faint smile: "In fact . . . Bernhard lived from one illusion to the next. No-no, what I'm saying may *seem* to be contradictory. But there, in fact, is no contradiction. For instance, every one of his inventions remained an illusion for some time—until they were made technically possible or proved impossible. Illusion like balloon flight. And second, when they had been made real in the *technical* sense of the word, another illusion arose, that in the *financial* sphere. And as you know, the illusion never became reality in that latter meaning of the term 'illusion.' But those that I would call balloon flights are one thing. Of course he imagined for several months that all the ships in the world (or at least half) would use Schmidt's rotors. And that Schmidt's gastroscope would hang on the wall of every doctor's surgery. And that all astronomers in serious observatories would do their observations through Schmidt telescopes. And he was no fakir who never paid attention to the financial side of his inventions. He certainly thought about the financial side. But I must stress: this was at the level of balloon flight. His workbench was at a completely different level. There, Bernhard would brook no illusions. There he was merciless with himself and with others. Ever since boyhood. So that when he told Father that the filament had glowed for an instant, it will have done so."

I ask: "But how do you relate to tales about how Bernhard achieved technical success at an early age?"

"For example?"

"For example that wonderful story that a few old people from Naissaar have told in Tallinn, and I don't know whether to believe it or not, about how at the age of twelve Bernhard found the base of a glass bottle in the sea, which had been smoothed by the waves, which he then polished himself and made an excellent magnifying glass out of it."

"Well, in that instance," says Erik Schmidt, "the tale belongs to the 'minor miracles during the childhood of the saint' type of story. It circulated in our family too. Most certainly. Not the fact that he had made an excellent magnifying glass out of it, but that he had *made some sort of magnifying glass out of it.* That is something else entirely!"

"Understandably. But then I've also heard that Bernhard was supposed to have—right from boyhood days—made huge lenses out of chunks of ice that could magnify a light several times."

"You know something," Erik Schmidt cries out with a laugh—"I wrote that story down myself from my father's reminiscences, and sent it to Dr. Peeter Müürsepp in Tallinn, and he printed it in one of his Schmidt brochures."

"So you think it is true?"

"Yes," Erik Schmidt confirmed, "the boy made lenses out of chunks of ice, a couple of feet across, as I can imagine. Why not? A hundred paces from the house there were all manner of chunks of ice washed up by the sea. You had an endless choice. Naturally, such a lens would make the flame of a petroleum lamp look unexpectedly bright. It didn't make the light of the lamp several times more powerful. We are both physicists enough to understand that. I remember reading in Tallinn during the war, or just before when still at school, Alexei Tolstoy's *The Hyperboloid of Engineer Garin.* You will have read it too . . . ?"

"Yes, I have," I admit . . .

"Well, you see. I was already thinking then, and you have no doubt done so too: it is in practice impossible to cut an armored warship in two with the light of a mere candle, however perfect the mirror that reflects the light from the candle. A mirror does not increase the energy several times over. Nor a lens, for that matter. It's against the laws of physics. But according to the laws of folk belief it is the only possible explanation. Once such laws kick in."

I ask: "But what do you make of the story that Bernhard constructed a spyglass during his childhood? Don't you think that all those lenses and so on point in too naive a way to his future as an optical scientist? Wouldn't he have been interested in all sorts of different technical things as a little boy?"

"Well he would have been. He experimented with dozens of things. And not only as a boy. But as for his Naissaar spyglass, I would put the question: Why not? When that too has lodged in the memory of my father. Why couldn't he have constructed one? We should perhaps ask instead: How could he *not* have built one? First, he was interested in observing things from a long distance away, right from early boyhood. We all like to do so to a certain extent. But his interest was more intense than the average person's. Owing to local circumstances. I am thinking of the sea's horizon with its constantly changing objects. This change was stimulating. And besides that, the silhouette of Tallinn and Paljassaare and the beach at Kakumäe. They were of course immovable objects at a distance that presented a challenge—they were a dozen or so kilometers away, still discernable to the naked eye but not really *visible.* And then, quite early on, he discovered the starry heavens—that too on the island. I also remember this very clearly myself—the stars were very clear, very pure, very tangible. Yet inaccessible. There were old naval spyglasses, which had long been replaced by new ones, in the lumber room of every house, just lying there waiting to be taken apart, put together again, and tested out. So Bernhard will have cobbled together a new spyglass from the pieces of old ones—what could be more natural?"

"What properties did his new spyglass have?"

"All the usual ones, of course. Can't have been a miracle device."

"But people say right to this day, or let us say now in connection with the growing interest in Schmidt, that with this boyhood spyglass of his you could see from the island shore at Lõunaküla how they were mowing the hay at the foot of the lighthouse at Suurupi on the mainland. Or even better: some girl from Naissaar, who had moved to Mulgimaa in the south of Estonia somewhere out Tarvastu way at the turn of the century, wrote down an even more amusing story. In some of the villages around Tarvastu people to this day say that the spyglass built by little Schmidt was so good that from the island you could see what sort of dresses the young ladies in Tallinn were wearing as they strolled along the beach at Kadriorg. So that some girls from Naissaar had looked through the device, which they had borrowed from Schmidt, and had sewn dresses according to city fashion."

Erik Schmidt bursts into hoots of laughter.

I say: "To more or less that same category belongs the camera that Bernhard is supposed to have constructed as a fourteen- or fifteen-year-old."

"Oh yes, of course," Erik Schmidt agrees, "but the question is, was it when he was fourteen or fifteen—or when he was sixteen? That is still the question."

"In what way?"

"In the way that . . . Look, I have noticed myself that in Schmidt folklore, both that of the family circle and more widely, people tend to shift the dates of what Bernhard did as a boy by a year or two. Usually nudging them in an earlier direction. And I think that the reason can be, on the one hand—how did you put it just now, the wishes of the *mythmakers* to accentuate the boy's special skills. All of this according to the principle that the earlier in life our saint performs his miracles, the greater a holy man he becomes. But on the other hand, I feel that making some of Bernhard's deeds occur earlier has arisen from the desire to make them more credible. In what way, you may be wondering? Because many of those who remember and relate the stories can themselves not believe that such a crippled boy as Bernhard could manage to build, for instance, a camera—*using only one hand.* So that for the sake of plausibility, the date of the story was nudged back to the time before he had lost it. In reality, the construction of the camera could very well have taken place *after* he lost his hand. Because according to what many people remember, he adapted the use of his left hand for all sorts of tasks with fantastic speed."

"How fast?"

"Well, as far as I remember: he would practice whole days at a time after he came home from the hospital. Drew sketches, wrote things, threw knives, tried to play the mouth organ, tied and untied all sorts of knots. And goodness knows what else. About a year afterward, he was perfectly capable of using his left hand."

"And so this camera clearly did exist," I comment.

"I imagine so," says Erik Schmidt. "The most important components were a viewfinder that he had obtained God knows where, plus the bellows from an old concertina. I still have a photo that everyone assures me was taken with the camera that Bernhard built using the concertina parts. Look, here it is . . ." Erik Schmidt takes from the shelf by the sofa a very white, very sterile photo album with plastic sleeves, and out of one a small, faded picture. "It is entirely my fault that I cannot tell you whose wedding it was and on whose farm. It was presumably taken at some wedding of Schmidts or Rosens. There were quite a few Schmidts married to Rosens, Schmidt boys to Rosen girls and vice versa, for several generations. It was taken at one such wedding. So for that reason I tend to think more and more that the picture was taken by Bernhard when his mother married Uncle Frans. That would have been in November 1898."

"What do you mean by 'more and more' . . . ?"

"More and more," says Erik Schmidt, "because it is rather a strange photo. Empty chairs instead of the bride and groom. And we know that Bernhard didn't approve of his mother's second marriage."

I say: "Mr. Schmidt, *why* he didn't approve of it is something we can talk about another time, but now . . ." And I take a faded photo from my pocket. "Look, this photo was taken, according to the information I've received, with that very same camera. Not by Bernard himself but rather in 1911 when Bernhard had already left the island. It is said to show the birthplace of a man, now very old, from Naissaar—one Aleksander Toom at a neighboring farm to Jaanipere. And this Aleksander Toom has, by the way, met both yourself and your mother, Mr. Schmidt. On the motorized boat the *Marmor I.* He was the assistant mechanic on the boat. In the years 1930 to 1931. When your father was the captain and you traveled with your mother in the summers. What would you have been at the time, fifteen or sixteen?"

We examine the two old dog-eared photos, faded to grayish green and brown, that are now unexpectedly lying next to each other on Erik Schmidt's oval, six-legged living room table. In one photo, through the yellowish-gray mist, the cut birch-branch wedding decorations can be made out in the corner of a low room, plus two garlanded empty chairs, bowls of potted meat on the table, plus five or six people sitting there whose faces are blurred. In the other, through a similar yellowish-gray mist that is like a cloudy sun-flecked veil, can be seen a long house with a glassed-in veranda, and two goats in the mist in front of the house. Over the picture with birch branches, and the other with a lawn, there hovers the nervous present-day shadow of a pomegranate tree in the yard in *Establiments.* Looking at these faded old photos and becoming aware of the bygone worlds shown there, I ask myself for the second time: Is not time itself one of those forms of energy that simply gobbles up objects? An energy field that greedily eats up forms of matter?

"Yes," says Erik Schmidt very quietly, "I can almost recognize the house. And the *Marmor I,* whose captain my father was, is clearly lodged in my memory. A nice small vessel. We shipped dolomite from Jaagurahu to Sweden and especially to Norway, a far as I remember. And sometimes we would sail with the ship fully laden plus two barges in tow also filled with dolomite."

I say: "Wait a minute. I now remember a story about one of those dolomite ships. A story from Bernhard Schmidt's youth that I've heard tell around our way. I can't now remember who told it. I've written it down somewhere. And what I want to ask is whether his family folklore recognizes it or not."

"Do carry on! What sort of story?"

"If I use the good works of saints as an analogy, I would say that this is a tale of Bernhard as the twelve-year-old Jesus in the temple."

"You are making the story rather interesting . . ."

"What else can an author do? In a word, the twelve-year-old or let us say fourteen-year-old Bernhard is sailing on that vessel. Back to Naissaar from Tallinn. Legend does not reveal what he was doing in Tallinn. Nor who he was traveling with. But he must have had someone from the family or from Naissaar with him. Otherwise the story of his encounter with the elders would have come from his own lips. And that doesn't suit this type of story. Who it was that saw it happen and told it isn't known. But for some strange reason the vessel in which this all happened has been fixed for posterity. It was the *Blitz,* a small steamer belonging to the Baltic coastguard, no doubt. Anyway, this vessel sometimes plied the route between Tallinn and Naissaar. It had been constructed to take passengers, and a large part of the deck was covered by a roof that formed part of the upper deck. When the weather was fine, the passengers tended to stay up on the roof. Around the small backward-sloping funnel, white park benches had been placed. A photo of this steamer still exists. And—I can imagine it to be a fine Saturday—a group of gentlemen from Tallinn were present. Merchants and engineers. The fact that there were engineers present is important. God knows why they were sailing. Maybe simply to get a breath of fresh air, or maybe on business. I have thought about the fact that a few years later they began to allot plots of land on that part of the island, around Lehtmetsa, and to build villas there. Maybe these gentlemen were sailing out in connection with all of this. Anyway, they were chatting away and clearly in a good mood. They had quite likely already visited the ship's concession stand and tasted the beer. And I can imagine that the islanders, insofar as there were any out on the roof, would have kept their distance from the city gents. Even somewhat demonstratively. To what extent is hard to tell with hindsight. Well now, the gents then notice a tug boat in front. The tug is sailing at ninety degrees to port, that is to say to the west of them, in the direction of the port of Paldiski, and dragging two heavily laden barges behind.

"Well, I can imagine that the distance between the two ships was decreasing, and sooner or later one of the gentlemen on the *Blitz* asked what the cargo of this other ship was. And so the merchants and engineers began to discuss the issue. Especially when the barges crossed right in front of their ship and the *Blitz* altered course to sail in a northwesterly direction when a hundred or fifty meters away, so that it was now sailing parallel to the barges. And a grayish-yellow mass could be seen through their open cargo hatches.

"One of the gentlemen said: 'This will be a load of old Girard's Port-Kunda cement. Portland cement. Needed in Paldiski to build the warehouses.'

"Another man said: 'No. Cement is more precious than that. They would transport it in barrels. I know. Four hundred and fifty pounds per barrel.'

"Someone asked: 'OK. But what stuff have they got there, then?'

"Someone said: 'What is it they've got there? It's, well, oil shale. I've heard about this stuff. Baron Toll from Kukruse manor house has allowed them to exploit the oil shale on his land, and some crazy Englishman has bought some for his ship. Wants to try it out as fuel.'

"Someone said: 'But take a look—what's in the barges looks to be something more fine grained than that.'

"Someone yelled: 'It's *sand*! Sand, and nothing else. They're building a jetty in Paldiski for the czar's sailing yachts. I'm telling you, it's sand.'

"One of the gentlemen summed up: 'Well, we can ask the captain to lend us his megaphone, then we'll get some clarity. But before we do—*wer gehört zur Zementpartei? Zur Sandpartei? Zur Brennschieferpartei?*'

"For each of the options, three or four of the gentlemen raised their hand. And only now did they notice an unfamiliar youth who had moved closer to them but had at the same time been peering over the railing at the barges. And the man with the questions—I think of him as a jovial man with a mustache and a bowler hat—was so involved with his own questions that he cried out to the youth as well:

"'*Und Sie, junger Mann. Zement? Sand? Brennschiefer?*'

"(By the way, Herr Schmidt, when I present the story to you in this fashion, you will understand that I, to a certain extent, to make it fit the novel, begin to wonder whether it hadn't in fact happened later. And you will have been wondering—for reasons of credibility? Maybe this actually happened in the summer of '95, when Bernhard had already lost his hand. Perhaps he needed that loss to have already happened in order to make him a little cocky. Or maybe the people of Naissaar, the ones that saw and heard all of this, needed the loss of a hand to immortalize their tale?)

"So, the gentleman from Tallinn repeated: '*Also—Zement? Oder Sand? Oder Brennschiefer?*' And looked quizzically at the youth in the sparrow-gray jacket. And only now noticed that the pale young man, strangely enough, had no right hand. Or maybe he didn't notice . . . Because the boy wrinkled up his sharp nose and shook his head:

"'*Sägespäne.* Sawdust.'

"'What? How d'you arrive at that conclusion?'

"'It can't be anything else. Those barges can carry 150 tons. And they are full to the brim. Think of the specific weight involved. They would have sunk like a stone if that had been oil shale or cement. Sawdust is the only possible cargo.'

"The engineers obtained a megaphone from the captain and shouted across the water:

"'Where are you sailing? What are you carrying?'

"And from the tugboat they shouted back: 'To Paldiski. Sawdust. Needed to build the warehouses.'"

"No," says Erik Schmidt and smiles, "such a legend is quite unknown to us."

"You see," I say with a measure of pride, "how mythology has thrived locally."

"A myth is a myth," says Erik Schmidt, and puts his whiskey glass down on the table, "at any rate that tale belongs in that category of folklore . . . Though you don't have to accept my way of dividing the subject up. You see, I have long been of the opinion that the traditions of folklore—it is these elements specifically that I am dealing with here—can be divided into two groups. Into two groups by their—how shall I put it—immortality factor. In other words, according to under which fundamental circumstances they have been preserved for posterity. I am sure that folk poetry theoreticians will have claimed something similar. My way of dividing things up is off the cuff. One of those endless reinventions of thc wheel. And let us admit that Uncle Bernhard was not wholly immune to making such inventions. And now it suits us to use them. Anyway—two divisions. One of which has at its core a maximum amount of implausibility. The principle being: the less plausible, the longer lasting the legend. Tall tales, if you like. And the other, when the core of the tale contains a grain of truth. Whereby this truth is itself divided in two. It can be a mundane, ordinary, usual, quite impersonal type of plausibility. Or it can be connected to an unusual and very real occurrence that actually happened *in reality.* Well, you can find a suitable name for such stories that are not in themselves mere tall tales. My Estonian is neither adequate nor flexible enough to do so myself . . ."

"Herr Schmidt," I now say without having to do any pretending, "your Estonian is quite perfect—and it's been forty years now . . . But for want of a better term, such stories could be called *true tales.* And should you wish to divide them up according to their mundanity or rarity, well, then you could call the former parish tales, and for the latter you could delve into the dictionary compiled by our great lexicographer Saareste, who investigated the vocabulary of the island of Saaremaa and came up with *marras,* a word meaning both uncommon and threatening, and you could come up with something like *looming tales.*

"Why not, why not? Very good!" says Erik Schmidt with the eagerness of the young inventor of neologisms, Aavik. And I ask:

"So you are prepared to consign this sawdust legend of Bernhard's to the category looming tales?"

"I certainly am," says Erik Schmidt.

"But don't you feel that the clear decisiveness of the young lad is just a little too sharp witted? While the engineers are portrayed as being a little too . . ."

"Why too sharp witted? Clever, certainly. Even to an unusual degree. But is this not natural, in your opinion? When we remember that the young man was not just an ordinary lad. No-no, that sawdust tale is not known in our family. Otherwise I'd have heard it years ago. But there is one thing that my father said often: despite his chariness with words, as a boy Bernhard did express himself with peculiar clarity. I don't think my father ever said this in so many words, but the drift of his argument was: Bernhard availed himself of apposite and precise vocabulary and his mind worked in the same way. I can't call to mind any instances of this. But I do remember that according to what my father told me Bernhard had something of a phobia for the old men of the village when they began debating biblical matters . . . Not because he in any way behaved like an arrogant boy. That wasn't his style. But for reasons of logic. And I fear that also because of his irony, which had developed early in life.

I ask: "Like when we used to come up with trying questions at confirmation camp and pester the clergyman with them—such as, could God create such a large boulder that He Himself would be unable to lift it . . . ?"

"I don't really know, maybe," Erik Schmidt comments. "When I went to confirmation camp that was also a popular question among the boys there. But I do think that Bernhard's questions were less tricky and more serious. I do seem to remember one such story. Told, if not by my father, then by someone else. As you are aware, a kind of evangelical spirit held sway on Naissaar at the end of the last century. I'm not sure whether this was connected in any way with the Congregation of Brethren or the Baptists. At any rate they held some pretty dogmatic prayer meetings. And once—I'm not sure at whose house this was—Bernard was present. Happened to be present, I could add, but he was definitely there. Because Bernhard tended to keep aloof from things religious, to a certain extent because Uncle Frans was regarded on the island to be, well, a religious man—he was after all the sexton. And at this prayer meeting one of the local firebrands had explained, let the Old Testament be what it is, but the Gospels are at any rate written down from divine revelation and are therefore absolutely true. Whereupon Bernhard (I imagine he was fourteen or fifteen at the time) asked from the corner of the room: "But what if something in the Gospels is patently untrue?"

Well, they didn't exactly shoo him away. I can't tell whether this means that they took him and his question more seriously than we imagine, or just the opposite, that both were too childish. But anyway, they asked him rather abruptly *what* it was in the Gospels that was patently untrue! And he drew their attention to—what was it now? Not at all to one of those subjects that are always disputed, such as believing in miracles and the like. Those are things that a believer and a nonbeliever cannot even start to discuss, and this was clear to Bernhard. Though many of us adults don't understand such things even on our deathbeds. No. Bernhard drew their attention to the *arithmetic.* That's right. In Luke's Gospel you can read that a few days after the Crucifixion there were two disciples making their way to Emmaus on foot. I read this again recently. In connection with my work on the altarpiece. Two disciples, Cleopas and another one, whose name is not mentioned. And then everything happened, Christ's appearance and the disciples recognizing him, and so on. As Rembrandt painted. And then these two went back to Jerusalem. And on this point Bernhard asked the old men: How many disciples did Jesus have? Well, the old men of course replied: twelve. But Bernhard asked, if you took away Judas Iscariot how many would you have left? Well, said the old men: eleven. Bernhard had said: "I agree." But Luke writes—check it out for yourselves, if you don't believe me—that when those two, Cleopas and the other one, arrived back in Jerusalem from Emmaus, *they found eleven disciples there and joined them.* And Bernhard had said: out of the total of eleven who were left after Judas's departure, there could only have been nine there at the most when those two looked them up. Could anyone explain this in any other way than that Luke wasn't paying attention?

"Well, the old men of Naissaar couldn't," says Erik Schmidt, and sips his whiskey. "I happen to have talked to theologians, both Lutheran and Catholic, when I was painting my altarpiece last year. The theologians said conveniently that the two were disciples all right, but not two of the twelve chosen ones. Even though you could understand that to be the case from the text itself. But regarding those old men on Naissaar, maybe one grunted that this was sheer clever-dickery on the part of the boy. Because the boy certainly dotted his *i*'s and crossed his *t*'s when it came to such clever stuff. He said: 'But if this is a lack of attention, then it cannot be the Word of God. God doesn't make such mistakes. So it could only have been *human* error. But if that is the case, then you cannot say that the Gospels as a whole are divine revelation; rather, they are the work of man.'"

I say: "So you see, we can't escape stories about the child Jesus in the temple. Although, this last instance was really the reverse."

"But we can," Erik Schmidt replies immediately with a smile. "Right now, if I try to explain to you what sort of character Bernhard actually had."

"Ahah!" I exclaim in surprise. "Perhaps you want to say that his way of thinking corresponded in some way to the childishness of Jesus at the time? Something rather demonical? Or what?"

"No-no-no, not that. Nothing demonical. But, of course, not like Jesus either. Because when it boils down to it Bernhard was *ordinary.* As far as I know. Or can imagine. Because I don't have or couldn't have any personal observations that would reveal his character. Except for what has sometimes crossed my mind: if he had been someone who talked without inhibitions in order to make contact with others, then I would have remembered some of his joking banter when I was a child, some of his puns, or that he was on all fours with me straddled on his back playing doggies. Such scenes are ones that people tend to remember of their uncles from childhood. But I cannot remember anything like that in Uncle Bernhard's case. Nor the reverse, for that matter. So all I can tell you about his nature—if it is of any interest . . ."

"Of course it is!"

". . . all I can tell you are things I've heard from others in the family. And the thing you can best orient yourself by, and the whole family was more or less unanimous on this point, was that my father and Bernhard were very similar. Both regarding their appearance and their character. I know my father's character *relatively* well. Children tend not to know such things. Their parents are too close and children's life experience too short for them to be able to see their parents' nature in context. Later on, when they have grown up, they can better pin down their parents' personalities. If they don't start imagining things about them by way of compensation. Whether in a critical or idealizing direction. I imagine that my relationship to my father was too average for me to have distorted my memories of his personality in any significant way.

So: my father was essentially a village lad. Later on he did become a sea captain, that is true, and by the end of his life he had seen a fair amount. But the village boy in him was there right to the end. He was ninety when he died. Uncle Bernhard died when he was fifty-six. And I think that the village lad was present in him right to the end too.

As an adult, I have analyzed my impressions of my father and it would seem that the thing he kept most from his village days was his power of observation. Observation, whose wellspring is a lack of knowledge as to what is *comme il faut* and what isn't. Yes indeed. I know this from personal experience. I too am a village lad by origin. From Lõunaküla on Naissaar. Even though I did attend high school in the town of Haapsalu. But my roots are in the village. I felt that fear of not knowing what was *comme il faut* throughout my youth. Still in Tallinn, still in Stockholm. Not until I was in France as a twenty-five-year-old did this begin to gradually fade away. Partly for personal reasons, partly because of the unprejudiced nature of France, or at least of Paris.

My father never quite got past the shy village lad stage. And I am convinced that this was exactly the same with Uncle Bernhard. My father managed to keep in balance his insecurity with regard to the world at large when he was in his own sovereign little world, that is, on board ship as a captain. He strikes me as having been a very polite, very sensitive captain. But a captain who nevertheless enjoyed absolute power in his own little world. And there—as I have heard tell—he was a very clear-headed man in the most critical of circumstances. Such as when a German aircraft started bombing his ship right in the middle of the Bay of Biscay. In July 1940. But that is a whole story in itself. What I want to say is this: my father's point of security in the wide uncertain world of *comme il faut* was his ship. When cut off from the world by the breadth of the swell, or at least the thickness of the ship's hull. *His* sea and *his* ship. And in the case of Uncle Bernhard, his zone of security was actually above the world. Or at least beyond it: his telescope, which enabled him to enter that realm, and his heavens. And the worse he felt in the world of *comme il faut,* the more sovereign he felt in his own. But as for this inner shyness that I have mentioned, I think it was more pronounced in the case of Uncle Bernhard than with my father. First and foremost because in Uncle Bernhard's profession he did not have to lead other people or be responsible for their actions. His profession steered him in a solitary direction. Two people can't look through a telescope at once, let alone a whole group of people. But second, his shyness and fear of other people stemmed from the loss of his hand. What that loss meant to him, despite his virtuosity with only one—well, there are no confessions in that area. But let's take the story that is beyond any kind of Schmidtologia, I'm thinking of the photograph that shows Bernhard behind the wheel of a car. His friend Grünfeld took the picture—Bernhard is sitting in the front seat with his left hand on the steering wheel. But Grünfeld reversed the negative, as you well know. The result: Bernhard is holding the steering wheel with his right hand. A right hand that stands out clearly against the dark background. We all talked about it at home with a kind of pitying smile. Wondering how much of a joke this was to Bernhard, and to what extent he loved showing it to others."

Erik Schmidt's very slim, very Swedish, and very hospitable wife, Kerstin, wheels the tea trolley soundlessly into the room and serves us strong, steaming Earl Grey.

"No, don't let me disturb you! Do carry on with your Estonian tales . . ." She looks at me in a sad and amused way, and at her husband—I can't really tell, but nonetheless—slightly reprovingly. "I'm used to it . . ."

And Erik Schmidt says, laughing: "Kerstin, we've got onto a topic that is not intended for ladies' ears . . ." Then to me: "Your next question was, after all, Uncle Bernhard and women, wasn't it?"

"It certainly was," I admit, "but if necessary, we can always . . ."

"Oh no," laughs Erik Schmidt like a schoolboy, "far from it! It's all gossip really . . ." And he continues gleefully in Estonian. "Besides, I don't really know anything at all about the women in Bernhard's life. Primitive visits to girls who took money from him were quite commonplace. They say that he had a long-term love affair in Germany. I can only speculate why he didn't marry. I imagine he was afraid of being tied down. Also maybe some kind of self-critical modesty. Because if he was in any way like my father in these matters—and I imagine he was—then he will have been rather awkward with women, yet surprisingly successful. Yes, sir. What that success depended on you would have to ask the women he was with. I can only think it is because of one trait common to my father and Uncle Bernhard, and that is a kind of old-fashioned neatness. This would, at least in prewar years, have impressed many women. For example—if we touch on the topic of the *comme il faut* problem—my father always used to sport more tip-top clothes than what you would call his social class prescribed. Even in his days at the naval school, but also when he was a boatswain with local shipping companies. Always a hard collar, a carefully chosen tie and pearl tiepin, a paste one initially, but a pearl nonetheless. Always a clean shirt, a decent suit, never without a vest, a bowler hat, an overcoat with a velvet collar, and so forth. Such a tradition was common to the whole of Naissaar. Or at least among the Schmidts. We used to have here, in the wardrobe inherited from my great-grandfather, a number of Sunday-best jackets and hats from the days when they used to wear knickerbockers. And Grandmother would, from time to time, put orange peel in the pockets against the moths. My mother continued the habit. So it became a kind of tradition. But my father aimed at wearing tip-top apparel—to a degree this was, of course, the spirit of the turn of the century. But mostly it was his village boy's worry about being *comme il faut.* And ultimately, habit. I am talking about my father, but I am sure that Uncle Bernhard was just the same. And in his mind, too. Except that my father was an ordinary person, while Bernhard was—well—at any rate, a . . ."

Erik Schmidt purses his lips over the edge of his whiskey glass and searches for the appropriate word. I want to test his attitude—maybe even his nature, and suggest:

". . . genius?"

"Well," he says slowly, but without embarrassment, "let us leave that for others to utter. And it has been said of him. As you well know. I will say of him, being a close relation, you understand (I hope this isn't too churlish, because the people of Naissaar have never been such), I would simply say: *an unusual person,* at any rate. Yes. Despite that he was very like my father. With regard to appearance you can see for yourself . . ." Erik Schmidt hands me the photo album and also places photos of his father and Bernhard side by side on the table. In his younger years Bernhard was more delicate and somehow more transparent than August. Later on, they grew in similarity. As Bernhard grew stouter with the years. And in the last photo taken of him in the summer of 1935 it is impossible, for someone looking only at photos, to tell them apart. If they do manage it would be by looking at their faces. August would by that time have been in his early fifties, and still had an easygoing, pleasant mien. For Bernhard, now fifty-six, the bitterness of experience has begun to show around the mouth.

"You can see for yourself," says Erik Schmidt, now sipping tea, "that the similarity between my father and Uncle Bernhard is so great—and also by inner criteria—that I would say, if it were not a rather cheap paradox, that *even their differences were similar.* And however forced it may sound—believe you me—there is a grain of truth in it."

"And what are you thinking of . . . ?"

"Among other things, the following. I have never heard that Bernhard ever had a serious interest in meteorology. Or weather forecasting, if you like. Or in any sort of skill at, or inclination for, prognosis. I can imagine that the weather only interested him to the degree that it affected his observations and photography, which the weather can help or hinder. Let's say on the Philippines. When he'd traveled halfway across the world. And then when he wanted to take photos at the appointed time, the sky happened to cloud over, and the whole reason for the voyage was to take photos of the sun. So, whether the sky was clear or not. Otherwise it didn't interest him one jot.

"On the other hand, my father was very sensitive to changes in the weather and took an everyday interest in it. Of course, being a seaman, he depended a good deal more, and more regularly, on the weather than did Bernhard. And his interest in the weather and changes in it (*Where will the wind turn tonight?* or *Will that wisp of cloud bring us rain or not?* etc.) was well known to his family. As were his forecasts. And even more so to his crew. I remember this from when I sailed with him once. He stepped out of his cabin in the morning and looked around on the deck or the bridge—looked in one direction, then the other. First with eyes screwed up and his nose a little wrinkled, then suddenly with a curious listening expression on his face. And said to the boatswain, 'At midday the wind will turn to the northwest and by dinnertime we'll have rain.' Or (after hearing on the radio that there would be a storm coming from the northeast that evening), 'But by that time we'll have left it astern.' Or, 'Rubbish! It'll have abated before it's even started blowing.' And so on. Practically speaking, without ever making a mistake. Year in, year out. So at sea the crew would listen to the weather forecast only to compare it to what the captain had said, then grin at the inaccuracy of the official forecast. Because my father would foresee changes in the weather not only for the next day but also often a couple of days ahead. And—nota bene—with an accuracy of a couple of hours on either side. I remember asking him when I was already a big boy, thirteen or fourteen years old:

"'Tell me, where do you get it all from?'

"My father thought for a moment, then said: 'You know, it's hard to explain. The symptoms are there in the sky. The only thing is—there are a hell of a lot of them. Taken individually, I don't grasp their significance. But when you take them together they give you a sure indication that this or that is going to happen.'"

I now ask: "And you imagine that Bernhard would tackle his own field of stellar optics in much the same way?"

"In exactly the same way!" Erik Schmidt says eagerly. "Of course Bernhard did have a scientific approach to things based on physics and mathematics. At the same time as my father was going only on experience. But even for Bernhard, a scientific point of departure, or shall we say the development of such, was not in any way a set course. Insofar as I've seen some of his sketches—there are plenty of them left among the material kept at Bergedorf, all the preliminary sketches and drafts. Sometimes surprisingly sketchy first drafts. When we compare them with the almost pathological precision with which the final *objects* were constructed. I have asked myself: How can this contrast be explained? Well, it would be easiest to say: the exacter sketches, the perfect blueprints, have simply been lost. But this just isn't particularly likely. Why should those specific ones happen to have been lost, while the vaguer drafts and sketches are still extant? If you entertain the thought of selective loss, then surely it would be the other way round. But the most plausible explanation is, in my opinion, that Bernhard never made any more precise and accurate blueprints. You see what I mean? Because he didn't need any. He could manage quite well with those scribbly drawings that he had made with a badly sharpened pencil on any old sheet of paper he happened to have handy. Or had drawn among notes and equations using the same scrappy pen with which he was noting these things down. He never used a ruler, either for the pencil or pen sketches, nor a pair of compasses. They are scribbled on paper; the cross-sections of concave lenses often look more like Jugendstil vases that have melted askew, while the convex ones look like a boat with pointed prow and stern drawn by a child . . . How was it that these sufficed for him? I think that once his mathematical and logical train of thought had reached, let's say, level *x,* he made what was to a certain extent a leap in the dark. Have you not noticed: everyone, or almost everyone, who has characterized his theoretical thinking—Schorr, Wachmann, and the rest—has talked in one way or other of *intuition*? And that's exactly what it was! Suddenly, intuitively, Uncle Bernhard would see the completed construction, the finished object, in his mind's eye. And could see it in such detail, and so clearly, that he immediately moved on to constructing the object manually. And he realized his own idea—I can't say whether this would be on every occasion, but for many at least he would seem to be moving forward with the sureness of a sleepwalker . . ."

I say: "So you see how we have moved from the question of Bernhard Schmidt's intrinsic character to what type of creator he was. In the case of men like him it is almost one and the same thing. And now, if you will allow, there is one of the questions I sent you that centers on *family matters.* You see, in just about every other matter, and with a bit of luck, you can find information, from indirect if not direct sources, about various things. Except, that is, for purely family matters. And in this area, Herr Schmidt, you are my only hope. Because I cannot go and look up your aunt Ester in Belgium or France—what was it she was called: Madame de Vernou de Bouneuil. If she were still to be alive, and if she would agree to speak to me. And if she knew anything. Although it is true that she might be able to provide interesting information."

"What question are you thinking of?" asks Erik Schmidt.

"How Bernhard got on with his stepfather."

"Why would you be thinking that there is anything to ask there . . . ?" Erik Schmidt fills our small cognac glasses. Kerstin has been watering the flowers in the garden for some time now. I explain:

"I do not actually *know* anything. I only have two small observations. The first is this: in 1901 Bernhard fills in a form that is needed by the technical college in Mittweida. This form has been preserved and its contents have been published on a number of occasions. On the form there is a question about whether the applicant has a parent or guardian. At that time, Bernhard's mother and stepfather have been married for four years. This all happened around the beginning of the century, that is, in the days when *the man* was regarded as the head of the family. Especially in such small conservative communities as on Naissaar at the time. But Bernhard writes on this form: *Maria Schmidt.* From which I conclude that Bernhard—now a young man of twenty-two—has *not* accepted his stepfather as such. Another observation: look at this photo . . ."

I place a small photo in front of Erik Schmidt, a serendipity find in Tallinn, which shows a dozen or so people standing around a grave. As the person who gave me the photo confirmed (and as can be seen on the ribbon attached to the wreath), this is the grave of Maria Schmidt in the cemetery in Naissaar. The photo is said to have been taken on March 23, 1930. I say:

"This picture was taken thirty years after the form in question was filled in. Look how they are standing around the grave."

(They are grouped rather unusually. It could, of course, be coincidence. Right next to the cross, Frans Henrik Schmidt is standing, that is, Maria's second husband and Bernhard's uncle and stepfather. Bernhard is standing to his left, but one and a half meters away. Immediately in front of Bernhard stand the sisters Olga and Berta. August is not in the photo. Maybe he is taking the picture.)

I say: "Consciously or unconsciously, he is standing a good distance away. This can mean one of two things—either a mark of deep respect, or a mark of deep animosity. And we may have to dismiss the possibility of deep respect . . ."

"Let's do so," says Erik Schmidt.

"Then all that remains is animosity. I mean to say: he has not managed to accept his stepfather even after thirty years. Such things do occur. Usually for some quite ordinary reasons. But what reasons could there have been for this animosity between Bernhard and his stepfather?"

"Well, I would imagine that they were the same type of reasons. Ordinary ones," says Erik Schmidt, "maybe a little more acute . . . Look, I don't necessarily think that a son has to get on badly with his father. Because of jealousy regarding the mother. As our wise Freudians have almost confirmed. The critical moment in father-son relations can occur with boys in a milder or a more severe form. But

I agree with the school of thought that in most cases the relation between them is quite normal. And when it is a case of a father who has died young, then there is almost some degree of idealization. And when, in such a situation, the elder boy, that is, the one shouldering the burden of responsibility, suddenly realizes that his mother is about to get—or has already got—a new husband, and a kind of shadow father for him, then it often happens that the boy feels doubly betrayed. And then revolts. Well, such a revolt never arose in Bernhard. As far as we know. But how much do we really know? Maybe his taciturn nature, something that was already talked about during his childhood, was in itself a form of protest. Was it? A kind of 'if I can't say what I think, you'll get what you deserve, and I'll keep my gob shut' reaction. Maybe his attachment to spyglasses, his interest in telescopes and binoculars, was also a kind of revolt. Looking at objects on the horizon, things light-years away—because there was something hurtful in things nearer home."

"OK," I say, "but you did say recently that Bernhard did not have the usual stepfather problems. So how do these things tally?"

"Because clearly Uncle Frans had two qualities that got on Bernhard's nerves. First, Uncle Frans was a big shot on Naissaar. Or shall we say that ever since his youth he had been pretty visible on the island. Handsome, energetic, enterprising. Such as the girls would make eyes at. Someone who was fully aware of his worth. So that, I don't know, but I imagine that Bernhard had an inferiority complex in addition to the usual dislike of stepfathers. And second, for Bernhard, Frans always remained a kind of joke uncle: he was, after all, only fourteen years Bernhard's senior. So that to Bernhard's mind, the man belonged less to his father's generation than to his own. And therefore seemed all the more unsuitable in his role of uncle . . ."

I think aloud: "Out of that feeling there must presumably emerge a kind criticism of his mother's behavior. Above and beyond the usual criticisms regarding stepfathers."

"That would seem logical," Erik Schmidt admits. "An accusation, whether spoken or unspoken, that by marrying Uncle Frans she was behaving even more light-headedly than widows usually do when remarrying. Because she had chosen this rather extravagant man. By the way, in the eyes of some village moralists this action was a plus for Bernhard's mother. I think because she had married her dead husband's brother, as Moses commands. But in the eyes of others—and maybe Bernhard's—this did not improve matters. And Frans was, after all, five or six years younger than Bernhard's mother."

I ask: "But his mother was—at least later on—nevertheless the central person in Bernhard's life, was she not?"

"Oh, sure she was," says Erik Schmidt. "And this is quite understandable. Because my grandmother was—or let's call her his mother—she was a person of standing on the island. From what I could see, the people of the island did not take badly to her second marriage. She had received—when she married her first husband at the age of eighteen—a dowry of five hundred gold rubles. That is true. But after her husband's long decline, there was precious little left. So in fact, Maria was a poor widow with four children and a rather ramshackle house; not that she suffered real hunger, but they had a pretty needy time of it. A husband was a real necessity for running their home. The practical-minded islanders understood this. Understood this and granted her more and more respect over the years. I get the impression that in old age she was one of the most respected women on the island. Because of her medical skills. And her sunny disposition. In my opinion, all of Bernhard's stays on Naissaar were in effect a return to his mother. To what extent, I cannot tell. Because the island was quite a strange place. The island and his mother were in effect the embodiment of each other."

▪ ▫ ▪ ▫ ▪

7

NOW I ALREADY KNOW THAT MY PLATE WORKS.

When the cigar between my teeth goes out, I walk next door to the precision mechanics to get a light. Not because I couldn't light it myself by striking a match. Simply because those sixty paces—along the corridor into the adjacent cellar and back—offer a change of air. The precision mechanics' Bunsen burners have already been roaring away since the morning. Sometimes I go along to them ten times a day. Not to chat, naturally. We rarely exchange any words at all. But sometimes I hear what they are chattering about. If I go in without knocking. Recently I heard how the senior mechanic Schmidt, Paul Schmidt that is, was telling young Schulze: "If Herr Schmidt is on a winning streak, he always says: the world will hear about Schmidt—not about me but about himself, I mean . . ." Then they see me and fall silent. And I think: hee hee hee hee. Quite likely I said that once when I was in a good mood. And now it's going to come true. Just a matter of time . . . ?

God Almighty, two weeks ago I managed to create my first little plate using the vacuum pump for the small teaching telescope, and I turned the telescope on a random object. It happened to be a sunny day and so I chose an object on earth, something that just happened to be in front of me. This was a gravestone among the bushes in the new cemetery, two hundred meters from the railings of the observatory. I focused on it and couldn't believe my eyes . . . it was as if every unevenness, every grain on its surface, whether black or pink, were *right here.* As sharp as if they were right under my nose and I was looking at them through a ten-times-magnification magnifying glass!

Only later did I ask myself whose gravestone this might be. And I remained in ignorance. As it was standing with its back facing the observatory and the name was written on the other side. And later I suppose I asked (or maybe I didn't) whether it was significant that the first thing I focused on was where we all end up . . . ? All silliness, of course.

In mid-February I had everything I had ordered for my coma-free telescope: the tube, all the necessary adjustment knobs and screws, a camera with all its bits and pieces, plus a tripod. A week later the new telescope was already standing on the balcony of the meridian circle building: the tube, or box, rather, was one and a half meters long, the aperture thirty-six centimeters across. At the same time my first series of photos was lying on Schorr's office desk.

God—I *must* be allowed some tiny personal feats of progress. After so many failed experiments . . . I will never forget the way in which Schorr looked at the photos . . .

He pursed his lips under his old-fashioned walrus mustache, a mustache resembling that of our own Estonian author Eduard Vilde, and raised his eyebrows so that his very serious director's face somehow became comically excited. It struck me then that it was as if he had just heard of the arrival of his eighth child after the preceding seven . . . He eyed the photos and looked me in the face. Eyed them again, looked at me again. Then he leapt up from behind his writing desk and toddled, short stout man that he was, toward me. He gasped.

"Schmidt—tell me—how did you manage it . . . ? Is this what you were telling Baade about . . . ? It's *incredible*! We must show it to Baade . . ."

He snatched up the telephone receiver and got Baade on the line in his workshop. Five minutes later Baade had arrived. Schorr stepped from behind his desk and beckoned to Baade:

"Look!"

They bent over the photos and were both silent for a minute. I had retreated to the window. For a moment I observed Baade's pale, concentrated, Red Indian face. Then I felt embarrassed observing them like that and looked out of the window. I saw: old mother Clara, our cleaner, standing in the courtyard of the director's residence and walking toward us carrying a bucket of hot water in one hand and in the other a long-handled mop. Then Baade asked me, as he looked at one of the photos:

"You've done these with that plate of yours? You managed to make it? As you said you would after that storm in the Sea of Andaman?"

I nodded.

"Do you realize what this means?" asked Schorr.

I nodded.

Baade said: "It means that Herr Schmidt's telescope will expand the visibly observable universe—well—by how much?"

I shrugged my shoulders. How was I to know? As it would be a great simplification to put a figure on it, say *x* times. When simplifying things consciously you can of course do this. But let them come up with a figure. When I myself have *thought* what it might be.

Schorr snuffled a little over the photos, and Baade said:

"Around ten or twelve times. This, at any rate, is an *explosion.*"

Schorr wiped his forehead with a handkerchief and straightened up:

"Professor Baade! Herr Schmidt!" He did not even now forget the order in which Baade and I should be mentioned, but I did not hold it against him because of all the directors I have ever dealt with he was the most easygoing. "Professor Baade! Herr Schmidt! On the occasion of this event—Herr Schmidt's explosive invention—and as Professor Baade has so appositely said—as I myself would also say—this Nova Proxissima—you must know how *little* I like it, especially considering the fact," he jerked his head in my direction then to the air between Baade and myself, "but on the occasion of this exceptional event—please—let us go in to my place and drink a glass of *sekt.*"

Well, on a good deal less suitable occasions I have not refused such a proposal.

We stepped out into the courtyard and walked through bare trees of the park flecked with snow in the direction of the director's residence. Schorr led the way with shorts steps, and as always only made little progress. Baade walked behind him with elegant long strides—as always. And I followed some ten paces behind, my hand in my trouser pocket. That is to say, as always, that too.

What people gossip about the director's residence is none of my business. I have not lived there. I first lived in the white employees' block, in an attic room. Until Professor Schwassmann began to covet the room for his maid. So I moved to a private flat. In a small red-brick building, as many were in that area. Right across from our main gates, in the home of a vegetable salesman. Whose name, by weird coincidence, was also Schmidt. Karl Schmidt, just like my father. They would not have managed to prize me out of my room in the observatory building had I myself not wanted to move. But I agreed. I had been thinking of moving for quite a while. Because a private flat would mean greater independence. That of course. But what they have said about the director's residence is as follows: that Schorr had had it built before the Great War using state money; a small castle, a small luxury villa with eight or ten rooms. At that time he was a bachelor—well, not quite as old as I am now, but still around forty-five . . . And he had moved all alone into this proud white house. Yes. While living there he not only managed to arrange his catalogue of the sky of the northern hemisphere but also took a wife . . . That too. He had started wooing his maid, a sprightly young thing who at first vacillated between accepting the offer from one of the works mechanics or from Schorr. He wooed his maid and in the end they had seven children . . . Well, I'm not one of Schorr's subordinates. I cooperate with him on a voluntary basis. I have a special relationship to him. But he became so dominant that even his underlings began calling him *papa.* And everyone forgave him his eight rooms because of the seven children.

During my three or four years at Bergedorf, I had actually entered only one of these rooms: the bedroom on the mansard. When Papa Schorr was bedridden with gallbladder problems, but wanted to hear about the progress of the polishing of one of the mirrors. *Now,* I entered after the others into the director's dining room.

Anyway. There was so much glitter from crystal objects in there that there was no end of raw material for precision instruments. There were no fewer than three couches upholstered in silk. Not to mention the armchairs and dining-room chairs. And the bottle of *sekt* that Papa himself went to fetch from the kitchen was a flagon covered with pleasantly cool condensation. He opened it with a pop and filled the three glasses. He looked at us triumphantly and announced:

"Dear colleagues! We will now drink a glass to Herr Schmidt's grand invention in the hope—what do I mean, hope—in the sure knowledge that Herr Schmidt's invention will once again bring fame to our Bergedorf!"

We drank up our glasses and Schorr refilled them. Baade said, and I thought I detected a slight tremor in his voice: "These photos mean that, to a certain extent, Herr Schmidt has shattered the limits of the mirror. What now prevents further development of the telescope is of a different order. It is the granular size of the photo emulsion. By the way, Herr Schmidt, have you yourself calculated this—it is possible to draw elementary conclusions from the increase in density of the stars in your photos—how far away are the most distant objects that can be seen through your telescope?"

I shook my head. I had in fact made a rough calculation as to the distance. But it seemed too much taken from the realms of fantasy for me to name it. Let them estimate for themselves, if they so wished. And Baade did just that:

"I would say—two to three hundred million light-years."

Schorr exclaimed:

"We shall not just at this moment begin to ask how Herr Schmidt has managed to take these remarkable photographs. That is to say, in what way he managed to construct his correction plate. I can imagine that the surface of this plate only deviates a few ten-thousandths of the thickness of the plate. But how one can polish such a plate to perfection is something that I cannot imagine. Nor, no doubt, can Professor Baade . . ."

"No, I am quite unable to do so," admitted Baade with a smile.

"Even if it is of primary interest," Schorr continued, "we will not ask him right now. Because I wish to speak about something else. Colleague Baade does not yet know this, but colleague Schmidt does. Erm, there have sometimes been certain misunderstandings between ourselves and colleague Schmidt. For understandable reasons. And do you know what he answered recently—when I kept coming in to him and said, rather critically, that he goes for walks too often, yes *too often,* in the Vierlande. And that just wasn't scientific activity. . . He does walk around there too on occasions. In order to observe the flight of the storks, I know . . ." (And I was thinking: what a creep. Is there anything he hasn't managed to observe!) "Sometimes he walks through the hayfields with a pole in his hand, and on that pole some wind propeller or other, whose effectivity he wants to check . . . But mostly I've seen him treading the paths of the Vierlande in the direction of the Holtenklinke and Curslack inns . . . And when I addressed him about the matter, do you know what he replied? Word for word: *Professor Director, sir,—when I walk through the greenery of the Vierlande, I am at any rate doing more scientific work than many a director as he sits at his green baize-covered desk!* Yes. Wham! So that I do have to admit that I felt hurt. But now, Herr Schmidt, after these photographs of yours, that is to say, after the completion of the device with which you have taken them—now, I have to admit . . ." He put down his empty glass on the desk and spread his short arms in a hearty manner, then said: ". . . it cannot be denied: *you* were right."

I looked out of the window. So that he would not notice the triumphant twitch at the corner of my mouth.

We agreed right there that the observatory would buy my telescope for five thousand marks. And that for the same price I would over the next year build them a second one. After that agreement there was no reason for me to hang around the director's residence any longer. Baade stayed and I left. So that by the time I reached the main building to retrieve my photos from his desk, old mother Clara the cleaner was already there. The eight photos were still there on Schorr's desk exactly as I'd left them: four in a row to the left and four to the right. So four pairs, the left-hand ones taken without the correction plate, the right-hand ones with. This meant that what looked like one large star in the left-hand photos proved to be ten to twenty smaller dots in the right-hand ones. And Frau Clara, a large-boned fifty-year-old woman, was standing there, hands on her hips, looking at the photos.

This sort of thing doesn't particularly surprise me. At the observatory there are around a dozen or more workers: mechanics, the janitor, the gardener, the driver, and cleaners. The more alert of them take a certain interest in the scientific work of the institution, out of good manners. And a number of people who entirely lack any scientific background nevertheless have unexpected interests and preferences. For instance in the case of the brush-binder, Vick. This short swarthy man with a walleye came to sell his wares to our janitor a couple of years ago. When he had sold something he asked to be introduced to the director. He asked Schorr whether he could be allowed to calculate the route of a specific comet. When Schorr, smiling a little ironically, had given him a few basic values, Vick also asked for a couple of blank sheets of paper. "So that you don't suspect me of using crib notes, you understand." And went and sat at an empty table in the library. Then he laid the strap with which he bound together his bundles on the floor. And before the eyes of a couple of young librarians was ready with his calculations in one and a half hours. Something that even an educated person could hardly have done any more quickly. So that Schorr took him on immediately to be responsible for calculations. When it is a matter of pigeonholing people that *entirely lack scientific background*—aren't I one of them? At least to a certain degree . . . ?

But I have never before noticed any interest on mother Clara's part. Now she is standing upright in front of the photos, her hands still on her hips:

"Herr Schmidt, do explain to me, which of these pictures have been taken by your magical telescope? They were talking about it in the office. But I can't make head or tail of it."

I hadn't really wanted to go into detail because I had a slight fear that she might make advances. And why not? In comparison to the wife of the director, I regard her as a good deal more suitable for flirtation. Hell and damnation. But I can't just brush off her question. I ask:

"What differences have you noticed between them?"

"If these are supposed to be the stars in the heavens—the left-hand pictures look like dried bilberries. And like little plums round the edges. But those to the right—they're not even as big as fly droppings . . ."

"So you see!" I say, a little disappointed nonetheless, "the fly droppings are done using my magical telescope."

"What are you telling me!" cries Clara in genuine surprise, and glances at me swiftly with her yellowed eyes. I still want to impress her nevertheless. So I take my ninth photo out of my pocket. I intended to show it to Schorr and Baade over the glass of *sekt* we were drinking, but desisted at the very last moment. It would have seemed too childish to show them it . . .

"Do you recognize what's in this picture?"

"Sure," says Clara. "That's Herr Manow's windmill. Here in Wentorf."

"And what would you say about the photo?

"Nothing special about it. A nice clear picture. No doubt taken as evening was drawing in. The windows of the miller's house are white. But otherwise it's all very sharp. You can count the ribs of the vanes. And the twigs in the tops of the trees. Didn't the miller's dog give you a bite in the leg? It was taken from so nearby."

I shake my head: "It wasn't taken from nearby. It was taken using my telescope. And you know where that's standing."

"What!" cries Clara with unexpected expertise. "You mean that this photo was taken from two kilometers away!"

"Yes, that's right. From a distance of two kilometers. And in the dead of night. Last night between one and three. In pitch darkness."

"Listen—Herr Schmidt—if that is true—then you are—the Wizard of Bergedorf . . ."

Hell—I was glad and embarrassed at one and the same time. I did realize that both the gladness and the embarrassment were foolish, but for some excruciating reason I was experiencing both at once.

Then the door to Schorr's office opened and in slipped the ever-blushing forty-year-old Fräulein Berger from the secretariat:

"Oh good, Herr Schmidt, you're still here. There's a telegram for you . . ."

She handed me the folded paper, glued at the edges. I had no reason to delay opening it. What did I have to keep secret? And furthermore I just knew that this message was going to be bad news. I ripped open the telegram and read:

MOTHER ILL COME HOME IMMEDIATELY BERTA

"Has something—bad—happened . . . ?" asked Fräulein Berger, and looked at me with her round brown eyes.

"Look at you—you've gone all pale!" cried Clara. "What did it say?"

I shouldn't explain anything to them. It's none of their business. I should simply collect together my photos and hurry home. I scoop them up but then hand them the telegram to read.

"You see," mutters Clara, "she must be seriously ill."

"Oh, so you'll of course be traveling home—to your island . . . ?" Fräulein Berger wonders. "But—how old is your mother?

I don't need to explain anything. But I say: "Oh, she's not seventy yet."

Old Clara says soothingly, "Well then, she's bound to get better . . ."

And Fräulein Berger bursts out in almost indiscreet surprise with: "Oh you've got such a young mother, Herr Schmidt!"

And I understand full well that after that cry I have now opened up the opportunity for them to also cry out that they have noticed, as Fräulein Berger had now pointed out what a young man Herr Schmidt must be, given how young his mother is—silly of me . . .

I give a wave to the ladies and hurry out of the office and the main building, and think, on my way over to the director's residence: it must be serious. Berta, with her own kidney problems, has seen so many bad times and suffered in silence that she would not send a telegram for some trivial reason.

Baade has by now left the director's residence, but Schorr is still there. I show him the telegram. I tell him I'm traveling home. Only when I've already said this does it occur to me that I should perhaps have asked formally for *permission* to do so. But I am, after all, a voluntary collaborator and I have never asked for such permission before. I accept the chit from Schorr for the two thousand marks I'll be collecting from the bookkeeper. I am just about to leave. Schorr says:

"I hope that your mother gets better. And that you're back in a couple of weeks' time . . ."

"I hope so too . . ."

"But listen," says Schorr, "while you are away—and it could happen that you are away for a long time—in order not to waste time, would you allow me to draft a brochure about your new telescope? And have it printed? And send it out?"

I shrug my shoulders.

"What shall I write?" Schorr wonders. "Let's say like this . . ." And he picks up a sheet of paper with text in large letters:

BERNHARD SCHMIDT
ASTRO-OPTICIAN
Bergedorf, Gojenbergsweg 108
WILL CONSTRUCT A COMA-FREE TELESCOPE
WITH A COMPLETELY SHARP FIELD OF VISION

"Like that. And then we'll have a photo of your miracle instrument. With the caption:

This is the Bergedorf coma-free telescope
Light intensity 1:1.75, aperture 36 cm, focal length 62.5 cm,
fully sharp field of vision 15 degrees."

"Is this all true . . . ?" asks Schorr, and looks with pleasure at his text.

I mutter: "Sure it's all true. But no one will believe it."

"Come on," says Schorr with a laugh, "everyone will see from the photo and our name—even if not immediately from yours—that this isn't a joke. And they will ask after us. What shall I put as the price?"

I shrug my shoulders. ". . . Ah, er, well, nothing too high . . ."

"OK, not *too* high. But it has to be a serious price nonetheless. We'll do it like this: the price, including a quadratic camera, a viewfinder, and a cassette (but exclusive of the directional tube and the mounting) will be 5,500 reichsmarks. Agreed?"

"Well, yes, agreed . . ." I say.

"Marvelous!" says Schorr, all smiles. "Everything will, naturally, take time. But if I'm not completely mistaken, by the time you return and your mother has completely recovered, as I hope, let's say in two weeks or a month—you will be a rich man. Oh yes, indeed. Because once we send out this brochure, orders will start coming in for your telescope, first of all enquiries, which are as good as orders—in unimaginable numbers."

I remain silent.

"Come on," says Schorr, "let's shake on it. On your departure and return."

Schorr is occasionally a little odd. I walk up to him and shake his hand. The fact that a left hand and a right hand do not fit together perfectly always affects me.

When I have been at the bookkeeper's and am already outside the grounds of the observatory and want to cross the street in the direction of Karl Schmidt's, that is, to my own place, I start thinking that I have, over the whole of yesterday evening and night, and the whole of today, not had more than a glass of milk with the precision mechanics at half past six in the morning. So I walk on four houses past Schmidt's and enter Land's bar.

Old Land is having his lunchtime nap right now, but his daughters, Emmi and Fanny, have kept my vegetarian dinner warm for me. I eat rapidly, fried potatoes and sauerkraut, and drink a mug of lager. And a handful of cranberries with the beer. As always—gooseberries in summer, cranberries in winter. A quarter of an hour later I am back home packing my things into a briefcase for the journey. There's not very much: a leather box with shoe polish and a brush, my pajamas (which I don't really like, am a little suspicious of; they remind me of a straitjacket), clean underwear, a couple of handkerchiefs, and a razor. That's all. And basic drawing equipment. I always travel as light as possible. Like Phileas Fogg. And today like him especially. While I do not have any passe-partouts with me, I do have in my pocket, well, not quite ten pounds sterling, but at least I have my two thousand German marks . . . I go out into the hall and take my rather worn black winter coat with its marvelous velvet collar (on Naissaar it also serves as a spring and autumn coat) and call out in the direction of the kitchen:

"Frau Schmidt! I'm off on a journey. For about a week. Maybe more. If I stay away longer, ask Professor Schorr for news. Goodbye!"

Frau Schmidt comes to the kitchen door, her face flushed from the cooking. She says something and asks something. I give her a wave and shut the partition door.

I go back to the hat shelf, take down my everyday black winter hat, and put it on. Then I happen to look in the mirror (it belongs to the host family and is in our joint entrance) and stop. That hat is hardly suitable for Naissaar and its sea winds. The wind would blow it off my head at every step and send it rolling across the snowdrifts . . . And it wouldn't really fit in out there among the fur caps of the local men. I am a gentleman to various people; that is true. But not for the people of Naissaar, not for them. And what is most important of all: I feel—when I go out to the island wearing my black fur cap (the peak is still shiny and without cracks)—then, and only then, can I hope that Mother will get better . . . God, what childishness . . . I don my peaked cap, the one I bought in some junk shop at Kalaranna in Tallinn, and run to the bus stop near the gate to the graveyard.

As soon as I am sitting in an empty carriage of the afternoon *S-Bahn* train that is humming its way to Hamburg, a rather pointless thought strikes me: *if only I knew what was wrong with Mother . . .* In fact that would not help matters. I am sure that Berta will do all she can with regard to medical assistance. But what conclusion should be drawn by the fact that Mother is clearly still on the island? And not in the hospital in Tallinn. It surely cannot mean that her illness is so trivial that she needn't be taken to the hospital—but is serious enough for me to be sent a telegram asking me to come home. And Mother *must be* on the island. Otherwise the telegram would say where she is. And she is likely to still be on the island because her condition is too serious for her to travel to Tallinn . . . There is, of course, another possibility, and that is that the pack ice prevents her from being taken to Tallinn. But in that case I won't be able to get to the island either. Oh, if only I knew what was wrong with her. And whether God will help her the way he helped her once before—in 1890 or whenever it was. I know of this principally from hearsay. In a word—Mother felt bad and went to Dr. Greifenhagen at the Deaconesses' Nursing Home for an operation. With the diagnosis that she had cancer. She was entirely convinced that she was going to die. So she had had her hair cut short and the clippings sent to someone to make small memorial plaits from—watch chains for the boys and bracelets for the girls. But after the operation she began to get better and finally grew well again. Up to now. Such a recovery could repeat itself, whether by way of a wrong diagnosis or a miracle—but it was pointless to place one's hopes in such . . .

The next morning in Stettin, I learned that the southern shore of the Gulf of Finland and the straits between the islands had already been free of pack ice from the second week of March. So that only bad things could be assumed regarding Mother's health.

My financial situation at the time would have allowed me to travel with the express steamer, the *Rügen.* Compared with sailing on some freighter I would have won ten hours. But the *Rügen* was not going to set sail until the day after tomorrow. So that I chose the slower vessel in order to arrive there quicker. After I had heard that a Finnish ship, the *Ilmatar,* was setting sail for Tallinn in three hours' time and that Captain Förbom had assured me he would do the best he could. Two days later, in the afternoon, we were already sailing past the Suurupi lighthouse and approaching Naissaar, so that the blackish Kabelikari and beyond that the yellow houses of the village of Lõunaküla emerged ever more clearly out of the spring mists. The wind was rather biting and there were white horses and chunks of pack ice on the surface of the sea. The ship raised the pilot flag and within a quarter of an hour the pilot boat was sailing toward us. On that boat were the Berg boys, Jakob and Kristjan. The winch rope was lowered and I was down in the boat in a few moments. A sailor from the *Ilmatar* lowered my briefcase down after me. I waved back to the ship, then looked into the weather-beaten faces of the Berg boys and asked:

"What's wrong with Mother?"

Kristjan pulled the sail to port and Jakob pressed his weight against the oar so that the boat swung round so violently that I was forced to grab the crossbench.

"She's had a stroke," muttered Kristjan.

"But—still alive . . . ?" I asked hoarsely through the rush of the waves.

"Alive," said Kristjan, ". . . except that . . ."

He said no more, and I asked no further questions. In twenty minutes' time, my neck wet with spray, I was in the boat harbor, and home.

Berta and Uncle Frans were in the house. And August's Johanna was there with her five-year-old Eerik. Mother was lying in bed in the back room, very small, very pale, and appeared to be sleeping. When I stood by the bed, speaking in a whisper with Berta and Frans, she opened her eyes slightly, only her left eye actually, there was something strange in that, and it was as if she recognized me when she saw me and tried to smile. But maybe this was my imagination.

Frans shrugged his shoulders and turned his stony face aside. Berta explained, as she gave me something to eat in the next room: Mother had cleaned the rooms on Saturday and then begun to bring in the ready-chopped firewood to the sauna. And she had taken it into the sauna, but not returned to the house. Until Uncle Frans, coming back from the boats, had gone to look for her. And found her on the floor of the sauna, slumped there among the logs, quite unconscious. He had carried Mother into the house and put her to bed. And this was now the fifth day that she had been lying there.

I cried: "But a doctor! Haven't you called a doctor?" I myself noticed that my two thousand reichsmarks had increased my pride and I was shouting this as if summoning a doctor to the island was the most ordinary thing in the world . . .

But it turned out that they had called a doctor. Johanna had phoned for one on Saturday from the village hall. And Berta had come from the city on Monday with the *Sextant* (this vessel sailed twice a week between the island and the mainland) and brought a doctor with her. The doctor had listened and observed and looked at Mother's arms and legs, shaken his head and said that Mother should *not be moved.* No trip to Tallinn. Not to move her was the main thing. Otherwise the hemorrhage could spread in her brain. The doctor had produced some medicine or other from his bag, which they were to spoon into Mother's mouth three times a day. But all those days, Mother had not had a bite to eat.

Berta and Johanna had taken turns to sleep by her, as Uncle Frans slept too deeply and snored too loudly. While Berta and Johanna had dozed off occasionally rather than slept. Women appear to sleep very lightly at a sickbed. I remember this from Mother's own sleepless sleep next to my bed in the ward at the Free Hospital. At any rate, I told the ladies that I would lie down on the wooden sofa in Mother's room so they could get a good night's sleep this coming night.

In the evening, when everyone had gone to bed and Uncle Frans's snoring could hardly be heard through the plank wall, I turned the petroleum lamp in the sickroom down as much as I could, took off my clothes, lay down on the wooden sofa, rested my head against the wallpaper, looked at Mother's pale, barely visible face on the lace pillow, and suggested—I don't really know to whom—to myself, the world, Mother:

She *has to* get better this time! You *have to.* I don't know how much you yourself want to get better. But it is likely that you do. You have been a very lively person up to now. Inasmuch as a prodigal son can say as much about his mother. You no doubt want yourself—despite all the disappointments and sadness you've encountered—to get better and live. But I *definitely* want you to! Not because the burden of my unpaid debts is especially heavy. Not because I feel that I could never rid myself of the burden of your death. But because my own joy has been too great these past two weeks for you to die right now.

Mother—I am ashamed to admit it, as if my reason right now is too trivial—but you do understand me, as always, as almost always, better than anyone else . . . better than Father, whom I do not remember . . . and better than Johanna, whom I would like to forget . . . Mother—understand me: you can't die *right now* because this is my final opportunity to bring you joy! To prove to you ultimately that I was after all born a son of yours, not just a fantasist, a dreamer—hell—a drinker, but a son who has given the world something! And who will now start giving you something back . . . God Almighty, my new telescope costs five and a half thousand German marks. That is almost six thousand Estonian krooni. And Schorr has predicted: an innumerable number of orders . . . Even if they are not innumerable, even if there are only ten orders, only five a year, that will make, say, of two years—some six million senti . . . Hell, I notice that my calculations have slipped from krooni to senti, just to impress you with the size of the sums involved. No, no, forgive me! Sixty thousand krooni! And I'm not backing down from that sum. That's for real. And that will be more than enough to finance all my experiments—and I'm now thinking quickly through them: my ship for sailing against the wind, which I have actually had ready for ages, but which I want to perfect, and for those five or six other things that are at the top of my list of plans. More than enough. I'll be able to pay those Berg boys who brought me ashore today, Kristjan and Jakob, for a week or two. I'll teach them to build a proper tranter's cart. Something we haven't yet got on the island. And then they can put a horse in front of it and fetch a few hundredweight of that fine black earth from the edge of Lehtmetsa or the cliffs at Kunila. I know that they know where to find it. And seaweed from the shore at Rävasaare. And they'll mix the seaweed with the soil and spread it out around our yard. That you have—a fantastic patch of earth. For carrots and whatever flowers you choose. Frans will dig over the garden twice a year. Spring and autumn. Good work for an old man. Better than going out hunting seals. And what else? You already have a sewing machine. And you have always said that your old Singer is better than two new ones. Maybe. And then I will fetch from town a wind turbine. Made by Meyer's. I'm familiar with the construction. The propeller *could* of course be perfected. But it'll do as it is. And I would of course fetch an iron pole. To serve as a mast. And a dynamo. And batteries. And then we'll put the turbine up here on the slope of the hill at Jaanipere. So that your house can have its own electricity supply. The more the wind howls—and it's howling now—the brighter the lights . . . So that you can see to sew as much as you wish, shirts and trousers for little Eerik, and whatever else you want . . . And I will be able to see enough to draw properly. And I will complete my plans for that *ship* that sails against the wind. Not a boat. I've already got a boat. As I have told you. And I will sail with it along the river Ryck and on the Greifswalder Bodden. Everyone looking on will marvel at the fact that my engine is so silent. But it won't have an engine. Just wind power. And I will now build that vessel. Well, a small one, of course. But big enough. With two tiny cabins. One for you and one for Johanna. But, that's true—you haven't actually met Johanna. You only know August's Johanna. You don't know mine. Nor do I any longer, for that matter. But I will again meet her by way of my ship against the wind. And we will become closer again. Because I now want that, now that the burden of constructing my telescope has fallen from my shoulders; I want it more than anything else; the ship and the closeness . . . And I will build the ship in such a way that it will not float but rather fly. The propeller and a very simple way of changing its function. It will fly—straight from our beach where we dry the nets, across the sea from behind the houses, across the yard all the way to Mittweida—and circle above the Lauenheim Mill (Johanna and I used to take walks around it), circle as long as it takes to get Johanna to come out there. Then I will take her on board. No-no-no! Not for her to confess anything to me. Nor me to her. Simply to look into her eyes. I might, if I really have to, ask: "Well . . . ?" And she will remain silent. But she doesn't remain silent. She is responding to me. She is clearly upbraiding me for something. She is making some sort of sound. I cannot understand what it is. How do you mean? She is still so young. But only compared to me. She's no longer a small child! But now she is crying like a small child. Or moaning, rather—or groaning: *aa-aa-aa* . . . God, have I really hurt her so much . . . ?

Then realization cuts through my chest like a knife. I wake up a moment later. I am not somewhere else. I am *here,* on Naissaar, in the back room at Jaanipere. And it is my mother who is groaning.

I rush to her. I don't know what to do. I don't want to leave her to wake up the other women. Though women have a way with the sick. On the bedside stool there are medicaments. I balance a spoon across the hole in the stool with which you lift it so that it won't tip over when I fill it with cranberry juice. I try to bring the spoon to Mother's mouth, but the juice runs out of the trembling corners of her mouth onto the bedsheet. Her right eye is shut. But her left one is still slightly open. The black pupil is shining through the slit. This one-eyed stare has distorted her face in a frightening way. But that stare clearly recognizes me.

Her very quiet, very—even whimpering—*aa-aa-aa* seems suddenly to trip up. It continues, but the rhythm has changed, it is somehow hoarser, heavier. Five days long she has not uttered a word, now she suddenly says—barely audibly, but I can understand:

". . . Help me . . . Help me . . . Help me . . ."

I understand: *now* she is dying. I can't do anything at all. What can I say to her? If this is the last thing I can ever say to her. And when every solace is false! I should place my hand on her forehead and say: "Mom, believe in the Lord. He is here. Right here. And he will take you into his grace." A lie! I could only say that if I believed it myself. But I don't! Not enough, at least . . . Or should I nevertheless? Despite the lie. At such a moment as this. Last words. But I can't . . .

So I whisper—I don't know whether she can hear me—the only thing I can say without lying (and maybe even this is a lie):

"Mom—I can't help you . . ."

But she's already gone.

I dared not put my hand on her forehead. But I held her left hand—and felt how her grip ebbed away and was replaced by an inevitable and irresistible peace. I closed Mother's eyes. Now her small face, insofar as the lamp, now turned low, showed, was symmetrical and almost happy again.

I sat with her for a short while. In some way she was still here. And in some way she was farther than three hundred million light-years away. That life, from which I myself had emerged, had stepped out from between me and nonexistence. I was standing quite naked before a void and had to cope with this emptiness all on my own.

An hour later I went and woke up Berta. It was five o'clock in the morning. It was March 19, 1930. Berta woke up Johanna, and Johanna, Frans, and they all began doing what had to be done. A telegram to Olga in Helsinki. Frans taking the boat to Tallinn to deliver the death notice, go to the priest, and get the food for the wake. I took relatively little part in all the bustling and squabbling. Only inasmuch as to go, two days later, to the village hall and let Jürgenson record my mother's death in the register. And during those three days before the funeral, as I passed through the village to go and wander in the woods and along the beach, I received, in the rather bleak and bare way they have round here, condolences and *medkänsla,* as the Swedish-speaking folk say on the island, and shook hands with their callused paws.

The funeral came and went. Half the island stood around Mother's grave in the graveyard under the fir trees. The ribbons on the wreaths described Mother as someone who had cared for and looked after the island. There was not enough room for all the mourners in the farmhouse at Jaanipere. But apart from the Vodka Soothsayer Villem, no one got drunk. Nor me. I could only relax a few days later. Not until I was walking along the southern shore, with fresh Tallinn newspapers in my pocket, and somehow excited, and Peeter from Laasu invited me in to have a natter.

What I was excited about was that I could read in the paper that a ninth planet had been discovered!

This toddler had only been discovered the previous month. And, alas, not using my new invention. Discovered in Arizona, at the Lowell Observatory. And not by some famous name there—Shapley or the rest of them—but rather by some greenhorn. That boy Tombak, or whatever he was called; Tombaugh, according to the way it was spelled, was said to have, until recently, been a cowherd on a farm and then *aus Liebe zur Kunst* had gone to work at the observatory. Using as his testimonial a letter full of spelling mistakes and inkblots . . . So it was the most sprightly chicken of the brood who had discovered the grain! But with regard to the grain itself, no one yet knows much about it. An object of the fifteenth order of magnitude. Its orbit taking some three to six hundred years to complete. So it's a pretty tiny object really. But the ninth planet nonetheless. And there are hardly any more to be discovered. So this Tombak's name will be famous for all eternity. Well anyway, my own name will be immortalized by my telescope too. Without my having actually discovered—what's it called now—X or Columbia or Pluto, that has not yet been decided. But incidentally—I could very well have discovered it. I already had my telescope ready during that critical week. So that—if I hadn't been photographing Wentorf Mill for a couple of hours . . . Yes, if I had pointed the telescope at that quadrant of the heavens where, when it boils down to it, hundreds of observers were looking for that dot—I would have had a considerable advantage over those hundreds. But I was busy taking pictures of Wentorf Mill for the whole of two hours . . . When it comes down to it, wasn't this a substitute for Lauenheim Mill, which Johanna and I used to walk around at night . . . ?

Just as I was thinking this perturbing thought, Peeter from Laasu hailed me from his garden gate:

"Hey—aren't you Smitt's Pärnard? Well, good evening to you. Don't you want to step inside—and take a sip or two of grog . . . ?

After that perturbing thought, I certainly did.

So I stepped into the Laasupere farmhouse. The old widower had kept his house pretty neat and tidy. He gave me a kitchen chair with a carved back, and I sat at the bare table.

"Well, any news from the big wide world?"

"Nothing at all. They've discovered the ninth planet."

"I see. Have they named it yet?"

"Not yet."

Meanwhile, the old man, his stubble copper colored, takes the pan of boiling water from the stove and the sugar bowl from the shelf and puts them on the table, and starts mixing the grog in a white ceramic jug. Not rum or cognac or arrack. Such drinks are not to be found in this house. Because Peeter has not worked as a pilot for ages. But what there is here, and plenty of it, is pure spirit. Ten-liter jerry cans filled with the stuff are often thrown overboard by smugglers when they are caught by surprise by customs vessels, and this jetsam is not retrieved until storms have worked the cans loose and wash them up onto the beach—so often that nearly every household has its supply of spirits . . .

"So it's not been given a name yet . . ."

"Maybe they'll choose Pluto . . ."

"Well, well. That's what Matson from Põhjaküla called his dog. Jaan, who came back from America last year. A little mongrel. And an eternal wanderer."

"The planet is tiny too. And wanders."

"So Jaan's mongrel's name will suit it."

"That's what they called the Greek god of the underworld."

"Oh, that too," mumbles Peeter. "Well, let's take a sip . . ."

We pick up our two small white flint cups. The grog is unexpectedly good. So we drink it down in one draft. And your body begins to purr with warmth on this bleak late afternoon. Peeter says:

"You've got some papers in your pocket too. Have you already read them—there should be something there about how they nabbed eleven Communists in Tallinn last week."

"Yes, I glanced at the article. But here you are, read it for yourself . . ."

I take the copy of *Päevaleht* out of my overcoat pocket and mix myself another grog. Let him read. If it interests him. God—I read these things too. Can't exactly shut your eyes to them. But they don't interest me! I cut myself off from all that. Because if you let politics enter your life—God damn—then you'd have to leave all your lenses and mirrors and telescopes and run onto the street and yell and shout . . . Here, in Mittweida, in Hamburg, all over the place. But nothing would change by all that shouting—by *my* shouting. My voice is too weak for shouting. No-no-no—explanation, mixing with people, speaking, convincing—ugh. Horrible just to think of it. Because I haven't a clue how to tackle politics. At my lathe, at my polishing bench—there I *know* things, there I feel with every fiber of my body what has to be done—better than what Strandman and Stresemann and Thälmann and Hitler all put together know about their politics. And what I do there, what I do at my cobbler's last, is something the world at least has a tiny bit of use for. If not with a hungering stomach, then at least with a thirst for knowledge. So I have only one political demand, and that is: *the right for the shoemaker to stay at his last.* But even to obtain that right I'm not going to go out onto the street shouting . . .

I say: "Peeter, let's talk about work."

He hands me back my newspaper. "Well, there's not much as we can do in that sphere. What work were you thinking of?"

I explain: "You know, I want to take a break with my spyglasses. Have a rest from those telescopes. I don't have any use for them here on Naissaar as it is. But I can do other things here. At my mother's funeral supper I happened to hear the men say that you'd bought a new boat in Tallinn . . ." I've downed two cups of grog and we're now well on our way to start talking of the thing that is bothering me most after the telescope—and I don't feel I've got any problems letting my mouth do the talking. "Look, it's about this boat I want to talk. How big is it really?"

"Not terribly big. Just over three fathoms long. That is to say, six and a half meters."

"But pretty narrow?"

"Well, yes. A good bit narrower than a fisherman would need. But I happened to spot her in Tallinn—and she's rather beautiful—and so I bought her on impulse. Three pairs of oars."

"It's not the oars that interest me. Do you have her in the shed behind the house?"

"Yes, she's right here."

"Could I have a look?"

It has already grown so dark that we take lanterns to the shed. But I can see, even in the light of the lanterns, that this is just the sort of boat I need.

So that when we have returned to the room and almost finished our third grog, we agree that he'll sell me the boat for a hundred krooni. Whereupon Peeter (he's the best man on Naissaar when it comes to working with wood) will do the following for that sum: he will take off the front pair of rowlocks and build a deck across the boat—on the condition that it is constructed exactly according to my drawings and has a small thwart. Then he will fetch the necessary equipment from Tallinn and we can set it up together.

"What type of mechanisms are there going to be? An engine?"

"No," I say. "A mast. A vane. The transmission. A propeller."

"Listen," Peeter asks, "are you going to continue with all that stuff you used to do when you were in short trousers? I remember—I am, after all, twenty years older than you—that already then you were messing about with your late father's fishing boat. Can't quite remember whether you still had your right hand or not, but that didn't bother you anyway. You stuck a mast on Kaarel's boat, and sails on the mast. And all the women and girls on shore laughed at how Smitt's Pänn had built a floating coffee grinder! But you explained that you were going to sail with it against the wind to Sweden or America or wherever . . ."

"Precisely," is what I say, but I have to admit that it still embarrasses me somewhat that my boyhood whims are still with me now that I am a fully grown man—a fully grown man, take it or leave it, but at any rate a renewer of telescopes of world renown. When I've drunk three grogs I dare to admit this to myself. But it is still a whim from my boyhood days. And so, quite obviously, I say to Peeter:

"Precisely. But I'm going to sail with it. You'll see in the spring. From Naissaar to Tallinn and Aegna. And around Aegna and around Naissaar. And then—who knows what I'll do then?" By this time Peeter has set before us our fourth steaming cup—I gulp down half of mine in one go and explain: "Then I'll turn the vane to a horizontal position—and I'll be flying . . . Hee-hee-hee-hee—everyone will think that I'll need at least one engine to achieve this, but I'm going to manage without! Yes, sir! A Spaniard, I don't remember what the rogue is called, Cierva or Sterva, has *almost* solved the problem with flying in this way. But not yet completely. I'm going to solve it completely. Then—I'll be flying—with that very boat of yours—everywhere . . . But now I'm going home . . ."

Peeter half fills my cup with the last bit, a drop of spirits and hot water. I drink it up standing, confirm the boat purchase one more time, look at my pocket watch—it's only eleven—and step outside. The wind has become pleasantly warm. The moon is shining bright. And I have only two hundred meters to walk. But the fresh air nonetheless plays such a trick on me that I don't remember a thing about how I got home.

At seven o'clock in the morning the alarm clock drives me to my feet in my warm and clean attic room. I scrape the stubble from my chin, wash my face, and come down to breakfast as I do every day.

Mrs. Wallenius, that is, Olga, has traveled back to Tallinn with Ester immediately after Mother's funeral, and then back to Finland. But Berta is staying on Naissaar to keep Johanna company. And Frans too. Frans seems to have accepted the death of his wife with Old Testament dignity, which makes me sometimes think to myself: the old man is *playing a role.* And is enjoying playing it.

This morning Frans has gone off to tend to the sprat nets, so that when I come downstairs there are only Berta and Johanna with her little Eerik sitting round the table. This little fellow with blue eyes and dark eyelashes from farther south is wriggling about on his chair in front of his dish of oat porridge. The women are already drinking their coffee, which means that I am late. I say "good morning!" and sit down, and at first I don't notice anything.

Berta is exactly the same as always. No longer in the bloom of youth. Just over forty. With a kind face, transparent somehow, bright eyes that seem darker than they really are. I don't really know anything about art, but privately to myself I would say her face looked "a bit like a Botticelli." For some reason, Botticelli's angels have stuck in my memory as somewhat snuffily delicate creatures. And then there's Johanna. Our captain's wife. She is still young. Not yet thirty. And as I've now dropped one artist's name, I can throw in another (because if everything is happening silently, as it mostly does with me, then): Titian. Johanna, I mean. A quite shapely figure. Her hair on the dark side with an auburn sheen. Clear, bluish-gray eyes. But this morning her gaze is somehow evasive. And her usually so dignified mouth is curled in a wry smile. Suddenly I notice it. And it worries me somehow.

Eerik starts on his plate of porridge, drinks up his milk in gulps, and runs away to Uncle Frans's workshop to play with the lathe. The women drink up their coffee. Berta takes the dishes to the kitchen and starts the washing up. Johanna sits down at Mother's Singer sewing machine in that same dining room and starts to sew a shirt for Eerik. I'm the last one to be drinking coffee. Then I too am ready and take my coffee cup and saucer in to Berta to wash. When I return to the dining room, Johanna looks at me with a strange expression of fleeting surprise, then looks down again at the white material under the foot of the sewing machine and starts pedaling again with greater energy than before. So that I stop and ask:

"What's the matter with you?"

"With me—nothing at all!" says the captain's wife. But for one split second her mouth creases in mocking laughter, which she immediately manages to suppress. So I ask again:

"What are you laughing at? What is it with you . . . ?"

I then glance down at my trousers to check. To see that my flies are not undone (Johanna has got that sort of expression on her face). Such things have happened a couple of times in my life. Even after I had become perfectly capable of buttoning them with one hand. But my flies are done up. Johanna says, her face suddenly flushed:

"Do you yourself not know what you did last night . . . ?"

". . . No. What did I do—in your opinion . . . ?"

"What do you mean—*in my opinion*? Do you *really* not know?" The captain's wife says this in a tone of voice that suggests that she simply doesn't believe my denial.

I shake my head. There is something lurking there in my subconscious, but I just can't grasp it.

"Good Lord! You tried to force your way into my room! Do you really not remember?" says Johanna in a rapid whisper. "It's just not possible that you don't remember! But as it happened, the door was on the hook. I don't myself know why I put it on. You came to my door at half past eleven and started trying to force your way in. I tried to make it clear to you that you should go away, because it really wasn't right for you to be doing . . . But you started talking to me in German—saying, why wasn't it right? How could it be that it was all right *in the past*! As if there had once been something between us . . ."

Johanna tells all this and blushes even more as a consequence:

"I try to calm you down, but things get worse and worse. I'm saying: 'Shut up now, you lunatic! You'll wake Eerik!' But you carry on yelling—and in German, like a complete fool. 'Aha, so he's called Erik is he? I always thought his name was Werner. So you've already got a new one?' And you press against the door so that the hook starts to give. And you won't be quieted. All I can do is jump out of bed and slide a table in front of the door. But I can see that this light table won't be heavy enough to stop you. So I am beside myself. Dear Jesus—what shall I say to August . . . ? But then I see in the moonlight: Eerik's box of toy wooden bricks. So I lift it onto the table and slide it under the door handle. Just fits under the door handle. So it can't be moved . . ."

"And then—did I shut up?" I ask uncertainly.

"Yes you did," mocks Johanna with a smile.

"What did I say after that . . . ?" I ask, not really wanting to hear her answer, wincing in anticipation at her answer (as if I already knew what she was going to reply)—and yet wanting to hear it . . .

"You declaimed: *Johanna—ich liebe dich*—and in such a stage whisper that it could be heard throughout the house . . ."

I mumble: "Well, at half past eleven everyone will have been asleep."

"No doubt. Thank God. Otherwise Berta would have brought it up at the breakfast table."

"Undoubtedly . . ." I am in agreement—and feel the street urchin inside me, the naughty boy lurking within the renewer of telescopes, and think it was rather a pity that this utterance wasn't heard more widely. But thanking the heavens that it wasn't . . .

But now I ought really to say: Johanna, you do nevertheless realize that you are not the only one on this earth who goes by that name. So you yourself will no doubt realize that it was not of course you that I wanted to meet on the other side of that door on the hook. And to whom I . . . Note: in the German language—said to you so that you could hear . . . Because tell me, when we have ever spoken German together? I did speak with my father now and again in German—so that I would pick up the language. But I have never in my life used that language with anyone else in our family. And I would have been even less likely to speak German to you, who comes from out Kunda or Narva way, or wherever it is that they don't know much German. So you can well imagine that I wasn't, hm, thinking about my sister-in-law—even if I did say what you would like to think I did . . .

That's roughly what I *should* say . . . But God Almighty, speaking is not my strong point on this earth, at least not when I'm sober. And if I did indeed manage to announce a declaration of love on the strength of Peeter from Laasu's grog, then it is a very rare thing . . . It is my second declaration of love, the first being the one to Johanna in Mittweida—foolishly or sensibly, but at least when more or less sober—a few weeks before I, how shall I put it, abandoned her. And this second one—here, now, yesterday night—to whom, that is not entirely clear. To Johanna in Mittweida once again? Maybe. But 100 percent? Maybe to *some* extent it was meant for my brother's pretty wife. And if that is the case, it would be quite impossible to retract it! To simply say: my dear lady, what you could term my *declamatory statement* the other night had absolutely nothing to do with you . . . That, in the present embarrassing situation would be downright insulting to any woman . . . And what right have I, after having harassed her at night (because that is, damn it, what I have done), to then go and add insult to injury the very next morning. But even worse would be for me to let words cross my lips that could mean, for her as well, that now, in the clear light of day, my words last night were meant for her . . .

Oh hell and damnation. I mutter:

"Johanna—if I bothered you in the night—then please forgive me." I mutter these words knowing that I am not being entirely honest, because I am nevertheless deriving a slight amount of enjoyment from the ripple of ambiguity that these words leave in the air, enough to satisfy any woman's vanity, and that of August's Johanna, so she feels a shameful, unacceptable, but nonetheless sweet quiver of excitement . . .

I mutter my apologies and turn on my heel, so as to leave the house, flee down to the beach or into the woods. But right then, something springs to mind. So I go via my room in the attic.

Ten minutes later I have taken my briefcase, a notebook, a pencil, and a ruler up to Peeter from Laasu's boathouse, and am squatting, noting down the exact dimensions of the boat I am about to purchase. What the hell am I waiting for? Wasting valuable time! I know that the *Sextant* will be sailing for Tallinn in ninety minutes. I shall cross a stretch of snow and slush and reach the small-gauge railroad tracks in a quarter of an hour. Stumbling from one tree stump to the next (there are only snowdrifts here and there in the coppices of young pines), I will be at the harbor, then on board, within three-quarters of an hour.

In Tallinn I could of course pop in at the Ministry of Education and get from Blees, from Nikolai, that is to say, Berta's husband, the key to their flat on Köler Street (Berta's husband is now some sort of secretary representing the interests of Estonia's Swedish-speaking minority). I could walk over to Liivalaia Street and the Ackerbergs would receive me with open arms. Or go and see Johannson or any other of our Franconian Society brethren. But no. This would be wasting time pointlessly. So I go straight to the appropriate shop and buy a good ruler, a couple of rolls of cartridge paper, and a box of thumbtacks. All of this drawing tackle is now in my briefcase. And I walk along the seafront at Mere Avenue to Mrs. Lindvet's boardinghouse and rent a room for a couple of days.

The place is familiar, and I have my routines. I have stayed here before. When I came to Tallinn in the spring to continue on to Naissaar and it had turned out that I was too early—when the ice on the sea was too weak to support me, but too thick for ships to break through.

At Mrs. Lindvet's I can allow myself everything I want for the next few days. No one here grumbles at clouds of cigar smoke. Nor that one of the guests sits up all night at the writing desk using up electricity and gets up to pace the room from time to time, not exactly scraping chairs and banging around in boots, but not in stocking feet either.

The landlady herself shows me to one of the five or six rooms, luckily to one where I have stayed before, and leaves with a smile. I pin the cartridge paper to the desk (nor do they mind thumbtack holes in the desk top) and get down to work. A kitchen maid comes up promptly at three with fried eggs and a glass of milk, and brings me coffee in the evening and at nine in the morning.

By nine at night the *Naissaar 2* has fairly well taken shape on the sheet of cartridge paper. The *Naissaar 1,* which I bought in Greifswald and rebuilt to suit my needs, had a very light construction. A plywood boat with a plywood deck, five and a half meters long. Plus a mast, a boom, and the rest. Peeter from Laasu's boat is also a relatively light vessel. The thickness of the planks is a mere three-quarters of an inch, as opposed to between one or two inches for normal boats. But she is nevertheless a seagoing vessel. And a meter longer than her namesake. And the various functions must also be increased in size by the appropriate amounts. The vane will now have two propeller blades. And the blades will be forty centimeters longer. So the aluminum tubing forming the mast must also be extended by the corresponding length. Ditto the transmission, which will be located within the mast itself to transfer the movements of the vane in the air down to the propeller in the water. The blades of the propeller will be more curved than before. There are a couple of benches in the low cabin—because this boat will not be built to achieve something, like the previous one, but built rather for the purpose of, well, what? You can't really call it sailing . . . OK then, *traveling* . . . Under the front porthole there is a steering wheel. It has the usual spokes through which I can put my right arm and steer the boat. To the left of the steering wheel is a gear lever, to enable me to steer the boat in the opposite direction if necessary, that is, in reverse. Such situations rarely arise. But as I have now constructed something as impossible to sail against the wind with as a boat, I have to be able to sail both forward and backward, just for effect . . . The whole of my boat is in a way the same as my mirror with its sixty-centimeter aperture . . . Everyone said: 1:1.75 is the outer limit for the light intensity. I said, sure: 1:1.5 is also possible. No it isn't! Exaggeration! Nonsense! Schmidt doesn't know his theory. *Und so weiter.* Until I started trying, just to prove them wrong. Calculating and testing. Hell. The depth of field just got bigger and bigger. And the area of focus smaller and smaller. So I cobbled together a lens to put in between. The measurements were still quite absurd: a depth of field of nine meters! The radius of focus fifteen millimeters! But I built it and the light intensity turned out to be 1:1.5. Exactly that. So some of them started shrieking that this was another miracle! And others, that sure, it was a miracle all right, but a *pointless* one. I said: be that as it may. But it is at any rate *possible.*

The reverse gear mechanism on my boat is very simple: two propellers, one behind the other. So there we are . . .

By the end of the week of staying at Mrs. Lindvet's boarding house I had clearly gone down in weight by a couple of kilos, there wasn't much I could lose, but drawing the details of the boat meant that I was in my usual pleasant fever of activity; I have even noticed that this light fever is contagious when it approaches those with a positive attitude to my efforts. Ackerberg at least was smitten by such a fever. I went to his place and gave him a brief glimpse of the sketches. I wasn't too keen on doing so, but it was necessary for the progress of my project. He looked them over and said to his wife (despite tendencies toward acting the father of the family and sporting a premature potbelly):

"Luise, don't serve us dinner just now. We have work to do. And I'm not sure when we'll be there." And he patted his daughter on the cheek, saying: "Karin, go and keep your mom company at the dinner table. That's right. Mr. Schmidt and I have some important work to do . . . What? No, good Lord, no beer drinking, nothing to do with the club . . ."

Jakob and I went to three factories: the Luther, the Arsenal, and the Ilmarine. In all three, he knew an engineer who would be suitable for the task. We showed them my drawings. We explained, that is, chiefly Jakob explained: cash payment, as soon as possible, as accurately as possible. The drawings were left at the three offices, the equipment orders were drawn up there: a propeller from the Luther factory; a turbine from the Arsenal, plus that moveable head by means of which the vane in the air could be moved in any direction, depending on where the wind was blowing. And from the Ilmarine factory the whole transmission plus the water propellers. In each factory the engineer picked a number of suitable workers who were to construct their appropriate items to the exact dimensions. At the Luther this was a sour-faced, bald man, Piilberg by name, who was said to construct propellers with great skill for the planes built at the flying club. At the Arsenal, his equivalent was the square-chinned Passup. When he had looked over the drawings, said "mmm," and gone back to his workshop, the engineer said to Jakob and me: "That chap does the most precision rifles in the world!" and looked at us with an expression that implied that we ought to start clapping. I said: "But, good Lord, we haven't yet heard that he's also shot a record with any of them." The engineer said: "Just you wait. The rifles already exist. All we need now is the men to shoot them."

At the Ilmarine, Jakob went to the office of an engineer named Eichen. He called up a turner from the workshop, whose name, if I remember correctly, was Drumm. He was said to be the best man to make my transmission. This swarthy young man, a little nervous, so it seemed, was, in the words of the engineer, *ein teuflisch präziser Kerl.* And precision had to be absolute for all my constructions. If I wanted my vessel to sail against the wind, as well as with it and across it.

There it was. But it would take at least another two weeks for the orders to be ready. So I had to weigh up whether enough days had now passed since the intermezzo with August's Johanna that I could sail over to Naissaar in the meantime and act as if nothing had ever happened . . . I weighed this matter up—and concluded that one week's absence should be enough. How long would I have to sit in the damned doghouse for my transgression? Enough is enough!

At least in Tallinn, at least while still in the Mine Harbor, I felt that it was enough. All the more so as the weather that April morning focused my attention on other things. The waves were quite calm. And a pleasant steady breeze was blowing from the southeast at, judging by the *Sextant's* flag and the skin of my face, ten to eleven meters per second. So I was thinking: an ideal wind to do a test run in my boat.

In this wind the vane would do three revolutions per second. That means that the back propeller would be doing twelve. That means that with a wind speed of thirty-six kilometers an hour, I would be able to sail against the wind at, well, let's say, seven, and if we take into account the perfect finish on the boat and a good quality varnish, then seven and a half kilometers an hour. Using the wind to sail against that very same wind. During the two weeks that the workers will be slogging away at my orders in Tallinn (given the rate of unemployment at present, I cannot see why it should take so long!). During those two weeks Peeter from Laasu and I could manage to build the decks and other features.

Then I raised my eyes to look at the shore that was now approaching—and I felt, with a start: no, no, no! Those rocks, those trees, the people on the quayside that I could already recognize, they are all nearly right in front of me—but I just can't cope with Johanna's gaze . . . Stupidity? Maybe. Can't be helped. Because I know my own denial mechanisms through and through. It's like a clock with an anchor whose ratchet wheel only allows it to be turned in the direction of denial. If you try to turn it the other way, the ratchet will break. So I made the decision: I will go on land and simply walk around in the woods for the two hours that the boat takes to reload. Then by the time it sets sail I'll be on board again. And I'll stay during the time it takes to get everything sorted at Mrs. Lindvet's boarding house in Tallinn. By then I will be able to face meeting Johanna.

Two hours later I climbed up the iron stairs back onto the *Sextant.* When I was halfway up, someone called out to me. A child's voice, one I instantly recognized. It was Eerik:

"Uncle Bernhard! Uncle Bernhard! Are you coming with us?"

Even before I actually clapped eyes on the boy, I saw his parents coming out from the deck cabin to the rail. There they all stood: August, Eerik, and Johanna. With three large suitcases and two strapped-up bundles.

"Nice that we meet again. But—I can't really understand where you've been and where you're going."

That was August shouting. Where he had come from and was going to became clear in an instant. He had come back to Naissaar the previous evening, to take his wife and son on a sea voyage during the high season. He was now the captain of the steamship the *Marmor*. It belonged to a stock company of the same name. Was now moored at the merchant quay in Tallinn. Was now going to fetch marble from Jaagurahu on the island of Saaremaa, and would then be sailing to the countries where the Marmor Company sold it: Denmark, Germany, Norway. The so-called marble was in fact really limestone. But almost completely pure $CaCO_3$. They used it for the production of sugar and cellulose . . .

"Uncle Bernhard—aren't you coming with us?" asks Eerik. As I have stopped right in the middle of the stairs.

Johanna asks nothing. Says nothing. I don't look her in the face. I do not say a word more to them. I simply wave, rather desultorily, I feel. And walk back to the quayside. Not before I've gone some thirty paces (at that distance I feel more or less liberated from the strain of the unwanted proximity) do I turn round toward them. They are standing next to one another at the rail. Eerik is already poking his nose over the edge. August takes his captain's cap off his head and waves it. Eerik sees that we are waving and waves too.

And then even Johanna raises her arm and waves to me.

Two weeks later, my mechanisms were ready. But owing to Peeter's sciatica, no deck building had taken place. I did at least get a telephone call from Jakob to say that my orders could be collected, and so I traveled to Tallinn. Jakob took a lorry belonging to his firm and picked up all the equipment from the three factories, and we drove to the Mine Harbor, where the sailors of the *Sextant* heaved it on board. All the equipment together cost two hundred and fifty krooni. But I could afford this easily owing to the sale of my telescope. On Naissaar, I transported it all from the harbor, with the help of Schulmann and his cart, to Peeter of Laasu's yard.

Peeter got on nicely with the task for a few days running. He sawed the planks and slats for the deck. But the next day he was virtually immobile again, and he went into the hellishly hot sauna to lash his backside with curative nettles, although for a few days running he could hardly even manage to get out of bed.

My situation had become a little ridiculous, but I could do little to change it. Ridiculous, in that I was totally at the mercy of Peeter and his sciatica. And he had himself said that he would not sign any agreement with me because of his periodic ill health, so he might not be able to meet the terms. Even I was loath to break any agreement at the time. The sheer zeal with which Peeter had started on the agreed tasks did in some way bind me as well. And he did not say: look, I'm not the right man for the job. Find yourself some other carpenter . . . Because I would find no more accurate carpenter on the whole island. Some more or less skilled carpenter, no doubt. But with such a man I would have to stand right over him a good deal of the time shouting orders. And Peeter is not giving up. He is, of course, sad that he can't get on with his work because of the nerves in his ass and because he is wasting my time. But it is clear that he *wants* to do the job. So all there is left for me to do is to wait impatiently and do things myself with the boat. Although I cannot do anything in the way of carpentry. I will be doing quite different things. I will be sitting upstairs in my attic room sketching away at drawings of my piece of fantasy equipment. That is to say, a really big Schmidt telescope for the Bergedorf Observatory. Incidentally, it should not yet be placed at that observatory. It would really be better if it was located far away from any larger cities, somewhere where the sky is clear. Right here, for instance—as I have imagined—on the King's Hill on Naissaar . . . With a good, let us say, 1.2-meter aperture, completely coma-free, and a field of vision of six degrees. For which the instrument we have now set up at Bergedorf, despite its perfection, would be by comparison merely a first tryout. And that real one, that big one, I could build without any difficulty at all . . . Well, what do I mean by "without any difficulty"? *With some difficulty,* naturally. But nonetheless. And using that you would be able to see—let's say the Pleiades, which I can, if I extinguish my petroleum lamp and open the window, I can see relatively clearly through the opening. These same Pleiades could be looked at, oh, how . . . Before my telescope was invented, you could see, under optimum conditions, a hundred or so stars within a field of one and a half degrees, plus a couple of thousand beyond. With the Big Schmidt you would be able to see all those hundred and fifty or two hundred or however many there are, but beyond those, in the background, let's say at least half a million . . . The question is simply the damned cost of it all . . . Because this would no longer be a question of five thousand marks but rather of one hundred and fifty thousand . . .

But by the way: Is there any unsullied patch of sky left over Naissaar . . . ? I'm not thinking of the glow from the windows of Tallinn.

What I mean is all the horrible things that have taken place on the island.

During the ten years that have passed since such things happened, I have been to Naissaar four times, spending some four months there on each occasion. And yet I have never gotten a clear picture of what happened. Well, I have never done any research into the matter. Nor really asked anyone. After I had noticed that what had happened in the winter of 1919 was something people did not *want* to talk about.

There were very few civilians on the island at the time. Of those that had been deported at the outbreak of the Great War, only a very few had returned. And these people didn't really get to know what had occurred either. The details remained rumors shut away, as it were, behind a triple barbed-wire fence. What was known publicly was the blood-drenched tip of the iceberg. And people didn't want to talk about that because it was common knowledge anyway. But even more so because what had happened was felt to shame the very soil on which it occurred. Such shame that it also somehow sullied the very heavens above that spot . . . By the way, this feeling of shame or pride about a patch of earth tends to be stronger on islands, as they have clear limits made by nature, than on the mainland, where such boundaries are less clearly defined.

Anyhow, what happened and is public knowledge is roughly as follows:

Around Christmastime 1918, two Red warships, the destroyers the *Spartak* and the *Avtroil,* were on a reconnaissance mission in the Bay of Tallinn. The war between White Estonia and Red Russia was at its height. And a British squadron had already arrived in Tallinn to assist the White government there. The Red cruisers were not aware of this fact and a battle ensued off the island of Aegna. The British captured these vessels and handed them over to the Päts government. The Red crew, 199 men in all, were imprisoned in Tallinn. Whereafter febrile activity ensued on Naissaar.

A triple line of barbed wire was placed around the old barracks on the edge of the woods beyond the harbor. And the staff headquarters were set up in an abandoned house. In other words, a prisoner-of-war camp was built on Naissaar and the Red sailors were brought there from Tallinn to isolate them completely.

How were they treated? The authorities gave assurances that everything was done according to the norms of the day. Rumors soon reached Tallinn suggesting: inhumanly . . .

Now, just a couple of days ago, Peeter was planing planks in the room at Laasupere for the cabin of my boat and offered me a grog to ward off the evening chill. He too drank some and then all of a sudden started telling the story.

The prisoners had been used for forestry work. The columns grew shorter by the day, as more and more were lying in the bunks in the typhus hut, or had ended up in graves at the edge of the woods. Peeter had seen columns of them on their way to work, with guards armed with rifles at the front and at the rear, on several occasions. During the day the prisoners built bonfires and warmed themselves around lunchtime. Peeter had once been given permission by one of the guards to warm himself at such a bonfire when he had been in the vicinity collecting firewood for the stove back home. The guard had muttered. "Go on then. But make sure that you . . ."

There were a dozen or so men around the fire. And they were boiling some sort of sludge in an old herring can. Peeter related:

"I asked them what that was, and one replied, 'soup.' I asked what sort of soup. He said '*indyukovyi.*' I didn't know what that was. Another man knew some Estonian. He said: 'turkey soup.' They grinned with their white teeth and licked their black lips. I didn't believe them. How could they have turkey soup out here . . . ? Then the man who knew Estonian explained: they had found a leg of turkey gnawed virtually bare in the slops hole outside the barbed-wire fence. They had managed to free it from the frozen earth with an axe. At the same time they found some potato peelings. And now the soup would soon be ready."

That was what Peeter had seen with his own eyes. The rest he only knew by hearsay. One very quiet morning following the early February thaw—a remarkably quiet morning for Naissaar—bursts of machine-gun fire could be heard coming from the woods in the northeast. And the next day, it was already afternoon, there was sporadic gunfire. Which went on for several hours. Until nightfall. Across the whole of the southern part of the island. And then rumors started circulating, God knows from where, maybe from the guards themselves, or from the soldiers brought in to assist them, or maybe even from onlookers—there were such people on the island. The commission that the provisional government had sent out to take over state property had been active in the harbor, around the fortifications and by the railway, for some time. This commission consisted of civilians, and some of the commissioners even had their wives with them. So suddenly there was an unexpectedly large number of people who might see things and dare to talk about them. In a word, rumors started circulating: from among the sailors of the captured ships, those that admitted to being Communists were weeded out. Over thirty of them. Those from the *Spartak* had been shot in the woods behind the enclosure on the morning of February 3. The ones from the *Avtroil* were to be shot the next morning. But when they started transporting the men to be executed on the morning of the fourth, they scattered under fire. A hundred or so armed soldiers pursued fifteen prisoners through the woods, some of whom were in rags, others wounded, until night fell. Until every single one of them had been shot dead in their various hiding places. People said that they had found the last of them in Kõrve-Toomas's abandoned net hut under a pile of old herring nets.

And such details could only have come from those who shot them. How this last one was pulled out from under the nets (or to be more precise, his corpse) and dragged by his feet across the yard into the snow with the nets still clinging to him. When the soldiers investigated, they found that he had pushed a cork float into his mouth and bitten on it so hard that he could no longer extract it. They cut the net away from around his stubbly lips with a bayonet.

Such was Peeter's story as he sat over his mug of grog; his pipe had gone out. And I thought to myself: this all happened some eleven years ago, but I am hearing the story for the first time . . . I have heard *something* about this before. But have never asked for any details. Because I have always wanted, without even being aware of it, to remain *free* of this event. So I am only now hearing all this for the first time . . . God, I am sitting here in Peeter's room at Laasupere and listening to it. And I am thinking: But why did he have that cork in between his teeth . . . ? And answer my own question: because after the desperate chase he had hidden himself under the nets and was panting. And he wanted to stop the panting, as the sound would betray him. But his tracks in the snow had inexorably done so already . . .

Peeter said that at dawn the next morning the dead were collected together and stacked up on sledges, then taken to the woods behind the enclosure and buried in a sandhill next to the first mass grave. Peeter said:

"There is not the slightest trace left of that second day. There were bullet holes in the floor of Kõrve-Toomas's net hut. But now that hut is gone. And the graves—at first there was trampled soil and loose sand. And bullet marks in the pine trunks from the first day. Now there is nothing. Only someone who knows precisely where to look knows what happened here. And anyone who starts digging around in a tree trunk with a knife will find a rusty bullet or two . . ."

Peeter spoke—and I was thinking: he is no doubt telling me all this because he hopes to *free* himself by telling the tale.

"In the summer, the POW camp was closed. Those still alive, some forty or so men, were sent elsewhere. To Pääsküla or wherever. And were handed over to the Russians after the Treaty of Tartu. So that once the camp had gone, some men put a juniper cross by the graves. But it was soon removed. By soldiers no doubt. So that the whole event would fall into oblivion. And, well, they didn't see the point of putting a Christian cross by the graves of unbelievers. But there were a number of more obstinate believers on the island—your stepfather and others—who put up another cross. And a third time too. Because we were in no position to judge the denial of, or belief in, God. And in the Christian world people's graves should be marked. But when the cross vanished once again, the men gave up. And now all that is left is heather . . ."

And it's true. I wandered through that area beyond the barbed-wire fence, which has now fallen to pieces. Well, when in the woods, you can expect something to turn up at every step. Hillocks. Depressions. Secret signs. A wood is not like polished glass. A piece of glass either has uneven patches or it doesn't. But even that fact is relative.

No. There in the woods on the edge of Storkärr there really is nothing. But I can feel that there ought to be something! A sign of some sort! No, not a memorial. Who would build one—to the victims of the Whites and Reds and Blues and Blacks . . . But some sign, a cross made out of juniper wood or something else: some kind of lightning rod, something *to discharge the tension* . . . Because I can feel it: the ground is still charged. The charge enters the soles of my shoes from the now rushing, now silent sand, and rises—both agitation and anguish, repugnance and witchcraft—from my feet into my knees, my groin, right up to my heart, my brain. The ground is charged. Charged with a barely noticeable but suffocating pain, shame, and fear. The whole island is charged with it—the whole world. But with such a covert charge that when you are moving around, walking, thinking of other things, you simply do not notice, hardly notice it at all. But as soon as you stop you feel it—try to grasp it, or are in fact grasped by it, hear its essence, sense its pressure—so that just a little more, just a tiny bit, and you are smothered by it . . . Light green pine saplings stretch up in the sunlight. But in these saplings moves the sap that comes from crumpled bodies that lie rotting under the earth, from twisted faces that are dissolving into nonexistence, and from someone's shame—presumably my own. God, what meaning—in cosmic terms—do the deaths of thirty men have, or my feeling of being smothered? But still, if I am, if we all are destined in cosmic terms to be sentient beings . . . That feeling that my island has been sullied by blood—the feeling that the whole world is rotting away—is in fact so powerful that if you begin to concentrate on the matter, you would arrive at the conclusion that there is no other way but to shut one's eyes and begin to yell . . .

Thank God that *I* can choose another way.

My boat is finished at last. My *Naissaar 2.* The cross ribs and deck made from planks half an inch thick. A bird's skeleton construction. And its aluminum Drumm mast and the Passup propeller mounting, with the necessary springs and stays attached. And a Piilberg propeller, precision work. Which I myself polished to perfection before it received its coat of varnish.

Around five in the morning there is not a soul about at the boat harbor. The horizon in the east is already growing light, but when I push the boat out from the jetty it is still some forty minutes before sunrise. The wind is coming from the northwest and is exactly what is required, very steady, from the same unchanging direction, and at eight meters a second.

I push the boat away from the jetty. I have let Peeter mount a rowlock on the stern so that I can have a support for the paddle and scull with one hand. Within five minutes I am beyond the relative lee of the shore of the island and take the wind propeller brake off.

The slim, glittering vane jerks into motion and begins to rotate.

Now it is doing three to four revolutions per second and its rotation surface is catching the wind. I pull the paddle on board and lean with my right arm on the fork of the rudder, constructed so that I can move it with that arm.

There we are. Behind the stern, there is a pretty white tail of foam. The propeller on the stern is doing some 1,000, then 1,200 revolutions per minute. The prow is lifting and sinking slightly, now that the boat is doing twelve to thirteen kilometers an hour, a good speed for a cycle trip over the waves that are bobbing toward the southeast. I steer toward the triangle of the distant façade of the ruin of the Convent of Saint Bridget at Pirita and maintain that direction for a quarter of an hour. Then I start maneuvers.

I turn the rudder so that the boat describes a circle with a one hundred meter radius. At the second half of this circle, I brake the vane and turn it so that it is parallel to the wind direction. So that the inertia of the moving boat gives the power for this second half. Then there I am bobbing on the waves, and the northwesterly, as steady as before when it was blowing on my neck, is now blowing straight in my face. A godly fresh, godly pure sea breeze, which is now blowing so vigorously that it almost takes my breath away. And then I turn the vane across the wind again. And fix the rotation surface and release the brake.

I know from experience what is going to happen, what *must* happen. Exactly the same as happened on the Greifswalder Bodden ten, twenty times. How could it not happen here in the Bay of Tallinn?

And it does happen! So that when I give the vane a little nudge with my hand it begins to rotate. Ten seconds later it is rotating at three to four revolutions a second. If the waves were not sloshing against the side of the boat, I would be able to hear a light pinging in the mast. Then I press the lever that engages the propeller down in the water. So that the boat, which has been pushed slightly backward by the wind, now gives a start, grows tense, and *understands*—understands the unusual but undisputable law of nature—and obeys it. Without demur. And inevitably. I can feel how the boat is trembling slightly at the unfamiliar situation—but obeys. And begins to move in a northwesterly direction, against the northwesterly wind. At a few centimeters per second, decimeters per second, half a meter per second, one meter per second. Given the strength of the wind, the speed will not increase any further. Maybe I can perfect the shape of the water propeller. But right now I cannot see any way of doing so. But at this speed I can also—at about one-quarter of the wind speed—say with full justification that I have found the solution to the problem of using wind power to drive a boat against that very same wind.

Those that were able to understand my calculations (of the few that I showed to anyone) were already congratulating me three years ago. Prandtl in the first instance. When I submitted my application for a patent at the Prussian Patents Department, he promised to send them his most glowing recommendation. He said in Greifswald right in my face: "Herr Schmidt—your boat is really a toy, but the principle governing it smacks of genius." So why the hell he never sent his recommendation, I do not know to this day. When they give patents to people that have invented tie clamps and curling tongs. But I never went to ask or plead. And incidentally: I doubt if any recommendation from Prandtl would have made the idiots at the Prussian Patents Department any the wiser . . . Why should I turn to them in the first place? Be that as it may. Schorr commented: "Herr Schmidt—why shouldn't you let them grant you state protection for such a grand machine as yours?" And, well: people are most regrettably not entirely free of human vanity . . . But it doesn't really matter. Neither the fact they didn't give me a patent on my boat, nor the boat itself. Because it is of course a toy. It can only be important inasmuch as *play* is important . . . At any rate it will allow me *to sail in any direction I wish, whatever the direction of the wind itself happens to be.* Faster in some directions than others, that is true. But still directly in any direction I choose without having to tack . . . And in no way is it a miracle. Beyond the precision involved. And, well, a certain amount of intuition. Australian aborigines have known about this for ten thousand years. Because in principle my boat is using nothing more than the boomerang effect. With a different application, that is true. It is a way of releasing the energy of movement from the trammels of the direction of movement. That's all.

But there is, God damn, something in being able to sail where you want, and not to have to depend on the direction of the wind.

8

FRAU JOHANNA BRANDT WAS BORN IN 1901. AND MATRICULATED FROM the Mittweida Girls High School in 1919. So that when we met she was eighty-four years old. The same age as Herr Kelter. And just as well preserved. But nonetheless in quite a different way. Age has turned Herr Kelter into a stringy, ironic, almost cynical old man. Frau Brandt—when she stands before me in real life, in her real context, it is hard to think of her as *Johanna*—has become an amiable, mild, maybe slightly melancholy old lady.

Her real-life context consists of an upper middle-class guest room in the detached house of the daughter of her cousin, the wife of a lawyer, on the edge of Lübeck, almost on the banks of the Trave.

"Oh yes. Irmgard has explained it to me. You are that gentleman from, where was it again? Bernhard's native land, and who wants to write a novel about Bernhard. But all of that happened so *terribly* long ago . . ."

Very well, I think to myself. At least she admits that it did happen.

She asks me to take a seat and places her hands (with only the double widow's ring on her right-hand ring finger) a little helplessly next to each other on the edge of the table. She is a good deal frailer than I imagined from Herr Kelter's description. But on the other hand, I was imagining her as she would have been some sixty years ago . . .

"And what is it you wish to ask me about?"

There is a comically perplexed expression on her small face. A hint of the redness of age on her cheeks. Maybe the veins have dilated a little, or she is shy, or it is rouge. She looks at me with her clear greenish eyes. Her hair is combed smoothly over her scalp and is of an even iron gray you rarely see in Estonia. But maybe she has dyed it.

I feel that I am not sure what attitude I have toward her. I feel a little regret, that is true. But I do not know whether this is because she left her illustrious husband and preferred to marry a mere bookseller. Is it the kind of regret that is condemnatory, occasioned by her own, Johanna's own insignificance. Or a well-meaning regret that stems from trying to make amends for the fact she is oversensitive about the issue, or the fact that her all-too-egocentric Bernhard abandoned her—and that she is now, over half a century later, his representative, now that she is an old woman, is somehow painful . . . ? She wants to know what it is that I want to ask her. But I can hardly in the first instance ask what I really would like to know most of all: tell me, which of you was it that broke off the relationship . . . ? I start explaining:

"You see, my good lady, one can find out about Bernhard Schmidt's technical achievements from a hundred different sources. Nowadays there are hundreds upon hundreds of such articles. Maybe, it is true, not about every single one of his inventions. For instance, I have found almost nothing written about his boat for sailing against the wind. Incidentally—he did do work on it while living in Mittweida—do you happen to remember anything about it?"

Johanna does not need much time to think. She answers immediately:

"Only that he sailed between Mittweida and Greifswald a few times. And that it—the boat or ship or whatever it was—was finished there. So he managed to sail on the sea with it, and was very satisfied with the result. But they never gave him a patent for it . . ."

I say: "Quite. And no one seems to know any more about it. There are only a few lines written on the subject. So you cannot really get a clear picture of the scientific and technical aspects from what has been written about it. But personal things, qualities—about such things you cannot find anything anywhere. Apart from the fleeting memories of a colleague or two. But in the case of such an introverted person as he seems to have been—what could his colleagues know compared with someone who really got close to him, a person such as you . . ."

Frau Brandt gazes at the pattern on the coffee table runner and says quietly:

"He was no more open with me either . . ." But it is evident that she does not a priori want to refuse me an answer, and adds: "I understand—I did experience *something* of his nature at close hand, closer than his colleagues . . . What is it that interests you?"

"To tell you the truth—everything. If you will allow, I would first like to ask: Was he always so reticent as people now say?"

Johanna thinks for a moment:

"I never met him again after the autumn of '27. How he was later on in life I cannot say. He could have changed a lot. I think he *would have had to* change a lot. But he would hardly have become any more talkative. And during the time I knew him, I can say: his flow of words was very uneven. Do you understand what I mean? He could be almost silent for a week at a time. And would hardly even utter a yes or a no. He would nod or shake his head. And literally for a week at a time. Then suddenly—especially when he had the right listeners—he could be all enthusiasm about some idea, always some technical idea, and would expound for half an hour, so that no one could get a word in edgeways. A whole hour even. Or one and a half. I don't think I ever heard him talk for any longer."

I ask: "Can you remember any concrete instance of this? Some place? Some details?"

"I do remember one such occasion," says Johanna. "I went to his workshop now and again. Sometimes I was even his assistant there. Sometimes, when he wanted to skip meals to avoid wasting time, I would bring him his lunch from the vegetarian restaurant. But his workshop was quite a large, untidy room. There were all sorts of objects and oddments there. Polishing lathes, whetstones, half-finished mirrors and lenses, equipment and tools for measuring things, books, and God knows what else. That has been written about in a few books. I'm sure you will have read them."

"I've read something," I say, and Johanna continues:

"The door would always be locked and he would be in there on his own. He would only rarely let anyone else come in. I had a special way of knocking that we'd agreed on." And I do not know whether she is doing so automatically from memory, or consciously so that I can hear what it sounds like—she knocks with her knuckles on the edge of the coffee table.

"One time I knocked and he let me in as he usually did. But once I was inside and he had locked the door behind me, he walked to the middle of the room and I saw that there were strangers in the room: Kuntze and Bräuer. These were two interesting types from Mittweida, admirers of Bernhard's and his friends, you could say. Bernhard would order the odd piece of equipment from the locksmith Kuntze. He was presumably the only man in Mittweida whose accuracy was good enough for Bernhard. Bräuer was a precision mechanic, a watchmaker by trade, and Bernard was especially impressed by his skill and exactness. Now and again, Bernhard even allowed him to polish a mirror when he himself was away somewhere. And that was indeed a sign of acknowledgment. And these two men were also sufficiently bohemian and philosophical. Kuntze was sitting at Bernhard's large workbench. But Bernhard himself marched back to the center of the room—so I understood immediately that he had been standing there before I entered, explaining something or other—and he continued in midsentence. About how an American called Michelson—he pronounced it in the German manner—was said to have invented a device that enabled you to measure the diameter of fixed stars. This device was the so-called interferometer. Michelson was said to have invented it some forty years previously, but now the idea had struck Bernhard to use it for a different purpose. Then he told them about how the interferometer worked—but they hardly understood anything of what he said. Even I didn't really understand much. Even though I had been studying physics that year at the university. In principle it's a matter of splitting up a beam of light and viewing it from various angles. Bernhard walked over from the large table to the smaller one and hectored Kuntze and Bräuer: Did they understand what this meant? And did they know what this star actually was, the one whose diameter Michelson measured? It was Alpha in Orion or Betelgeuse! And did they have any idea how large it proved to be? That it turned out that its diameter was three hundred times that of our sun! Even if it was not very dense—it was large anyway, so that if you imagine the sun as its center, then not only Mercury and Venus but also Earth would be orbiting *within* it, at a depth of some sixty million kilometers *inside* Betelgeuse! And even Mars, with its elliptical orbit, would for a large part be orbiting within it!

"While Bernhard was telling Kuntze and Bräuer all this he was pacing back and forth, and was snapping the fingers of his left hand in his enthusiasm while holding his right arm behind his back. Enthusiastic about the fact that, thanks to Michelson, we now knew the diameter of Betelgeuse. Despite the fact that the star was some five million light-years away from us.

"I remember Bernhard standing in the middle of the workshop and looking with flashing eyes now at Kuntze, now at Bräuer, and suddenly he burst into laughter . . . You know, he used the least crude language of anyone I've ever known—I imagine this was because of the old Herrnhuter traditions of the island—but . . . (you know, I believe that a *writer* could be interested in such trivia), but in his moment of excitement, he allowed himself a little . . ." And God, the eighty-four-year-old Johanna blushed slightly—"a little frivolity. So Bernhard burst into hoots of laughter and said: 'So that old Michelson—he is, after all, seventy years of age—measured Old Mother Beetle Juice's rump—*bitte schön*—with his measuring lath.' Then Bernhard seemed to grow abashed, fell silent, and said hastily: 'But now, gentlemen—*Schluss der Lektion*—back to work, to work, to work . . . !' So that Kuntze and Bräuer left the workshop with polite rapidity . . ."

"And how did he behave after this outburst?" I ask in the most matter-of-fact voice I could muster.

"Quite normal again afterward. For several weeks," says Johanna. "On that particular occasion—he indicated with his thumb that I should clear away the salad bowl and put it in the cupboard, and he carried on polishing his mirror. I ran a wet rag across the floor. That had to be done several times a day in the workshop. Then I started to read something, and after three hours had passed he said: 'Nine more minutes. We're going to make it.'—'Make it where?' 'Make it to the Chaplin and Jackie Coogan film.'"

I now ask: "Frau Brandt—you mentioned, if I am not mistaken, Bernhard and his old Herrnhuter tradition. I have asked several people, but have never got a straight answer: What *was* Bernhard's attitude to the church, religion, and God?"

"Listen, he hardly ever said anything about such things . . . He did say that in his childhood he had belonged to the congregation of the Moravian Brethren on Naissaar. Had it not been established on the island some fair while by then? And that his stepfather had been the local preacher. And, by the way, maybe his reticent nature stemmed from that tradition. He once said that it had been drummed into him during his childhood that lying is the greatest sin of all. And added, from personal experience: *but most of what we say consists of lies.* With regard to his relationship with the church, or religion, or God—I really don't know a thing about it. That was presumably too personal a matter. I mean to say . . ." Johanna thinks a brief moment, then continues: "During the years we were together, it did happen a couple of times, let us say once in a blue moon, or on one of the first days of Christmas, that he would say in passing: I dropped in at the church yesterday. But I never pressed him to say why he went, whether out of good manners or for religious reasons . . . A third possibility could only be that he went in order to smile at the naïveté of people from his superior scientific heights. But that is impossible. That was not his way of doing things. Because, do you know, when I think about it, he did show a certain interest in the Bible. Although this was neither a religious interest nor an ironic one. It was somehow a third way . . ."

Johanna falls silent and I say: "A very interesting observation. How did this interest manifest itself?"

Johanna says: "Well, in the first instance, the fact that he knew unbelievably many passages from the Bible by heart. And loved to quote them. This can, of course, be explained by what he learned as a child. But I do remember a little circle we had in Mittweida called the Serious Bible Scholars. They were, for the most, simple people. Several half-educated folk, but a few academics as well. Yes, this happened rarely, but Bernhard did go along to their meetings on a few occasions. And not to make fun of anyone, or when drunk, but when he was stone cold sober."

"But nonetheless—for what inner motive?"

Johanna shrugs her shoulders. "I imagine that he just happened to be interested in how people try to tackle their problems. I think that if there had been in Mittweida, apart from that little circle of Bible scholars, the usual associations that were to be found in larger cities—theosophists and anthroposophists, the Oxford Movement, and so on, Bernhard would have gone along, but without any commitment on his part . . . I did hear that later on he . . ." Johanna stiffens slightly in her armchair at her own words, looks inquiringly at me, then smiles rather apologetically. "Well, you will now think that I tried to keep an eye on him even when he had moved to Hamburg later on. But I would say: no! I only heard things about him now and again and quite by chance. At least, not with any initiative on my part. Simply because some of my girlfriends in Mittweida thought that anything they knew about him *had to* interest me. In a word, people told me that out there at Bergedorf he did go a few times to such an odd group as . . . What was it now? The Order of Good Templars . . ."

"Sorry," I interpose, "but who were these Good Templars?"

"I didn't know either," Johanna admits, "but then one of my girlfriends explained that it was some sort of zealous teetotalers' association that originated in America. And a few of my girlfriends added that in Bergedorf Bernhard had even more need of their knights in shining armor than he had had in Mittweida."

I then say: "My dear lady, that was of course not what I wanted to ask you in the first instance, but now that we've broached the subject, could you clear up something for me once and for all? I'm thinking about the role played by alcohol in his life . . ."

"But what kind of question is that?" asks Johanna, a little bit wearily. "I mean to say, I cannot tell how things stood during his Hamburg years. Those girlfriends I've mentioned could not be relied upon to supply impartial information. I can only speak about his years in Mittweida." Johanna pauses a brief moment as if weighing up how to express herself so that I will understand. Then she says, almost curtly: "Well, despite his being a genius, there was a lot about him that was infantile. At least, rather infantile. As with most men of his caliber. Sometimes he would hit upon the most childish of pranks . . ."

"Such as . . . ?"

"Such as? Well, in the early 1920s in Mittweida he had this friend. Engineer Czygan. A Czech or a Sorb or whatever. For instance, it could happen that Bernhard would turn up at midnight at Czygan's place, wake him up, drag him out of bed—but completely sober—because he had had some technical brainwave. And Czygan would be all enthusiasm. Because he was of the same ilk—if you like—a fool or mad or a genius. And so they would start discussing Bernhard's idea.

It could happen that they went to the bar. But it could also happen that they would, as Bernhard put it, go for a stroll under the starry heavens. Until the gentlemen felt their stomachs rumbling. Then, at four in the morning, Bernhard would roll up his trouser legs and go fishing in the pond. And would catch one. So they would build a fire out there in the Schweitzerwald, and Bernhard proved to be a dab hand at frying fish, the son of a fisherman that he was. And then at five in the morning they would wake up the landlady of the Hop Flower bar by banging on the door, and ask for some salt for the fish, this being in his eyes the most normal thing in the world. If this wasn't childish, it was at least a kind of student prank. At the age of fifty. And, every three or four months, he would be on the bottle, three or four days in a row. That too. Although he was never to be seen drunk in a public place. And then—nose to the grindstone again. I am not exaggerating when I say: twenty hours of work a day. An exceptional strain on both body and soul. Polishing mirrors and lenses is hard work. Even physically. And especially heavy because of the exceptional self-control that you have to exercise every single second. Oh yes, I'm telling you this from personal experience. I'm familiar enough with this sort of work . . ."

I say: "Yes, I've heard that Bernhard had worked in his younger years in opticians' workshops in Berlin. And I am very grateful. You have given me very good insight as to the human side of Bernhard. But allow me to return to another question that we have touched on in our conversation. What do you think: Did Bernhard—given his own, shall we say Baptist or Herrnhuter background—believe in God or didn't he? Even in our century there have been a number of major physicists who have believed in God."

"I don't think so in his case," says Johanna slowly.

"And why do you think not?"

"Because I remember," says Johanna, lifting her bright gaze from the tablecloth, "Bernhard said once that when he listened to Händel he would believe that God existed."

I then ask: "And that would mean that as he will have listened to Händel only a fraction of the time, then he will not have believed in God for the rest . . . ?"

"Maybe it's like that," Johanna allows, but not quite satisfied with this response, continues: "The way you have expressed yourself sounds a trifle odd—but there is truth in it. Because do you know, I can remember that he once said: 'I have the starry heavens instead of God. Like Herschel. Incidentally.'" Johanna admits this with a little sad coquettishness. "Bernhard did not say and I do not know to this day where it was that Herschel said this. But Bernhard at any rate said that the starry heavens are the best antidote to the fear of death. If I think my way into the heavens, I become so tiny and trivial, that my death will be of no significance whatsoever . . ."

Frau Brandt fingers the fringe of the table runner.

I do not know what it is that urges interviewers on at such junctures. I am urged on by nothing more than chance, which brings questions to the forefront of my mind. And I now know that a suitable moment has arrived. I say:

"Frau Brandt, could you not tell me something about your husband, I mean Herr Brandt?"

She looks at me as if a little shocked. As if I am not supposed to know that she also had a husband. As if she has to resign herself to the fact that I must have known. But that mentioning him is somehow unseemly. She says:

"But that hasn't got anything to do with Bernhard . . ."

"Oh but it has, my dear lady," I say, expressing as much disagreement as courtesy will allow. "Because you affect Bernhard more than anyone else. And Herr Brandt in turn affects you. So that . . . So that I would be most grateful if you could perhaps show me a few photos of Herr Brandt. And I would be even more grateful if you could show me some pictures of yourself during your Mittweida years."

Johanna is slightly put out, but soon gets over it:

"If you will allow me, I would first like to offer you a cup of coffee. But both the coffee and the photos—inasmuch as there are any—are upstairs in my room. Let's go up . . ."

She walks in front with an old woman's steps, light as paper, and I follow.

The room is slightly oppressive owing to the low ceiling and the slant of the roof, but is otherwise pleasantly lit, situated as it is on the top floor of the lawyer's dwelling. A door opens out onto a tiny balcony.

"Look, you can see the river."

She opens the door and leads me out. Down below, a hedge marks the boundary of the plot and beyond it there is the green rug of a lawn covered in red maple leaves. And if you lean quite far over the balustrade, you can see a glittering gray strip of the river Trave to the left.

When I step back into the room, the cups have been filled from a thermos and there is a bowl of thin biscuits on the table. With a photo album lying next to it. Johanna speaks between sips:

In 1929, she and Werner moved from Mittweida to Dresden. Werner had transferred the bookshop he had inherited from his uncle to that city. In 1944, the flat and the shop, along with most of the city, were destroyed in the bombing, and Johanna had rescued a few bundles of belongings and moved to Irmgard's place in Brunswick. And had stayed there. Initially because it was impossible to find a flat in this devastated country. Then later because Irmgard had a baby, and needed a babysitter while she worked as a schoolteacher. As soon as Irmgard's husband was back from the war, he had had the sense to specialize as a lawyer in war reparations claims and began to earn good money from this. He had sought compensation for Johanna for her destroyed property, but the amount she got in the end was tiny because by now the place she had claimed lay in another country. The compensation was not sufficient to start a new independent life. Johanna had given her small sum to Irmgard, and it had been invested in the new house that they had built in the mid-1950s. In Lübeck because that was where Irmgard's husband was from. They guaranteed Johanna the room we are now sitting in for the rest of her life in gratitude for the help she had given (including her childcare activities).

Johanna says, with a slight smile: "Neither they nor I realized at the time how long they were guaranteeing the room for . . ."

The excursion into her past is at an end and I feel I must now suggest:

"Could we return to Herr Brandt?"

"Oh yes," says Johanna—in words that suggest that she had forgotten in the meantime, but in a tone that confirms that my request had been at the back of her mind all along. She places a photo album with a green velvet cover that has seen better days on the table, and opens it at a certain page.

"Well, here they both are for you to see . . ."

And there they both are. To the left, a photo of Bernhard that is already familiar to me. I am a little disappointed that it is not a photo I have never seen before. And even among those I have seen, I would have preferred another, one that would exemplify the ideal mentioned by Herr Kelter regarding Bernhard's appearance: a willful peasant lad who has starved his way to becoming an intellectual, but has remained the same nonetheless. But the photo in Johanna's album does still show the same man. Even though in that photo (Kurt Schröder, Mittweida, Rochlinerstraße 24. Fernruf 305)—even though he is wearing a jacket that looks a little like a tuxedo, a pocket watch on a chain, and a hat with a silk band in a dandified manner. With the fingers of his left hand stuck into his trouser pocket and the back of that hand so brightly lit that the photographer must have realized that his model was particularly sensitive on this point . . .

And so the one to the right is Werner Brandt.

This is a portrait photo and taken with the subject much more in the *foreground* than with Bernhard. But this unfortunately corresponds to their roles being reversed then, at least in Johanna's time.

Werner has dark hair combed straight back over his scalp, but luckily not slicked. He has full, dark eyebrows, and compared with this energetic line of brow, his gaze is one of uncertainty. But maybe this stems from the fact that he is wearing those horn-rimmed spectacles, fashionable at the time, but that give someone looking at the photo some decades later the impression of vacillation. The photograph has been taken to show the right side of his face in semi-profile (it strikes me that in this album the two men are turning their backs on each other), so that the viewer sees a man in a gray summer suit with a nose that is neither sharp nor blunt, a soft mouth that is giving a fleeting smile and a neck that has been shaved surprisingly high. There is no doubt that this is a man with civilian ideals who has just been to a military barber's.

"When was this photo taken?"

"In the summer of '43. When he came home on leave for the last time."

Well, it was all so long ago and Johanna is so old that she can answer in complete tranquility. Or in tranquility at least. For both reasons, that of time past and that of age, to be exact.

"And when did he die?"

Johanna replies, completely calm:

"Soon after he went back out there."

"In Yugoslavia?"

Johanna nods.

"But do tell what sort of man he was."

Maybe there is not the slightest hint of irritation in Johanna's voice. Maybe I only imagine it to be present when she says:

"A very decent sort of man. But absolutely *ordinary.* Ordinary men are, after all, the most respectable . . ."

And it suddenly strikes me that *now* is the time. I can now ask without ruining my chances of getting an answer. I say:

"But Frau Brandt, do explain—if I am to write a novel about Bernhard this is very important—and do say if you do not wish to answer, but I would be most grateful if you did: Why was it that you preferred, well, an absolutely ordinary man to an absolutely unusual one?"

Johanna looks out through the window at the gray sky and remains silent. And I count the seconds out of interest. Or rather the second-long moments that experience has taught me are suitably long. Johanna remains silent for eleven seconds. Then she says, rapidly, in a somewhat flat voice:

"Bernhard's strangeness was simply *too* strange for me. Because I myself belong to the group of ordinary folks."

I try to catch the content of her thought, but I am not quite sure of myself: "Are you thinking of, let us call it his lack of discipline? I mean things like that business with the engineer Czygan."

"Good Lord, yes—such things as well. But principally—I know what I'm saying will sound ridiculous, but actually quite the contrary. His exaggeratedly disciplined manner. If you can call it that."

"Are you thinking of his bouts of intense work lasting several weeks at a time?"

"Yes. Unfortunately. With all respect for his work! And you may think that I *understood* how to have respect for it. I myself wanted to become an expert in the same field. And I managed to. Well, not to such an extent. Not like him, quite obviously. I am, after all, an ordinary person. But I did learn the skill through and through. And grew in so doing to respect the way people do their work. But despite all my understanding and respect—in the end his working frenzy just became intolerable. His drinking bouts—or as he himself called them—days of relaxation or work-enabling days, those were things I could have tolerated. Because when he got tipsy he was neither violent nor disgusting. He could be amusing for hours at a stretch, would get ever more spirited, and would then suddenly disappear somewhere. That is to say, he would go somewhere to sleep it off. I'm telling you: I have no idea what stories they told about him in Hamburg. When he carried on like this in Mittweida—a few days every two or three months—that was quite manageable. But I soon saw this happening: the number of normal days grew fewer and fewer. What do I mean by normal days? Simply days spent as normal people do. As ordinary people would spend them in those days: work from breakfast till lunch. Maybe in the polishing workshop. Then lunch, maybe a bit on the odd side, but in a vegetarian restaurant. Then normal small pleasures, an hour in a café, a visit to the cinema, and an evening with a novel, or with that new invention, the wireless—you remember how it was?—I don't suppose you do. With earphones, through the earphones news, music—well, rather tinny, but good music anyway—even perhaps Bernhard's Händel . . . But such days became fewer in his life. Despite all my efforts. And instead came his work frenzy. I've already mentioned: days and nights on end with the smell of tar and glass dust. Shaving less and less frequently. Clothes more ragged as time went on. And if he were at home for the odd hour, he would be—how shall I put it—irritable, because he felt bound by his hands and feet, or happy, but as if in a fever, totally absorbed by a mish-mash of technical ideas that were bubbling up in his head—precision screws, aerial cameras, periscopes, some new profile for a propeller, some sort of merry-go-round built on new principles, God knows what else . . ."

"And all of this became, how shall I say, too colorful for you?"

"Yes."

"So that in 1927, when he had finally moved from Mittweida to Hamburg, you say that you stayed behind because *you* yourself had had enough . . . ?"

Johanna is silent for seven or eight seconds—saying this is no doubt not easy for her:

"Yes."

I leaf through the photo album, to the front for pictures of Bernhard Schmidt, and to the back for those of Werner Brandt, and I marvel at Johanna's steadfastness long ago and her honesty right now. In those days she was not yet the mild old lady whose mouth showed the bitterness of experience at the corners. In those days she was, as can be seen here, a bright-eyed young woman with shimmering hair, a young woman with a touch of romanticism in her white dress of simple cut, like in David's portraits—but nevertheless a young woman with such a clear gaze that I feel slightly sad at something or someone.

But right now Frau Brandt's frankness has given me an impertinent idea, a slightly base professional idea. I think rapidly to myself: women this old tend to be surprisingly candid about their former love affairs. Maybe on being asked she would tell me about something only *she herself* among those still alive could know about Bernhard . . . I say in as neutral a voice as possible:

"My dear lady, with the exception of Bernhard Schmidt and perhaps a few close colleagues—and of course a couple of historical background figures—I have altered the names of people in my novel. For that reason I would like to hope, if you so agree . . . Look, in the novel it is unavoidable that Bernhard declares his love for his beloved. And it would be invaluable, with regard to authenticity, if such words were to be the actual, genuine ones. Tell me, what sort of words did he use?"

Johanna looks out of the window at the gray sky and is silent for a moment. But I can see immediately from her face that she has *decided to tell*! And so she does. Very calmly. Perhaps in a slightly condensed manner, having remolded the phrases over the years to form more of a unity than they had in reality. But assuredly and honestly:

"Bernhard only expressed his love to me on one single occasion. We had been close for many years. But everything had somehow occurred without words. At least without *such* words. So I remember quite exactly how he expressed himself on that single occasion.

"We had come in from a walk. A summer's evening. From a stroll to the windmill at Lauenheim. We used to go there when he had the opportunity. But this time I had observed that he was more restless than usual. And then, in the beech grove, he stopped suddenly—I remember the rush of the millstream could be heard very clearly. He stepped up to me and asked:

"'Johanna, are you acquainted with Hörbiger's glacial cosmogony?'

"I said . . . But listen, I will now have to explain to *you* the writer what this phenomenon was. Because it has now been forgotten completely . . . Look, in those days it was ridiculously popular among dilettantes and semi-educated people—it was cosmogony and mythology rolled into one. It explained every cosmic phenomenon and half of all phenomena on earth. And, by the way, the birth of galaxies. Anyway, according to Hörbinger, there were two opposing principles at work in the universe: the Neptunian and the Plutonian. Or, let's say, the principle of ice and that of heat. And everything that occurred in the universe was because of the struggle between them. One of the basic claims of Hörbinger was that there existed gigantic stars, several hundred million times the size of our sun, that are of both the one and the other sort—that is, the ice sort and the heat sort. And their collisions would give birth to new galaxies. And so on. In other words—as a scientific theory it was completely absurd, but as a poetic mental game it could be called magnificent!"

Johanna stops talking and looks down at the table, and I think, as the silence continues: Did she expand on this piece of information from the periphery of the history of ideas in order to educate me? Or to avoid giving me a straight answer, after all? In order for me to finally realize her unwillingness to answer me, which she herself only realized halfway through her tale? But curiosity stiffens my resolve, and I pretend not to understand:

"Very interesting. And then . . . ?"

". . . Oh yes . . . ," says Johanna, returning from her memories—and I am beginning to think that she did after all want to acquaint me with the various concepts in order for me to understand what is to come . . .

"Anyway, he asked me whether I knew anything about Hörbinger's teachings. And I replied: do you know, Bernhard, when it is you who are asking such questions, I never dare to say yes. Because for you knowing something means knowing it very thoroughly indeed . . . But I do of course know roughly what they are all about. Not so much a theory, but a myth.

"Bernhard said, and again almost angrily:

"'But I would like it to be true!'

"But why?

"'Then I would have an image.'

"To what purpose?

"'So that I can express myself!'

"You know," says Johanna, "I wanted to ask, *what it was* he was trying to express, but, I don't know—perhaps I anticipated his reply, so I didn't have the heart to ask. What I did ask was:

"'What kind of image are you thinking of?'

"He said: 'The meeting between the Plutonian and the Neptunian stars. And how a new galaxy is born.'

"I said: 'But the *image* already exists! So what if . . .'

"'But that must not be allowed to be a myth! It must be true!' he yelled. As childishly and angrily as could be. And now I could no longer resist. I asked:

"'So what is it you want to express?'

"And he croaked: 'That I love you, fuck it!'

"It was so dark by now that I can hope he didn't see my wry smile. I took his hand and said: 'Bernhard, I've known that for several years.'

"He cried: 'I see!' and let go of my hand and ran off. Well, I didn't go running after him. When I reached town, he wasn't in his workshop, nor was he at home. Nor at the Lindengarten. He turned up only three days later—he had gone away that very evening to pay off some old debt to Herr Fauth . . ."

Johanna says no more, then, a short while later, in a voice that shows she has returned to the present:

"I don't know what you can do with that for your novel, but that was the way that Bernhard Schmidt declared his love to me . . ."

And I am thinking: and pretty soon, after they were standing there in the gloaming in the beech grove in Lauenheim (I wanted to ask how soon after, but I didn't dare), Johanna had said to Bernhard that now *she* had had enough—and chose, instead of him, Werner with the dark eyebrows and the uncertain gaze . . . I would like to ask whether she had know her Werner long. But that is not of any direct importance for my novel about Bernhard Schmidt. Before I ask that, I really ought to ask how Bernhard reacted to her leaving him. With a double dose of work frenzy no doubt, or even longer "relaxation" after what had happened . . . I ought to ask *how* it was that Johanna came to take the step she did, what went through her mind, what she weighed against what, what feelings, hovering between affront, disappointment, desire, or despair she felt—not only for the sake of my novel but also for my own sake, so that I could get to know for what reasons women do such things. Or would at least have done so sixty years ago. But I cannot bring myself to do so. It is only me who is imagining that at this point something that had previously remained undamaged in Bernhard was now destroyed, something that would have come to fruition could now no longer do so. But whether it could have happened is something I simply do not know. It is good enough that we grope our way toward *what actually happened.*

I ask simply this: "Frau Brandt—you mentioned, if I am not mistaken, that Bernhard traveled away the same evening that he declared his love for you, well—by way of that glacial cosmological image—to a Herr Fauth's place? This wouldn't just happen to be the same Philipp Fauth who was one of the authors involved with glacial cosmogony, would it?"

Johanna cries out: "Well, well—you've actually heard of him then?" And only then does she realize the obliqueness of my question! "No—you couldn't have . . ." And I think to myself: strange how old people can, as in a dream, blunder through space and generations, however good their memories otherwise are . . . Johanna says: "Yes, it was that very same Philipp Fauth. He was an untiring observer of the heavens. Especially the moon. And used to order mirrors and lenses for his telescopes from Bernhard."

"So in some strange way," I point out, "he must have sucked the juice of his observations out of his cosmic ice using Bernhard's instruments!"

"That's true," says Johanna, "but Bernhard is in no way responsible for that." I think: it's almost moving to think that this old woman is rushing to the defense of her lover whom she abandoned some sixty years previously . . . But I can nevertheless not really forgive her for abandoning him. I feel that I should try to penetrate the essence of this action, but as I have already said—I don't want to, I daren't, I haven't the heart to do so. So nothing remains to be done but to thank her and get up from my seat. In any case you always think afterward of hundreds of questions that you should have asked, even important ones. And a barely perceptible shadow of dissatisfaction at my abrupt departure hangs over Johanna's leave-taking. We are already downstairs again, in the hall, near the mirror of the hall stand, when I take out my diary, write down the contact details for my Hamburg stay, and rip the page out:

"Frau Brandt—just in case—here is a phone number you can ring for the next ten days. And the address you can send letters to. If you do remember something that I have forgotten to ask, but which springs to mind and you consider important . . ."

Once I'm standing in the hallway I briefly shake her parchment-brittle but nonetheless warm hand, and cannot help thinking, though I try to fend off the vain thought, that however *indirectly* this may be, this has something of a direct touch of the sorcerer's hand of Bernhard Schmidt himself . . . And once the door has shut behind me and I am standing on the street, I cast a glance back at the lawn strewn with maple leaves, at the house, and what Kurt Tucholsky once said springs to mind: *it is a most peculiar thing to think that you have done something for the last time in your life.*

On the fourth day after this conversation took place, my friend in Hamburg handed me a letter at morning coffee from Johanna. Here it is:

> My dear sir,
> You asked me a number of rather odd questions yesterday and I, accordingly, gave a number of rather odd answers. But it is not my strange answers that concern me now. I can imagine that you will in any case alter them in a hundred ways. Chop them up, piece them together, change them. You will not fail to use poetic license—if, that is, you use them at all. Whatever the result may be, there will be so little left over in its original form for me to worry about. But there is nonetheless one matter that is causing me concern. That is to say—*one* of the answers I gave you. Because all the other answers, however subjectively and oddly I might have answered your questions, they at least corresponded to the truth. Except for one. When you asked me this one, I felt no good reason to answer it differently than I had sixty years before, both to other people and ultimately to myself. But this morning it suddenly struck me—and I still feel this—that now is the time for the truth to come out. I shall never meet you again. That knowledge releases me from the pain of my admission. But this admission exists nonetheless and has been preserved in some way because of the memories of Bernhard. Do what you wish with it, according to choice. What else can I say to an author? Only this: authors are rarely, if you will forgive me, worth the truth, but they should be allowed to know it, all the same. And so: it was not I that left

Bernhard. It was he that left me. It was only the fact that my pride had been hurt to the very marrow of my bones that has caused me to forever deny this fact. What really happened was as follows:

A week after that sole declaration of love, which I described to you, he invited me out into the town park, so that I could help him take the glass spheres down from the trees. He did not like questions, nor did I ask him any. But I already had an inkling that this meant he was going away—he had recently been several times to Hamburg and talked of moving there. And after what he had told me the previous week I never doubted for a moment that we would be going to Hamburg together. We loaded the spheres into two baskets. When we were ready, it was already dark. Then all at once he took me by the hand and said: "Johanna, I'm leaving for Hamburg now. For good. But you are not coming with me. You will stay in Mittweida."

I do not know why he did this. He did not explain and I did of course not ask. At first I was struck dumb with shock, then pride sealed my lips. Much later I understood: there was something in my behavior that clearly got on his nerves. Maybe the fact that I explained that I wanted to help him love Germany. I remember noticing at the time how he *gave a start* at these words. But it was what I really wanted. I spoke about it. In the same way as he talked about his Naissaar. For everyone loves their native land. At least, so long as it is an unlucky land.

A little while before this, when I was looking for a book in the Brandt bookshop, Werner Brandt had said to me: "By the way, Fräulein, when you get fed up with ironing and pressing Schmidt's trousers, I shall ask for your hand in marriage." I was ill for a whole month. Then I went to the bookshop and said to Brandt: "OK. I'm now fed up with ironing Schmidt's trousers." And I shall also set down in writing in this letter, so as to free myself of the utterance, that I said to Werner: "I'm leaving that dirty old man!" And Werner said: "Let's go to the parish registrar and sign the book."

Soon after that I moved with Werner to Dresden. I am not saying that if Bernhard had written to invite me I would have left Werner on the spot. Because my pride required that I remain loyal to Werner. But I do know—every morning that Bernhard was still alive, and for several years after that, my heart would flutter every time I leafed through the post: maybe a letter from Bernhard . . . I would hardly have gone, had he invited me. Because the life you have chosen is a binding commitment. Or . . . God knows.

So there we are. I have nothing further to add. I hope that you succeed in writing your novel. But as far as I have heard, such things take an immense amount of time. So that I at least will never read it. Because by the time it is translated into German, I will already be what Bernhard once said about himself when in a jocular mood—a tiny star in the Telescope constellation.

I wish you all the best.

Yours,
Johanna Brandt
Lübeck, October 14, 1985

■ □ ■ □ ■

9

"OH—HELLO, HERR SCHMIDT! ONCE AGAIN MY SINCERE CONDOLENCES on the death of your mother. I was very worried, as you were away for such a long time—five whole months! And I am very glad that you have finally come back. *Tomorrow,* Herr Schmidt, we must have a talk about how we are to proceed . . ."

At that point, I noticed on Schorr's friendly face a certain inexplicable perplexity. Feeling themselves to be directors and behaving accordingly are things that Germans can do easily and convincingly—especially when they have been directors for quite some time. And Schorr always managed this perfectly. This really was the first time that I noticed that the old boy was in a bit of a quandary, that something was disturbing his self-esteem and was making him squirm. And he did indeed lay out the reasons for this the very next day. Even before I could have brought myself to ask.

At nine o'clock promptly, as soon as he had arrived for work, he sent Fräulein Berger to my workshop to fetch me. He even came to meet me in the general office and led me in a fatherly manner into his own private one. He asked me briefly about my journey (he had already written a letter at home about my mother's death and sent his own and his colleagues' written condolences to Naissaar). Besides, he had repeated his condolences when we met the previous day. So there was no further need for him to express them once again. At least not regarding my mother's death. But if the content of what he said touched upon this, it was for quite a different reason.

"Herr Schmidt—back in March I did what I had promised to do on your departure: I had a brochure printed to advertise your telescope. Exactly as we had discussed together. And I sent it out far and wide. To everyone I thought fit . . ."

"I see."

Now I too remembered. It all came back to me in an embarrassing way, the fact that during the whole time I was away I never actually forgot about Schorr's utopian predictions; despite Mother's death, despite my summer games with the propellers for my ship against the wind, the anticipations of the director had stuck in my mind: when you get back, you will, in one way or another, be a rich man! Thanks to the orders that will have arrived in the meantime . . .

"Well? And the results?"

I asked this in quite a haughty manner, in an ironic tone of voice. But not so ironically, I hope, that it was against my interests; my hopes and fears and the feigned superiority could be detected through that tone of voice.

"The results—how shall I put it—are scandalous," muttered Schorr, and looked down at his writing desk. "Not one single order! Over almost six months! Not even an inquiry as to what the instrument you have invented can actually do! I have to admit: I am agog! I really cannot understand the passivity of the world in this matter at all. Can you?"

So that was that. I now had to comfort him. What else could I do? To a degree, I also comforted my own disappointed self in so doing. I said:

"Yes, I do."

"Well, well, well! And whatever could the reason be?"

"The skepticism of experts."

"It should be the experts who, in the first instance . . ."

"Listen, some chap called Schmidt offers to sell weapons experts a minipistol he himself has invented—length 62 millimeters, weight 120 grams. Guaranteed bull's eye when shooting at a ten-pfennig coin at a distance of ten kilometers. What do the experts do? The experts chuck the project into the wastepaper basket. They cannot even be bothered to insult Schmidt with a letter."

Schorr burst into laughter, and he laughed, now loudly, now quietly, for all of half a minute.

"Herr Schmidt, you really are in-cor-ri-gi-ble! But we do have to decide *what* we are going to do now. In order to draw the world's attention to your new invention."

What could I answer to that? I could hardly start explaining that he should do such and such in order to draw attention to my invention. I could not say write, for instance—and, of course, include your name and titles: professor, doctor, director, and national consultant—a thoroughgoing article about aspects of my invention . . . *I* simply could not make this suggestion. Because he would be incapable of writing such an article. He didn't even know how my invention had been put together! He knew no more than the most cursory details: *roughly speaking,* how many thousandths of the thickness of the plate this involved, and so on, and so forth . . . But whether this was a matter of one side or both sides of the plate was something he just didn't know . . . Even less how to actually construct such a plate. He hadn't a clue about that. Nor did anyone else, for that matter. From time to time, I even thought that I myself didn't know. Despite the fact that I had succeeded in polishing such a correction plate three times over. Despite the fact that I myself had thought from time to time that semi-inexplicable events were at play whose repetition I was incapable of achieving ever again.

And second, the idea of myself suggesting this (that Schorr should write an introductory article about my telescope) was made impossible by the fact that I was the very last person who could suggest this to him. This would have been worse than farting in a public place, worse than letting off stink bombs—inasmuch as I had heard endlessly from Mother and Father, Grandmother and Grandfather, that self-praise stinks . . .

But he sat there across his green desk from me, my director in need of solace, with his thin drooping mustache, his short arms crossed on his belly, his pearl tiepin slightly askew—and looked at me, repeating:

"Herr Schmidt—what must we do?"

I grunted: "Work."

Only when I had said this did it occur to me that I was, in a sense, mocking the director. It was as if I was paying him back for the upbraiding I had received on occasion from his lips. At times when he wished, in his straitlaced German way, to interfere with my routine.

When he accused me of doing too little work—and on each occasion hastily apologized. Because he then remembered that just before those couple of beery days of mine, which he had heard about in Bergedorf yet again, I had for three weeks in a row, and more or less round the clock, been polishing the world's best forty-centimeter mirror for him . . . *Et cetera.*

I simply grunted: "Work!" But he, for heaven's sake, did not perceive this as mockery. Which he had, in my opinion, every reason to do. Perhaps he was simply too worried by our lack of success. Perhaps he thought his conscience to be so childishly clear, that it would never occur to him that I could be taking the Mickey . . . Goodness gracious me, a director did, after all, have certain disciplinary duties vis-à-vis his underlings—and he was carrying them out in as paternalistic and at the same time polite a fashion as he, Schorr, could do in the face of this willful and unpredictable mule, descendant of sea pirates, Schmidt—who was then likely to—*et cetera.*

In other words, I replied: *work.*

And that is what we did. Schorr started a large-scale project to comb the heavens of the northern hemisphere using my telescope. And I first of all completed the construction of a second example of my telescope. And so, for the following two years, there were a whole lot of other things to do as well . . .

Incidentally, Wachmann, that well-brought-up young man, who has by now been *Dr.* Wachmann for some fair while, once asked me if I were not prepared to explain to him the details of the theory behind the correction plate along with the concomitant technology for its production. So he could put it all down on paper and publish it for the scientific fraternity. Ah, yes. He suggested that writing it all down might just be a little too much for me to cope with, and kindly offered to assist. To a certain extent, he and the others regarded me as a wizard, half incapable of writing, someone who was even himself not fully aware of what he was dealing with . . . Wachmann's offer was of course completely genuine. But it did hurt me a little. So I said:

"Do you know, Herr Wachmann, it is better that each and every one who deals with such matters derive his knowledge from personal experience."

And I have to admit that when this nice young chap Wachmann agreed without demur, in his well-brought-up way—("That is undoubtedly true, Herr Schmidt")—his agreement irritated me to such an extent that I felt insulted by it, so that I tried to resist the temptation to insult *him* myself. What I said was:

"And besides, Herr Wachmann, I do not think it wise to cast pearls before . . . you yourself know before which creatures . . ."

Wachmann concurred with this too in his well-mannered way.

In fact, it became an unreal year. The year 1932. The whole country was being governed under a state of emergency rule, the *Notverordnungen.* Six million unemployed. Herr Brüning both covertly and overtly brandishing his knout to the Left, at the same time as the Nazis to the Right began to yell ever louder. Until Herr Brüning was dragged off his chancellor's stallion and Herr von Papen's very dodgy government rose to power. And in the background—the SA in their brown uniforms and their unwashed faces, even if you only looked at the street scene in Bergedorf. Then rumors of an internal struggle within the ranks of the SA, even rumors of murder, but mention of this was toned down for the general public. Then the rising alarm, emanating even from people who otherwise behaved perfectly sensibly: that *the Jews* were to blame! Hovering above all of this was a febrile and suffocating atmosphere, at first, it is true, merely an almost tangible foreboding of terror that seemed to rise up from the present situation. Brrr . . . Amidst all of this I learned to adopt the old art that has allowed me to live more or less independently for a very long time: listen to what is said, because you cannot entirely avoid doing so, but do not react in any way to what you have heard. Read the papers, naturally, because if you shut your eyes you are no longer alive—but read them in such a way that things you have no control over remain at *another* level, a level that, compared with my way of life, could be in another galaxy . . .

It really was an unreal year. Because at the same time great discoveries were made in the field of science! Hubble confirmed that the spiral mists are constellations equivalent to our Milky Way. And their aberrations toward red in the spectral continuum, which increase with distance, are proof that the universe is expanding! Compared with this, Piccard's 16,940 meters is a mere trifle—but in fact the balloon flight of the stubborn Belgian also expanded our world. To a certain degree it was even more important and tangible. Because it is not only an expansion of sight, thought, and theory—but also for mankind in the sheer physical sense . . .

But concerning the theory and technical side of my invention—this was too important a matter to leave entirely to chance. I had written it all down in the autumn of 1930. On squared paper that I had cut out of a couple of exercise books, a little like the work of a stenographer when it came down to detail, but accurately enough for a specialist to understand. And I've now got it here with me, rolled up and tied with a piece of string, in my room in greengrocer Schmidt's house. And the greengrocer knows where it is: in a shoebox on the hat shelf of the wardrobe. And knows what to do should anything happen to me: he must take it to Schorr. Every sheet of paper found there in my room must go to Schorr. This above all.

In those days I never thought about the fact that something could happen to me. Neither with regard to my health or in any other way. I remember that there was something wrong with the cupola of the large Repsold refractor. They put up scaffolding around it and I clambered up to take a look. That must have been in the winter of 1931—it was a bit icy and slippery up there . . . When I had come down again, Paul—our Paul Schmidt, that is—looked at me a bit oddly and said:

"Herr Schmidt—please, don't climb up there. You're no longer that young . . ."

And I thought: hell . . . A fifty-one or -two or -three-year-old man is in his most vital years . . .

Nor did I have doubts about my physical condition in other respects either. So me and my colleagues had a few nice parties. I didn't celebrate with them as a rule. When relaxing I often got on better with complete strangers. But there were exceptions. Such as when, for instance, we would teach one of our number a lesson. Well, here's an example.

Baade was a fine young man. A brilliant chap. I liked him for other reasons too, as he would pit himself against old Schorr's rather narrow-minded approach in the most elegant of ways. His way of thinking was simply more modern with regard to scientific matters. But he did make me laugh with some of the things he got up to. People are odd, after all. Alongside very serious aspects of character, they can have unbelievably childish traits. Baade, for example, loved, despite all his unusual intelligence, to play practical jokes on his friends in a silly student sort of way, maneuver them into a series of traps. With imaginary things, trick questions, activities that proved to be idiotic. And he was always absolutely convinced that *he himself* would never fall for such things.

Anyway, it must have been the spring of 1931. Because the Nazis were not yet much in evidence and Baade had not yet sailed off to America. One pleasant Saturday evening in spring we went on a bar crawl around Bergedorf until dawn. Baade, Wachmann, the Swede Malmkvist, who was our apprentice, and me. Our money ran out in the end, although we knew that Baade must still have had some tucked away, so we started provoking him so that he would buy a few rounds for the rest of us. But he didn't swallow the bait. He smiled, said he was tired, and strolled off home. We happened to be sitting in Land's bar at the time, and Baade lived nearby at the observatory residences. And it so happened that our mailman, in full uniform and with his leather bag over his shoulder, dropped into the Land bar for his morning coffee. We knew him quite well, and we thought of something. Collectively, as such ideas tend to arise. Malmkvist went outside and found a largish brick. We got some packing paper and glue from the bar. Malmkvist happened to have some Swedish postage stamps in his pocket along with a blank cash-on-delivery form. We ordered another coffee for the mailman, we still had enough money for that, and then the mailman took the parcel with him, which by now had been "franked" by the Uppsala post office, the franking drawn in black ink: a parcel for Professor Doktor Baade from the Royal Observatory, C.O.D. fifteen marks. We had even written a suitable rhyme to insert in the parcel. I don't know who wrote it. Not me, in any case. And Malmkvist wouldn't have known enough German. So it must have been Wachmann, but I fear he would deny it.

We left the bar and stood behind the hedge to see what would happen. We could see: the mailman rang the bell of the Baade residence. Baade appeared at the door in a dressing gown and with tousled hair, went back to his room for the money, was given his parcel, and went back inside. And the mailman brought our fifteen marks to where we were standing behind the hedge. So we went back to Land's and had some cognac with our morning coffee and chuckled, imagining Baade back in bed opening his parcel out of curiosity and finding the brick and reading our rhyme, cursing in his well-brought-up way:

Im süssen Unschuldsbade
badet Doktor Baade,
während wir, die Frechen,
bei Land sein Geld verzechen . . .

That is to say:

In a sweet bath of gullibility
Doctor Baade is bathing,
while we, with all temerity,
at Land's his money are spending . . .

That same summer Baade traveled with his friend Minkovski to America. He had had a pretty bitter exchange of words with Schorr. Because Schorr had wanted to keep him. The old chap was incidentally one of those unusual types who managed to get geniuses to work for him and managed too to put up with them, even when they proved to be cleverer than he himself was. But California had offered Baade opportunities that he simply could not have in Bergedorf. People said that the financial crisis would soon be over, but initially it seemed that the reverse was true. For Baade it didn't really make much difference, but for his friend Minkovski, who was Jewish, the trip came just at the right time. The Weimar Republic was to last one more year, and it was becoming more and more obvious in which direction things were moving.

I don't really know anything about the ancient world. But it has nonetheless electrified me somehow. Maybe because the history of the ancient world was one of the inevitable subjects taught at high-school level, but that instilled in me, later in life, the fox's attitude to the grapes in Aesop's fable . . . And of course, my interest in very old things, compared with my interest in things very far away, is to an extent symmetrical. So that I felt that Blegen, with his excavations, brought Troy a thousand years nearer to us than Schliemann did with all his hypotheses, and that it was as if my telescope had been employed within the subject of history.

But with regard to my telescope: after the small, rather sad party we had on the eve of Baade's departure, Walter (i.e., Baade) came over and asked me if I couldn't give him a short description of my instrument that he could take with him to America. I did, of course, agree. For if there was anyone that had contributed anything to my ideas about the correction plate, it was Baade. Maybe during our chat in the Sea of Andaman Baade had contributed 1 or 2 percent to my idea. That for starters. And second, Baade was 200 percent reliable. And third, there was not the slightest chance that I could reproduce my instrument in its Bergedorf variant right now in Germany, and even less of a chance to start to build the larger version for which I had been scribbling down notes for the best part of a year. So I invited Baade home to my place, shoved an extra stool under his right buttock on account of his stiff hip, and placed my shoebox in front of him:

"Note this down!"

And he copied my notes. He understood the whole business pretty quickly. With such a grasp of things that makes me like certain people. Only at a couple of points did he mutter "oh" or "ahah" and ask me whether he had understood some point correctly. So by the time I recalled this episode toward the end of 1932, the details of my Bergedorf instrument will have been lying in Baade's desk drawer at Mount Wilson for about eighteen months. But I had no idea what he had done with them. I had to draw the conclusion that he was not yet sure if my telescope had any prospects of ever getting built even over there.

And then, in 1933, the whole of *Machtergreifung* washed over us (though we had no idea at the time how much it would change our lives). This big-mouthed guy with the Chaplin mustache and the drooping ass—about whom that old gent Hindenburg had said not three days before, "minister of postal services at the very most"—had suddenly, because of the hardening of the old gent's arteries, and the devil knows what other circumstances, become the chancellor. And let loose his gray and black and brown hounds on the German people. That is to say on *those that did not themselves howl with the wolves.* And on the Jews most of all. And never asking how many of them howled with the wolves. Because out of sheer self-preservation a number of Jews made attempts to howl with the wolves. No, by no means all of them behaved as did Einstein. The ruins of the Reichstag were still smoldering when Einstein declared openly that he disapproved of the new regime, and dropped everything, the Prussian Academy, his lecturer's post, his tower, and left. But Richard Courant, a young Jewish chap from Lublinitz in Silesia, and as people said later, a brilliant mathematician, wrote a letter to James Franck saying that . . . the letter was circulated by Franck's family in Hamburg and a copy made the rounds at our observatory. And I have the tiresome habit of remembering texts I have cast an eye over . . . Courant wrote that he was in the first instance shocked at how people like Einstein were expressing themselves and how the internal affairs of Germany were the subject of anti-German agitation using lies and slogans taken from lavatory walls. So that even if Einstein doesn't feel himself to be German, he had nevertheless experienced many good things in Germany and should take personal responsibility for, and try to calm, the unrest that he himself had given rise to. The way Einstein had behaved would only lead to anti-Semitism not limiting itself to attacks on unpleasant writer types and other degenerates but would also lead to attacks on the Jewish people as a whole, even if they were good Germans in their way of thinking or members of their family had shed blood during the recent war . . . Courant wrote: nor can I believe that such an unjust attitude will prevail for long, not at least among the leaders, especially Hitler, whose speeches have, of late, made an entirely positive impression on me personally . . .

When such tragically naive instances of howling with the wolves occurred among the Jews themselves, what is there left to say about other Germans? Even such a respectable person, with regard to common sense and status, as Otto Hahn could be mentioned, and he said at the time that he had every reason to believe that the arrests were carried out in Germany only in such instances where it involved people who proved to be Communists *and just happened to be Jews at one and the same time.* And he explained that he was sure that Hitler was not responsible for the atrocities attributed to him . . . It was of course the case that he said these things to a newspaper reporter in Toronto, and that he would be traveling back to Germany a month later . . .

But I myself didn't expound on such things to anyone. Thank goodness I didn't need to. Because I was neither a Nazi nor a Communist, neither a German nor a Jew. I could allow myself the pleasure of being a bystander. Luckily, no reporter ever asked me anything. But the word *pleasure* is, of course, a rather inaccurate term. Because when you put together all the pieces, the course of events would instill fear in any thinking person. By the way, a few dozen people were taken away in our little town of Bergedorf during the first few months. Not only Communists, who were entirely outlawed by now. But also insignificant former Social Democrats who had opened their big mouths against the Nazis. And what was cynical about this operation was that they were purportedly being interned to protect them from the wrath of the people . . . ! There were supposed to be thousands of them in Oranienburg, in the vicinity of Berlin, and in other camps. A month after the *Machtegreifung,* an edict was published termed the "Statute on the Protection of the People and the State." The signatures of *Reichspresident* Hindenburg and *Reichskantzler* Hitler were neatly applied side by side. And in this statute it was literally stated that such and such clauses of the constitution have now been annulled. The only thing that was not set down in writing was that such annulments were unconstitutional. But what was added was a detailed description of what such annulments entailed: the suppression of Communist violence included measures involving the limitation of personal freedoms, of the freedom of speech including freedom of the press, of organization and congregation. What was allowed was the opening of letters and other postal items, the reading of telegrams and eavesdropping on telephone conversations, searches and confiscation, plus the circumscription of the ownership of property—as the statute stated—beyond the scope of the law that usually applied in such cases. In a word: the Nazis were allowing themselves almost unlimited means to ensure that they remained in power. So the word *pleasure* is perhaps inappropriate in the circumstances. But for heaven's sake—in this whole vortex of madness—my being a *bystander* did for the moment give me a feeling that cannot be described as other than the pleasure of the street urchin. Thanks to the secret protection that I enjoyed at the time. Well, here's one example: from July onward all civil servants were obliged to use the greeting "Heil Hitler!" I thought immediately: but I am not, technically speaking, a civil servant! I am working *in voluntary collaboration* with the observatory. So this did not apply to me. So they can wipe the appropriate orifice with their *Hitlergruß*!

Schorr invited us all to the library and read the circular pertaining to the new statute out to us. A little nervously, which we all noticed, having worked for him for a good while, but quite neutrally. And the news was received in precisely the same manner. Presumably we were all thinking, or to be true to the facts, most of us were thinking: listen, if everyone were to say out loud what they think about this circular, that is, let us not allow such risible shit to enter our mouths, our eyes, our minds! then the changes would simply not happen . . . But everyone kept their peace. As if they were all foreigners and bystanders. But I did notice an ironic quiver at the corners of Wachmann's mouth. And thought to myself: none of this rubbish affects me . . . And there were, luckily, not those types of person working in the observatory who would take such ordinances seriously from start to finish. The driver and one of the young mechanics did try for a couple of days, but then abandoned their efforts. Incidentally, when some party representatives turned up at Schorr's office, he raised his arm appropriately. Almost with demonstrative zeal, to my mind. But only for a moment. But unfailingly. And when writing an official letter he will end it with the required "Heil Hitler!" Because the statute states clearly: if this is not done, suspicion will fall on the individual concerned that he is in willful denial of all that Germany stands for . . .

But no one requires anything of me. Sometimes I even regard this as almost a pity. At the New Year, Schorr mentioned that he was expecting the party bosses to turn up. He had applied on a number of occasions for finance for the large variant of my telescope. He had used this argument, which should have been a salient one under the present circumstances: the large Schmidt telescope will make it possible for German astronomy to get twenty years ahead of America! In fact he did not himself seriously believe this argument, but he did say: if anything will convince them, it is that. And these gents had to turn up at some point. And so they did. I saw the Mercedes with its nickel-plated spokes and hub caps through the window of my workshop, plus the gents in their brown trousers and shiny jackboots. Schorr did not call me to talk to them. Maybe their conversation was planned in that way. Maybe he began to fear that I would in some way ruin the whole plan by the impression I gave the *Genossen.* And thank the Lord that the meeting proceeded in that way. But I still think it was a pity. Because in my mind's eye I was greatly amused at how I behaved there in Schorr's office. Or in fact . . . could have behaved . . .

Fräulein Berger, blushing even more than usual today, has been sent to fetch me. Walking in front, with her stride that grows more like that of a Valkyrie every day. That is the principal reason she conceals her Hammonia backside beneath her brown skirt! She knocks on the door to the director's office and opens it. Schorr says to his guests: "Gentlemen, here is Herr Schmidt, whose invention we have just been talking about . . ." Maybe he mentions the scale of the sums of money involved and maybe the joker even says: ". . . whose brilliant invention we have just been talking about . . ." I cannot be shielded from such expressions of his. And there they are, sitting on his sofa and in his armchairs, the gentlemen, three or four of them, who have just eaten a perfect meal, have just been to the barber's and are all spit and polish, in their mustard-colored uniforms (God knows which specific uniforms, as every third male individual is wearing one nowadays), wearing red armlets with a white patch containing a black swastika, some *Gau-* or *Schau-* or *Sauleiter* or other, with maybe some little lecturer with them. At any rate, they have no more serious specialist to take along. Because they can't be dragging their Lenards or Starks round the whole country. Lenard and Stark are indeed serious physicists with whom they have found a common language. But neither of them has studied anything in the field of optics, or stellar optics. Let them stick to their specialisms and try to help "German physics" crush "Jewish physics." In fact, Lenard is said to have said from his chair at Göttingen that physics is a racial phenomenon and is determined by one's blood . . . How can Nobel Prize winners end up spouting such idiocies? . . . Anyway, I shall not be meeting these gents in Schorr's office. And if they do have a specialist with them, he'll be some fourth-rate individual, some ex-technical college teacher, like our new minister of education—Rust or whatever he's called—who was dismissed a number of years back because of his bad nerves and problems with his students, and has now risen, because of his membership in the right party, to become a university lecturer . . . There they sit on Schorr's leather sofa and in his armchairs and raise their hands as I enter—*Heil Hitler*! Everything they know about me comes from Schorr. And from his lips not one syllable has been uttered that could suggest that it is perhaps unwise to greet me in this manner . . . I am standing before them. My right shirtsleeve is rolled up to my shoulder under my jacket. And I jerk up my right arm to acknowledge their greeting. The effect is exactly the same as when I have tried this out in my room at home: the sleeve of my jacket (it is after all lined with satin) slips down to my elbow, revealing my stump. Onto which my knitted sheath has been rolled. Just as if there is a tarry cap over it. And I say with a straight face and quite incomprehensibly to these conquerors of the globe, with a Jewish accent and in Estonian:

"Ai itle!" ["I'm not saying!"]

Is there another language on this earth that offers such Satanic opportunities for expressing oneself?

But I was never afforded this opportunity. I was not even invited to have the chance to use it. And I'm hardly likely to have used it should I have been given the chance. Neither with the bosses (when they come to visit) nor with anyone else. I was silent and remained a bystander. Or to be more accurate: it wasn't that often I even got the chance to be a *bystander.* I simply looked on from a distance. And imagined this was somehow looking down from above. Anyway, I kept silent. As silent as the great boulders of Naissaar. Like the rocks at Põlendiku. Like the fields at Väikeheinamaa after slash and burn. Completely silent, completely cold. Apparently, at least.

But I couldn't resist taking a glance at the newspapers. Nor could I avoid hearing what the people around were saying about current events. Even though such utterances were mostly made in a whisper and increasingly as hints. Why was this? In fact, you could even say that people uttered things ever more loudly and noisily. Depending, of course, on the exact nature of the utterance. Both types of opinion tended to constrict my throat. Even though I for my part kept quiet on this score.

I remember going to Schlei for a haircut. In those days I would go there for a shave as well. Actually, I could do the shaving myself without the least problem. Although people would go on about it rather a lot at the observatory. Five years ago, when Baade and I were on our way to the Philippines, Mrs. Baade bought me an electric razor without asking me first. Thinking that I would need one because of my handicap. And Baade happened to catch me—and this was even before Cuxhaven—throwing the thing overboard. I needn't, of course, have actually thrown it overboard. And I should naturally have picked a more suitable moment to do so. So that no painful explanation would have been necessary later on. But at the barber's, I tended to let him shave my beard. And on this occasion too.

Instead of old Schlei himself, his son had been working there for several months and training three apprentices. The old chap's hand had shaken so much these past few months that his son had taken over. And he now shaved me as befits an old and regular customer. He was a rather brusque thirty-year-old who occasionally had a whiff of beer on his breath. And on that occasion I suddenly noticed: under his white smock he was wearing mustard-colored knickerbockers and brown jackboots. And I thought: so it has come to this. His business. And I said.

"Please cut my hair. And do my beard afterward too."

In order to avoid having to make conversation, I buried my face in some magazine I'd picked up from the table. But Schlei Junior was in a talkative mood. Had I been following the papers these last few days? I shook my head. But he had been at the center of events and eagerly explained: he'd just come back from Berlin! He'd been in Berlin for two weeks! He circled my head from behind and snipped the hair from behind my ears as he said, his face flushed: he had been marching on the Tempelhof Square on the first of May—along with one and a half million others, celebrating National Workers' Day! That celebration of the dissemination of Communist poison—the first of May—now no longer existed! From now on it would be National Workers' Day! At Tempelhof, one and a half million—and in their hearts—sixty million honorable Germans!

"Herr Schmidt—you cannot imagine the speeches! What unity! What power!"

I muttered: "Mmmm . . ."

The next day he had been sitting with a couple of thousand other handpicked people—I can't remember where exactly—and declared the dissolution of the free trades unions. In their stead, the *Deutsche Arbeitsfront* had been created.

"Herr Schmidt! What a feeling of liberation! The last purulent Communists, the last of the Social Democratic shits, the last snotty liberals and Jews—the whole bunch: a kick up the ass and into the ditch with them." He was clipping, snip, snip, snip, and tidying the edges. ". . . boot up the ass!" He stamped on the floor with his jackboots—but then gave an awkward little bow and mumbled, "I do apologize, Herr Schmidt . . ." So that I nearly burst into laughter at the residue of the petit bourgeois kindergarten disciple that still lurked within him . . .

I muttered: "Mmmm . . ."

On the tenth he had helped a couple of thousand students at the university to throw decadent literature onto the book pyre. And Doktor Goebbels himself had made a speech by the light of the bonfire ("Herr Schmidt, he isn't half a sharp little devil!")—saying that from these flames, where the sickness and shame of the German printed word was reduced to ashes—from these very same flames would arise the gigantic light of the liberation of the German spirit! *Und so weiter* . . . "Simply magnificent, Herr Schmidt!"

I muttered "Mmmm," and asked: "Who'd written the books that they then burned?"

"Oh, the devil knows," said Schlei, and I wasn't sure whether it was the devil or Doktor Goebbels who was now speaking—"books by Jews and their lackeys. All that garbage that prevents the renewal of German might."

And I remembered: the most recent person who had been declared to be a lackey of the Jews in the newspapers was Max Planck . . .

But I didn't utter a word. All I did was mutter *mmmmm*—over and over again until Schlei had finished cutting my hair and had moved on to my beard.

This was duly being lathered, and it was a boundlessly pleasant moment. The shaving foam smelling of lavender was being applied from my throat to my temples, and I had the feeling that I was completely covered in it. And this took away every duty I had to react and rendered me quasi-invisible. But then Schlei began to scrape off my protective layer with his cut-throat razor. Starting on my cheeks, moving on to my throat. Despite the particularly sour stench of beer he did this with professional assuredness. And expounded, as he was working:

"You, Herr Schmidt, are one of my father's oldest customers. And we know you, even in other circumstances—hmm—through and through. We know that you are a foreigner. But just as good as a German, really . . ."

I clearly must have given a start. He stroked the blade over my

Adam's apple so that the stubble rasped, and said: "And at least you're not a Jew, as far as I know. You are, as our professors have assured us, one of Germany's current grand masters of stellar astronomy. And as a human being . . ."

But what I was like as a human being was something I didn't immediately find out. He took an abrupt step to one side, tautened the whet strap, one end of which was hanging on a hook on the wall, sharpened the razor, tested the blade with the tip of his thumb, *siuh, siuh, siuh,* drew the sharpened blade across my throat, and then said: "And as a human being—ho, ho, ho, hoh—a friend of beer, like every good German must be. So do not be afraid. *You* are someone we will accept in our newborn Germany. On the condition, of course, that you don't start messing around with some whore of a Jewess or other."

My lips were covered with shaving foam and I said nothing. I limited my reply to another mutter. And I remember thinking: just last Saturday evening, in the Die Sonne tavern here in Bergedorf, some thin mustachioed type had sung:

Am dünnen Faden hängt ein Schwert
sich auf mein Kopf zu laden.
Denkt bloss nicht daß das Schwert mich stört!
Mich stört noch nur die Faden . . .

Upon a thread there hangs a sword,
could get it on my head.
Do not think that I fear the sword!
What bothers me's the thread . . .

But of course I kept my mouth shut. Then, as now. I refused the hot towel, paid my *Mark fünfzig,* and left. But the next Saturday, in the Die Sonne, I did happen to ask about the man who had sung the sword-and-thread song the previous week. I really have no idea why I was asking him now, when two weeks ago I would not have cared a jot about the man. I don't usually go around asking such questions. The landlord glanced swiftly to both sides with his bulging brown eyes and leaned his reddish mustache over the bar, closer to my ear:

"Don't ask, Herr Schmidt. They came to fetch him when he was sitting at one of the tables here on Sunday. Was dragged off. You get my meaning. Never came back. And I myself was taken a couple of times to the *Sicherheit* people. Why the fuck are people singing anti-German songs in your bar? In the future, keep your ears open and come here to report to us. How the fuck should I know what it is I should inform them about or not . . . ?"

But all of this did not really make me particularly afraid. Not at least before June 30 last year. When Hitler announced, over the space of two days, that he was post factum the supreme judge of Germany. After that, he had seventy leading members of the SA shot. Who were said to have been plotting to overthrow the state. Plus another thirteen people whom he simply didn't like. These are the official numbers. Unofficially, people say that some eleven hundred people were murdered. This was, of course, horrible. Of course it made you jump. But it didn't frighten me as such. Because what did *I* have to do with it all? I did not belong to the SA. I did not wear a mustard-colored shirt. I was—gray. Gray as lamb's wool, gray as the sea, gray as dust, as glass dust. Gray, gray, gray. Not brown, nor a gay lilac. It was whispered abroad that this proclivity of Röhm and Heines and the other leaders of the SA had been condoned by Hitler for the past fifteen years or so. I had nothing to do with such men. Well, I lived here in the Third Reich, this third dimension, if you like, that is true. But for me, for this complete bystander, there was within the third dimension a completely sovereign fourth one—if you like, an independent Fourth Reich—my own level of being. Quite untouchable by the functionaries of the Third. As long as I always remained elusive . . .

Nevertheless, last summer, the week after June 30, I caught my first glimpse of the abyss. The first inklings of an apocalyptic vulnerability.

I had been sitting, standing, crouching time and time again at my polishing lathe for two weeks running, more or less night and day. I decided to take a break for a few days and go to the Holtenklinke that evening to build up my potential a jot. But before that, in the early morning at daybreak, immediately, now—I wanted to take a walk in the fresh air.

I left my workshop, started to stroll through the area beyond the back gate of the observatory, and was soon up on the Gojenberg ridge. There below, about thirty meters down, was the Vierlande plain, which was covered in the grayish mists of dawn right down to the river. The top of the ridge was several meters higher than the tops of the trees growing below and somehow stuck up out into brighter air. The trees and bushes were so wet that this could not have been because of dew alone. It must have rained in the night, but I just hadn't noticed. And now all this water glittering like silver on the foliage, plus the river mists, rising into the air. So that the observatory could not count on any reliable results for the next night either.

I stopped, took a deep breath, and discovered that now, at around six o'clock, the morning air was close rather than refreshing. And I saw, fifty meters away, among the bushes and wearing his dressing gown, Paul Schmidt. Our head of precision mechanics. And he was doing exactly the same as I was: making his way through the wet foliage of the bushes and wiping the moisture off his face and forehead. He had not yet noticed my presence. So I wondered whether to slip back into the bushes or walk over to him. I would have preferred to flee into the bushes. Then stand motionless, my lips slightly apart and every nerve tense, and watch from the shelter of the bushes as he passed by. But playing the wild animal in this manner did seem just too silly for words. If indeed Paul had not already spotted me. A tall, dark-haired, somewhat horse-faced man. An autodidact. Had done his apprenticeship at the Zeiss factory. But quite a wise fellow. And, by the way, quite rich too. Some small factory in Westphalia. Run by his brother. But Paul himself—was hellishly stingy. Thrice as stingy as the average German. But with odd quirks. When Wachmann got married a couple of years back, Paul suggested that they absolutely had to go on their honeymoon. Wachmann had asked—as he himself told me—how he was going to travel. When railway tickets were so damned dear. Paul had replied—by car! It'd be cheaper in a small car to suit the occasion! But Wachmann had cried: Where would he get a car from? Buy one. But I haven't got any money! Whereupon Paul said quite calmly: then I'll lend you some. And he lent Wachmann God knows how much. Three thousand, probably. With which Wachmann bought an old Opel, and they really did go on their honeymoon. And this gesture had been so odd, coming from Paul, that I got over my urge to hide in the bushes and went over to him.

We both said "Good morning, Herr Schmidt" simultaneously, and both laughed dryly at this. Paul said:

"Nothing odd about our meeting here like this, one of us overdoing the work, the other not being able to sleep, and then calling each other Herr Schmidt. Neither of us would mix the other up with anyone else. But have you heard what happened on the night of the thirtieth in Munich? You haven't? Well, not everyone who got shot that night was an SA man. Schleicher and his wife, Klausener and others. And they were big names. Everyone's talking about it. And lesser-known figures. As is always the case. People who had said hostile things about the Führer. And for whom the command was issued: shoot them. Along with these there was a certain doctor of medicine from Munich named Ludwig Schmitt. Schmitt with two *t*'s, you will note. The police went looking for him the other night but couldn't find him. Later on, it emerged why. By then, he had already been in a concentration camp for a couple of weeks. But an order is an order. So *doctor phil.* Eduard Schmid was found as a substitute for *doctor med.* Ludwig Schmitt. His name was admittedly written with only one *d* instead of two *t*'s. And he had never said a wrong word about the Führer. And lived at a completely different address, and was fifteen years older than the other one, as is written in his papers. But an order is an order. And Dr. Schmid was shot. The *d* one instead of the *tt* one. Herr Schmidt, what do you think of that—what should we Schmidts with *dt* think of that?"

I remained silent. Paul said: "Excuse me, I'm going to have a pee in the bushes, then see if I can get back to sleep for a little while. But you should think about this. Ho-ho-ho-hoh."

I walked back home, that is, to the house of greengrocer Karl Schmidt, went to my room, kicked off my shoes and threw myself fully clothed onto the sofa (which I would otherwise do only if I had been having a serious bout of beer drinking)—and strange things began to happen to me.

. . . I was undeniably myself, that is true. But I did not immediately realize which of my changeable egos I was at which of the changeable moments. Though I understood full well what it depended upon. Very simply, and quite mechanically out of this whirlpool of Schmidts, that Schmidt, that is to say, Paul Schmidt, had been released into the air. Then someone mentioned, behind my back, that Schmidt—and I did not grasp which one—had to be killed. And I understood only too well from where the guillotine motif entered my muddle of consciousness: the *Fallbeil*—they would never use such a disgusting French word as *guillotine* in National Socialist Germany—the *Fallbeil* was now a legal instrument of execution in the case of serious criminals. If anything can still be termed legal over here. The first to die in this way was the pathetic fool van der Lubbe, who set the Reichstag building on fire. God knows, maybe it was Goering himself who committed the arson. But the one who was killed was van der Lubbe. And now, behind my back, someone was explaining that a certain Schmidt must die . . . it would be interesting to know which one . . . In the strange earth-brown light of dusk between gray planks, a group of Brownshirts has assembled, smelling of sweat and beer. But they are not pushing particularly hard against me. Because between themselves and me stands a whole group of different Schmidts: Paul, in his dressing gown, and Karl, my greengrocer landlord, in his blue smock and jute apron, and Dr. Schmitt, the thorax surgeon or whatever he was, wearing a striped concentration camp shirt; I have never met him but instantly recognize him. And next to him Eduard Schmid, a Sanskritologist I think he was, in his blood-stained vest with bullet holes. He is, in any case, already dead, so it can't be him they want to execute now. He himself realizes this and smiles a shy smile. Then Schlei the barber steps forward from somewhere. He has a sheet of paper with the appropriate order. He says, smiling through his ginger Hitler mustache: "Please listen!" and reads aloud:

"The *Fallbeil* will now be employed to execute the Schmidt who resides at the address Gojensbergsweg 108." And I say to myself: that's terrible, I can't deny it, but it would be interesting to know why they want to chop the head off my landlord . . . But I can feel as I mutter this question that my lips become as cold as ice because of the fear rising in my innards. Because I already know—despite the fact that I am a mere bystander, I already know that the man condemned to death is none other than myself. So I ask:

"Herr Blei . . ." For some reason I say Blei instead of Schlei (maybe to suck up to him, and to intimate that if it has indeed come to this, I would prefer the bullet to the guillotine), and he doesn't get angry at this. "Herr Blei, would you like to tell me *why* I am to be . . . ? I haven't, after all, set light to anything! Have I?" (Hell, it would seem that I am no longer sure.)

He opens the small door in the gray plank fence and there in another yard surrounded by an identical plank fence stands a guillotine, blade raised. Schlei leads me gently by the shoulder, and when we have reached the guillotine, he says:

"You have not set light to anything up to now, Herr Schmidt. Certainly not the Reichstag. In your thoughts you have indeed been more inclined to piss on it, in order to extinguish it. But you are nonetheless *guilty* of a terrible crime. During the recent *Eintopf*-day that the Führer has introduced to combat starvation and misery, you sold to both bars and eating houses in Bergedorf 3,976 kilograms of carrots, which you had bought up from the farmers of the Vierlande . . ."

"Here, wait a minute . . ." I try to protest, but he continues:

"You sold the carrots at twenty pfennigs a kilo, as you were supposed to. But when they were weighed at the Reich's weighbridge to check, 110 kilos of them were already black! Black as sticks of gunpowder!"

"Wait a minute!" I cry, and I now burst out laughing with relief. "I am not Schmidt the greengrocer! Can you not, Herr Blei, see that?"

"Of course I can. And that just makes matters worse," he says. "For a greengrocer it would have been sufficient to put him in a concentration camp for a few years. And his misdemeanor would be regarded as a routine case of inaccuracy. But in your case, that of someone who wants to be world famous for his precision, this amounts to the most heinous crime that could be committed against the heroic people of Germany. Just imagine what would happen if your black carrots had exploded in German kitchens! I can tell you this: not *every* Jew would have managed the likes of this!"

I cry out—or, as I myself hear, am hissing: "Herr Blei? What do you mean by 'every Jew'? Are you trying to say that I may be a Jew?"

He spreads his arms: "So what if you are? Do you have any convincing proof that you are not? In fact, the proportion of Jews among polishers of glass is so high that your very choice of profession already raises suspicions. And there's that woman too. Your woman whom you have concealed from the whole world. Oh yes indeed. Johanna Krüger. We know all about her. She also studied glass polishing and physics. What kind of German woman would study those sorts of things?"

"My God—Herr Blei—is this all of any importance? I have never given all of this a moment's thought . . ."

He pushes me up to the guillotine ramp and presses my head down onto the block.

"*Now* it is no longer of any importance."

He presses my neck down a little more. I cannot say that he is doing this with brute force. With patience, rather. A measure of tolerance that he is showing to an old customer. And struggling and wriggling just wouldn't be dignified.

So there I kneel with my face resting on the block and I see (and wonder what kind of eye I must have in the back of the head to see this) how Herr Schlei lifts his hand to the rope, which is hanging in the air, and *pulls.* I can clearly hear the short whirr of the blade, and the thud—as it severs my head from my neck.

I do not know how long it took for me to come to. I do not understand—was the rush of air and the thump nothing more than Karl Schmidt's little van? My landlord always backs his van out of the garage and straight across the road with the same sudden anger. So I'm still alive? I look at the striped wallpaper of my room in astonishment and see the open door of my wardrobe and the shoebox on the shelf inside. There is surely something important in that box. Right now, I'm not sure what it is . . . But anyway, I'm still alive. I try cautiously to move my hand—and it moves. I feel at my throat. The veins are sore and my neck is wet. I bring my fingers in front of my eyes: the liquid clinging to my fingers can be nothing other than blood. But all it is is the sweat of fear from the nightmare I have just experienced.

10

THIS ALL BEGAN IN NOVEMBER. IN OTHER WORDS, ONE MONTH AGO. IF I remember rightly, it was the day after the *Völkischer Beobachter* had announced that the nation had expelled from its midst such traitors and blackguards as Erwin Piscator, Leonhard Frank, Klaus Mann, and others, some eleven blackguards in all.

The next morning at nine, Fräulein Berger came into my workshop. Would I go and see the director immediately? I asked her, as I pulled on my jacket, what was the matter. She didn't know. Or at least said she didn't. Which, given her unflinching loyalty, wouldn't mean anything anyway—and she could even have been ordered not to know anything. I asked whether the director had visitors. And I thought to myself: maybe there'll be some of those mustard-trousered swastika-armbanded types sitting there (for whom, as Fräulein Berger will be present, I will not be able to roll up my shirtsleeve and practice my arm-stump greeting routine . . .), or there could be sitting there (as times have become harsher, and they would understand nothing else) a number of expressionless faces in gray coats from the SD who wanted to arrest me. For what reason? Well, if they're there already, they will of course know for what reason. But Fräulein Berger shook her head: "No-no. The director is alone."

A nervous weariness had been perceptible of late in the hitherto amicable behavior of Schorr. So much so that even I, who was perhaps the only person in the whole observatory who treated him in an unceremonious manner, had made do on occasion with not turning to him for assistance, and managed without disturbing him. Schorr's retirement date was not far off and it sometimes felt as if he wanted to leave right away. If Baade had not lingered in the United States and had been ready to take over the running of Bergedorf, that is. Or if the other candidate for the post (and this had recently been the talk of the observatory) had been acceptable to the Nazis. This other candidate was Professor Otto Heckmann from Göttingen. Schorr had tried to get the authorities to accept his candidature, but it had been made known that Heckmann upset the authorities on two counts. First of all he was a practicing Catholic. But what was even worse was that he continued to teach Einstein's abhorrent theories practically to this day, even after Einstein had played his dirty tricks . . . Which had not improved Schorr's mood of late.

But that foggy autumn morning, he received me with a smile on his face. So that I did not imagine that his summons boded ill in any way.

"Good morning, Herr Schmidt. Do sit down."

I took a seat at his writing desk, on the edge of the leather armchair.

"At your service."

He looked at me with such a sly expression that his intention to surprise me was patently obvious.

"Herr Schmidt—we've received an inquiry!"

"For what?"

I did actually understand: *we had received an inquiry*—this in effect meant that someone wanted to order something from the observatory and the director assumed I would be fulfilling the order. All manner of things had been ordered from us—mirrors, lenses, prisms, instruments, corrections to same . . .

Schorr cried out: "For what? For your telescope! With the same specifications as in the brochure! Can you imagine?"

I didn't start cracking jokes. I did not feign a superior kind of amnesia. I really did need the four seconds to recover. So deep had the hope been buried during these four years. On the surface I did of course remain completely calm:

"And who has been making this inquiry?"

"That is, how shall I put it, what is so intriguing."

"Well?"

Schorr raised his eyebrows, narrowed his eyes and said in a stage whisper through his mustache:

"The Russians. Moscow. Tekhnoproimport. I have no idea what kind of setup that is."

I said: "Must be some kind of technological import center. Or something of the sort. Well—if they're asking you, you ought to reply. That we agree, on such and such conditions."

"Wait-wait-wait," said Schorr. "*We*—that is to say *you,* in this instance. What conditions would *you* agree to?"

Indeed, if there was anything I could give concrete answers about, it was this. Should be crystal clear. However deeply I had buried myself in mundane concerns, I had nevertheless weighed up such matters a thousand times.

"There is nothing to it. A contract has two important components: the delivery date and the price. I don't like rushing things. I need time to correct things if necessary. I want to construct a first-class instrument. The deadline would be nine months from the date that the order is signed. The price—oh, I don't know. You can say . . ."

Schorr jumped up from his seat and paced back and forth behind his desk.

"Listen, if you were satisfied with five and a half thousand four years ago, then now, given a further rise in prices—not less than six thousand. And besides . . ." Schorr turned to gaze out of the end window of his office—through it, a hundred paces distant, you could see the façade of the director's residence with its windows covered in condensation, and its whitewashed walls, and Schorr was looking intently, as if looking into the rooms from this distance, into the kitchen where his energetic wife was bossing the skivvy about, and into the bedroom where five of his seven offspring who still lived at home were indulging in a pillow fight. He said rapidly:

"Please remember—*I* have not suggested this to you. I would propose: do not take payment in German marks. Not to mention rubles. Let them pay you in Swiss francs. And into a Swiss bank account. In reality the payment will come in a year's time. All currencies are unstable at present. Except for the Swiss franc. And were you to choose rubles, you'd hardly get anything for them!"

I mumbled: "But they're not likely to be paying out in francs—as they're all starving in Russia."

"But you can at least *bargain*!" said Schorr, turning toward me almost angrily. "You talk about starvation. They know all about it. Are you going to start playing the benefactor? You have—you said so yourself—only two thousand marks left to your name. For that money you wouldn't even be able to buy Wachmann's old banger, should you wish to do so. And what else have you got? That shoebox. Which you're going to hand over to me. If we die in the wrong order. And that shabby jacket. And that's it. You don't possess anything else. But they have one-sixth of the earth's surface, as they keep telling us. And all the gold in Siberia! No, no. You'd be a fool!"

Again I mumbled. "OK, I'll think it over . . ."

And he finished—in a quieter voice now:

"And bear in mind: don't bring any francs over into Germany. It can happen any day that the order will go out: any foreign currency belonging to citizens is henceforth the property of the *Volksgemeinschaft* . . ."

"But I'm not a German citizen . . ."

"Well, you should know by now how much that fact protects you. I would be inclined to believe that it makes your situation here even more precarious. But that is not the main consideration."

"So what is?"

"What is? You'd actually be prepared to make this thing for the Russians . . . ?"

"Why shouldn't I . . . ?"

"Oh dear, oh dear. I understand your plight completely. I am just as interested as you are that your instrument will *one day* be sold all over the globe. It's just that . . ."

"Just what?"

"It's just that the whole of your correspondence with Moscow will go via the SD. As you already know . . ."

I said. "Well, yes, if it goes via that institution, that will be in what is now termed a legal manner."

". . . Quite. Does that not bother you?"

I had already given the order to the appropriate muscles to crease my upper lip, which was meant to express contempt at the present situation, and shook my head at the same time. Which was all meant to indicate that such contemptuous circumstances were not going to worry me. But then I took a look at Schorr and changed my mind.

This thickset little man—his well-meaning boyish enthusiasm was now veiled to a large extent by worry, and the fact had been long apparent that he was the *only* person in the whole of Germany that would stand by me. And I felt it was worth making an exception to my rule. My rule that I would never comment on anything. I said:

"Of course it's disgusting. But one should not let oneself be disturbed by it, it ought in fact—oh good Lord . . ." I couldn't find the right expression, as to what someone should do, and Schorr said:

"Very well. I understand. But what I wanted to say was that if they find out, by way of your answer, that you are willing to sell your invention to the Russians, then they can stop you. Whether before the agreement is signed or afterward. What I mean to say is, they can allow you to sign the contract, but can prevent it from being implemented."

I said: "Can. But why would they wish to do so?"

"I fear that their logic is exceedingly straightforward. They would argue like this: if the Russians are ordering this instrument despite their straitened circumstances, then they need it for something. They need it very much. But anything they need that much is something that National Socialist Germany must not give them."

I asked, of course only to wriggle out from under Schorr's uncomfortable train of thought:

"How important for them could it be to indulge in stargazing?"

Schorr said with touching frankness: "We both know that it could be a matter of life and death for a very small group of people." He paused, then added: "Besides, we have what are termed all-round specialists. You know whom I'm thinking of. And were one of those, some suitably high-ranking guy, to think that your telescope had military potential . . ."

I cried: "What military use could a *telescope* be put to? All we can see through it is maybe that Mars' neck has become a threatening red color."

"Ah but things aren't as simple as all that," said Schorr. (This I already knew myself.) He continued: "For instance, in the *Bergedorfer Zeitung,* our local *Käseblatt,* someone published a photo of the mill at Wentorf a few years back. With all the details. The distance and light conditions under which the photo had been taken. So that any average layman, if he had any interest at all in the subject, could conclude that some part of that telescope also constituted the world's most powerful camera. And such a piece of apparatus could be of interest to military intelligence . . ."

I said, out of sheer cussedness: "OK, weight: two hundred kilograms. Hung round the neck of some intelligence officer. For taking photos in the dead of night!" But naturally I understood at the same time that the idea of a military use for the telescope could very well enter the heads of people who dealt with such matters. And not only, as Schorr put it, of the all-round specialists, that is, those arrogant party hacks who had been crammed into such jobs. I said:

"Oh, they can forbid it, all right," I conceded. "They can do anything they want. But I nevertheless want to give it a try. So I would like you to help me write to Moscow. With the language, you understand. I will have to write in German. I would make even more mistakes were I to try to write in Russian."

"By all means," said Schorr. But I heard from his voice that he was more worried than his eagerness to be of assistance betrayed. So that I looked him inquiringly in the face. At first he looked aside, then looked me in the eye:

"Herr Schmidt . . . I can do no more than warn you . . ."

He paused for so long that I asked:

"About what specifically?"

He said, almost in a whisper: "About your willingness to sell a telescope to the Russians—whether you get to build it or not—just that willingness could be interpreted as a betrayal of the Fatherland. And that could have the direst of consequences . . . The worst of which being . . ."

My God, this was of course plain to me already. Because of the absurd atmosphere that now held sway in Germany. So it was with a greater degree of blindness, and self-protection, that I blurted out:

"Herr Schorr—In the case of Germany, only someone who is an ethnic German and indeed a citizen of Germany could betray the Fatherland! And I am neither the one nor the other!"

"Listen!" yelled Schorr. "You're a genius of a guy—but you are arguing like a second-year law student from back in the days of the Weimar Republic! . . ."

I laughed: "Ha-ha-ha-hah . . . They can't guillotine me in this country!" And I did hastily add, as the thought had entered my head: that the Dutchman van der Lubbe had indeed been guillotined—I added hastily: "All they can do is deport me. If they consider me to be *ein lästiger Ausländer.* But even that is not likely to happen. Because Professor Schorr . . . ," I bowed before him in a swift music hall gesture, "will say when it is necessary, and *where* it is necessary, that I am one of the stars of German stargazing! Ha-ha-ha-hah!" And then seriously, and with emphasis: "No, no, Herr Schorr: I *must* take the risk."

"Very well," said Schorr as he sucked in a tuft of hair from the right side of his mustache and started chewing it, so that I could even hear it crunching. "Very well, Herr Schmidt. We shall take the risk."

The next day Schorr and I drafted a reply to send to Moscow, and Schorr typed it up himself in his office. It would have been faster for Fräulein Berger to do it, and it would—maybe—thus reach its appropriate destination through the mail all the more quickly, but it did not need to fly there with *such* haste. When it came to the crunch—what difference would it make? Anyhow this was our reply:

Bergedorf-Hamburg
Gojenbergsweg 108
November 22, 1934

Tekhnoproimport
Tochpribor Department
Moscow
Pr. Khudoshestv. teatra 2

I have been informed via the Director of the Hamburg Observatory, Professor Doktor R. Schorr at Bergedorf, of your inquiry concerning the construction of a 1:1.75 coma-free telescope, with a field of vision of 36 centimeters, a mirror diameter of 44 cm, and a depth of focus of 62.5 cm, as set out in the brochure.

I am the person that produces such coma-free telescopes and would like to inform you herewith of my willingness to construct such a telescope, including a quadratic camera, focusing equipment, and a cassette without a guiding tube and without parallel mounting. The delivery date is nine months from the date that the order has been confirmed. The price, inclusive of packing, will be 7,000 Swiss francs, to be paid by check into a Swiss bank account. The first installment of the payment is to be received in conjunction with the order, the second half when the instrument is handed over in Bergedorf. The place of the exchange is to be Bergedorf Railway Station.

Yours faithfully,
B. Schmidt

In reply to this letter we received—that is, I received—three telegrams during the space of one month. The first offered me three thousand Russian rubles instead of the sum demanded. In the second telegram this offer was repeated, and the third offered five thousand German marks. I replied on each occasion that I stood by my original offer. I had chosen—or, in fact, Schorr had—the sum of seven thousand Swiss francs because, by current rates of exchange, this was the equivalent of some six thousand German marks. And six thousand was under the present circumstances a just price.

A couple of afternoons after I had sent my third telegram (where I still stood by my original conditions), someone knocked on the door of my workshop. I could hear from the sound and the rhythm that this was not one of the young precision mechanics or even anyone from the observatory. So I ignored the knocking. Which was then repeated, loudly and unpleasantly. I continued to ignore it. A moment later I heard from behind the door footsteps and voices, and young Schulze saying rapidly and confusedly:

"Herr Schmidt! Open up . . . The police want to . . ."

Whereupon I went and opened the door.

On the threshold stood a broad-shouldered man, wearing a gray overcoat, who could very well have been the boxer Max Schmeling's younger brother. He did not hit me in the face with his fist. But did stride so self-confidently into the room that I was obliged to step aside. Under the powerful ceiling light he turned round and looked me straight in the face:

"Herr Schmidt?"

"Yes."

"Bernhard Schmidt?"

I replied "yes," and did think: so you see, we have managed to learn something. Neither Karl nor Paul would no longer be shot here . . .

"Do you have your passport with you?"

"I do."

"Show it."

I did understand that I was behaving like a second-year law student from the Weimar Republic (a second-year one, because any third-year student from that era would have understood the futility of his actions)—but I still had to ask:

"Do you have any document that gives you the right to ask for my passport?"

He looked at me and smiled in a repulsive manner with one corner of his mouth.

"*Ach so.* Here you are."

He thrust his card with the SD stamp under my nose, and I said with feigned satisfaction, which disgusted me:

"Right . . ." As if I even imagined that the bearer of this card really did have the right to check my passport. Or, the devil knows, maybe he did. It was, after all, their business.

I pulled out my Estonian Republic passport for foreign travel from a drawer in a cupboard, where it happened to be lying under empty cigar cases, and handed it to Schmeling. And anticipated an explanation at this point that it concerned a foreigner, and so on. But no. He glanced at it with his leaden eyes, then at my face, and handed it back. That is to say, they already knew I was a foreigner. They had collected information about me already. Which was not difficult to do. I had rung from Bergedorf on several occasions to the Estonian consulate in Hamburg, once to extend the validity of my passport, the second time to speak in general terms with the man running the consulate, a Mr. Karp, about which ships sailed to Tallinn. And on Thursdays, I had attended meetings of the Estonian Club in Hamburg. Not regularly, admittedly, but quite often nonetheless. When a dozen or two club members would meet on their *jour fixe* in rooms belonging to the Finnish Club. I would, for instance, be sitting at the chessboard along with Karp, my ears open to news from home—newcomers from Estonia always ended up here. Sometimes even interesting ones. One or two of them tried to get to know me and to see my workshop, as the odd member had heard about me. I refused them all. Except for one kind young man, Arindi, or whatever his name was, a stipend holder at the university, some sort of linguist or other, who managed to talk to me round a year or eighteen months ago. I myself invited him to my workshop. Anyway, the SD no doubt kept an eye on all foreigners' organizations. So that my passport was nothing for Schmeling to get excited about. He said:

"Put on your coat and come with me. We want to have a word with you."

I have to admit: as I put on my coat, I felt that if I wanted at that moment to light a cigar, I would have to control myself so that Schmeling did not see that my hand was shaking. And as I walked toward the gates of the observatory (he adopted the usual routine of allowing me to walk in front, him following behind), everything I had heard of late was at the forefront of my mind, not exactly piercing me through, but making itself felt like the pressure of the tip of a pencil pressing hard and stiffly into my consciousness, obstructing my breathing to a slight extent . . .

One former member of the Reichstag, Seger, had managed to flee from the Oranienburg concentration camp. And had ended up sending—Social Democrat as he no doubt was, and a typical old-fashioned German opinionated old dogmatist—a detailed description to the High Court in Leipzig about how he and other prisoners in the camp had been treated. Imagining in his futile manner that the High Court was still the same type of institution that it had been until lately, at least to some extent. So that it would be obliged to take up the matter. And this did not of course happen. I have no idea what happened to Seger. His only chance was to flee abroad. But his description of concentration camp life was somehow picked up by the foreign press, and some parts seeped back into Germany. And I had myself seen some of them. And according to them, terrible things occurred at Oranienburg and presumably elsewhere as well. For instance. A new batch of prisoners had arrived at the camp, among them two leading Social Democrats, Ebert and Heilmann. Ebert was, by the way, the son of the one-time president of the Weimar Republic. Plus a number of leading Reichsradio men. Their heads were shaven, but a few ridiculous strands of hair were left on their pates, so that they looked comical. They were ordered to strip naked and put on old rags that had been picked out for them. Then they were made to line up in front of the other prisoners. An SA *Standartenführer* gave a speech to all the prisoners. Speeches, especially insulting ones, are all the rage right now. "Look at those criminals who have stolen from the state! Especially that fat red-haired Jewish swine! (Heilmann was a Jew.) They've all stolen money from the honest German people and thrust it in their own pockets, boozed and scoffed down food for years on end and built themselves villas. But now they will get what they deserve!" And their job was to empty the latrines for twelve hours a day and even in the middle of the night, which was in effect a hopeless task because of the overuse, and during their "free" time they would have to take part in a kind of steeplechase that had been set up for physical education in the backyard of the camp. They would have to crawl through a bent conduit some seventy-five centimeters in diameter and climb over three-meter-high plank fences. According to Seger, in the camp they also used windowless concrete boxes in which the prisoners were forced to stand up . . . If I remember rightly, the longest time recorded by Seger was 192 hours . . .

All of this pushed into my innards like some glowing bar of pressed coal dust. In all truth, I felt such fear that I have to admit to myself—damn it—that I clearly was no *hero* . . . Because for what other reason was I pressing onto this glowing bar in my insides, thinking we'll have to see what they will do. But really *none of this has anything to do with* me . . .

We walked out through the observatory gates and I saw among the bushes a long-nosed BMW waiting, with a chauffeur at the wheel. From the presence of a chauffeur, I worked out that Schmeling must be quite an important figure. No young whippersnapper would be driven around by a chauffeur. On the other hand, any official who came *himself* to fetch me couldn't be that high up in the ranks. So he must have had just the right rank to come and fetch me. He didn't strike up a conversation with me in the car. This was clearly because it was not *comme il faut* to converse in the presence of the chauffeur. At any rate, I looked at his coarse neck and his angular cheekbones as he sat next to me, and tried to imagine how things would develop from here. So as to be prepared to some extent.

Seven minutes later, the car turned into the narrow courtyard of the Schloß Bergedorf, and we had arrived. My boxer led me through the police station and up some stairs and told me to sit and wait on a wooden sofa in a bare corridor with brick walls.

I waited there for almost an hour. Luckily, the sofa was one of those traditional inlaid ones made by village craftsmen of the Vierlande—you can find such marquetry all over the place in Bergedorf—so

I occupied myself by thinking: Is it not a brand of extremism, the extremism of precision, that gives an art form its open sesame moment . . . ? But I know nothing whatsoever about art . . . If only August had been here, he's pretty good at painting . . .

Looking at the patterns in the sofa, I managed to kill time for that nervous hour. Then Schmeling came back and took me into some office. It turned out that my assumptions had been wrong. If I continue to use German models for the people I met, the boxer type Schmeling had brought me here, but the man now dealing with my case was like the actor Gründgens.

Because you could almost imagine it was the actor himself sitting there behind a massive bureau—even more massive than that of Schorr—and pointing politely at a leather armchair. This was Gründgens as I remember him on stage at the *Hamburger Kammerspiele* a few years previously. And when I saw him in his famous role of Mephisto at the German Theater in Berlin—Baade, and even more so his wife, had dragged me there. And recently, as photos of him appear as the director of the Reichstheater in all the papers. Gründgens to a tee. With curiously lithe movements, somewhat snakelike. A pale, thin, somewhat masklike face. Almost expressionless. Or maybe unexpectedly maniacal. Maybe a cocaine addict . . . At any rate, someone who had come out here from Hamburg or even from Berlin, as such types simply do not build their nests in holes such as Bergedorf.

"Herr Schmidt, is this the first time you have had dealings with the German police?"

He knows I'm Schmidt, but I don't know who he is. As if he knew, as if they all knew, that it makes no difference who they are—Meyer, Müller, Schulze, Schmidt. Wait now, for heaven's sake—if it's a Schmidt then at least not Bernhard, not Erhard, not Otto, not Paul, not Karl . . . hell, there's something wrong with that list . . . But I don't have the time. I've got to answer him. Because I don't want to make things difficult for myself. I could reply: "With the National Socialist police—yes, the first time!" That would be telling the truth—and would no doubt please Gründgens. Stressing the distinction between Germany as it was before and is now would constitute a small plus point for me in his eyes. And were I to continue in that vein . . . But for that very reason, I should not start off like that. I say:

"No."

"What was the reason the first time?"

I think: ahah. That is almost impressive—that they have taken the trouble to root that information out . . . I say:

"Because of the idiocy of the Kaiser's police force in Mittweida."

I cannot see from Gründgens's face whether he is analyzing the extent to which the words *Kaiser's* and *Mittweida* eliminate any suspicion that my utterance refers to the actions of the German police *here* and *now.* I myself feel the ambiguity of my reply: I am a little fearful, as this is dangerous, but also proud of the fact that the comment has a little edge to it. I am both enjoying and rejecting my boyish pride. The corner of Gründgens's mouth quivers, but he continues:

"And what did this idiocy consist of?"

"The suspicion that the glass spheres that I had hung up in the park—in order to do checks on the optical efficiency of my instruments—were in fact a means to send signals to enemy aircraft!"

"Whose aircraft might they be?"

"Russian."

"Well, there you see," he said, "how we have come full circle. Now you want to sell your telescope to the Russians."

He lets his words sink in.

I have heard people say in Mittweida (i.e., have heard one young physics teacher, the blabbermouth Kneipp, say) that Schmidt was supposed to have gone to court with Zeiss in Jena, and won the case, flying in the face of all the Zeiss lawyers. Something to do with some aspect of his work. Without employing a lawyer. Thanks to the fact that he was in the right, and that his logic was as hellishly precise as his polishing. All nonsense, of course. What actually happened was the following. Some law consultant at Goerz (nota bene, Goerz, not Zeiss) went to Mittweida and more or less forced his way in to see me and accused me—Bräuer and Kuntze happened to be present—accused me of having broken an agreement that had been signed with Goerz. In the case of some concave mirror or other. I said that there was no such agreement. Prove that one was signed. I said that earlier on, a couple of gents had come over from Goerz and asked under what conditions I would sign such an agreement. I told them my conditions, and they traveled back. So if they claim that an agreement was *signed*—let Goerz produce the text. Their legal adviser threatened to take me to court. I said that that would be the best way of arriving at clarity in this matter. The guy went off and no court case of course followed. Just a little correspondence back and forth. So what is being rumored in Mittweida some fifteen years later is sheer nonsense. But this nonsense does tickle my sense of humor in such a way that I reply to Gründgens:

"My dear sir. First: even if it were possible to send some sort of signals with those spheres, and if the planes to which I was sending them were present, and I had indeed sent such signals, then that would be to the advantage of imperial Russia. While selling a telescope *now* would be—if that is the case—to the advantage of Communist Russia. So that this closed circle of logic that you are eager to demonstrate does not exist. There remains only a highly improbable coincidence. Second: the Kaiser's police force in Mittweida, with their lamentably circumscribed view of things—and you are likely to be aware of that fact—were soon assured of the fact that their accusations were simply ridiculous. And now sir, you must understand that my selling this telescope lacks any suspicious political grounds entirely. Because there are agreements that are of use to both parties—even of use to everyone . . ."

Gründgens—he is wearing an elegant dark-gray civilian suit—raises his refined right hand in its white cuff. He makes no ironic comment. He does not issue a command. He simply said:

"Stop, Herr Schmidt. You are by no means as taciturn as people say. You simply cannot be allowed to sell your telescope to the Russians."

I say: "Ahah," and think rapidly. "In that case, there is no point in indulging in argument, not now at least . . ." And I continue:

"And in whose interests is it that I cannot do so?"

He says—and without that Prussian note of command in his voice, almost familiarly:

"In the interests of National Socialist Germany."

And I say—in a voice muffled by strain, as I myself can hear:

"Well, if you, sir, are the supreme arbiter of such interests and say that I am not allowed to sell, then I cannot do so. I will inform Moscow that I am not allowed to, and that will be that. So what is the problem?"

"The problem lies," he says, "in the fact that sending the message 'I'm not allowed to' would be insulting. The only reply you can send that would not be insulting to Germany is 'I do not wish to.' But it is now too late for that. Take note: your contact with Moscow has been terminated."

For a couple of seconds I feel that there is something strange about these words and am, at the same time, thinking: Why strange? Because nowadays it is an everyday occurrence that someone says: your career is at an end! Your freedom has been terminated! Your marriage has been annulled! Your life will come to an end at six o'clock tomorrow morning!

Gründgens speaks: "We chose the method that is most convenient for you. We could see from your correspondence and telegrams that the Russians would give in sooner or later and go along with your conditions. Seven thousand Swiss francs, on the deadline of your choosing, into a Swiss bank account. So we broke the whole thing off. All letters and telegrams from you to them, and from them to you, have been intercepted by us. We have taken the responsibility for the whole matter on ourselves. You have been entirely freed of any responsibility in the matter. The Russians will curse the Nazi bastards who are curtailing the freedoms of German citizens. You have been freed. To develop new ideas for the glory of Germany. By the way—the minor fact that you did not wish to deposit the money you received from the Russians in a German bank account but rather in a Swiss bank, is a subject we shall not broach. Nor the fact that you are a foreigner among us and are living *demonstratively* on the strength of your Estonian passport. As I say, nor that. But do you know why it is that we are shutting our eyes to such matters?"

"Because they are of no significance."

"Oh no! They are in no way insignificant. But I shall tell you thanks to what. Because in principle we are a *sincere* power. In every sphere where sincerity does not damage us. You see, even naive little Professor Schorr mentioned things to your advantage. But you are protected from us by the principle that you have on many occasions uttered, sober or inebriated. Oh yes indeed. This is of great importance. That only *one* man on this earth is of any true value. Do you believe this?"

"I do."

"Well, you see. You yourself do not yet know what this means. But sooner or later you will arrive at the conclusion: it is the pure principle of leadership in its potential form . . ."

Jesus Christ! I really must keep my trap shut now, remain serious!

No smirking! No bursting into laughter! No crying out: listen young man you can shove your ramblings up your ass! My principle is rather that of the anarchist, the utter lone wolf who would go and place a bomb under the *Führer* . . . That rather!

I am a nervous person by nature. Have been all my life. Especially in recent times. For some reason. But despite all this I manage not to react in any way. I am immoveable. Do not give a twitch. Like the Põlendikukivi—the Burnstone—in the hayfield on Naissaar amid the firestorm. And then—I do not know whether Gründgens's words give me backbone or whether my temerity is rising (if the latter is the case, I really am stupid)—I say:

"There is just one thing I would like to add. With regard to the sale of the telescope. *My* interpretation of Germany's interests."

"Yes? I'm listening." Gründgens leans over his bureau toward me. I clearly notice too late how attentive he has become. I say:

"In my opinion the sale of the telescope would be entirely in the interests of Germany."

"I *believe* you when you say you think that. Otherwise you would not have agreed to sell it, now would you . . . ?"

Gründgens leaves a provocative question mark hanging in the air, but I ignore it. I say:

"First, the Russians would see stars they are unable to see now. Their astronomers would know a little more than they do today. The world as a whole would know more than now—by a tiny bit. And to the same extent we" (I want to say *you* and *me,* but my mouth balks at using such intimate terms so I say *we,* which can mean anything, can even mean people in general), "and to the same extent *we* will feel more at home in this world. And second, the Russians, with every step forward they make with this telescope, will know that it is thanks to German technical precision. They will regard it as German technology. So the world would obtain a little more knowledge by way of this instrument, and would believe a little more in the perfection of German technology. Is this against the interests of Germany?"

Gründgens laughs so heartily that I begin to feel ashamed at my quarter-truth, my three-quarter lie . . .

"Ha-ha-ha-ha-haa! Not bad. Only, the thing is, you know, that no unified world exists. Until the hegemony of Germany has been achieved. We are attempting this by peaceful means. Our *Führer* has assured us of this a thousand times. But we could be forced to declare war. And then we will wage war. And your telescope—or at least its guiding principle—could be of use for military purposes. That you know full well. So—let's call it a day."

He picks a small printed form up from the bureau: "Sign here. This is your assurance that you will remain silent—absolutely silent—about the contents of our little conversation."

I sign the form. He says:

"This does of course mean that you will meet our demands." He looks at me with his light-gray fishlike Aryan eyes. I sense that the corners of his mouth are quivering . . . as he continues:

"Galileo was shown a number of instruments to convince him. Do you remember? We do not have any such instruments here . . ." (I feel he is stressing the word *here* a little more than the others.) "As you can see. Neither on the bureau, nor in the drawer . . ." He pulls out the bureau drawer quite a long way, maybe some forty centimeters, and looks at me. On the veneer base of the otherwise empty drawer lies a Mauser with a magazine equipped to hold nine bullets. Gründgens glances at it, smiles engagingly as he shuts the drawer. "Oh, that was quite by chance. Goodnight, Herr Schmidt. And we do hope that you will continue to produce first-class instruments for the benefit of German science."

I get up. He too rises. And stretches out his hand to shake mine as a farewell gesture. For a split second I search for a solution. Then I find it. I stretch out my right arm toward him. He gives a slight start. I am thinking: even the likes of him are not invulnerable—but we are nonetheless a thousand times weaker . . . He shakes my empty sleeve. He does not reach as far as my stump. Not that far. Thank God . . .

Once outside, in the darkness, on the bridge to the northeast of the castle I suddenly feel that my knees are shaking; I'm freezing, yet a red-hot hammer is pounding my temples. The wave of nausea hits me so suddenly that I hardly have time to reach the balustrade. I have had nothing to eat since morning, and apart from the bile that keeps on coming up my throat, as if sandpaper were being rubbed up and down my gullet, there is nothing to be relieved of.

Depression is the best word to describe the weeks that followed. Depression, which was not relieved even by work. Indefinable things bothered me. From that December evening onward, I had the feeling that the taste of bile persisted in my mouth. However much I brushed my teeth with Chlorodont. The taste of bile lurking in the background of every other flavor. And it wasn't so much bile as verdigris, the almost imperceptible taste of verdigris. The taste of copper vessels and old storage batteries covered in green mold. The taste lingered in bread and in the egg dishes I ate at Land's, near the old Jewish woman's laundry, on whose door was posted a notice: *"Deutsche! Wehrt euch! Kauft nicht bei Juden!"* Every time I went out for a meal, I couldn't help noticing it. But as for the taste of verdigris, I once asked the girls at Land's why they didn't clean the copper pan in which they made their scrambled eggs properly with Sidol. The girls looked quite uncomprehendingly at me, blushed, and explained:

"Good Lord, Herr Schmidt—no one would put eggs into a copper vessel! Egg dishes are always made in a clean iron pan . . ." So I in turn blushed and changed the subject . . . But I even began thinking that the beer tasted of verdigris. At Land's but even at the bars: Die Sonne, the Holtenklinke, and the Drei Eichen. Even the cranberries I took from a jar in Frau Schmidt's pantry. Even those.

On the morning of Christmas Eve I went to our old Church of Peter and Paul. I went round the ring, along streets whose grass strips were covered in rime frost, streets that were already full of the bustle of the forthcoming holiday, so that the church might be reasonably empty when I arrived there to collect my thoughts. As is generally known, next to this church is the house where the organist Hasse had lived, with a small gray plaque on the wall: "In this house was born on March 23, 1699 the composer Adolf Hasse, *et cetera.*" And I thought, as I had thought two hundred times before: this Hasse was, during his lifetime, so we are told, more famous than all those Bachs, Glucks, and Händels. But nowadays, just about no one remembers him. And presumably I—oh I know, I am destined to enjoy the opposite fate. During my lifetime, just about no one has ever heard of me. A few schoolchildren will nudge one another and whisper: "Hey, look, there goes the *Linsenschmidt* on his way to the bar . . ." And that's about all . . . But one hundred, even three hundred, years from now I will be more famous than all those Hales and Richeys and Pickerings . . . Every time I have gone past it, I have thought literally: just you wait, one day the world will get to know the name Schmidt . . . That morning (the sparrows were rustling about in the bare wild vine around the small windows of Hasse's dwelling) I suddenly felt so clearly that my heart stopped: *my ridiculous hopes are completely in vain* . . . People simply *don't want* to see further than they are used to doing. It has been demonstrated that they don't want to. My God, not even specialists want to do so. Schorr sent off the brochure about my telescope in several hundred copies. No one has ordered it. The only interest that anyone has shown in it has been forbidden. And what will Schorr achieve with it in the long run . . . God knows whether my invention will ever be brought to the attention of the world at large. Because the world is marching in the direction of apocalyptic insanity. I've seen this insanity. Those brownshirt marches, all those tens of thousands of Schleis with the eyes of fanatics . . . Rumors are already circulating: Hitler is spitting on what is left of the Versailles Treaty and is rearming Germany again. My Gründgens (I give a start every time he springs to mind) did after all say: we will attempt to achieve this by peaceful means—that is, German hegemony. But they could force us to go to war. That much is clear. As soon as they feel strong enough, they will immediately feel they have to wage war. And then they will. Until such time as someone denies them access to some tract of land or other. Without that bit of land they will consider they do not have enough *Lebensraum.* So everything will be trampled to bits . . . I know from the previous war to what extent things can be trampled to bits. Knocking things back at least ten years. And a new war would make that twenty. And by that time it will be too late for my telescope. If by some miracle I am still alive then and my shoebox has not burned to ash and the ashes scattered across the turnip patches of the Vierlande . . .

I didn't even notice the fact that I'd entered the old doll's house church. No doubt in the secret hope that this particularly childish space would give me back that slight feeling of security that I had felt every time I entered before. And why only that slight feeling? No, for a fleeting second even a complete feeling of security. Which consists of the perception of two opposing tendencies: sinking back down into childhood, almost into nonexistence, into the ferns and bear's moss of Kuningamäe Hill, that is, the King's Hill, on Naissaar—and rising, flying, hovering over the pinewoods of Naissaar and the dust of solar systems and galaxies . . . I have felt this very intensely when standing in front of a number of the paintings in here. Owing to their strangely translucent colors and even more to the painted wooden relief that decorates one of the sides of the hexagonal pulpit.

Pastor Behrmann has said this to me: this pulpit was put there in 1586 and is said to be one of the finest in the whole of northern Germany. Women from Naissaar, if they had been at all familiar with what can be found in this town, would have said, and Berta straight out: that pulpit looks like a powder box.

One side of the pulpit is fixed to the whitewashed wall like a swallow's nest. One side is open—from there stretches the twelve-treaded stair up from the tiled floor of the church. As for what the three remaining depict—God knows, I really can't say. But the one I am thinking of in particular represents Christ's ascension into heaven. In other words, the events described in verses fifty and fifty-one of the twenty-fourth chapter of the Gospel according to Saint Luke: *Then he took them out as far as the outskirts of Bethany, and lifting up his hands he blessed them. Now as he blessed them, he withdrew from them and was carried up into heaven.*

In this painting the blessing has already taken place. There are four of the disciples who have sunk to their knees in awe, arranged more or less symmetrically, in pleated golden raiment, their eyes raised to the heavens. The sky is black as pitch. But a little way above the black stripe of the sky, a cloud is shining. A lumpy cloud, full of holes, fills the vaulted top of the painting like an arched white head of a mushroom. Even more like the head of a mushroom, because something golden and slightly pleated is hanging from the center of the cloud, as if it were the short golden stem of the mushroom. Except for the fact that from the lower end of the cut-off stem something is dangling. And although I have known for a long time what these two slightly formless objects are, I cannot take my eyes off their unexpectedness: the two objects, that seem to be two roots, two wings, or two leaves, there against the pitch black background, but only a handbreadth above the heads of the disciples—turn out to be the Redeemer's pale and naked feet . . . I have on several occasions thought that anyone who has seen the bare feet of Christ taken down from the cross in Mantegna's depiction in Milan can imagine that he has seen the ultimate artistic rendering of those feet. But no. The anonymous master who carved the reliefs on the pulpit here in Bergedorf has succeeded in creating something extraordinary. Christ's naked feet are dangling here so helplessly, so humanly, so surprised is He by what is happening to Him: He is being translated into heaven. Although He Himself has to know that this is going to happen to Him (for the Gospels are full of utterances from His own lips that foretell this), at the actual moment of the ascension itself, He regards it as a miracle. We cannot see the surprise on His face, for nothing more can be seen but a little of the soles of His feet, His heels and the golden hem of His mantle just below the ankle. But all His helpless and blessed confusion is in those feet. Exactly the same marvel that I feel in miniature, when sitting here before the pulpit. Well, not for the same reason as Christ—as now God the Father is raising Him up into heaven (I cannot really imagine how this is effected, whether by stretching out a finger, as Michelangelo depicted it, or hauling Him up by the scruff of His neck—the way Wachmann tore me loose from the railings)—no, no, I don't feel anything like that, but before that image I have always felt that sinking into the moss of my childhood coupled with the feeling of rising into the galaxy.

That morning I did not have this feeling.

I sat on the narrow pew in front of the pulpit and waited for this feeling to well up. But it didn't. I could smell the somewhat sour odor of rot coming from the old wood of the pew, and the smell of the rags used to wipe the floor. And the mothball smell from an unknown old woman's winter mantle as she passed me, because to my annoyance there were already ten or so people in the church. I sat there and smelled my own damp, sweaty, and unwashed shirt—I had been sitting at my lathe day and night for a week and had not taken the trouble to go home and change. And suddenly I noticed that the saliva that had seeped into my mouth, my own saliva, tasted of verdigris. So distinctly and so undeniably that my heart gave an extra beat: the alien world with its taste of verdigris had therefore managed to swallow up mine . . . And if here, before the picture of redemption, the charm no longer worked—what would happen outside? On the square? On the streets—where my Schmelings would be driving around in their BMWs, the Gründgens in their Mercedeses, and columns of my Schleis, arms raised, would be marching in their thousands—on the Holtenklinkerstraße, where notices hung with the message: "Germans! Defend yourselves! Do not buy from Jews!" and on August Bebelstraße, where you could already imagine the nameplate at the corner reading: Adolf-Hitler-Straße . . . ?

I sat there motionless for half an hour. And I felt that this stillness was protecting me. That any movement would inevitably mean coming into contact with something horrible. I understood that from now on I had to defend myself from the outside world, as well as from what had penetrated me, becoming to an extent part of my inner being. I got up half an hour later—I could hardly cower here all through Christmas—and went to visit Spiering, to the Weißer Schwan bar on the Sachsenstraße. At eight in the morning the door was still locked, and Spiering's flower shop next door was not yet open. I continued knocking until Frau Spiering opened up the door to the restaurant. As I was a regular, she made do with a little grumbling. I told her I desperately needed some flowers. She walked round the outside and opened the door to the shop. I bought seven of the most beautiful pink roses. At Christmastime such roses cost three marks apiece. I thrust the roses into Frau Spiering's arms and bade her put them in the bar and do what she had done before from time to time, but never on the morning of Christmas Eve.

An hour later everything was all right. Or, should I say, as all right as it could be under the present circumstances. I was sitting in the quiet, dark little back room of the Wießer Schwan. I had eaten a fried egg with raw onions (more than I had ever eaten in my life on such occasions) and had drunk down three or four mugs of beer. Along with the cranberries that Frau Spiering had brought to the table unbidden in a glass dish. And I had beaten down the abnormal taste of verdigris in my mouth to normal proportions. When I stuck out my lower lip and blew my breath up my own nose there was, naturally, the smell of copper. But, thank goodness, not to such a frightening degree as a couple of hours before.

At around eleven the first guests arrived. Some were strangers, some familiar. In fact, they were all strangers, but I knew the names and jobs of some of them. And there were those whose names and jobs no one knew for sure. Such as the thin bald man with the large Adam's apple who was always trying to strike up a conversation with me when I had been imbibing. Kürtz—Kartz—Kertz—Kurtz, the devil knows what he's called. And the devil knows which Hamburg paper he works for. He slouches down at the next table to have his meal:

"Well—Professor Schmidt, already started celebrating . . . ?

I ignore him.

"The holiday's started—with fresh onions, I see."

I ignore him.

"Listen, I've heard that *Estonians* like to eat a lot. True? Butter and bacon and pork and all that sort of thing. It's the Germans who are always starving. You know that, don't you? Eh?"

I ignore him.

"And now we're still starving. That's obvious enough. Hi-hi-hi-hiii: What does the turnip mash from the one-dish eating house taste like on Thursdays, eh?"

I grit my teeth—I feel that by doing so I am pressing the taste of copper out from my gums into my mouth. So I say:

"Jolly good."

"I see!"

"Yes, it does. I've been a vegetarian since birth."

"Really? Didn't know that."

"Didn't do your homework."

"How d'you mean . . . ?" he asks, foolishly struck by the comment.

"You should know."

"But why do you think that I should know such private tittle-tattle? Eh?"

"A journalist should."

"*Ach so.* Well," Baldy mutters, and uses the waiter's arrival as an excuse to end the conversation.

And so on. Optician Schröder's apprentice, the one with the big chin—don't know his name—came over to my table. His cylinder lathe had begun to go wrong. I teased him:

"But what do you need a machine for when you do the polishing? Do it by hand. You'll never get a machine to do it properly!"

He smiled and said that I ought to go and say that straight to Schröder's face, and what he basically wanted was for the machine to function as it should. I said that I could take it to one of our precision mechanics. He complained that he had already been there, but that Herr Schmidt, Paul Schmidt, had refused to waste his precious time on that machine. That wasn't his job. Then I said, OK, well bring it to me then. As it was a new Kärger, I would be interested in having a look at it. I could, after all, spare that much time.

And so on. At one o'clock I got up and walked, slowly, but very straight, up the stairs to the attic room that Frau Spiering had made ready for me. For God's sake, I didn't have any designs on that kind woman whose hair was prematurely gray. I didn't really know what she looked like. A white pinafore and something with gray and lilac spots. And a voice that was somewhat accusatory, but gentle nonetheless . . . No-no, I managed to perform what little I would do quite discreetly with ladies of the Reeperbahn. And a long time has passed since I was so vain as to think that it was for reasons more than mere cheer that the good lady had put a little Christmas tree in my room and three electric candles on the table. I knew this to be only a token of the nature of German hostesses—as there was a note under the edge of the ashtray: be careful with your cigar!

I draped my clothes over the chair back, went to bed, and got up again at five. In my sleep I had traveled from Dresden to Mittweida with some kind of bundle in my hand. Until I understood this bundle to consist of Werner Brandt's clothes. Werner Brandt's clothes covered in blood. Because I had just shot Werner Brandt and had to deliver his clothes to Johanna. Johanna was in my room at Frau Knechtel's, behind the screen. I couldn't see her, but knew she was there. When I was about to place the bundle behind the screen, I stopped to think: How did I manage to know that there are nine bullet holes from a Mauser in Werner's clothing—yet don't know who actually killed him? I said: Johanna—surely you're not so blind, so naive, such a poor judge of human nature to suspect *me* . . . ? Johanna did not reply. I cried: Johanna, stop playing tricks! If that's what you think, then go straight to the police and report me . . . I nearly yelled: *Johanna*—and awoke, as I have mentioned, at five in the afternoon, in the attic room at the Weißer Schwan.

The taste of verdigris and bile had not vanished from my mouth, but had become still stronger. And I was so hungry that my body ached. I put on my clothes, went downstairs, and was served a portion of fried potato slices by the boy behind the counter. But I couldn't eat the stuff. It tasted as if copper coins had been fried till they were leathery. So I put on my overcoat and went to have a look at the next bars, to see if they had anything worth filling my stomach with. At around four in the morning I arrived back at the Spiering place to get a few hours' sleep. The rest of the time I walked along streets whose shop windows were decorated for Christmas, still walking impeccably upright—to Doll's, to Behrens', the Drei Eichen, Wiesemann's, and the railway station restaurant. The result was the same everywhere: nowhere was the food eatable. The first mug of beer was tolerable, even though it still tasted of copper, but I just couldn't get the second one down me.

On the evening of Boxing Day, I gave the waitress at Spiering's her money and sent her out of the back door to the shops. She brought me a razor, a shaving brush, soap, clean underwear, and a white shirt. On the morning of the twenty-eighth she ironed my suit and I went to work at the observatory. On my way there, I popped in at Land's and tried again to eat some of their potato salad, but did not succeed. When I got to the basement, the young precision mechanic boys were eating their breakfast. As they did every morning before seven. The married ones had eaten breakfast at home and drank coffee there, the bachelors would bring bread and sausage from the shop and eat here. And the thought entered my head: the only thing that had not up to now tasted of copper was something I hardly ever drank—milk. I asked them whether they had a bottle of milk for me, and they had. Young Schulze poured me out a snow-white mugful from an untouched bottle. And it tasted absolutely pure. So I drank the whole bottle. And young Schulze's blue eyes glittered in his pink face because he was able to do me a service. But I did not start work. I went to Dr. Schrader's morning surgery on the Hansastraße. The old gent received me with routine affability:

"What is it that has started aching, Herr Schmidt?"

"I have a physiological or psychological question."

"Which is?"

"Tell me, how long can a fully grown man, doing a normal day's work, survive on consuming nothing but milk?"

"Only milk?" Why would you do that?"

"As an experiment."

"Well, you know, that would depend on a number of things. The constitution of the man in question. The nature of his work. The quality of the milk. And, self-evidently, the quantity of milk. If a few glasses or bottles of milk were drunk every day. Then I would say, more or less: you would hold out for two or three weeks. Then you would, little by little, have to stop working. A week later you would have to stay in bed out of sheer weakness. Well, yes, let's say—you could manage for up to two months. Calculated from the start of the experiment. But we do of course remember Gandhi's last hunger strikes—milk is more nourishing than orange juice . . . But do tell me: Why would this man want to take part in such an experiment?"

Dr. Schröder looks at me penetratingly—but I can't just tell him: my dear doctor, he is not experimenting. He has to. Because everything around him is poisoned. With the exception of milk. The poison no doubt is the result of human actions. Words, breath, the emanations of bodies. What does the word "emanation" mean, anyway? It is but a word. In reality bodies emit things, through the skin, through clothing, through the soles of the feet. It is, in effect, a vapor. A phenomenon not unlike the moisture of people's bodies. The diameter of such droplets would be from one to a hundred microns. And it soaks in everywhere. As moisture. Into substances, objects, organisms. And evaporates again as circumstances alter. From the substances and objects when the temperature rises (this is quite logical). And out of organisms, presumably when emotional stresses increase. Or leaks into them all the more. But *why* some are poisoned, presumably many, but one person for sure, that is, me, while others are not affected, but are instead enlivened, nourished, stimulated, *why* this is so—that I really do not know. I can only hazard a guess: any given person rises up out of the soil where he is born. He is—in purely chemical terms—a part of the soil, a part of the chemistry of where he comes from. And in a number of cases, cases that are clearly statistically rarer, the human body totally rejects the foreign chemicals that surround it. The environment has become chemically more alien and the body is therefore less tolerant of it. The surroundings have become chemically less acceptable. Or completely—*intolerable.* I myself can, in the first instance, offer nothing but observations and assumptions. I have no unified theory. If I could arrive at such a theory within the space of the next two months, I could maybe . . . But I have to give Dr. Schröder an answer right now. He is already regarding me with a look of undisguised suspicion. So I smile forcedly and ask:

"Does the name Dr. Karell mean anything to you?"

Dr. Schröder shuts his eyes, scrolls through his memory, then shakes his head:

"No-o-o."

I say: "That doesn't surprise me in the least. He was a compatriot of mine. A man from the last century. But a renowned doctor. One of his discoveries was what was termed 'Karell's Milk Therapy'". . . (God, I know something like this exists, but haven't a clue what it actually consists of!) "We in Estonia use it to this day. And a friend of mine wants to try it out. On account of gastric ulcers. But in a radical manner. So there you are . . ."

I lay Dr. Schröder's two-mark consultation fee on the corner of the table and smile with relief. I return to the observatory, but the relief at not having to endure Dr. Schröder's gaze doesn't last more than ten paces. Because all the while, as I walk along the cold and slippery Hansastraße, against a backdrop of decorated shop windows, I am thinking: *that means two months . . .*

I go down into the basement of the observatory. I know that the precision mechanics will notice me, but I cannot get past them by any other route.

"Good morning, Herr Schmidt . . ."

"Good day, Herr Schmidt . . ."

"Have a good holiday, Herr Schmidt!"

The master mechanics and the young lads all greet me—some for the first time in some days, others for the second. I grunt something in reply, slip past, lock the door of my workshop behind me and think: *they* still know nothing about this . . .

I open the door again (hopefully they won't notice my vacillation) and beckon Schulze over from the adjoining room:

"Herr Schulze . . ." (He was no more than seventeen when he started work here, but is by now twenty-three, and I have called him Herr right from the start) "Herr Schulze, if anyone asks after me, anyone at all, tell them that I'm not here. Say that you *saw* me go out."

He nods assiduously and I lock the door again. I am standing in the middle of the room, looking at the lathe. On it there is a forty-centimeter concave lens that I have just started polishing. For a camera that Schorr has ordered, though I do not know what he will be using it for. Maybe as an excuse to pay me something extra. He does not limit himself to giving me moral support. But this latter act means that he does invite me into his office—the last time just before Christmas—offers me a cigar, and relates:

"Herr Schmidt, I can tell you here in confidence this: a man from the Hamburg Senate gave me to understand last week that with a bit of luck we shall be receiving that one and a half million during the first half of next year! Yes, indeed! And then Baade will return from California and take over here at Bergedorf. And I will at last—at last—be able to devote my time to purely scientific research." (And I think, rather mean-spiritedly, that, well, it is questionable whether the world will see the point of that—and I feel ashamed of my thought, however justified . . . But he continues.) "Because the main thing is, Herr Schmidt, and this is what I was wanting to tell you, the main thing is: you will then be absolutely indispensable to us. You really will! Because then you will be doing here what no other man can do. You will start supervising the construction of *Der Grosse Schmidt*! You understand: at each step dozens of technical problems will arise! And I have never in my life met another person who can conjure up solutions to such problems *out of thin air* as you can!"

I don't of course believe him. Because I believe nothing at all anymore. But I feel it would be embarrassing to remind him just *how often* he has told me this. And nevertheless, I do feel a tiny, tiny, tiny bit of warmth at his words . . .

I stand there in the middle of the workshop and smell the pitch—I have put the tin on the electric hotplate to warm up—and think: Dr. Schröder said to me this morning, *two months* . . .

It is absurd, but presumably and sadly quite true.

I polished till eight o'clock without a break. Then my knees were so weak and the first puffs on my cigar went so much to my head that I would have fallen over had I not gripped the stool tightly. I drank half of the bottle of milk that Schulze had brought me. It was, thank goodness, quite without any aftertaste. And my polishing had gone perfectly the whole day, despite everything. So I put on my overcoat and hat and went to Land's to have another try.

The girls at Land's fried an egg and potatoes for me, as usual. While they were doing their work in the kitchen, I took small sips of beer out in the taproom. Because of the taste of verdigris, it was as before with the beer. I could manage about one mugful. But when the girls came to the table with the food from the kitchen—all prepared in the most hygienic manner and with a paper serviette next to it—I nevertheless felt that I wouldn't be able to get it down my gullet. It was irreparably bitter and bland. While the girls remained in the taproom I pretended to eat, and wondered what to do. When they vanished into the kitchen I remembered: I had kept a rolled-up cellophane bag from the bakers in my overcoat pocket for the past week. So I took the bag, poured the food into it, and took it home. For Karl Schmidt's long-haired yellowish sluggard. There was a message on the hall table at home: I should go to Schorr immediately in the fourth telescope cupola. That was where my instrument was mounted for Schorr's observations.

I shook the dog food out into the mongrel's bowl. While he was gobbling it all up and lashing my legs with his tail, I leaned against the wall on my elbow, shut my eyes, and thought: *Two months . . . Doesn't matter what sort of news Schorr has—it just doesn't interest me.*

Schorr came over from his telescope, ordered Wachmann to take the next batch of photos, and took me aside. First: Where had I been these last five days? He had been looking for me from morning till night. I just couldn't answer him. And then this:

"But tomorrow morning at nine you will have a visitor. He was here already this morning and we had a long talk and he wanted to meet you. But you weren't here. So he's coming again tomorrow morning. You have to be in your workshop. I must travel to Hamburg. He's coming alone. I've already shown him where your door is."

I couldn't bring myself to answer. Visitors are something I hate. But if I had to, then I had to. If I had started telling Schorr about my two months, he would maybe have left me alone. But I kept silent. Then asked:

"Who might this visitor be?"

"Some professor. An astronomer. Of the statistics of the evolution of stars. But he absolutely wants to meet you. A serious sort of guy."

"From which observatory?"

"Oh, didn't I say?" Schorr looked startled. "That's the whole point. From your country. From Tartu."

"From *Tartu*?" I heard myself say this in a whisper, but almost in falsetto. "What's his name?"

"Oh dear . . . New names aren't my strong point."

I said—and surprised even myself with the strange eagerness in my voice:

"If it's the evolution of stars—then—would it be Rootsman?"

"That's it exactly."

I promised to be there at nine the next morning and went my way. And I remembered . . .

During the spring of '26 I spent several weeks in Estonia. A short while on Naissaar, then in Hiiu, on the outskirts of Tallinn, at the home of the Wendachs, that is, cousin Lilly and her husband. And then I went, at Grünfeld's suggestion, to Tartu. It was only a suggestion, inasmuch as when the conversation turned to Tartu, he had said: "Why don't you travel down there. Then you will have seen it with your own eyes . . ."

And I went. To that city that had once been thought of as the Göttingen of Livonia, and was in fact rather a decrepit town. At least for a visitor who arrived with the superiority of having been to Germany itself, and with the inferiority complex of a craftsman.

I sat for an hour or more in the old Tartu Observatory and talked to two gentlemen: Öpik and Livländer. They made rather an odd trio, the two of them plus Rootsman, as already mentioned, who was the director there and dropped in before I said farewell. I would have said that they formed too solid a trio for the hundred-year-old Fraunhofer Tube, under which we had taken a seat on stools. Right now, I feel that I knew of them back in Mittweida days, even before I'd actually met them. Not in the same way as now. As I have actually met them in person. Öpik with his proofs of spiral mists proving to be galaxies, Livländer with his astrometrical ideas, and Rootsman with his attempts to calculate the age of stars. Because if there is anyone here in Bergedorf who reads the *Tartu Observatory Chronicles* (subscribed to on my initiative), then it would at least be me. But in those days, nine years ago, such young guys—even though the Fraunhofer Tube was the best telescope of its kind a century ago—such young men would have needed other instruments. Because one or two of them, for instance Öpik, was one of the world's leading astronomers . . . But they blew clouds of the smoke from my German cigars up at the blotched ceiling and admitted: Tartu University did not have the money for any new equipment. And, incidentally, even if they had

had the money, they would not have ordered anything from *me.* But, of course, from Zeiss or Goerz. Because that trio consisted of serious academic figures—even though Livländer was almost still a boy in short trousers—so that when I mentioned Mittweida, it made an almost pitiful impression on them. You simply feel such things. But they said with one voice that should the Tartu Observatory ever need new instruments, they would turn to me in Mittweida in the first instance . . .

"You are, after all, one of us," said Öpik, and smiled with his musical prodigy's button mouth.

Well, so much for that. But tomorrow morning Professor Rootsman—I remember him well—will come to see me . . . A stumpy little man, his head a little crooked, and what could be a little covert humor revealing itself in the corners of his mouth. His eyes so wide apart that certain neo-Lavaterians would exclude genius from his mental makeup. So he has come to Hamburg—and wants to meet me . . . !

I stand in the middle of the snow-covered pavement of the Gojenbergsweg, between the gates to the observatory and the corner fence to the greengrocer's kitchen garden, with Alpha Cygni shining down on me. I fill my lungs with the light, fresh, and frosty air and at once everything is clear to me: they're looking me up after all!

It is most likely that they want to order my telescope for the Tartu Observatory. My current Hamburg model. But I do know that it won't stop there. I *feel* that this will lead to new work, returning home, untold opportunities . . . Now, now, steady on—but why shouldn't things be limited to the ordering of one single telescope . . . ? Of course! And I can in fact build it for them right here in Bergedorf. Deliver it at the railway station to one of their representatives in, let's say, nine months' time . . . But why should I do that? When I could actually build it in Tartu. Oh God, they want my telescope and they must have it! Six thousand marks, that is exactly eight thousand Estonian krooni. If they've come to order one, then they must have the money. They know my price. In fact—I could even lower it just for them! Never mind *could*—I *will.* I will build the instrument for the cost price plus a minimum of living costs. And *over there.* I have hardly anything from here to take with me. Maybe a dozen of the polishing discs that are most comfortable to use. Even the lathe and the steel cylinder for pressurizing the correction plates are things I can get made over there for a few dozen krooni. I don't really need anything. Except for a few discs of high-quality glass. Everything I need would fit into a suitcase. In Tartu I can live in the little room behind the refractor on the right side. Its tiny windows facing north, and always an even, cool temperature. And if I get on with the job, it'll be finished in six months' time. But my God, this morning Dr. Schröder said two months . . . That's a load of nonsense! It *has to be* nonsense! Or maybe it isn't. Because even now I'm weak at the knees from lack of food. And when I know that I can't keep anything down except milk—that milk bought by Schulze—plus a few gulps of beer. But God Almighty—that is the state of affairs *over here*! *Over there,* at home—why didn't I think of it before! There—on Naissaar, in Tallinn, in Tartu—I am an organic part of the outside world wherever I happen to be! My body will not reject home-baked bread because it tastes of gall or verdigris . . . Even though there is poverty there too, and Pharisees and veterans from the Estonian War of Independence, and a political police force . . . But for someone who sees *through* all that—as if it were dust that happens to have risen from the highway of history—someone like me, will not be poisoned over there to the extent that he is being poisoned over here . . . And over there I won't be needing Dr. Karell's phony milk cure at all! If I do (but I know that such a need will never arise)—if necessary Berta can maybe send me bread and potatoes and herring from Naissaar to Tartu . . .

From six in the morning I am there in my basement workshop. A little shaky on account of the weeklong semi-fast and also—why deny the fact—on account of my excitement. I look around my workshop in the uncompromisingly harsh light of the electric lights. At the mess created by all manner of everyday work practices, where I nevertheless know where every glass disc and small object can be found. For a brief instant a quite pointless thought travels across my brain: if I were to try to tidy up in here? Such a ridiculous thought that I feel embarrassed by it . . .

I have been polishing for one and a half hours at a stretch. Then I remember: the door to the workshop, which is virtually always locked, ought to be open now, as Professor Rootsman is on his way here. Principally because his knock would not be likely to force me to stop work and to go open the door. Second—well, the door could be left unlocked.

I go to unlock the door, and carry on polishing. Ten minutes later someone knocks. Ah-ah. A man of European punctuality. Not one of those traditional Russian delays I experienced during czarist times. And it would be overdoing things to actually be polishing when he enters. I switch off the lathe motor:

"Yes!"

Without myself noticing, I have half risen up from my stool. Ho-ho-ho-hoh. Not on account of the arrival of the Lifesaver, the Long-Awaited One. The Redeemer. But spontaneously. A guy coming from afar. All the way from my native land. I repeat:

"Yes!"

And then he steps inside. Rootsman himself. Of course. A little more portly than I remember him. Some five or six years younger than myself. The very same man. And I feel with every fiber of my body that within a minute, five minutes, everything will have fallen into place.

He closes the door carefully behind him (clearly, one or two of Schorr's remarks have implied that I am very pedantic in some respects). He shuts the door behind him, turns, and comes over to me. Well, I've said yes to his visit. Now it is his turn to open his mouth. And he looks at me, his eyes set wide apart, smiles, and says:

"Guten Morgen, Härr Schmidt! Äine Fröide Sie Kennen zu lärnen. Höitzutage kommt äiner sich schon unjebildet vor—in där Astronomie—wenn är Härrn Schmidt nicht mit äigenen Augen jesehen hat . . ." i.e., in a painfully provincial Baltic-German accent: "Good morning, Herr Schmidt! A pleasure to make your acquaintance. Nowadays you tend to be counted as quite uneducated—in the field of astronomy, that is—if you have not seen Herr Schmidt with your very own eyes . . ."

I sit back down on my stool and remain silent. He looks around and says:

"Und dieses hier ringsum ist wirklich alles, womit där Häxenmäister von Bärjedorf säine Wunderstücke färtich bringt . . . ? Also muss man es glouben." That is to say: "So, what I can see around me really is all you have used to make your little miracles . . . ? So one has to believe it to be true."

I silently gesture toward a stool. He takes a seat. He is speaking German with an even more pronounced Baltic accent than I do. Then he starts plying me with questions. Politely, but wearily. Evidently out of sheer curiosity, which does not suggest a great deal of knowledge of optics. And I am obliged to answer. I reply as succinctly as possible. And as he is speaking to me in German, twice German, thrice German: *Ja. Nein. Mhmh. Allerdings. Nein.*

I hear his questions as if they are coming from afar. I hardly hear my own replies at all. I perceive them as small movements of the mouth and throat muscles through the gray fog of disappointment. I can hear him speaking:

"Und was ich sich besonders bitten möchte: zäigen sie mir ihr Teleskop. Am Tage—aber dann auch nachts . . ." "And what I would really like to ask you: Could you show me your telescope? During the day—but also at night . . ."

I hear myself saying:

"Das hat Professor Schorr ihnen gestern schon gezeigt. Gehen sie hin, schauen sie. Tags oder nachts. Ich habe nichts hinzuzufügen." "Professor Schorr will have shown it to you yesterday. Go to him, have a look. By day or by night. But I have nothing to add."

I do not look in his direction, to avoid seeing the stiffening of his face. I rise and say: *"Ich bedaure, aber jetzt bin ich in Eile."* "Please excuse me, but I have work to do."

I follow the professor, who has frozen in incomprehension, to the door of my workshop and lock the door behind him.

I stand there for a moment leaning on the door trying to fight down the blow that has hit me. I know that it is due to a lack of food. Then I remember: I still have half the bottle of milk that young Schulze brought me this morning. I go into the back room of the workshop, where there is the door to the toilet, an electric hotplate, a sink, and one or two cupboards, then I think in an entirely businesslike manner, without despair and maybe with provocative mettle: now I really have been condemned to death, haven't I? But let's wait and see . . .

I take the half bottle from the cupboard. There is no fridge, but there is a small flap out to the fresh air, so that milk will stay fresh for a few days. I fill a small, clean enamel mug to the brim, noticing that my hand is shaking alarmingly, and drink—and immediately spit the milk down the sink. I go—and someone observing me might have said *reeling from the blow*—to my workshop, open the outer door and yell:

"Herr Schulze!"

Young Schulze comes almost at a run from the precision mechanics' room. Behind him through the doorway the faces of Schmidt and Rode can be seen. Schulze stops in front of me:

"What is it, Herr Schmidt?"

I say—I know it's not his fault and it is true in a way only I can understand—but I just have to say it to someone:

"Herr Schulze—now even the milk you buy me is poisoned . . ."

11

MY SECOND AND LAST MEETING WITH DR. KELTER TOOK PLACE A WEEK after the first, and no longer in his home but instead at Wirth's on the Gerhard Hauptmann Platz in Hamburg, a small café that has plastic tables with patterned holes. And I was once more obliged to admire the vitality of the old man. He was not only prepared to answer my questions; but for some good while he didn't even give me the opportunity to ask them. Because he began by himself asking me questions:

"Ah. Do tell me with whom you've been talking in the meantime about Miracle-Maker Schmidt. And what you have heard!"

"Well, I have, for instance, talked to Herr Wachmann . . ."

"Yes-yes-yes? Really. He is, after all, one of our somewhat unexpected Schmidtophiles. He has written quite a bit about him. In *Sterne und Weltraum*. Twenty years back, wasn't it?"

"Yes. Your memory, Herr Doktor, is astonishing."

"Ha-ha-haa. It was an astonishing article."

"In what way?"

"Well, maybe because Wachmann there assures his German readers, and with a degree of pleasure, that Schmidt wasn't a German at all. While in Estonia itself, twenty years ago, people were still quite indifferent to that fact."

"Dr. Kelter, I have to admit that you are very well up on everything to do with Schmidtiana."

"Listen," says the old man, sipping at his coffee with relish, "as I have already told you: my moderate interest in Schmidt has only been superficial. And it was originally merely the residue of my own father's interest. But tell me, how did Professor Wachmann respond to the questions you put to him? And what was it you asked him?"

"His response—was a very good one."

"*Ach so*? What did you manage to charm him with?"

"I am not talking about how he treated me, but rather how he related to the questions, that is, to Schmidt. And in that respect he came over as quite generous."

"Oh yes? For example?"

"Do you know Professor Wachmann personally?"

"To a certain extent."

"Then you will know: Professor Wachmann is—well, as far as I can judge by comparison—very academic, very stiff, very much the gentleman . . ."

"Yes," Dr. Kelter admits, "when such a guy has such an immense amount of experience, and two comets named after him . . ."

"Quite," I concur, "and Professor Wachmann's objectivity was therefore all the more impressive. He talked to me about Schmidt on a couple of occasions. For a total of some seven or eight hours. He unearthed invaluable documentary evidence. Photos, manuscripts, letters. You were wondering what I asked him, and what he answered. Well, one of the finest answers was this. I asked him: Herr Professor, you worked with Schmidt and were quite close to him. You were one of the few people who were often in his workshop. Let us remember that charming tale that you told about how Schmidt stopped working and went off for a short while leaving you standing at the lathe, and you used the opportunity to do a couple of polishing rotations. And he came back, touched the mirror, and said: 'Hm, someone's been doing something here . . .' In a word, you were present on many occasions when he was working. I can imagine that you had to assist him now and again with *secondary tasks,* because of his handicap—lifting things, putting them in place, fixing them, measuring . . . Do tell me, did it happen that he would occasionally ask you for such assistance?"

"Well-well-well?" asks Dr. Kelter with interest. "And what did Wachmann reply?"

I say: "He said very quickly, with great assurance: 'Schmidt—never. Because he could in fact do even these things better than me.'"

"I see," says Dr. Kelter.

"So Professor Wachmann said literally—*he could in fact do even these things better than him.* Even where Schmidt was clearly handicapped. So one should add, in one's thoughts: not to mention the things where he didn't suffer a handicap. I begin to think that such an admission would require quite a high degree of respect for the person in question, plus a good portion of aloofness from personal considerations."

"Yes, yes, yes," says Dr. Kelter, curling his lower lip, "that would mean that Wachmann in his old age has been swallowed up by Schmidtophilia . . . And what else did he come out with?"

"Mmm . . . various things. Things that partly covered the time after Schmidt's death."

"For instance?"

I search my memory: "For instance—he told me something that I could only grasp in part owing to my lack of specialist knowledge. And I didn't dare to ask him too many extra questions. But I would imagine that you, Dr. Kelter, being a specialist yourself, will be able to grasp the essence of it. Professor Wachmann said roughly this: that those who later began to examine the correction plates made by Schmidt could not work out how it came about that his plates were markedly better than those produced by others using his vacuum method with the greatest of care. When plates were made by others, there was still an element of distortion—which, if I remember rightly, Professor Wachmann termed *reflective images.* These were, as far as I have understood, unavoidable according to optic laws. But they did not arise in the plates made by Schmidt himself. So the results were therefore better than one would have expected from a physics point of view . . ."

"And then?" said Dr. Kelter, now absorbed by the whole issue.

"Professor Wachmann in Hamburg and—if my memory serves me well—Professor Fricke in Heidelberg had begun to look into the matter. In other words, they had begun to investigate it some fifteen or twenty years after Schmidt's death. I have to admit that I did not actually ask, but you have to reckon with the fact that the Americans were onto Schmidt's secret already. They would no doubt have known it when they were building the Big Schmidt on Mount Wilson, that is, around 1940. But Wachmann and Fricke did, after all, arrive at their conclusions quite independently. From what I have understood, Schmidt's trick was that he had used the vacuum method on the surfaces of his lenses only up to half the curvature necessary, but from both sides. At any rate, the relief of the lenses had such a minimal aberration that no one noticed that he had worked on both sides of the lens. And I am now taking this into consideration and am asking you, Dr. Kelter, if I have understood Professor Wachmann correctly."

"Oh yes, you did, you did . . ." (so that I need not seek further assurance) "but what *more* did Professor Wachmann say?"

"Well, there was a whole lot more. The main thing being: he showed me documents. Incidentally, all the things I learnt from Professor Wachmann were by no means the most surprising. The things he mentioned were, in the main, known already. If not by me personally, then within the field of Schmidtologia. By our own Schmidtologist Peeter Müürsepp, for example."

Dr. Kelter orders a small glass of vermouth and a bowl of bitter almonds. "So what was it that was most surprising to you?"

"Professor Wachmann, being the most important living source of Schmidtologia, told me a thing or two as well. But I managed to find yet another living source."

"Ahaa. You are thinking of old Professor Frank?"

I swallow out of sheer astonishment. Dr. Kelter is also aware of that name associated with Schmidt that has been so long forgotten.

"No. I was told about Professor Frank, and I wanted to look him up. But it turned out that he was too old and too sick."

"So whom did you find?" asks Dr. Kelter—with interest, it is true, but with the kind of interest that is somehow guarded, reluctant.

"Herr Alfred Schulze."

"Schulze . . . ? Dr. Kelter does a quick flick through his knowledge of Schmidt. "Don't know him. One German in seven is called Schulze. Who is this man?"

I tell Dr. Kelter everything I have heard about Alfred Schulze, and have observed myself when I met him. That he was not a scientist at the observatory. That he wasn't an academic. But had been one of Paul Schmidt's precision mechanics in their workshop down in the basement at Bergedorf. On the other side of the wall separating that room from Schmidt's workshop. That he had come to work in their den at the age of seventeen and had risen, some thirty years later, to become the head of the workshop. And who met Bernhard Schmidt every day, almost every day, for nine years running. With the exception of Schmidt's months on Naissaar and his "days for the raising of his potential." And was now a few years over the age of seventy and had been retired a few years. But as a former worker at the observatory, his name was in the card index. When my pressing need to know more about people who knew Schmidt during his time at the observatory was still alive, I think it was Professor Weigert who remembered his name. And found his address and telephone number in the register. I say:

"A very decent, very unassuming, yet very open man. And definitely very observant."

"Well, well, well," Dr. Kelter is amused, "I detect here an element of—how shall I put it—proletarian solidarity between Schmidt and your Schulze, and yourself?"

"Yes maybe," I have to agree with a smile, "and why ever not? Is this something bad in your opinion?"

"That all depends on you, and you alone, my dear writer . . ." Dr. Kelter gives a jovial grin. "On how far such solidarity with your characters drags you away from the objective truth. Maybe artistic people think differently, but for me, an old pragmatic, the only yardstick by which to measure a work of art is objective truth. All other artistry is mere flimflam. And too much solidarity and sympathy can give rise to distortion and exaggeration. Let us point out this tendency of yours—I noticed it on a number of occasions during our previous talk—the tendency to declare Bernhard Schmidt a genius . . ."

"Now wait a minute," I interrupt, slightly hastily. "This is in no way a tendency of *mine*! I have been reading, here and now, in Germany, in old newspapers, things written on the fifth, tenth, fifteenth, and so on, anniversary of Schmidt's death. How many times do you think he was called a genius in these articles?"

"How many?"

"I found the word used twenty-one times."

The old man gives an almost hearty laugh.

"But what confirms my claims about your tendency better than your statistics? For what reason have you totted up all the times he is mentioned as a genius? In order to affirm your tendency. And only for that reason. You were clearly in such pressing need of . . . a new

Estonian genius that you did not shun even the most tawdry material: the endless bla-bla-bla of the newspapers."

I cry: "Not only that! Even a number of professors . . ."

"But principally the newspapers," says Kelter imperturbably. "Because the newspapers know only two colors: *either* black *or* white. If the papers regard someone as a scoundrel, the papers will blacken his reputation, if he is a saint, he will be whitened up. How you end up in one or the other category is a question of sheer chance. Schmidt has now, at any rate, been entered in the column for saints and is coated at every step with the whitewash of genius, so that not a smidgen of the human being in question remains. But in general," Dr. Kelter sips his vermouth and continues, now with provocative zeal, "have you not noticed that in every historical myth there is one rule—and this could almost convince us of the existence of justice in society, or, to express it with a little more pathos, the existence of the *attempt* at reaching justice in society? This means that anyone who has been successful in life will be dealt with in terms of myth in a narrow-minded, demanding, and intolerant way. He who has suffered slings and arrows will be enveloped in the myth of the saint or hero. Or the genius. And take note, this act of falsification to restore equilibrium is all the greater depending on the degree of misery or glory endured during their lifetime. Do you get my meaning? If any particular life has its coefficient of pluses and minuses, then the corresponding myth will be roughly the same, but essentially of the opposite order!"

"For example?" I ask.

"An example? Standard ones: Christ. Suffered hunger nearly all of his life. Was betrayed by everyone. Not only by Judas but also by Peter. Only one little whore remained faithful to him to the end. And at the age of thirty or so he was lashed, then crucified. But myth has made him the Son of God and the Redeemer. An example of the opposite type: the Sun King of France. Ruled over Europe's richest country for seventy years. Founded the *Académie française.* And the *Observatoire,* by the way. Slept, in his time, with the most beautiful women. And created a style that other rulers have tried to emulate for two hundred years. But in myth nothing of him remains but an unintelligent, moody, and unhappy fool. And so on, and so on. Do you want any more examples? You don't? Nor are they necessary. In a word: what can at first glance be taken as the justice of society is actually its diametric opposite. Myths about lucky, happy people are little more than the workings of envy in those doing the remembering. And those myths that deal with unlucky, unhappy people are the result of the pangs of conscience of society."

I say: "After that pleasant excursion into the philosophy of history—may I now return to Alfred Schulze?"

"By all means, by all means," says Dr. Kelter. "What more did you hear from Schulze?"

"You mentioned just now, Dr. Kelter, that I clearly needed to find some new Estonian genius. And that would not be 100 percent wrong. For 98 percent, I was looking for the protagonist of a novel. But for the remaining 2 percent, a new Estonian genius—and why not? With regard to Schmidt's Estonian nationality, no further proof is required. That matter is as clear as a bell. But I still thought: it would be interesting to know how his colleagues down in the basement at Bergedorf viewed him. As an Estonian, a German, a Baltic German, a Germanified ethnic Estonian, a Swede, an Estonian Swede—which of these was he? I wanted to ask Schulze. But I only managed to get out the first part of the question: 'Tell me, *who* was this Schmidt in your opinion, that of the precision mechanics, that is . . .' when Schulze, his shining blue eyes looking straight at me, said quietly: 'Obviously a genius.'"

Dr. Kelter does not burst out into a laugh of Homeric proportions. Not that. But he does smile a wry and slightly nervous smile:

"And such a vox populi therefore, in your opinion, weighs more in the balance than the rubbish you have read in the papers? Is this vox Dei, in your opinion, the highest voice of appeal? For what reason?"

I say: "Because, Herr Doktor, it simply *carries* more weight. I read principally the local papers. From Bergedorf and from Hamburg. It is only natural that they would boost the reputation of local heroes. I would even say that this is inevitable when public opinion has been contaminated and the law of the entropy of thinking sets in."

Kelter interrupts me in triumph—a split second beforehand I realize that *now* he will be triumphant.

"And so local papers tend to praise people from their town? But with regard to his own colleagues, guys in the next workshop who are already praised in the local papers, and a number of professors as well, this would have been important to Schulze, seemingly such a simple guy . . . don't you think that the tendency to wrongly boost a reputation could arise in such a fellow? Among *simple* colleagues. Maybe without wishing to do so, maybe deliberately?"

I say: "Not in one particular case."

"And when is that?"

"When a man is genuinely at a level where he should receive praise."

"Well there you are then," exclaims Dr. Kelter. "So even the garbage you read in the papers is true?"

"But of course."

"But in what way does what Schulze say carry greater weight than the garbage written in the newspapers?"

"First, because the papers know a good deal less, objectively speaking, than what Schulze knows about Schmidt. No reporter had the experience of working alongside Schmidt for nine years in a row. And besides, reporters are rarely that reliable."

"How do you mean?"

"Simply this: I received the impression that Schulze was a particularly credible person."

"In what respect?"

I set out my case: "Maybe in this. He mentioned that he had seen Schmidt almost daily for nine years. Often a dozen or so times a day. When Schmidt came by to relight his cigar at their Bunsen burner. But when I asked Schulze to characterize his conversations with Schmidt, he said this: 'Look, he didn't talk very much with me. His conversation was minimal. And, in any case, he would mostly talk about some *thing* or other. Some fitting or other item that he had ordered from us. And what he did have to say he would say to master craftsman Rode. There were four or five of us there, I was the youngest. But he would only address the master craftsman himself. On very rare occasions he would burst in on us and talk with great enthusiasm about some scientific problem. Was instructing us, so to speak. Or felt that having only himself as an audience was not enough. But otherwise—he would come in, nod, light his cigar, and leave. So that in all of those nine years, I only exchanged a few words with him.' That's what he said. And what I want to say about that, Dr. Kelter, is that it is something no reporter would ever admit. Each and every reporter would have confabulated or cobbled together some story about his lively conversation with Schmidt. But, Herr Doktor, would you now be so kind as to allow me to put *my* questions?"

"Gladly."

"So: you mentioned during our previous talk that you met Schmidt again in Hamburg, a couple of months before his death. That would be in 1935?"

"Yes. Since we last met, I have been freshening up my memory and have checked my archive—and this was later than I said, in late October 1935 in fact. I had arrived back from Kiel. The *Weddingen* had been built for our fleet of submarines, and our firm was busy with the periscopes . . ."

I asked in passing: "Was that by any chance the fleet that the captain of the frigate *Dönitz* was in command of?"

". . .Yes, maybe it was . . . ," said Dr. Kelter, even more in passing. "And on the trip back from Kiel I dropped in at Bergedorf. Stellar optics was, after all, more important for the Kelter company than periscopes. And like Professor Schorr, I was hoping that at long last his observatory would get its money from the state and there would therefore be some work for us there. But Schorr shook his head. They had not been able to find the money. And I wasn't very surprised, because 1935 marked the year that Germany began to rearm on a grand scale. We know a good deal more about that now than we did then. At the same time, Baade had written from California that he had got money for the Hale and that they were already building Schmidt's telescope with a thirty-five-centimeter lens, and that they were planning another Schmidt telescope, the *Big Schmidt,* with a 125-centimeter lens. And it was only natural that I, with my old weakness for all things that Schmidt did, asked about him. Schorr said that Schmidt had been ill of late, and out of sorts. He had visited a Bergedorf physician on several occasions and was following a strict diet. But he did keep on drinking almost as much beer as before. I did not ask what was actually wrong with him. Because in the same breath Schorr said that Schmidt was working as he always had done—periods of intense work alternating with intense relaxation. And that he was near the completion of a new variant of his telescope. Not of course comparable to what Hale was planning in California, but at any rate bigger than the Schmidt Tube there at Bergedorf—the diameter of the correction lens was sixty centimeters, if I remember rightly."

I ask: "But didn't you then meet Schmidt face to face?"

Kelter looks me straight in the eye, as if the vain old man was going to start confessing the sins of youth, sins he is slightly ashamed of but nowadays feels to be rather amusing nonetheless:

"Yes. You see, Professor Schorr invited me to dinner. And it would have been quite normal for me to go. But it so happened that for one reason or another I declined and said I was unfortunately in a hurry. That I had to get back to Hamburg to take the train to Berlin an hour later. For some reason. But as I strolled down to the bus stop by the observatory, the thought suddenly struck me that even before I got to the restaurant car on the Berlin train, I wouldn't mind having a bite to eat. So there and then I stepped inside the restaurant . . ."

I ask: "What restaurant?"

"Right there. Some five or six buildings down from the gates of the observatory."

"So you would mean Land's?" I suggested for clarification.

"I don't know. Maybe. But what I wanted to say, now that it is in fashion to take a peep at underlying motivations: I didn't so much go in there to get a bite to eat but rather in the hope, the instinctive hope, that I might meet Schmidt."

"And he was there . . . ?"

"Yes, he was . . . ," admits Kelter triumphantly.

I don't ask anything. I wait. And Kelter continues:

"You want to know what he looked like. I have to say: bad. He was unexpectedly thin, and had a bitter and nervous appearance. He was nonetheless perfectly shaved, and his hard white collar was as clean as eight years before in Mittweida. But his suit was very creased. It had been in such condition back in Mittweida. So he somehow seemed to have gone downhill with the years. Of course, Schmidt, despite his white collar, clearly always had the propensity to surprise people with his appearance. I remember, some years after his death, that someone who had been there described how Schmidt had turned up at the Baade family home in order to get into a car along with Professor Baade to drive to Hamburg and from there sail to the Philippines. At the beginning of his Bergedorf years. In '29. When he had just left Johanna's care, and his most important work still lay ahead, and nothing should have been noticeable of his decline. He turned up at the Baade house with his luggage for the Philippines. And do you know what it consisted of? A medium-sized bundle wrapped up in newspapers, with a piece of white string around it. A bundle, wrapped up in the *Hamburger Fremdenblatt.* Schorr told me later that this was the newspaper that Schmidt read regularly and that could often be seen sticking out of his pocket. But on that occasion Frau Baade had gone with them in the car to the port and had them stop on the way and buy a suitcase for Schmidt. He had protested—take it as you will, a protest or a bad joke: no, no. He didn't need a suitcase! He was going on a voyage to Manila and his bundle was wrapped up in real Manila string! But Frau Baade had nonetheless managed to cram all his stuff in the suitcase. Using the excuse that the tropical rains would otherwise soak Schmidt's things right through . . . So Schmidt agreed. Maybe out of the fear on his part that any refusal would conjure up rain in some magical way just as they were about to make their observations. He had smiled slightly: 'You are so right, *gnädige Frau.* Statistics suggest that when we carry an umbrella, we are less likely to encounter rain.'"

I ask: "Dr. Kelter—you mentioned the *Hamburger Fremdenblatt* . . . That is rather interesting."

Dr. Kelter grasps my meaning with surprising astuteness:

"Certainly! The *Hamburger Fremdenblatt,* that newspaper for foreign residents, could be found all over the place . . . on his table at home, on his work stool, in the pocket of his overcoat. See what I mean? That would be a theme for a writer! If the writer wished to move the plot in a particular direction: the *Fremdenblatt* as a clear sign of *Fremd bin ich hierzulande . . . !* I am a foreigner here in this country!"

I don't rise to the occasion at this mildly provocative jibe. I ask:

"And how did your meeting go?"

"Well, to a certain degree he looked bad," Dr. Kelter continues, "but he did recognize me immediately. You could see that from his face when he turned toward me. I went straight up to him and said:

"'I see, Herr Schmidt, that you have recognized me straight away after all those eleven years, as if I haven't, hmm, matured in any way. May I join you?'

"Well he could hardly do anything else but nod his head. He was not so badly mannered that he would have shaken it. I put my coat on the peg and sat down opposite him at his small table. He was sitting there quite alone eating. With some distaste, as it seemed. A green salad of some sort. I said:

"'Herr Schmidt, I heard from Professor Schorr that happily your health seems to have been restored . . .'

"I hardly expected any answer, I knew him well enough. Nor did he reply. So I carried on talking:

"'But the most surprising news is that you are developing some new kind of telescope!'

"He munched his salad and looked down at his plate.

"'Is this true?'

"He gave me a swift glance. Like a street urchin who is about to trip you up a second later:

"'You consider Schorr a liar?'

"I ignored this question. I said: 'So it's true. And what dimensions will it have? Depth of field? Luminosity? And what new features will it have?'

"'Didn't Schorr say?'

"I had to admit: 'No. Schorr simply said that the correction plate had to have a diameter of sixty centimeters. He said no more than that.'

"Schmidt continued to chew his salad with a degree of irritation, then said:

"'The rest will become evident.'

"I took his secretiveness in my stride. I did understand him to an extent. The lack of trust that an inventor has for specialists. As he didn't want to go into detail with regard to the specifications, I put my next question so that he would have to mention them. Within which specialty were the experts equipped, and what would they be using his new instrument for? From what he replied it would be possible to get some idea about the new telescope. So I asked:

"'And who is it intended for?'

"He had finished his salad. He took a swig of his beer and put in his mouth—can you imagine—some reddish berries, some kind of wild gooseberries, and said finally:

"'Everyone.'

"You know, I just didn't have the heart to pursue that line of inquiry. But his work was of genuine interest to me. You will, as an author, understand this. And he irritated me too. Maybe you understand this as well. I asked:

"'And when will it be ready?'

"He took a long draft of his beer from the stein. 'Next year—God willing.'

"Then I was no longer able to suppress my curiosity:

"'But what new *tricks* will you be introducing?'

"And he continued, as if not hearing my question:

"'But I can't fully bank on next year. I have to go to Holland quite soon . . .' And he carried on using relatively long sentences of several words, quite deliberately in order to draw me away from my question about tricks. And also of course because by then he had drunk a good deal of beer:

"'I've got to go to Leiden. Invited by the observatory. They have a new telescope. The Cassegrain. Ordered from England. But the picture it gives is poor. They want me to look it over. Hertzsprung has asked me. Haven't a clue how long that will take. But I can't refuse.'"

I interrupt Dr. Kelter's musings. I say:

"But . . . the fact that Hertzsprung—he was after all the director of the Leiden Observatory—invited Schmidt would suggest that he was in good shape."

"Well . . ." The old man purses his lower lip skeptically. "Maybe. But Hertzsprung didn't have to know exactly what shape Schmidt was in during those months or weeks. They all knew of him *in general terms.* Everyone in the wider circles of specialists. But how far from, or how near to, *delirium* he actually was by that time, was something they didn't need to know."

"Delirium?" I ask, shocked.

"Well, yes, delirium, dementia, depression—I am using the expression, *exempli causa.* And furthermore, I think that whether he was in top form or not, he would have managed to get the Leiden telescope fixed. Sure. I would like to say that you authors tend in general—if you'll forgive me—to be out after cheap sensation. Anyway, I can tell you about one matter. Baade, Walter Baade, has talked and written about it. I do not now remember to whom or where, but it was Baade. About Schmidt. Quite likely in Baade's impressions of their trip to the Philippines. When they were about to set up their instruments, which had already been shaken about by the voyage, without any expert help. Or it may have been a more everyday impression that he got at Bergedorf. Baade was, despite his satanic precision, despite his Schmidt-like precision, something of a poet. To cut a long story short, Schmidt was called over to—well—diagnose a telescope, as something had gone wrong. And what did he do? Schmidt walked slowly round the instrument. Stopped and continued walking. Then went up to it in an unhurried manner and touched it. Stroked it. Knocked on it. Not hard and with his knuckles, like a palpating doctor. But very gently, with his fingertips. And *listened* to how the telescope rang. He tried this in several places, a dozen places. Until he stopped at one spot and said: 'Here.' And there it was. Could be anywhere. The lens was askew, or the screw on the mirror was too tight. According to Baade's poem, that was what happened. You understand: I myself, of course, cannot help smiling at all of this, but you, as a writer, can at least pretend to take it seriously!"

I think to myself: all well and good. I will think about the extent to which I will take Baade's word for it. But I shall not take an old man's jibes, Kelter's jibes, so seriously that I feel I have to react. I ask:

"And how did your meeting at Land's proceed?"

"It didn't," Kelter admits. "Schmidt had drunk up his beer, rose from the table, nodded, put on his overcoat, and left." And it strikes me that Kelter is saying this all of a sudden in a slightly muffled, slightly creaky voice—as if he were still to this day angry at Schmidt's impolite departure.

I say: "So he traveled to Holland pretty soon after your meeting . . ."

"Yes." says Kelter. "Because of this conversation of ours, I had a look in the Brockhaus. There it says that he died in Hamburg on the first of December 1935. He cannot have been in Leiden for a very long time. Not more than three weeks . . ."

"Even less." I comment. "I found a postcard that Schmidt himself had written, lying among Professor Wachmann's papers. This was sent from Bergedorf to Hertzsprung at the Sterrenwacht in Leiden. And it turns out that he traveled to Holland on the fourth of November and got back on the eleventh. That is barely a week. But tell me, Dr. Kelter, what do you know about his death?"

Dr. Kelter takes a toothpick from the porcelain cup on the table and picks at a piece of almond between his teeth:

"According to the well-meaning articles I've read—and I think you know this already—Schmidt arrived back from Holland with a bad cold, became really ill, was admitted to the hospital, and died ten days later from pneumonia."

I ask: "You said 'well-meaning articles' . . . ? What about those less well-meaning ones?"

"There just weren't any spiteful articles at all," says Kelter, and pops another bitter almond in his mouth. "Because, you see, the Schmidt myth already existed in embryonic form during his lifetime. You could say that as soon as the man himself died, his *myth* took on a life of its own. As often happens. An author ought to be familiar with such mechanisms better than someone dealing with optics. But whatever the truth of the matter: those who did write about Schmidt's death—I can't say I've read every line—they were all, some to a greater, some to a lesser extent, writing under the influence of the *myth.* Those more under its influence wrote about the pneumonia, and so on. Those who resisted the lure of the myth—at least some of them—mentioned a surfeit of Dutch gin in their *in memoriam* pieces. And what was not set down in writing, but did of course circulate by word of mouth, was even more colorful. As always. Some wrote about a heroic cold occasioned by overwork plus the November wind. The wind from the North Sea blowing into the open cupola of the Leiden Observatory. Ah, that observatory—have you by any chance been there? You haven't? It is about ten kilometers from the North Sea Coast. Others—others wrote more wryly about that selfsame Dutch gin, waxed pompous about his beer in Hamburg, and said: delirium tremens. At least Dr. Eggers at Bergedorf said that."

"To you personally?" I ask, and feel I have put this question a little nervously.

"No, no, not to me. But I have chatted with people from Bergedorf for years on end after Schmidt's death. I cannot honestly remember who brought up the name of Dr. Eggers and his diagnosis."

"So in fact it wasn't pneumonia?"

"You know," says Dr. Kelter, "pneumonia was certainly present. At least according to documents . . . But I'm wondering now—what did your Schulze have to say about Schmidt's death? Did you not ask him about that? He was at Bergedorf at the time. He should have more exact details. If his hypertrophied respect for Schmidt did not prevent him from mentioning them . . ."

I explain: "I did, of course, ask him that too. And he told me more or less the same as I had already found among Professor Wachmann's papers. There is a letter there from Professor Schorr to some lady relative of Schmidt's in Estonia. And also Schorr's letter to the head of the hospital or the doctor in change. From those letters it emerges that Schmidt came back from Holland pretty ill. He had complained to Schorr about severe headaches and put them down to the bad cold he caught in Holland." (I take my diary from my pocket, look for the right entry, and carry on speaking—because why shouldn't Dr. Kelter, who would not presumably know this, share in the information. He not only can, but must!) "The conversation between Schmidt and Schorr took place on November 21. Schmidt had therefore been ill for about ten days by then. Four days later, on November 25, he went insane. According to Schorr's letter, he had turned up at the observatory, bawled out several people there (I couldn't find out exactly who) and physically attacked someone (nor do I know who that was). He had ripped off all his clothes and started raving. According to rumor, Schorr writes, he had been on a 'beer excursion' in Hamburg from the twenty-second to the twenty-fifth. Paul Schmidt and Gressmann brought him back home around lunchtime on the twenty-fifth and put him to bed. At around half past three in the afternoon Schorr went to his home and found him in his socks in the greengrocer's hallway, brandishing a pocket torch and talking incomprehensibly. Schorr succeeded in calming him down a little, forced him to eat something and drink some coffee, and then, with the help of the greengrocer, put him to bed again. That evening, the greengrocer came to Schorr's house complaining that Schmidt had got out of bed and was raving once again. Schorr rang for Dr. Eggers. He came, took a look at Schmidt, and rang for the Saint George Infirmary ambulance. Four men took the raving Schmidt to the ambulance and they drove off.

On the twenty-sixth, Schorr phoned the hospital and inquired after Schmidt's state of health. He was told that Schmidt, in his continuing state of agitation—as they put it—had been sent on to the hospital at Friedrichsberg. In other words, to the lunatic asylum.

On the twenty-eighth, Schorr wrote a letter to the head of the

Friedrichsberg, one Professor Rittershaus. Here he inquires as to the chances of Schmidt ever recovering and includes a few details about Schmidt that might be of use to the doctor treating the patient. This is, in its own way, a moving description of what Schmidt had achieved during his lifetime. Schorr writes that Schmidt is one of the world's leading optics experts, someone who has specialized in the construction of concave mirrors for use in astronomy. With his one remaining hand he has polished mirrors that are works of art, and which no one could hope to emulate. And that he has also obtained success in various other fields such as aviation technology, gastroscopy, instrument building, and similar."

I put my diary back into my pocket and ask:

"Dr. Kelter, do you not feel that Professor Schorr is *exaggerating*—with all those superlatives?"

"So even you think that!" Kelter agrees. "Of course he's exaggerating. His exaggerations are the epitome of those of a myth worshipper!"

I ask: "But do you not think that there may be a completely non-mythological reason for these exaggerations?"

"What sort of reason? Beyond naiveté."

"If he was trying to protect Schmidt from something—by accentuating his achievements?"

"Against what?" asks Dr. Kelter, and I feel that he is a little on his guard. But maybe I'm imagining this. I say:

"You, Dr. Kelter, have had a better chance of getting a picture of all such threats during that epoch, compared with my efforts. But let us focus on the order in which Schorr lists the fields in which Schmidt has succeeded. Especially the concave mirrors. That's clear enough. He polished them for Schorr and others by the dozen, and their superlative quality was Schmidt's bread and butter. But look at the remaining triangle. Point one is aircraft technology. In which field we know that Schmidt never really achieved any success. The only thing that could perhaps link him with such is his camera for aerial cartography. But this has nothing to do with aircraft technology in the strict sense of the term, and this really belongs under point three—instrument construction. Point two is, according to Schorr, his gastrophotography. His enteroscope. This also really belongs under point three, as it is a simple instrument. But at least an instrument for which Schmidt sought to take out a patent at the time. He didn't do so for his aerial photography equipment. Because he presumably never completed it or thought of it as important enough. *Point three itself* is Schmidt's instrument-building activities. Which means his telescope, which is the most important by far. In other words, Schorr regards point three as the most important one. The second point is an invention that was never actually built. And yet he mentions as his first point a field in which Schmidt had not really done anything at all. Why?"

Dr. Kelter says: "Well—why do you think?"

I say: "Would it not be because at the time aircraft technology was most important from the point of view of the *state*?"

"So what?" asks Dr. Kelter, now concentrating wholly on the matter.

I say: "If that were the case, then any merits in the field of aircraft technology would offer him better protection than the other fields. Would this not be why Schorr pushed this up to first place?"

"Protection-protection-protection!" cries Dr. Kelter. "Against what? Against whom?"

"An argument involving the state," I say, "implies being an opponent to it. Doesn't it?"

"What are you trying to say?"

I reply: "Some state rules or other that could have proved dangerous to Schmidt at the time."

"Such as?"

"I don't know. All I can do is ask: if Schorr put aerial technology at the top of the list for the sake of state considerations, why did he then put gastrophotography in second place—rather disproportionately? If he thought that he could use Schmidt's nonexistent contribution to aerial technology to influence people—who on earth would he be influencing with gastrophotography? Because here too his contributions were minimal compared with those belonging to telescope construction."

"Well, who would be influenced by that? In your opinion?" Dr. Kelter now demands, somewhat provoked by my reply. Or wishing himself to provoke.

I ask: "Don't you feel that he would have been thinking principally of doctors when it came to medical advances?"

And what now happened was something I had not dared to hope for up to that point. Dr. Kelter places his glass on the table:

"Ahaa! You are referring to the fact that Schmidt was taken in a raving state to Friedrichsberg on the twenty-sixth and died there four days later of lung inflammation, according to his file—so that we might very well be dealing here with a case that formed part of the euthanasia program! Mightn't we? But listen, that is absurd! The euthanasia program was not implemented until 1940, certainly not before 1939. But Schmidt died in 1935!"

I say: "I am far from being convinced that Schmidt's case was the only one. The question is only the degree of impossibility, or possibility. At any rate you have to take the following into account: December 1935—that is, after all, nearly 1936. That, as my first point. Second: the program that was implemented from 1939 onward could very well have been applied *selectively* even before that. And earlier than that could have been in the development phase. And this must have entailed a number of practical experiments. *Someone* had to do such experiments on *someone, somewhere or other.* I read that the euthanasia program was actually made public in July 1939 by the Reich Chancellery. Hitler signed the document on September 1. (Incidentally, it would be interesting to know whether the clock time was before or after the outbreak of war . . .) The text that forms the introduction to the program said the following: *to expand the rights of listed doctors so that those who are regarded as incurably ill, according to human judgment, after a thorough examination of the level of illness can be allowed to die by mercy killing.* Can it not be concluded from that passage that all the medical and legal foundations, the measures and institutions needed, had been put in place and were ready, on the shelf so to speak, to be implemented? But third: you used the word 'absurd.' In the case of Schmidt. At the same time that it was you yourself, Dr. Kelter, that linked the Schmidt case with the euthanasia program, and that shows that it is not that absurd, after all . . ."

"You did, after all, serve me up with the necessary associations," growls Kelter, "and it is absurd, however you look at it."

"But you are not the first," I say, "who has had such associations with Schmidt's death. I have talked with several people. Here in Hamburg. A forty-year-old lawyer. A sixty-year-old publishing executive. A professor of history of the same age as yourself. When they too had listened to the details that I got to hear from Alfred Schulze, they all asked: listen—what was going on here . . . ? They were all thinking of the same thing. And the publisher added that according to rumor, Friedrichsberg was an institution that, at least later on, put such things into practice."

"I see!" grunts Kelter. "I've never heard that before. But what are the details that Schulze told you?" Kelter poses the question with a degree of skepticism, but also with interest.

I reply: "Nothing really special. But still. He said that Paul Schmidt, the head of precision mechanics at Bergedorf, had gone to the Friedrichsberg hospital to visit Schmidt. When exactly, was something that Schulze obviously did not remember, but sometime between November 26 and December 1. And quite by chance he did manage to see him. Schmidt had been put in what was termed a "rubber chamber." He had not recognized Paul. He'd carried on raving. Paul was told that this raving had been continuing for several days and nights, without a break, for the whole time that Schmidt had been at Friedrichsberg. Injections of sedatives had brought only brief spells of relief. So in Schulze's words, he had more or less raved himself to death. And had all this time, according to the orderlies, been bawling and throwing out insults in some incomprehensible language. Paul had listened for ten minutes and concluded that this was no doubt Estonian."

"Yes, yes, yes," says Kelter, "all very dramatic, and a suitable episode from which a writer can derive some symbolic meaning—but what in all this suggests the use of euthanasia?"

"A number of lines of reasoning in this story," I say, "do suggest to a minuscule extent that euthanasia is just a tiny bit less unlikely, but no more. Simply put: if Schmidt had lain there quietly and given a pleasant impression, euthanasia would have been less likely than with someone who behaved as he was doing. *If* there was some doctor in the wings who was looking for an excuse to apply what were still top-secret edicts by way of his experiment, he would have to choose the most suitable candidate. And here there was suddenly someone who had been raving incessantly for the fifth day running. This symptom alone would not have made him the perfect candidate. But when he asked for his patient file from Dr. Eggers, it then transpired that this raving old man was in fact prone to delirium and was a chronic alcoholic. He had no relatives. He was a foreigner. Evidently, a foreigner who knew no German. And he was—given his recent bar crawl and bout of illness—a degenerate. He was, according to an entry that reeked of archaic usage in his patient's file—a lens polisher. But as he lacked his right hand, he was a Category-X invalid who couldn't work as a lens polisher, and was thus a burden on National Socialist Germany owing to his handicap. And this same old man had now been raving for five days in a row. Shouting volleys of abuse in his incomprehensible language. We don't actually know, but there is reason to believe that he did, amongst all this, utter words that were recognizable to a German ear—most disgusting words and very holy names, whose juxtaposition in the yelling of the lunatic simply forced the Nazi doctor of the experiment to spring into action!"

"Ha-ha-haa," laughs Kelter, though in a relatively subdued manner, "that almost sounds convincing. If you need help in this quarter, I can add that the atmosphere in Germany at the time had long been ripe for such campaigns: mass compulsory sterilization was carried out from 1934 onward. And so on. But in Schmidt's case, your version of events is nevertheless *impossible*!"

I do of course ask why.

"Because of Professor Schorr's letter, which you yourself mentioned. The one he sent to the Friedrichsberg hospital on November 28: the greatest optics expert in the world, and so on. Once that letter had arrived, they wouldn't have touched a hair on Schmidt's head!"

I have to concede: "I would have hoped so myself. But you do admit that without that letter things could have gone badly wrong, even for Schmidt . . ."

"Why do you think that?" cries Dr. Kelter. "When the letter was there!"

I say: "*If* it was ever there."

"Why shouldn't it have been?" cries Dr. Kelter. "When you saw it with your own eyes!"

I say (in order to torment myself and the old man a little): "I saw a copy of the letter in Professor Wachmann's hand. A carbon copy. It was dated November 28 and was clearly in Schorr's handwriting. But at the bottom was written *'Heil Hitler! Ihr ergenbenster.'* And there was no signature. Nor any initials."

"What significance does that have?" Kelter wonders.

"Well, it doesn't need to have any," I reply, "but it *could* mean that the letter and the carbon copy were written out by the secretary on the twenty-eighth, but that Schorr himself was not in the building at the time. So the letter was not signed until the following day, when the copy had already been filed. We can imagine that the letter was sent from Bergedorf on the twenty-ninth, and arrived, in an ideal scenario, on the thirtieth at the appropriate post office in Hamburg. Only if the post was distributed on the morning of the thirtieth could it have been lying on the desk of the head of the hospital at Friedrichsberg before the early closing on Saturday afternoon. The next day, the first of December, was a Sunday.

"We can imagine:

"A northerly wind was blowing on the Sunday morning—according to weather reports. This plastered the north-facing windowpanes of the brick-built Friedrichsberg Hospital with freezing snow. That we can imagine . . . And the letter, of which we are speaking, was lying there unopened among the post of the previous day, on the head of the hospital's desk. At six or seven in the morning, and using his own private skeleton key, a doctor who was hardly known, even to the duty staff, entered the corridor in which the rubber chambers are located. This was a youngish, very featureless and taciturn man who had hardly exchanged a word with either the staff or even the patients in his care during the brief time he had been in the building.

"The gray-faced doctor stopped in the dark corridor at the barred observation window of the third chamber. He switched on the lamp that lights up the room and observed the man who was wearing a dirty patient's smock and lying in a distorted position on the brown rubber floor whilst fending off something or someone with his healthy hand, babbling to himself all the while.

"A minute later the doctor left the corridor and locked it again with his key, then returned with the duty orderly three minutes later, carrying an injection kit. He put the box on the table, picked up the filled injection needle and pointed to the door with his chin:

"'*Aufmachen. Vorsicht.*'

"The orderly stood behind the doctor, ready to suppress any attack on the part of the patient. But the patient was too sedated from the previous injection to be dangerous. The orderly thought idly and professionally: 'What damage could this old one-armed codger manage to do to anyone after four days of raving? Nothing but yell. The likes of him should get a crack on the head and then he'd be quiet as a lamb until evening. But it has to be done so that no one sees it happen. So it can't do any harm for the doctor to give him another whack on the skull, so early in the morning . . .'

"The doctor pointed with his chin, this time to the orderly—'*Weggehn*'—and the orderly left. Not until about twenty minutes had passed did the doctor emerge into the main corridor from that leading to the rubber chambers, while pushing a notebook into his pocket, silent as always.

"At eight o'clock, when the orderly peeped into the third chamber to see whether to put the morning's soup slurry in, or not to bother (for the past four days he had got the soup back in his face from the patient), the patient was lying on the rubber floor in such an odd position that the orderly decided to look inside the chamber.

"He was dead.

"And Schorr's worried epistle telling of the world's leading optics scientist was not opened until Monday morning . . .

"You see, Dr. Kelter—we could imagine that things turned out that way . . ."

I don't really know how much of this is what I actually painted in words for Kelter, and how much stems from my imagination. Dr. Kelter remained silent for a good while, then muttered:

"But you know, mister writer: such fantasizing is simply insensitive and irresponsible. Do tell me whether Schulze told you anything objective about Schmidt's death."

"Well now—not really," I say, "apart from describing one long episode that occurred long after his death. Do you know, Dr. Kelter, where Schmidt's grave is located?"

Dr. Kelter shakes his head.

I explain: "Alfred Schulze told me this. Schmidt had once mentioned to someone, Schulze didn't know when and to whom, where he wanted to be buried. He wanted to be buried in the new cemetery in Bergedorf itself that was just the other side of the railings to the observatory grounds. And at the very eastern tip of that cemetery. I asked Schulze if he knew why. I had an inkling of what the answer would be, but couldn't believe my ears when I heard it: 'Because the eastern tip is nearest to the land of my birth . . .' I asked Schulze why then he wasn't buried on that spot. His grave is right next to the railings to the observatory, but a few hundred meters to the west. Schulze explained that Schmidt was indeed first buried at the eastern tip of the cemetery. They had moved his grave to where it is now only some twenty years later. In 1955 when the Hamburg version of the Big Schmidt had been constructed. At that point, the directors of the observatory had decided that the grave ought to be in the cemetery at the nearest point to his telescope.

"Anyway, as Schulze put it, the telescope has been a few thousand kilometers away, down in Spain, these past fifteen years. Which is certainly even further away from his native Naissaar . . ."

■ □ ■ □ ■

12

AS FOR MY TRIP TO LEIDEN—I WON'T ACTUALLY BE ABLE TO DO ANYTHING for their telescope. It's an ordinary industrially produced piece of garbage. The mirror is so impure that it's disgusting even to look at. I wrote a list of the chief defects. Eleven items. We were going to run through the list with Hertzsprung to agree in which order I would tackle them, how long it would take, and how much it would cost. But then I started running a temperature. No doubt due to the wind against my damp skin up there in the cupola gallery.

All the Dutchmen, with Hertzsprung at their head (who is, in fact, a Dane), are saying with one voice that I could just as well stay in their guest room, get better, convalesce, make myself at home there. And I am thinking: Would that mean feeling as if I were on Naissaar . . . ? Impossible! Then they brought some medicines or other. Brontosil and other odds and ends. Because the fever just wouldn't budge and my headaches became worse. So I asked for a bottle of their famous gin. They brought two. The fever did not subside, but the ache in my eyeballs, temples, and neck did ease a little.

Today things could still start throbbing, but not with the pressure in my eyeballs that was driving me crazy, so I can now focus on matters beyond my window. Their observatory is situated in a loop in the southwesterly part of the old city wall, and round about are the botanical gardens of the university. At this time of the year, the autumn wind gives the surface of the moat grayish gooseflesh. I can imagine that because of the fever my own flesh looks much the same. You can see almost as far as the university through the bare trees surrounding the greenhouses. The *peace and quiet* is quite extraordinary here. Even deeper than in the seven hectares of land that make up Bergedorf. And I can understand why. Because ordinary human life continues even beyond the stone walls of the botanical gardens. A little more lively, jerky, tedious out there than in the botanical gardens where there are three people strolling about right now, but entirely without tension, entirely natural. While through the railings at Bergedorf, the tramp of hobnailed boots on the cobbles penetrates, oh hell, both literally and metaphorically speaking . . .

Of course the thought flutters through my aching head: it would be easier to breathe if I were to stay here . . . Indeed why the hell should I continue to squat over there in Germany? When there are no prospects of ever starting to build the big version of my telescope. And when no one beyond the gates of Bergedorf shows the slightest bit of interest in my smaller version . . . OK, Dr. Schröder did explain to me at length some while back that the taste of verdigris in my mouth was, to a large extent, a figment of my imagination, and managed to cure me with goodness knows what sort of pills. So that starving to death would no longer be a threat were I to return to Germany. So I would not need to flee to Naissaar any longer. (I should say to Tartu, but I would rather not think about that carbuncle of disappointment.) So, neither to Tartu nor all the way home. But I could in principle leave Germany . . . And yet I cannot. Because without making requests I would never find anywhere else, maybe not even in any of the world's other observatories, such an understanding man as Schorr. And I cannot force myself to voluntarily collaborate with anyone else in my work. As they say: you can't teach an old dog new tricks. So that once I get my sixty-centimeter job finished, I will have nowhere else to go if I leave Bergedorf. It would be impossible to *offer my services* to that pleasant guy Hertzsprung. On conditions that they would accept. Because even if they were to welcome me with open arms (and they would) tensions would arise sooner or later, and neither side would budge . . .

Or should I have given it a try . . . ? When Hertzsprung came yesterday after lunch to inquire about my health? And when I said to him: "Herr Professor—I am grateful for all your hospitality, but right now with my flu and, I fear, oncoming bronchitis, I am of no use to you. I'm going home—yes, yes, those six or seven hours on the train won't harm me—and will come back when I've recovered!" Maybe I should have used the opportunity to add: *"And then—if you haven't anything against the idea—I could stay here . . . ? Because I won't be able to stand it much longer over there, as I imagine you can understand . . ."* But what I said was: "Late this evening, I'm going to take the train—Utrecht—Arnhem—Wesel—and I will be home by tomorrow morning. No, no, there's no need for anyone to accompany me. That little suitcase of mine is no problem at all . . ."

And now I'm here. In an empty compartment of a second-class carriage. With my suitcase, strangely enough. The same one that Frau Baade had me accept six years ago. Up to now I've only done one trip with it—to the Philippines. I've used my briefcase on all other occasions. And wrapped everything else up in copies of the *Hamburger Fremdenblatt.* But this time there was nothing else for it than to root it out again. Herr Goebbels has turned the *Hamburger Fremdenblatt* into something that you can no longer wrap your odds and ends in. Without it feeling that you are an accomplice to the violence all around . . . All quite idiotic, of course. As we accept it with every step we take—by the very fact that nobody or almost nobody has gone and hanged themselves!

But now I'm here. In the jolting and jerking gathering darkness of a second-class compartment, exposed to whining and clanking and the smell of coal smoke penetrating in through the window, my headache growing worse again, my senses dulled by the gin, feverish. How high my fever is I do not know for certain. This morning, at the observatory, I measured it with the thermometer I was given yesterday, and it was 101.8. Hertzsprung forced me to go and see a doctor. He recommended an injection of Omnadin that would reduce the fever, but I refused. Normalizing your body temperature with an injection is sheer self-deception.

And now I'm here. The darkness with its pinpricks of electric light slips by outside the window. The sky is heavily overcast, but the wind buffets the carriage like a meteor shower—today is the first night of the Leonides—and so I squeeze my eyes shut. Because otherwise I would, willy-nilly, start following the flashes of light with my eyes, as you would a meteor shower, and then I would see just how much my eyes still ache, twice over.

What I know is this: three kilometers before Emmerich runs the border. On the platform of the last station in Holland the stationmaster will be standing. He looks pink and calm in the light of the night lamp. Our eyes will meet and I will feel my eyeballs being penetrated by a dull ache once again. When I open them wide, with the haste of a passerby, of a drowning man, in order to catch a last glimpse of the Dutchman's quiet, rescuing face, he will already be past. And I will feel, all of a sudden, that I cannot breathe—at the thought that we have arrived at the German border. But that I must fill my lungs completely with air in order to be able to put up with what is to come . . .

Before the halt, long before it, I get up from my seat, pull my jacket over my pajamas to protect me from the feverishly cold shivers, take my suitcase down from the top luggage net, put it next to me on the seat, and unlock it. Because this halt indicates the German customs, and I don't want to have to open my suitcase *on their orders.* So I cower and sway there with my suitcase open beside me, my feet resting on the floor in my slippers, and await the arrival of the customs officer. And as I lounge there and am dozing off, apocalyptic visions go through my head: some kind of huge flat faces, giant shaven heads, that I don't recognize, but that should be only too familiar to me, hanging there in the half darkness over the Golgotha landscape, with bats and flying fish gliding in and out through their eyes and ears . . . Some kinds of trees that look like human monsters looming up in the darkness . . . Some sorts of faces of the *Übermensch* turning into cannon . . . Then I recognize them: they are variations on Eduard Wiiralt's *Visions of Hell.* This picture was printed years ago in an issue of *Välis-Eesti,* the magazine for Estonian émigrés. But I have not received a copy for several months. The German authorities have no doubt banned it from being brought into the country. Maybe because Wiiralt's work is *entartete Kunst* in their eyes . . . Oh, what a world, what an *entartete Welt* . . .

Suddenly I realize that the train has come to a standstill, and I can hear hobnailed boots on the platform outside: *tramp-tramp-tramp-tramp,* and I gasp for breath, causing me to think: perhaps I'm gasping so as to inhale some more of the air of freedom that I can hold beyond the border. Or because someone yelled *Halt!* outside my compartment window and I gave a start out of fear, and grow angry at my own fear. Hell and damnation. What kind of word can you hope to hear from that *Halt!*-yeller? (I can see neither him nor the person addressed through my window, but it is a matter of indifference as to what uniform he is wearing.) What word do I expect him to say right now? When his blunt language is self-evident. When *halten* is the seed, the germ of that language: on the one hand, *anhalten—festhalten—stillhalten—strammhalten,* and on the other, *Maul halten—Atem halten . . . aushalten . . .*

Then the customs and passport officers enter my compartment. Two men in black uniforms. And who act like idiots! The compartment is lit up brightly with a painful light. I have put on all the lamps. And the guys—unless they are blind—should be able to see that my suitcase is right beside me on the seat. And that the luggage net above me is empty. But they don't see this. They walk up to the door—tramp—tramp—and point at the luggage net. Complete idiots. Morons of routine. Indicating that I should take down my suitcase from the net. They cannot see that I already have. They are blind. They must be able to see this with their eyes. But their brains are so blinded by routine that they cannot see it. I ignore their gestures. What should I say to them? I raise the lid of my suitcase for the first of them and hand my passport to the second. Only once this second man has accepted my passport and stamped his little lilac stamp in it by the light of the corridor lamp "*Eingereist 11.11.35*" and the other man has rummaged through my suitcase, perfunctorily, formally, but rummaged nevertheless, which is one of the rules of the new regime, only then do I realize, and I must even be blushing through my fever: they are not complete idiots! The complete idiot, if not elsewhere, then certainly in the Germany of today, is me! Because they were not pointing at the luggage net, where my suitcase was not present. They were greeting me in the German manner . . .

And now I'm here. In the only damned office in the whole of Germany where people understand me. I explain:

"Herr Schorr, I've been ill all these days."

"All those ten days you've been back from Leiden?"

"Yes."

"What's wrong with you?"

"My fever just won't go down. Every afternoon it's at least 100.4. And I've got a splitting headache."

"Jesus! Why are you walking around then? Go home and go to bed!" cries Schorr, quite concerned, almost accusingly. "You look pretty bad. You haven't even had a shave. We've never seen this in the whole of twelve years. Why don't you go to bed?"

"I've been in bed," I say. But fail to mention that otherwise I wouldn't even manage to stand up now. I fail to mention that I've hardly eaten anything. For all those ten days . . . Fail to mention that the taste of verdigris has returned. The *poison* has returned. Back to milk only again. And maybe beer . . . I fail to mention all of that. Because Schorr would not understand. I say:

"But in the meantime I've had a new idea. Regarding our six-hundred-millimeter job. I'm going to my workshop to check it out . . ."

"What sort of idea have you got now?"

Oh yes, Schorr always wants to know such things. He's quite pushy in that respect. But because of his discreet nature, not *so* pushy that I wouldn't say:

". . . Listen, I've got to check it again . . . ," and then in order to change the subject, "and I heard—that the tax authorities have rung the observatory . . ."

"Do you need money?"

". . . have rung the observatory and said that I have to pay twice fifty marks for some fee or other. And I need a little to live on too."

We have an arrangement. A discreet arrangement that only the two of us know about—I am allowed to withdraw money from my savings book only with his permission. When he suggested this arrangement a couple of years ago, I felt deeply insulted. I felt so hurt that I went weak at the knees and was not even able to jump up out of the armchair and leave the office, so I sat there for a little while. And thanks to that, I could hear what his suggestion entailed:

". . . Herr Schmidt—I promise you that you will get the sum you demand every time you ask. But I do think, I imagine, that if you come to me with the request it will encourage you . . ." (he didn't say force me, and I noticed that) ". . . to weigh up how much you really need on each occasion. Or if you indeed need anything at that particular time. This would give your work capacity a treat. I believe, Herr Schmidt, that we both think, you and me, exactly the same way about this matter."

My better self understood that Schorr was trying to support this half of me. So that both parts of me replied in concert, the one ironically, the other sincerely:

"Very well. Because, Herr Schorr, a person is only a *completely* sovereign being if he is able, in that game of sovereignty, to relinquish that sovereignty. In all other instances he becomes the prisoner of sovereignty, is that not the case?"

He was a little uncomfortably surprised, and muttered: "Maybe that is the case," and from that time on we have put our little arrangement into practice.

He takes my savings book out of his desk drawer and hands it over to me. I go to the cashier, get my two hundred marks, and return the savings book for his safekeeping that same afternoon. He puts it back in the drawer and says:

"Herr Schmidt, I shall be going to Berlin this evening. I will be away until the twenty-fifth. Make sure you are healthy by the time I get back."

And now I'm here. Or maybe not?

Because I don't really know where I have come from and how I ended up here. And when the point of departure of a movement remains unknown, and if the nature of the movement remains unclear, you cannot say anything definite about where the mover finds himself at any given moment. Hell—that at least is logical!

I get the feeling that I was walking one morning—today, or yesterday, or the day before—past the Die Sonne bar and calmed my mind and fortified my body. Because I was in desperate need of some calories. And there are plenty of them in beer. And quite unexpectedly my self-esteem took a turn for the better. As the beer swilled away my headache—well, not completely, but pushed it somewhere farther away. And then I was suddenly at the Domfest festival in Hamburg, which was in its last week on Sankt Pauls Sandplatz.

I walked past those unreal booths at the market place, between the goods vehicles and the colored tents. Pies and lemonade, beer and wine. Hexagonal glass bowls rotating and filled with the small pink scrolls of lottery tickets. A shooting range for air rifles, and dodgems. All sorts of foolish things. But I had to walk around here. When my legs began to give out I stopped and convinced myself: Schmidts always walk tall. At the stall for knife throwing, where I would have got one hundred points as usual if sober, I only got ninety-one. But even that score gave me a cigar as a prize. I remember lighting it, then smoking it right to the end in two puffs. The cigar made me feel sick. When my legs became threateningly weak, I had a beer at the next booth. Then rested my legs by sitting on the saddle of the wooden donkey on the merry-go-round. Then walked on again. And the more I walked and drank beer, and let the heavens turn around me, the greater my tranquility grew. And everything got all mixed together, objects and people, tents, booths, signs, stalls of knick-knacks, the donkeys and horses of the merry-go-round, and people's faces.

Faces, ever dimmer, ever more of them. Even some familiar ones: Gressmann and Schmidt, Paul that is, but none of them see me. In the blurred muddle before my eyes, I see one or two things with unbelievable clarity. A man with a brownish flecked jaw, a narrow forehead, and bulging eyes, his uniform cap pushed back over his neck, and the brown collar of his soldier's smock round his sinewy throat. And women's faces, floating past by the tens and hundreds. And there—beyond them in the crush—God Almighty, Johanna . . . Johanna, quite untouched by the seven lean years, the latest bleak pharaoh years—and it could well be her (it *has to be* her!)—Johanna, with her green eyes, her abundant reddish-brown hair, God Almighty, the same woman I have, in secret, all those years, the whole time, every day . . . I run after her. I shout: *Johanna! I am freed of all my inhibitions! Johanna!* But she cannot hear me. She is moving away from me. She vanishes between the tents and the trucks. I catch a glimpse of her between the earthenware jugs and the lottery bowls . . . Johanna! Why don't you stop? Listen to me! I shall tell you why . . . Just listen to me—and you will understand why . . . And then, just as I rush between the booths, just as I reach out to touch Johanna—because it has to be her, just beyond the blue and red striped canvas of a tent—there is the brown-jawed man with the bulging eyes on my tail:

"Halt! Sie! Wohin stürzen Sie? Sind Sie besoffen? Oder verrückt? Oder beides? Sie zerschlagen ja meine Ware!"

He grabs my left hand and twists it up my back. He seems to do this professionally. But I am already completely free. Completely free of all fear. And there on a stool between brittle pitchers and bowls lies an axe. But I cannot seize it, as my left hand is in his grip. I kick over his pottery table and wrench my arm free, so as to grab the axe. I now have a hold of it—a completely free man!—but by then he has gripped my arm once again. And someone shouts, as I wallop him with the stump of my right arm:

"Stop it! Herr Schmidt!"

And now I'm here, here no doubt, obviously here: in my room in the greengrocer's house. Gressmann has been sent from the observatory and Paul, Paul Schmidt and the greengrocer Karl Schmidt, are trying, stupid though it may seem, to get me into bed:

"Get a good night's sleep, Herr Schmidt. It doesn't matter. You got worked up about something. They knew you were angry about something by the way you were talking. Don't worry. Nothing will happen. Half of what you said was in Estonian anyway. Just get into your pajamas and have a good rest . . ."

It is Paul who is saying this. The greengrocer is not as gentle. He is angry and silent and snorting.

And I trick them. I turn on my side and pretend to go to sleep. My head aches terribly, but I ignore it. I wait for them to go in silence and shut my door after them. I can hear them talking in the hall. Oh yes: I can see through the wall how Paul Schmidt put his shaven chin to Karl Schmidt's reddish ear and mumbles:

"What the fuck has got into Herr Schmidt . . . ?"

And the greengrocer mutters in reply: "Fuck knows. This has never happened to him before, however much he's been drinking . . ."

And Paul mutters: "Just started to yell without warning, right in the middle of the Domplatz: 'A Reich of cockroaches! Cockroaches' Reich! Two-meter-tall cockroaches!' Thank God that Gressmann called for help and got us out of the fix."

Then they are gone. I wait for half an hour. I feel how my heart is pounding in my eyeballs, each heartbeat is like the squeeze of nutcrackers. One with barbs on the inside. But I ignore it. I wait the number of minutes necessary, then get up. I will not try to leave through the door. The door is the usual way out, but not in a case like this. I slide down from the window into the yard . . .

And now I'm here. I'm not really sure where. Nor how I got here. If you don't know how you got somewhere, you don't know where you are either. *That* is logical, damn and blast.

I slipped out of the window down into the yard, and my plan was as clear as crystal. I didn't take my telescopes with me. Schorr had paid me for them and they were staying with him. But on the lawn behind the meridian house stands my ship for sailing against the wind. No one has paid me for that. No one even knows it's there. Even less the fact that it doubles as a flying machine. I cross the cobbled road hastily, down the graveled lane of the observatory park and across the cold grass. The glassy gray grass cuts painfully into my bare feet. Luckily this affords symmetry to my headache. At any rate, the trail I leave after me must be bloody. But I do not turn round to look. I have never felt sorry for myself. Quite the opposite. Very much the opposite. In fact, so much the opposite, that . . .

But my plan is eminently simple. And not even the feeling that my head is about to explode can stop me: I shall go behind the white plank fence of the meridian house and jump into my boat. Which is an airplane as well. I will get the air propeller going and turn it to a horizontal position. And fly away. Over the bare treetops and the gravestones of the cemetery. To Hamburg. To the Domplatz. And I will land behind the tents. So that the giant cockroach, the giant wasp who twisted my arm will not see me. Actually, he can see me if he wants. If he only dares to look. Because I am descending from the heavens like the angel in the book of Ezekiel. And the cockroach, however loyal a member he is of the National Church, is lying face down in the mud. And there, before the tent, Johanna is standing waiting for me. She really is waiting for me. In fact she has been waiting for me for years on end. And I lift her into my ship. When I embrace her in the air I press my frozen face against her glowing one—God Almighty, this really is the principle of ice meeting heat! And this *is* the birth of a new galaxy—and we fly off to celebrate to my island—Yes, we do. We fly away! Out of sight of all the cockroaches.

But when I go round the plank fence by the meridian house to jump into my ship, the cockroach is standing there blocking the way. The same cockroach that prevented me from running after Johanna on the Domplatz. And he, the unhappy creature, has not seen either my ascent into heaven or my landing, and is filled with his own idiot's pride and attacks me and twists my arm up my back again.

Then I wrestle with him as Jacob did with the Lord at the ford at Jabbok. And why should the devil be an easier opponent than the Lord? And yet he is weaker than the Lord. And I would have got the better of him. But other cockroaches come to his aid. Three or four of them. Running. From the fourth cupola straight across the grass, where people never run. But they're not completely stupid: they do know my name. They are shouting in their strange, hoarse, beetle voices:

"Herr Schmidt! Herr Schmidt! What's got into you?"

Then they attack me again. I struggle as much as I can. But I am no match for four or five of them in their smooth brown masks, tough legs, and stiff chitin shells—especially without my ship and its flying properties. The pant as they twist my arm up my back. And now I'm here.

I am in my room in the greengrocer's house. The cockroaches have gone. I am sitting at the table and Schorr is sitting opposite. Two cups of coffee are steaming in front of us. Schorr is cutting the bread, spreading the margarine onto two slices, slicing the liver pâté; picks up a sandwich for himself and hands me one:

"Eat something, Herr Schmidt. And drink some coffee. Headaches are always worse when your stomach is empty. And then go to sleep. That would be best for you."

He eats his own sandwich with gusto in order to demonstrate his point. I bite off a mouthful, out of politeness, and feel my nausea rising. But I manage to wash it down with a gulp of coffee. But I find it impossible to eat any more. Schorr munches calmly, then says:

"Everything's all right. Eat your fill, then relax—and everything will return to normal."

And I think to myself: "But Lord Almighty, it would be *terrible* if everything returned to *normal.* My only hope is to be free of such norms at last." And all at once a suspicion enters my head: isn't this didactic and soothing Schorr with his munch-munch-munching, despite all my experiences of him up to that point to the contrary, really on the side of the cockroaches?

When in principle I am an entirely free man—now that I am entirely free—should I not ask him about this? But I don't dare. It would simply be too depressing, too embarrassing, if he were forced to suddenly say to me: "But come on Herr Schmidt, could there ever be a question of my being on the side of anyone else but theirs, and manage to keep my job as director of the observatory and feed and clothe seven children—how shall I put it—as if honey just dripped out of a pipe?"

So I refrain from asking anything, but am craftier than he is:

"I am most grateful, Professor Schorr, for all your concern. And especially for the four sachets of headache powder. I took them all at once. And now I am going to sleep."

And that is what I do. At least that's what it looks like. He waits a short while for me to fall asleep, draws up the covers under my chin—silly old man, drawing up the covers when he thinks I'm asleep—so he just cannot be on the side of the cockroaches—and goes quietly on his way. And in half an hour I will leave the house.

This time I am prudently wearing socks. So that the frozen ground won't hurt my feet so much. And so I can sneak out quietly through the greengrocer's entrance hall. In my woolly Naissaar socks. I have long been an expert at finding stopgap solutions. But just as I am taking down the torch from the shelf in the hall (it is still light now, but when I fly off with Johanna from the Domplatz, dusk will have fallen and I will need a torch)—as I grope for the torch in the hallway to the greengrocer's house, Karl leaps out from his room. And he is definitely a cockroach man. And this is patently obvious right now. Because he doesn't say a word, simply pants like an asthma patient, swiftly locks the front door, and pulls out the key. Then he struts back into his room and I can hear him locking it from the inside. I rush across to the door leading to the kitchen—that too is locked. So now I am trapped in the hall amid four locked doors. And across the window near the door there are bars an inch thick. I cry out:

"Herr Schmidt! Herr Schmidt! . . . I grit my teeth and feel how my eyeballs and temples are filled with the fire of the strain . . . "Herr Schmidt, you are a cockroach after all—a cockroach and a bastard—along with all those other cockroaches and bastards."

"Oh dear! I see!" the greengrocer yells back from the kitchen. "If that's the case, then listen, and I will tell you: you—you yourself are a cockroach in a foreign country! You yourself are a drinker and a bastard! Despite all your disgusting pretense at being a man of honor! And now you've also gone off your head . . . *You yourself,* don't you understand?"

I am standing in the middle of the hall trying desperately to remember what, where, and who they were who shouted in this repulsive manner—yourself, yourself, yourself—one of them blind, the other cursed by half of the gods. But nothing comes to mind. Instead, I get a liberating idea. Strange that I never thought of it before, ages ago. To protest! Nothing more is needed. Protest against the situation I had been forced into. But the protest must be total. Absolutely concentrated. Absolutely genuine. Such a protest would loosen the tongue of the door lock. Or break down the door. Or the whole room. But the protest has to be total. So that I myself am not needed for it to be made. At least not in the hall mirror here. That old man with his twisted mouth, biting himself in the lip, he really must be a little bit *crazy* . . . There is the stove that Schmidt is stoking in the living room. Next to the mouth of the stove hangs a small axe with a metal handle on a brass hook. Frau Schmidt uses it to break up the briquettes. If one of the ten she puts in the stove happens to be inconveniently large. I take the axe from the hook and sash the mirror. I smash myself to pieces in the mirror and prize out the shards that have not fallen to the floor with the blade of the axe. I put the axe back on its brass hook. I can hear the greengrocer bawling at me from his room and how his wife is trying to calm him down: "Karl, for God's sake keep quiet. He could break down the door and come in and kill us . . ."

I stand there in the middle of the hall, screw up my eyes, and focus to concentrate in order to achieve my ultimate protest. I grit my teeth and make the decision: I will reject everything. And now I begin to list the things I will reject: human-sized cockroaches, warmongers, warlike beetles that make you want to spew. The violence of cockroaches that has been used against me. The jackboots that trample on people's faces. The magnified, hissing lies of the cockroaches, babbling in fantasy . . .

Then the front door is unlocked from the outside and four giant cockroaches come inside. A smaller white cockroach can be seen behind them. He says he is Dr. Eggers. I ask them what right they have to stop me from seeking concentration. They do not reply. They turn their brown masks on me and hiss. They twist my arms up my back and try to drag me with them. And then I resort to all that is left for me to do in this total protest: I start yelling. I bawl them out, kicking:

"I reject, reject, reject the violence of the cockroaches against the people! Against me and everyone else that the cockroaches, whose faces the cockroaches are pushing down into the mud! I reject—the jackboots that trample on people's faces!"

"He doesn't need his boots," mutters one of the cockroaches. "We'll lug him over to the car and that'll be it."

From that point on I start yelling without stopping.

And now I'm here. I do know where I am: the cockroaches have turned their inner room inside out and I am being kept prisoner in it. It is all the color of cockroaches and only seems to be solid. In fact its solidity is elastic enough, and your fists bounce back at you. But my method consists of yelling. Someone said that I yelled for four hours at a stretch. Or was it four days and four nights? I don't know. What difference does it make? Only after the injection I calmed down a bit for a while. But as I yell I list the things I am refusing: cockroaches marching over your face, jackboots trampling on your face, huge cannon that gobble up the money that should be used for building telescopes, inflated stupidity, dung heaps that threaten to reach to the stars . . . I reject, reject, reject—humiliation and torture; I reject the ideology that turns people into cockroaches—God, I know that when I have yelled all these things out of me my protest will grow and become total and will crush the cockroaches' space. So that I will be able to walk away and fly off with Johanna . . .

But it is hard for me to keep on yelling without a break. I am not much more than a yelling grain of dust filled with fever and a blinding headache. *An injection,* even if it ruins the perfection of my protest would give me a moment . . . So let him come—the gray-faced cockroach with his needle . . . Let him come . . . Three hundred million light-years . . . A grain of dust beyond infinity—and yet!

13

Dear Sir,

I called to mind just now our recent conversation about Schmidt and it seemed to me that a couple of things should be added, a couple of things of which you are not aware. If you know about them already, then please ignore this letter.

So, first, they are matters that contradict the naive interpretation that would suggest that Schmidt, with all his inventions, was in any way a victim of the situation that held sway before World War II. No. Quite the opposite. The history of science contains many paradoxes and Schmidt's case just happens to be the most striking and not only because he had only one hand.

When he died, the construction of the large version of his telescope had not yet started. You already know that the Big Schmidt was not ready until 1948. But the Americans did manage to find financial backing and with Baade's help they constructed a forty-eight-inch Schmidt mirror. If I remember rightly this was in 1940. By then, the United States was not yet at war, but the war in Europe had started. By 1942, the United States had joined in, and for that reason the conditions for scientific research were growing ever more hopeless. Baade stayed in America as a citizen of an enemy power, virtually under police surveillance. His American colleagues were moved over one by one to war work. At the same time it transpired that the Mount Palomar Observatory was no longer suitable for the most accurate observations—the sea of lights from Los Angeles was creeping ever closer.

But every week Baade would turn up at the police station to register—his papers made him out to be an enemy national—and he understood that while his situation was indeed annoying to an extent, it did nonetheless afford him a unique opportunity to work in peace. Observing supernovae with what was after all the world's best telescope. All that disturbed his work were the lights of Los Angeles. And, of course, talk of Japanese planes that were conducting sorties in the direction of the American coast. And for fear of these planes, it was decided to black out the whole of the southwest coast of the United States. Los Angeles switched off its annoying lights—and Baade, almost a prisoner-of-war, could work for three or four years under ideal conditions with the ideal equipment. And as he was, shall we say, a scientist of the utmost ethical decency, he would underline the fact at every opportunity that his discoveries were made possible only because of Schmidt's invention. Well, it has of course to be said that Schmidt derived no material or moral advantage from this. But such advantage should surely not be our ultimate goal, should it?

Second. Cast a glance at the September 1984 issue, I think it is, of the *Astronomical Review.* There it is written that a NASA team has just published its final report. The report concerned a question put to scientists as to which type of telescope could give us, in the near future, a new alternative chart of the heavens to replace the fifty-year-old one taken at Palomar. In principle, the photography involved would no longer be taken from Earth but rather from a spaceship somewhere beyond the earth's atmosphere with all its aberrations. In other words, stellar photography at a hitherto unknown level.

The NASA team took a look at all the telescopes that had come into use after Schmidt's day, that is, over the previous fifty years, and concluded that the best instrument was none other than the Schmidt telescope itself.

I hope that this item of information will fit in perfectly with what I would call, if you will forgive me, your somewhat amusing system of Schmidt patriotism. And you will, no doubt, wish to apply this term to me too. With regard to the bad conscience of the welfare society that I, in your opinion, should be concerning myself with in the case of Schmidt (and maybe in general).

Kind regards,
Dr. Friedr. Kelter

Villa Wolkenlos
November 22, 1985

■ □ ■ □ ■

WRITINGS FROM AN UNBOUND EUROPE

For a complete list of titles, see www.nupress.northwestern.edu.

Words Are Something Else
DAVID ALBAHARI

Perverzion
YURI ANDRUKHOVYCH

The Second Book
MUHAREM BAZDULJ

Tworki
MAREK BIEŃCZYK

The Grand Prize and Other Stories
DANIELA CRĂSNARU

Peltse and Pentameron
VOLODYMYR DIBROVA

And Other Stories
GEORGI GOSPODINOV

The Tango Player
CHRISTOPH HEIN

In-House Weddings
BOHUMIL HRABAL

Mocking Desire
DRAGO JANČAR

A Land the Size of Binoculars
IGOR KLEKH

Balkan Blues: Writing Out of Yugoslavia
EDITED BY JOANNA LABON

The Loss
VLADIMIR MAKANIN

Compulsory Happiness
NORMAN MANEA

Border State
TÕNU ÕNNEPALU

How to Quiet a Vampire: A Sotie
BORISLAV PEKIĆ

A Voice: Selected Poems
ANZHELINA POLONSKAYA

Estonian Short Stories
EDITED BY KAJAR PRUUL AND DARLENE REDDAWAY

The Third Shore: Women's Fiction from East Central Europe
EDITED BY AGATA SCHWARTZ AND LUISE VON FLOTOW

Death and the Dervish
The Fortress
MEŠA SELIMOVIĆ

The Last Journey of Ago Ymeri
BASHKIM SHEHU

Conversation with Spinoza: A Cobweb Novel
GOCE SMILEVSKI

House of Day, House of Night
OLGA TOKARCZUK

Materada
FULVIO TOMIZZA

Shamara and Other Stories
SVETLANA VASILENKO

Lodgers
NENAD VELIČKOVIĆ